What
Goes
Around

What Goes Around

ALEXANDRA CAREW

KENSINGTON BOOKS
http://www.kensingtonbooks.com

KENSINGTON BOOKS are published by

Kensington Publishing Corp.
850 Third Avenue
New York, NY 10022

All Kensington titles, imprints and distributed lines are available at special quantity discounts for bulk purchases for sales promotion, premiums, fund-raising, educational or institutional use.

Special book excerpts or customized printings can also be created to fit specific needs. For details, write or phone the office of the Kensington Special Sales Manager: Kensington Publishing Corp., 850 Third Avenue, New York, NY, 10022. Attn. Special Sales Department. Phone: 1-800-221-2647.

ISBN 0-7582-0434-5

First Kensington Trade Paperback Printing: August 2003
10 9 8 7 6 5 4 3 2 1

Printed in the United States of America

PART ONE

London
Winter

One

"Spare some change, please?" The boy looked about eighteen. He'd wrapped himself up in a quilt outside Monument station and was rocking backwards and forwards to keep warm. By his side were a lame dog and a box marked HUNGRY in which there were a few scattered coins.

"Spare some change please, Miss?" he repeated as the girl in a thick wrap-around cashmere coat, knee-high suede boots and pair of Gucci sunglasses approached. Guiltily Cat Wellesley shook her head. Without thinking she tightened her grip on her handbag, and then realizing that she actually had less money than he did, let it relax again.

At this rate I'll be joining you in a week or so, she thought grimly, catching sight of herself in a shop window. Talk about appearances being deceptive. She looked like the sort of woman who'd belong to an expensive gym and was on first-name terms with her hairdresser and manicurist. But it had been a full year since her thick dark hair was last deep-conditioned and trimmed to shoulder length, and long before that since her smooth pale skin and almond-shaped green eyes had last seen a facial.

Cat Wellesley was broke. She had overspent her savings and underestimated the time it would take to revive her career. She had three bulging credit cards, an ever-increasing overdraft and just weeks to go before the mortgage broker would force her to sell the little flat she owned on the New Kings Road. For a split second she could see herself there, beside the boy, her clothes and possessions sold.

Cancel that thought! She hissed at the errant mind that would plunge her into such doom. She refused to believe it would happen. Inspired by a book on positive thinking she'd just reread, she recited her current mantra:

I, Catherine Wellesley, have a fulfilling job at Trafalgar Broadcasting. I manage their international channels, run a team of people and am responsible for the program schedules, on-air promotions and a generous acquisitions budget. I am successful, respected by my team and highly regarded by management. I am in love with Dominic Pryce. He is crazy about me. He says I am the best thing that has ever happened to him. He is utterly devoted and faithful. Together we have just bought a fuck-off loft apartment overlooking the river in Docklands. We are the kind of good-looking couple who eat in smart restaurants and appear in the lifestyle sections of the Sunday papers. We are very much in love and planning a family. I have a fantastic life. Everything is perfect.

With a heavy sigh Cat pushed through the swing doors of the Rubens Brothers Investment Bank where she was currently temping as a secretary.

Climbing up the escalator she recognized Dominic Pryce ahead. She had kept track of when he arrived most mornings and would try and time her arrival to coincide with his. Some days it worked and they rode up in the elevator together, chatting awkwardly about the weather or his first appointment. Other days it didn't and she would have to check his diary to estimate when she might get her first glimpse. She'd even started adjusting her visits to the loo to avoid missing him. On a good day she'd see him four or five times; on an excellent day they'd have face-to-face contact, which she noticed was happening more often lately. But then there were the disappointing days, when all she'd get were a couple of misspelled e-mails and a phone call, and she'd trudge wearily home with only the morning to look forward to. She had even begun to resent the weekends because they took him away from her and to a life she could only imagine.

She knew he was separated and she knew he had children. Apart from that she knew little, but had made up a life for him in her own fantasies—a kind of parallel existence in which he was constantly by her side. He would wake with her in the morning, complain about the time she took in the bathroom and then chat to her as they walked toward Fulham Broadway. And on her way home in the evenings as she passed restaurants she could no longer afford—there he was, taking her out to dinner and suggesting romantic weekend breaks in Venice. In the supermarket she'd linger over the lamb cutlets and expensive bottles of wine, imagining the meals she might cook for him one day. Then the fantasy would fade and she was just Cat again: lonely, broke and studying the cut-price bargains at the back.

Forcing her way past the Rubens staff in their dress-down-Friday casuals, Cat made a bolt for the elevator and scraped in beside him before the doors shut. He looked surprized to see her, as if it were unusual for her to turn up. Under his winter coat he was wearing a pale blue Oxford cotton shirt, a fairly conservative tie and one of his navy double-breasted suits. Dominic Pryce did not believe in dress-down-Fridays.

"Dominic, how are you?" She flushed.

"Fine thanks." He nodded. He looked anything but. His skin was a pale olive, although this morning it was looking slightly green, and his hazel eyes were set in a frown, as if he had just remembered something terrible. He smelled of cigarettes and aftershave: he wore Opium, and possibly a bit too much of it. It reminded her of souks and spices and mysterious Middle Eastern alleyways and conjured up images of rough sex in a Bedouin tent. His hair was black but going patchily grey and Cat longed to run her fingers through it.

"You know it's my last day today?" she tried, willing everyone to disappear and the elevator to break down for a couple of hours.

"Is it?" he frowned. "I thought you were here for longer than that."

"No, Sophie's back from her honeymoon on Monday. So off I go into the sunset." She hoped she sounded romantic and mysterious. She hoped he'd fret about never seeing her again and spend all day figuring out how to contact her. But she was one step ahead of him, and had lined up a little surprise for the end of the afternoon. On receiving it, she had persuaded herself, his spirits would soar, doves fly, bells chime and he'd know she was the only woman for him.

"Well, that's a shame," he told her. "You've been really efficient—I've had no complaints."

Complaints? The very word reduced her from sex goddess to secretary. Had he not noticed the *obvious* sexual chemistry between them?

"I should think not," she snarled. The elevator had reached her floor and she slipped out. "And you're late for your ops meeting." She could just see his eyes rolling as the doors shut.

Irritated, she walked toward the open-plan administration area where she had been working for the last four weeks.

"Morning, Cat." Jackie, the department's senior secretary, pretended to cry. "I can't believe it's your last day already." Like many, Jackie had worked for Rubens for several years, her loyalty bought by generous year-end bonuses and a range of perks that would have been unthinkable at a TV station. She came from Essex, was married with a baby daughter and had a voice that could deafen at fifteen paces. She was funny, warm and indiscreet, and Cat had become very fond of her.

"I can't either." Cat took off her coat, revealing a short black mini-skirt and tight-fitting turtleneck sweater. "I've got to call the agency today, get a new assignment." She could at least pretend she was on *Mission Impossible.*

"Look, I don't want to see you go, you know? I was thinking about it on the way in. We've got this backlog of staff data inputting to do. If you're interested, maybe you could do that for another week?"

"Oh I'd love to. I've been dreading the thought of starting somewhere else."

"I'll have a word with Vince once he's out of the ops meeting. I'm sure he'll agree."

Rubens had been Cat's first assignment since joining the Savoir-Faire temp agency. The decision to sign up had followed a humiliating low point when her debit card was refused at the supermarket. She had gone home to a withered baked potato and a rejection letter from the BBC and had decided then that it was time to swallow her pride. It hadn't been easy. She had felt like a spy walking into the Savoir-Faire offices, looking around herself twice in case she was seen. She had taken her first ever typing test and had then felt strangely flattered to be told she was good enough to work for some of the agency's more valued clients, like Rubens.

She approached her month there like an actress who'd been given the role of an efficient secretary with a mysterious past. She was determined to enjoy it for the new experience that it was, and on a deeper level felt it had to be good for her soul. She decided to base her persona on Miss Moneypenny: coolly efficient on the outside, yet smoldering with unexpressed passion within. She didn't want anyone to know about her background, but would have liked them to suspect that she was different all the same. She must have been the first temp who wore better clothes than her seniors, after all. But as she made coffee and photocopied documents and heard herself being referred to as "the temp," her self-esteem had begun to fade, and with it her belief that she would ever rise to anything else again.

"You wasn't looking for a full-time job, was you?" Jackie asked.

"Not really, no." Cat was aware that Dominic Pryce and the department head Vince Parker were walking toward them on their way to the meeting room. "I've been through a rough patch lately, but I'm gradually getting things together." She hoped she sounded enigmatic and alluring.

"Cat, we've run out of cookies in the kitchen, could you call catering for me?" Vince called out, making her feel about as alluring as a school lunch lady.

"Will do, Vince." She could at least laugh at herself. Despite all her efforts, her new colleagues managed effortlessly to put her back in her place.

"Dominic?" She swung around to face him, crossing her legs as she did so, a come-to-bed look on her face. "Anything you'd like from me?"

"No, nothing thanks." He looked a bit startled. She watched as he entered the meeting room, bumping into someone on their way out, and sighed. *Of course.* Dominic was too cool to eat cookies. Dominic probably lived in Islington and ate seared tuna with udon noodles and wasabi paste. He enjoyed modern art and Wagner, and spent his free time absorbed in classical Russian literature.

If it were as easy to record fantasies as it was to read personal e-mails, the powers-that-be at Rubens would have been shocked at how much time Cat could spend tearing open the buttons of his shirt and embedding her face in the black curls of his chest. God, she hoped he had a hairy chest. The greatest thing about secretarial work, she had discovered, was all the mental free time it gave her. As she photocopied documents, she was kissing Dominic. Every trip to the stationery cupboard was an opportunity to tear off his clothes. And while taking parcels to the mail room they'd be having frantic sex on her bed in full view of the upper deck of the number 22 bus.

She ordered their cookies and tried to remember at what point Dominic had stopped being her not-bad-looking, slightly abrasive boss and had become the sex god he was today.

It certainly wasn't in her first week, which, despite her good intentions, she'd spent scowling resentfully at anyone who'd so much as asked her the time. But some time the following week they'd made a connection—it must have been the morning he appeared by her side and told her to cancel everything because he was going home for the day. She fantasized that he had just stormed out of a meeting on a point of principle. Dominic seemed the type that would. All day long she'd covered up for him, rearranging meetings and telling Vince that he had been taken ill. The next day he'd thanked her and the mood between them changed. He struck her as vulnerable, boyish even—someone who needed the support of a good woman. She never did find out what had happened that day, but from that point, yes it must have been that point, he was to dominate her every waking thought.

She handled his appointments possessively, refusing to arrange anything before ten as she suspected he was a slow starter. Should anyone dare to suggest an early breakfast meeting she'd turn it into a lunch, and preferably on their expenses. She typed, photocopied and filed for him without complaint. And when she received his e-mails written at two in the morning, she'd gently chide him for working such long hours, while secretly rejoicing in the mounting evidence that he was single.

Throughout her final week Cat had been planning today's *tour de force*. She couldn't leave without even trying. It scared her, but what had last Sunday's horoscope said? *Opportunities can only come into your life when you put yourself somewhere they'll find you.* It was time to put herself somewhere he'd find her all right. So that evening, as she e-mailed him Monday's diary, she was going to add her home phone number at the bottom, saying it was in case he needed her for anything. It would seem innocuous enough— efficient, really. She couldn't just walk down the Rubens escalator for the last time, knowing she'd never see him again, she just couldn't do it. She had to create an opportunity and then pray he'd have the sense to follow it up.

Of course, if she were to stay on another week the masterplan would have to wait. But what was another week when they had their whole lives ahead of them? Cat had convinced herself that Dominic Pryce was the one for her. Why else was she having to temp when she'd once run a TV channel, for goodness sake? Everything had been leading her to this point, to this experience, this moment. Dominic Pryce was her man. It was the only way she could explain how she'd gone from high flyer to office junior in one swift year. Nothing happened by chance. And Dominic, whether he knew it or not, was meant to be hers.

She poured herself a coffee and opened up her e-mail, where amongst the internal messages requesting stationery and meeting rooms was one from her friend Lorna in Hong Kong. Lorna ran the press office at Frontier, the TV network where they'd met, and was one of the few people to know about Cat's latest career incarnation. She'd written about the opening of a new club in Wanchai, her latest row with boyfriend Andrew and a forthcoming trip to Vietnam. But ominously her e-mail ended: *And your best friend, Max Carnegie, is coming to London for a few days. He's staying at the Park Royal Hotel if you want to swing by for a drink.*

Max Carnegie in London! Cat's stomach did a double somersault. She felt like a therapy patient being plunged into regression after years of intense work. Just as she was beginning to let go of the past, here it was, turning up in her own city to mock her.

She typed out a quick reply: *Any idea what Carnage is doing in London? Buying programs, channel deals? Who's he seeing? Tell me more!*

She had often fantasized about running into Max again. She'd be looking glamorous, successful and about seven pounds lighter, and have a handsome man like Dominic on her arm. She imagined talking to him with a slightly puzzled look on her face, as if she could barely remember his name, and then Dominic pulling her away and reminding her that they were late for their flight to Paris, or Istanbul.

But had she run into him tomorrow, Cat would have been humiliated. Cat Wellesley had failed to get a decent job, despite exhaustive research, umpteen letters and seven interviews. The girl who once spent hundreds on a jacket because she was feeling bored could now barely afford to feed herself. Cat Wellesley was a failure.

"Is Dominic around?"

Cat bristled. That was all she needed. Sandy Clapp was a project manager who worked for Pryce. She had pale blue eyes, cheekbones that could cut paper and the flattest stomach Cat had ever seen. She was wearing a white open-collared shirt with a short navy blue skirt and high-heeled pumps. Her hose had a huge run down one leg so it looked like she'd just been ravaged in the stationery cupboard. Her dark blonde hair was pulled back into an unsuccessful ponytail and Cat noticed she was wearing chipped purple nail polish. She looked like a woman who'd still be wearing yesterday's underwear.

"He's still in the ops meeting," Cat told her. Sandy huffed as if it were Cat's fault and stalked off. Cat caught Jackie's eye. "Which charm school did she get thrown out of, anyway?"

Jackie wheeled her chair closer and lowered her voice, safe in the knowledge that all the directors were in the meeting room. "I've known that girl for almost seven years now and not once has she ever acted friendly. She doesn't care about what the likes of you or me think." Cat flinched. "All she thinks about is work. And I know she works hard, but I've heard that Dominic helps her out more than he should."

"Does he?" Cat felt a stab of jealousy. "Why would he do that?" But she knew the answer already. She had always suspected that something might have happened between Dominic and Sandy, but would push that thought to the back of her mind. She had no evidence—it was a simple gut feeling. And while over the years she had learned to trust her gut feelings over logic, this was one she had rather gone into denial over.

"History between them," Jackie mouthed before rolling her chair back to her desk as the meeting-room door opened, littering the corridors with its occupants. Cat took a deep, calming breath, but still felt an irrational sense of anger, as if Dominic should have denied himself a past and waited for her—someone he didn't even know existed until four weeks ago.

"Where am I supposed to be right now?" The smell of Opium was behind her—quickly she traded Sandy in for a hundred camels and gasped as Dominic licked honey off her nipples.

"Oh, lucky you, you have a one-to-one with Sandy," she hissed. *What timing, Universe.*

"Oh, OK, thanks."

She looked up at him expectantly, but there was no reaction. What was he meant to do, burst into song? "Then there's the data systems review," she added awkwardly, hoping he hadn't noticed. "And then you have a spare half-hour. You could have lunch."

"Thanks, Cat," he sighed. "Or maybe I could just catch up on some work."

"Would you like me to fetch you a sandwich?" she asked sweetly.

"No, no, I'm OK," he frowned. "Oh, I nearly forgot." Sandy had joined him in the admin area clutching a notebook and a packet of cigarettes. "Could you do seven photocopies of this manual for me?" He handed her a ring-bound dossier.

"Oh, I can think of nothing I'd like more." She ignored the look of contempt on Sandy's face.

"I know, I'm sorry. I'll make it up to you."

"You will? I can be very demanding, you know." She kept her eyes on him as he led Sandy toward the smoking room.

"I have no doubt," he called from the corridor. "As are all women."

Cat wanted the moment to freeze in time. Had Dominic just flirted with her? And in front of Sandy?

"He likes you," Jackie whispered.

She waited a second before turning to her colleague. "You think so?"

"Definitely," she said knowingly. "He just told Vince how impressed he is with you. He wants you to stay on."

"Well, how nice to be wanted!" Cat beamed, as somewhere in the distance bells started to chime, doves flew and a pair of angels high-fived each other.

"Shall I show you what we need done?" Jackie leaned across and searched for a file on Cat's screen. She smelled of hair spray and Listerine and homeliness, which felt oddly reassuring after Sandy's hostility. "Here you go, there's the master list of all staff, in alphabetical order. Now if you check this off against this file," she pulled a box file off the shelf, "you can find addresses and contact numbers and type in the right information. You might need to chase a few people up for their details as well."

"Think I'll manage that," Cat said as Jackie disappeared to answer the phone. Feeling like a detective she scrolled down the list to the Ps until she found Dominic's entry. The address section had been left intriguingly blank but there was a phone number which she copied onto a Post-It note. Then for the hell of it she went to the Cs and found Sandy, who apparently lived in Clapham. Cat had always disliked Clapham.

While Jackie was in the loo she retrieved a phone directory from one of Sophie's cluttered shelves and scrolled down the page of London codes to find his. If he didn't live in Islington, then she saw him in either Highgate or Hampstead. She could picture his house. It was a newly renovated period terrace which he would have had designed in the minimalist style. It was austere and white, and he probably had a passion for ethnic African art. The list was in alphabetical rather than numerical order and it took forever to go through; she was long past Hampstead, Highgate and Islington before she found it. Bloody hell—Tooting Bec! The love of her life lived in Tooting Bec.

Cat sat back, stunned. Suddenly the goat cheese salads with balsamic vinegar he ate turned into burgers, chips and vinegar, and the tony wine-bars became cheap curry joints. Dominic lived in South London? In one short phone code he'd become a different person altogether.

But still she wanted him.

Two

"For someone who's temping and about to lose her flat you seem in an incredibly good mood." Joanna Kendall Ward poured a generous splash of Chilean Merlot in Cat's glass. Cat sometimes wondered whether it had been a good idea telling her friend about her latest career move. Jo knew a lot of people in the industry, and liked nothing better than to drink and tell stories. And the demise of Cat Wellesley's career was one hell of a story.

They had first met some two-and-a-half years earlier when Jo joined to run Frontier's network promotions unit in Hong Kong, and since their return to London she had become one of the few people Cat met up with on a regular basis. Cat had found it hard adjusting to London life. Her old friends all seemed to have got married and were starting families and moving out to the country, and Cat found they had little remaining common ground. She had tried, but as her money ran out and the job hopes faded, Jo seemed to be the only person she could really talk to.

Jo was a solid girl in every respect. She was strong-built with large bones and a sensible bobbed haircut who dressed classically in chocolate-colored suits and flat shoes, looking oddly out of place in the edit suites where she worked. She was also highly practical, tending to dismiss Cat's more ethereal way of looking at life, and was gradually heading toward a management position at DigiSat, the satellite network run by the intimidatingly successful Suzi Barratt.

"Maybe I finally got bored with being depressed." Cat leaned forward to avoid being hit on the head by a leather backpack. She invariably liked the idea of going to crowded Soho bars, but rarely enjoyed the reality. "Seriously, I feel like I've turned a corner. Have you ever had the feeling?" she started cautiously. "That you turned left when you should have turned right? That you had a choice and you took the wrong road, that you might have got the life you always wanted had you gone the other way?"

Jo looked at her blankly.

"Because that's how I've been feeling," Cat pressed on. "That somewhere for me there's a great life out there, and that I could have found it by now but I let it slip by, and since then I've been struggling to find the right way again."

"But at what point do you think you let it slip by?" Jo frowned.

"I don't know." Cat paused to think, taking a large sip of wine. "Leaving Hong Kong? Maybe I should have hung on in there, joined a different company?"

"But there was a recession in Hong Kong, you wanted out."

"Yes, I know I did." Cat paused, trying to clarify the point she was making. "But mostly it was because of Carnegie, and Declan. Maybe it was going to change and I missed it? Maybe I should have hung on in there a bit longer? But the point I'm making," she noticed the look of relief on Jo's face, "is that I no longer think there's just the one path. I think we're allowed to make mistakes, but that the Universe then creates a different outcome for us."

"What are you on about?" Jo was beginning to look impatient.

"Well, I can't help thinking that I was meant to go through all this just to meet Dominic, and that now I've found him my life's going to fall into place."

"And how do you figure that one out?" Jo filled her glass and then looked like she'd like to drown herself in it.

"Well it sounds far-fetched, I know, but I can't help thinking this was all meant to be. That in some way, on some level, I was meant to meet him. I mean it would explain why every job I've gone for has been blocked, wouldn't it? It would make sense of this whole strange period of my life. I mean me?" She lowered her voice, taking a quick look over her shoulder. "Temping as a secretary? In a bank? It's ridiculous. A year ago if someone had said I'd be doing this I'd have laughed in their face. I've really been questioning it lately, you know? Why haven't I been able to get a job yet? Why, when I'm perfectly well qualified and have got tons of experience? And you know what I think? It's because the Universe didn't want me to just yet, the Universe was forcing me to meet Dominic."

"Er, Cat, maybe it was because you're not that well known in this country? Maybe it's because the bulk of your experience was gained in some dodgy satellite outfit in Hong Kong? Because this country doesn't recognize any experience that wasn't gained here?"

"Yes, yes, yes," Cat said impatiently, irritated that her friend didn't understand. "But they're superficial reasons."

"Cat, when will you just accept that if you're not known, if you didn't work with so-and-so who knows what's-his-name, you're not going to get in? It's got nothing to do with any universal force."

"I have to believe it does, Jo, I have to. Else what's the point?"

"The point is you had a good run in Hong Kong and then a bad one in the UK. These things happen. End of story. Your time will come." She saw the look of deflation in Cat's face, and poured the remains of the wine into her glass. "Shall we get another bottle?"

"Silly not to." Cat sat back, frowning.

"Have you heard anything from Trafalgar yet?" Jo tried to bring the subject back to firm ground.

Cat shook her head. "But I will, I have to."

"I never did find that article, you know."

"Oh, I have it with me." Cat rummaged in her bag to produce the folded magazine clipping she'd been carrying around like a talisman. TRAFALGAR TARGETS INTERNATIONAL MARKET blazed the headline above a photo of chairman Sir John Maudsley.

Jo studied the clipping, frowning. "That's a shocking photo of Sir John," she said. "He looks like a retired ballet dancer."

Cat could see what she meant. Sir John had an elongated, thin face, pale blue eyes and almost non-existent lips and in this shot was looking upwards, a somewhat fey expression on his face. "A cravat would finish the look off," she agreed.

"Cat, I hate to sound negative, but what if you don't get this job?" Jo folded up the cutting and handed it back to her.

"I refuse to think like that," Cat said simply. "I believe in the power of positive thought." She smiled as she saw her friend's eyes rolling. "It has to come through—it's what I keep putting out to the Universe, I have to believe it will happen. When people think negatively all they're doing is attracting that negativity. It's like telling the Universe you'd like all this shit to happen to you. I've been doing that these last few months and it's been getting me nowhere. So now I'm thinking positively and already two good things have happened—Dominic and the Trafalgar announcement."

"Well, that's all very well. But," Jo paused, not sure whether to ask, "what if it doesn't work out? What then? How much longer have you got on your flat?"

"A few weeks." Cat's face darkened and she took a large sip of wine. "Then either I sell or they re-possess."

"It doesn't bear thinking about." Jo shuddered.

"If the worst happened," Cat started, "I think I'd sell up and go back to Hong Kong."

"What?" Jo looked like she'd just swallowed a wasp. "You'd go back?"

"I know, it's funny, isn't it? But I miss the place. Lorna's still there, there are new channels in development, and not just at Frontier. I'd go back. I'd have some money behind me and I'd just sit tight until I found something."

"I can't believe I'm hearing this. What about Dreamboat?"

Cat smiled, embarrassed. "Well, in fantasyland he comes too. Rubens have offices there. I don't know." She began to backtrack, regretting her admission. "But there is a pull, you know? I just have this nagging feeling, I can't describe, like there's unfinished business or something. I want things to work out here, you know, but if they don't, that's what I'd do."

"Have you ever thought about borrowing from your parents?"

"Are you insane? I've got more pride than that. I'm old enough to bloody support myself and I can't let them know it's got so bad. I have to see it as a challenge, an experience I'll be stronger from. You know, I'm having to budget for the first time." Her voice brightened, as if she were describing a thrilling new hobby. "With my weekly paycheck I have to pay bills and a pro-

portion of the mortgage. I live on baked potatoes and sell-by bargains from the supermarket. The other day I got some nice
chicken pieces that were on special offer." She added proudly,
"I'm starting to appreciate the simple things in life."

"I don't know how you can stand it." Jo shook her head in disbelief.

"Maybe because I don't really believe it's happening to me, it's
like a game. Like temping is just a game. But Hong Kong could
become a reality." In her mind she could picture the harbor, feel
the wind on her face as the ferry bumped her toward Kowloon;
she could smell the frying tofu, hear the cries from the market
stall-holders and feel the sweat on her back.

"You might run into Carnage."

"He's in London at the moment." Cat was back in Soho with a
bump and a cold shiver. "I'm trying to figure out why."

"God knows, let's just pray we don't run into him."

"Hmmm," Cat mused. "I keep thinking there must be something I can do."

"What do you mean, do?"

"I don't know, like send a gift-wrapped box of dog shit to his
hotel or something."

Jo sighed. "Cat, get over it and move on with your life. Stop
obsessing about him, he stitched everyone up in the end."

"Not like me he didn't. Anyway it's easy for you to say, but
you're not the one stuck here doing secretarial work, are you?"
She took a large sip of wine. "I keep thinking there must be something I can do, nothing terrible, just something subtle and funny
that would humiliate him but that couldn't be traced back to me."

"Not very positive is it, coming from one as enlightened as
you these days?"

Cat smiled. Jo had her there. "Call it his karmic dues," she said
loftily. "You reap what you sow. He fucked up so many lives that
he deserves some kind of come-back." She drained her glass and
Jo swiftly topped it up again.

"You should definitely get an interview." Jo changed the subject. "And this could be a turning point, but it'll be your doing,
not some bizarre universal force."

"I like the idea of it being a universal force," Cat said stubbornly. "I like the idea that I'm not entirely alone." She regretted it instantly, thinking she sounded self-pitying and lonely, neither of which she was.

"You're being philosophical because you're down," Jo told her. *And shitfaced*, she wanted to add. "Once you get this job and you're dating Dreamboat things will be different."

"Oh God, I hope so." Cat sat back with her glass, knowing the alcohol was beginning to depress her, yet not wanting to stop.

"And you're sure he's not married?"

Cat shook her head. "Separated. Two kids."

"Shame about the baggage."

"True." Cat paused, drinking more wine. "I think he had an affair with this girl in the office, Sandy."

"Oh dear. Are you sure it's over?"

"I think so." She sighed. "I hope so. Oh I don't know. He's such a tortured soul. I don't think anyone's ever made him happy. It's like we're both lost souls right now. But if I can rescue him, maybe in doing so I'll be rescuing myself. We can save each other, become proper people together, you know?"

Jo looked unconvinced. "He sounds like hard work to me. Is that what you need right now?"

"I don't know, I don't seem destined to make my life easy somehow, do I? Maybe you're right. He's just so bloody gorgeous, I can't bear the thought of someone else getting him." She took another large sip of wine. Her words were beginning to slur.

"Sometimes, I get the feeling that one day he's just going to reach into my chest, rip out my heart, squish it with his bare hands and then trample it into the gutter with the heel of his shoe." She took another huge swig of her wine. "Oh God, I have to have him."

Three

"**I** am never ever going to drink with you again, Cat Wellesley." It was Jo on the line.

"Oh please," Cat groaned. "I fell asleep on the effing bus and woke up in Putney Heath again."

"At our age we should know better."

"Our age? Darling, I've been twenty-six for years. Did we have fun last night? I can't remember."

"Well, you kept on about Dominic being a lost soul, and how you're going to rescue him."

"Oh dear," Cat sighed. "Did I mention that Carnegie's in town?"

"Yes, you did. About four times. God, Cat, can't you remember anything?"

Cat gulped her tea, frowning. "You know me. It's all a blur."

"We were trying to figure out what he could be doing here. You wanted to know if he was seeing anyone at DigiSat."

"And is he?"

"Not that I know of. Why would he?"

"I don't know, to unload a bit of Frontier? Set up a joint venture, a new channel?"

"I doubt it. But hell, I have a breakfast meeting with Suzi Barratt on Tuesday, why don't I just ask her?"

"Do you?" Cat was suddenly interested. "Did you tell me about that?"

"Yes I did, Cat. She has these big monthly network meetings and as my boss is going to be off skiing, I have to attend in his absence."

"Sounds scary to me. Would you seriously ask her?"

"Don't be ridiculous, I'll be too busy cowering in the corner. And worst of all, it's at 7:30 in the morning."

"Oh my God, that's revolting." Through the dull thud in Cat's head, an idea was slowly creeping in.

"Tell me about it. I'm certainly not going out drinking with you on Monday night. Look, I have to go, there's a man coming to look at the boiler and I'm still in my pajamas."

Cat hated it when Jo got efficient on her. She'd been hoping for a long lazy chat over endless cups of tea. "OK. Talk soon," she said abruptly, feeling slightly let down. "And tell me how Tuesday's meeting goes."

Despite the thick fog of her hangover, a rather interesting idea was developing. But would she have the courage to see it through? She paused idly for a moment, staring at the sorry-looking terracotta pots on the terrace. One day they'd be full of geraniums and fuchsias and pansies, and she'd be sitting out there in the sunset drinking a bottle of chilled white wine with Dominic.

Before then, though, she had a hangover to get over, some housework to be done and an idea to think through. Max must never be able to trace it back to her, that was the main thing. She had to make sure he'd never find out who was behind it.

She went to the door and arched her neck down the stairs. There was an envelope lying on the mat, and pulling her dressing-gown around herself, she tiptoed down, flinching as her bare feet touched the cold wood. On her way back up, she opened it, expecting yet another rejection letter.

Instead it was from Trafalgar Broadcasting, asking her to phone in to arrange an interview. Cat read the letter over and over, feeling a sudden surge of excitement. She was at a turning point, she could feel it. Having languished in the wilderness for months, she could finally see a future.

In her bedside table she kept a deck of tarot cards, bought in a New Age store years ago. The accompanying book explained the basic meanings but urged the reader to meditate on each card and intuit its message for himself. This she tried to do, shuffling the deck and allowing just one card to "speak" to her, but invariably she'd forget its meaning, or fail to intuit anything of any relevance, and would guiltily return to the book for clarification.

"Give me some inspiration," she whispered, shuffling the cards. "Give me a hint that everything will work out OK. Please Universe—I would like a job with Trafalgar and a relationship with Dominic Pryce. I want to be happy, I want to live again, not just exist. I want to go out for dinner, to go to the theatre, to be a normal person again. Please Universe, surely I've done my time?"

A card jutted out as if wanting her to read it and she turned it over. It was the Hermit.

She'd drawn this one before. The Hermit represented withdrawal and solitude, a search for something. Its key message, she remembered, was one of patience: waiting for the solution to come to you, and not going out in search for it. It was a time for silent observation, introspection and trust: *set your house in order*, the book had said, *and wait on the guidance of your soul*.

Set your house in order. A sign from the Universe that she should get on with the vacuuming. There had been times when Cat had wondered what the point was of doing housework, and days when she felt she had nothing even to get up for. But in truth she had more pride than to let herself, and her flat, go. She was too meticulous; she loathed untidiness and couldn't bear to watch the dust gathering on the mantelpiece over her fake gas fire. *Set your house in order*. Regardless how desperate her life seemed, she always did just that.

Every Saturday she would clean the bathroom, arranging all her products in descending height, turned at an angle against the tiles, just so. Then she'd dust, take her old papers to be recycled, vacuum throughout and wash the kitchen floor. In the cold of winter she likened herself to *Doctor Zhivago's* Lara, who kept her house in order despite war, revolution and deprivation. She'd walk tall and proud, belying the hardship she faced every day. And what of poor Tonya, who deprived herself of heat and food and had to share her house with thirteen peasant families? Cat's hardship was pretty tame by comparison.

She needed more tea to shake off her hangover. Putting the

kettle on again, she noticed Precious, her neighbor's little ginger and white cat, looking in through the French windows from the terrace. Gently she opened the door and let it in.

"Hello, you." She stroked the cat's head. "Won't they let you in? Is it too cold out there? Would you like some milk?"

The little cat jumped up appreciatively, brushing its body against Cat's leg. She went to the kitchen, feeling rather pleased that over the weeks it had chosen to become friends with her. She filled a little bowl with milk and put it down on the kitchen floor. The cat sniffed and promptly ignored it.

"Hey, Precious, guess what? I've got an interview with Trafalgar Broadcasting. Yes. They're interested in me." The cat peered behind the sofa before heading up the single step to her bedroom. Gracefully it slipped under the bed as Cat returned to the kitchen.

"What exciting things shall I do today, Presh?" she called out, pleased that it gave her an excuse to talk aloud. "A spot of shopping? A gallery or exhibition? A slap-up lunch with friends? I've got it!" She smiled as the little cat wandered down toward her. "I'll do some vacuuming, wash the bath, nip around to the supermarket for the bargains, get a cheap bottle of wine and stay in and watch TV! Now there's the thing."

She bent down to stroke the cat. "Can you believe what's become of my life?" she whispered. "I bloody can't." She scratched under its chin. "But it's going to get so much better."

Four

Cat was on her way back from the Rubens' canteen, clutching a chicken salad sandwich, when she ran into Pryce.

"Dominic, how was your weekend?" she asked, taking in his suit, his tie, his shirt and the renegade bit of hair that refused to be gelled back.

"Fine, thanks, I slept through most of it."

Definitely no girlfriend, then, she thought. "Good for you. Look, do you mind if I'm a little late in on Thursday? I have a job interview to go to."

"Oh, no, that'll be fine, I'm sure."

She was disappointed that he didn't ask her more. She was itching to tell him about the appointment she had just made with Trafalgar. In her fantasies this request had led to a long conversation about her life and her work and resulted in a dinner invitation to a romantic West End restaurant.

"Thank you, it's an important one," she tried.

"They all are." He looked pained, turned around and smashed straight into a filing cabinet behind him. She didn't know whether to check if he was all right or to pretend she hadn't noticed. Clearly embarrassed, he carried on walking away from her.

He likes me! She thought in awe. *He's awkward in my presence.* She almost skipped back to her desk where Graham Clark, a junior manager, was hovering. Sophie, Dominic's secretary, newly tanned and visibly proud of the ring on her wedding finger, had spent most of the morning catching up on office gossip, and seemed happy for Cat to continue with her duties.

"Sorry to bother you, but you couldn't look into some flights for me, could you?" Graham asked.

Cat had rather a soft spot for Graham. He was in his early twenties and had joined Rubens a year ago as a graduate. During her first week the annual bonuses had been announced and he had wandered around the department with a dazed look on his face, as if he found it hard to believe that anyone thought him worth so much extra.

"I need to go to Hong Kong the week after next," he added apologetically.

"Do you?" she asked. "How wonderful. Have you been before?"

"No, I haven't. It should be exciting."

"Certainly should. I lived there for a couple of years."

"You lived in Hong Kong?" Jackie swung around in her chair. "I never knew that. You are a dark old horse."

Little did she know. "Haven't I mentioned it? Yes, it was great."

"So what was you doing there then, same sort of thing as this?" Jackie asked.

"Er, no, not exactly. Administrational stuff mostly." *Running a department, managing a multi-million dollar budget* . . . She turned back to Graham. "Do you know where you're going to be staying?"

"The company uses the Marriott. Do you know it?"

"Oh yes." Cat smiled. "Very well." A warm memory of a spacious elevator, a man called Declan Moran and two shocked American tourists wafted through her mind. "It's a nice hotel. Give me your dates and I'll see what I can come up with."

"Thanks, Cat." Graham handed her a sheet with his proposed itinerary. From the corner of her eye she could see Dominic Pryce racing down the corridor toward her, his tie flung over one shoulder. She wondered if it made him go faster. Their eyes locked briefly, and Cat was aware of Jackie saying, "Hong Kong, eh? What a life that must have been. So how long was you out there for?"

"About two years," she replied, still watching Pryce.

"And what made you come back then, was you missing home?"

"No, not at all." She turned to face Jackie, aware that he was coming into their area, and would hear everything she said. "My contract ran out," she lied.

"And are you glad to be back?"

"Not really, no." Cat smiled. "It's actually been quite tough. But I'm an eternal optimist, you know, and things are looking up."

They locked eyes again.

"Glad to hear it." He smiled awkwardly. "Could you make three copies of this for me?"

"My pleasure." Cat smiled. For the first time, she felt vaguely in control. Dominic Pryce had smashed into a filing cabinet. He felt awkward in her presence. Finally Cat had a sense of power.

At the photocopier, she watched, mesmerized, as the document reproduced itself and spewed out into three different racks, pausing only to jam itself a couple of times. The memory of Declan Moran made its fleeting daily appearance in her mind, and she held on to it affectionately for a second, enjoying the warm familiarity of his features and his smile. Then she released him, let him go as she had all those months previously. She wondered when the day would come when she'd realize that it had been a full week, a fortnight, a month even, since she had last thought of him. And in a perverse way it frightened her that she might become so detached as to forget him completely, and finally accept that he no longer played a part in her life.

But she was accepting it, and it surprised her how she could now think of him without feeling either pain or jealousy. He had made his choice and she had finally moved on, reaching the point where she could remember him, and the past they shared, with a simple sense of affection.

She watched Dominic as he talked animatedly with Graham Clark. Was it because of him that she had let Declan go? Or had that process started earlier, before she'd even joined Rubens? She paused to admire the line of his back, the strength in his shoulders, the emotion in his face as he talked. Their meeting had been random, chance. She could have joined any agency, and Savoir-

Faire could have sent any of their temps to do this job. It could only be evidence of a greater force at work, that in her loneliness a guiding hand was nudging her toward a better future.

Without warning, her better future had a minor coughing fit, making a rasping, phlegm-filled sound redolent of a Hong Kong street vendor, then smiled sheepishly in her direction and headed back toward his office.

She finished her photocopying and returned to her desk. The area was quite clear. Sophie was chatting to the girls in human resources, Jackie didn't look all that busy and most of the senior managers were in meetings. Cat took a deep breath. In those last few seconds she had seen her future and released her past. Now it was time to have fun.

"Jackie, you couldn't do me an enormous favor, could you?" she asked.

"Course I could, love, what is it?"

"Well, this friend of mine's arrived in London and is staying at the Park Royal Hotel. We've got this sort of long-running joke going that we leave hoax messages for one another. He really got me last time and so I wanted to wind him up. It's just, you know, he'd recognize me."

"So you want me to make the call for you then?"

"Would you? I've written it all out here." She handed Jackie the sheet of paper she'd worked on all weekend. "He's probably in a meeting so you'll go straight through to his voice mail. Of course if he picks up you could always wing it, otherwise just hang up."

"No problem." Jackie scanned through the script as Cat dialled the hotel, her stomach turning over. As the number started ringing, Cat handed Jackie the phone.

"Hello, I'd like to leave a message for a guest of yours if I may," she started confidently. "A Mr. Maximilian Carnegie. Carnegie, yes, that's right. Could you connect me to his voice mail please."

Anxiously Cat checked around the office, praying that no one should interrupt them.

"Hello, this is a message for Mr. Carnegie," Jackie read. "I'm calling from the office of Miss Suzi Barratt at DigiSat Communications." Jackie threw Cat a puzzled look. Cat nodded encouragingly. "I apologize for the late notice but we have only just found out that you're in London. Miss Barratt would very much like to meet with you regarding digital strategic considerations and was hoping that you would be able to attend a breakfast meeting with her tomorrow morning at 7:30 at our offices in Twickenham. If I don't hear from you, I'll assume you can make it. Thank you very much." She passed the receiver back to Cat, who practically threw it back on the phone.

"You were masterful, Jackie," she said.

"So what are digital strategic considerations anyway?"

"Nothing. A bollocks term I just made up, but it should appeal to him."

"And what if he goes out there?"

"He won't, he'll figure it out," Cat assured her, returning to her desk.

He'll be totally and utterly humiliated, that's what, Cat thought. *And I've only just started.*

PART TWO

Hong Kong
Three Years Earlier

Five

Maximilian Carnegie kept Cat waiting for over an hour before arriving, unannounced, in Frontier's reception area. A vision of puffed-up importance and perma-tan, he wore an immaculately tailored suit, an extremely conservative blue tie and a pair of pretty terrible tasselled shoes. His skin was remarkably line-free for a man Cat guessed to be around forty-five and she caught herself wondering if he'd had a face-lift. He had a square chin and intense blue eyes, which looked as though they could read her every thought. His hair was silvery grey and what could only be described as bouffant, rising up like waves from his forehead. Given the level of humidity, which had flattened Cat's hair the minute she'd stepped out of her taxi, this was little short of miraculous.

"I've gotta go to a reception," he told her without bothering to introduce himself. Clearly she was meant to know who he was. "We can talk on the way."

Cat hesitated, caught off-guard.

"Are you coming or do you intend to sit here all evening?" He looked vaguely irritated.

"Of course I am, I'm sorry." She jumped up, stretching out her hand. "Catherine Wellesley."

"I know who you are." He shook her hand, unselfconsciously admiring her tall, slender body, freshly tanned from a Thai beach. She was wearing a pale blue suit, and was suddenly aware that its skirt was too short and her bare legs too long. They walked in silence through the main entrance toward a waiting car.

"So what brought you to Hong Kong?"

"I was made redundant when my company was taken over. So I packed my bags, rented out my apartment and spent the next six months travelling around Asia."

"That's a brave move." At their approach, Max's driver leaped out of his seat to open the car door.

"Where did you go?" Max asked as they climbed in. She was just about to answer when he leaned forward and gave the driver the name of a hotel to head for, and she stopped herself, feeling slightly foolish. It was as if he was deliberately trying to unnerve her.

"India first," she tried. "Sri Lanka, Nepal, then to Singapore and Malaysia and finally to Thailand, where I spent the last six weeks."

"The last time I was in Thailand, I stayed at the Amanpuri in Phuket. Did you go there?"

She smiled. A place like that would have been unthinkable on her budget. "No, I stayed on Kata Beach, somewhere simple." It had had sheets on the bed, a bathtub and hot water, and Cat had revelled in its relative luxury.

"Henry Kissinger was in the next villa to mine," Max added proudly, as if this fact reflected well on him. Cat said nothing, just nodded with what she hoped was an admiring look, wondering why the president of a TV network would be trying to impress an out-of-work beach bum.

"So you want to settle in Hong Kong?"

"Very much so. It has this incredible energy. I want to be a part of it."

"You'll need all the energy you can get if you're gonna work for me." It sounded like a threat.

"That's fine," she told him. "I got bored with lazing on the beach. I've had enough of my own company, you know? I want to feel involved again, to be a part of something. I need a challenge."

"That's exactly the attitude I'm after," he said in approval. "Because at Frontier I'll have you running around like a headless rabbit."

Cat went to laugh out loud, but turned it into a cough instead.

There was an awkward silence. Max seemed to be more interested in admiring her legs than in finding anything out about her.

"Who actually is behind Frontier?" she asked awkwardly, trying to distract him.

"Desmond Tang, one of the richest men in Hong Kong and founder of Tang Bauhinia Holdings, one of Hong Kong's biggest corporations."

"And you're launching how many channels?" she asked and tried to pay attention as he explained the channel strategy of the network, the carriage and distribution methods and the projected audience figures. Nodding self-consciously at what she believed to be appropriate moments, Cat tried to appear attentive and intelligent, but could not help but take in the extraordinary sights of Hong Kong through the car window.

It had been just six days since she had turned up at the infamous Chungking Mansions on Nathan Road, on the Kowloon side, and secured a tiny room with a fan, a shower and the odd cockroach for company. She'd spent the first couple of days securing her interview and getting to know her new city. She revelled in Hong Kong's color, in the heat that took her breath away, in every bead of sweat she felt trickling down her back. She found intriguing the constant smell of cooking: the fat, the spices, the unidentifiable pieces of meat she saw displayed on street corners. She loved the clashing neon lights, the stalls that stayed open all night and the range of things on sale, from fake Rolexes to tailored suits. And at sunset she'd head out to the harbor, to the clock tower by the Tsim Sha Tsui ferry terminal, and gaze across at a view she'd only ever seen before on postcards, and count the days until her appointment with Max Carnegie.

"So your role as I see it," he continued in his laborious American drawl, "would be to maintain the on-air promotions, scheduling and operations of the barker channel. Then, once the remaining channels are launched, to develop a creative services department to implement an effective cross-channel promotional strategy and appropriate sales and marketing support. Are you interested?"

"Oh, definitely." Cat tried to sound enthusiastic as she raced to engage her sun-drenched brain and work out what he had just said. "I'd love to do it."

He escorted her into the bar of the Regent Hotel, conveniently close to the Chungking Mansions. It had rained heavily earlier in the day, and the last thing she wanted was to ruin her only decent clothes getting back. Sipping a mineral water she watched as an army of suits swooped in to shake Max's hand. Clearly Frontier was the hottest news in town and there were a lot of people eager to be a part of it. All she wanted was a firm offer, but whenever she thought it might be close someone else would interrupt, and his attention would yet again be distracted.

The one sight that kept her attention was the view. It was becoming clearer now—Hong Kong was beginning to make sense. As much as it still looked like a giant postcard which had been placed in front of her, she was beginning to recognize landmarks, buildings she'd passed on her wanderings. There was Central, the commercial district, dominated by the Bank of China Tower with its goalpost-like spires at the top; to its east, Wanchai, full of night clubs and seedy bars that reminded her of London's Soho. Above Central was Mid Levels, a mainly residential area full of tower blocks and the odd Colonial style building, and beyond that The Peak, Hong Kong's most exclusive residential area with its breathtaking views and lavish villas. It was something to aspire to, Cat thought, sipping her mineral water and wishing it was a Sauvignon Blanc: a beautiful house with a view, far removed from the tiny room where her life here had begun.

"Miranda Elliott, Red Dragon Advertising." An attractive blonde with an English accent woke Cat from her dreams. She was wearing a Chanel suit and too much gold, and handed her a business card.

Cat introduced herself, offering her hand. "You're involved in Frontier's launch?"

"We're handling one or two sponsorship deals," Miranda answered crisply. Her coral lipstick matched her nail polish, and she wore huge pearl earrings. It was not a look Cat had been familiar with in London. "Do you have a card?"

"No I don't, I'm afraid, I'm not even sure I have a job yet." Cat laughed apologetically, wondering if a woman like that could ever become a friend.

"Oh really?" Miranda lost interest, turned away and began talking to the person on her left. Smiling, despite herself, Cat scrunched the card into a ball. Her action caught Max's eye.

"You're obviously no one here without a business card," she said sheepishly.

"So we'd better see what we can do about getting you one now, hadn't we?"

Cat had already worked out a figure to ask for, basing her calculations on her most recent salary, and adding a healthy pay raise. She had then converted it to Hong Kong dollars and rounded the figure up, wondering if she dared go that high. But having just spent an hour in Frontier's reception area, watching in awe the number of immaculately dressed women who darted from one work station to the next, Cat had decided to increase that figure by twenty per cent. She could always come down.

"That sounds reasonable enough to me," Max told her as she tried to disguise her amazement. "And when can you start?"

"Tomorrow?"

"That was the right answer. Be at the studios at nine o'clock."

Having taken a taxi before, Cat hadn't realized quite how far out Frontier's premises actually were. Based in a sprawling grey industrial complex, it was a good walk from either the ferry terminal or the nearest MTR underground station. As she passed factories, low-rent housing complexes, a cheap shopping mall and the odd dead rat, her enthusiasm began to wane. By the time she had reached the complex the sweat was pouring down her back and she was wondering whether to turn and run.

There was no air conditioning in the main entrance, where she had to bypass a group of Chinese workers unloading crates, but the Frontier offices themselves were at least cool. They were painted a pale and lifeless grey and were full of people who looked like they'd been there for years, but who in reality could have only just started themselves.

Cat's first task was to make sense of the so-called barker channel, which was free-to-air and highlighted each of the five pay-TV channels on the network. They were Score, the sports channel, Vibe, a music video channel, Frontier Kids, Variety, an entertainment channel and Movies Galore.

Cat's barker channel, which was to eventually become Variety, was topped up with entertainment programs bought by an acquisitions department Cat rarely saw. They seemed to work through the night, negotiating deals on long-distance calls to Los Angeles, and then secretly depositing program information on her desk by morning. Some days she'd come in to find a bunch of TV movies and ageing series had been acquired for her; other days, disappointingly, she'd find just a single documentary on dolphins, or a profile of a Taiwanese artist she'd never heard of.

Cat learned to her dismay that Saturday mornings were considered just another working day, but one on which casual clothes at least were acceptable. The morning officially ended at one, but inevitably continued until late afternoon or early evening. It was extraordinary how hard people worked—it was as if they had signed a contract agreeing to sacrifice their lives for the company. She felt like she had unwittingly entered a competition to see who could stay on the longest every evening, because no matter how late she left, there was always someone else tapping urgently on a keyboard or slumped over a document at their desk.

There was no time to apartment-hunt, so she migrated to a motel nearer the office, where she rented a larger room with a comfortable bed, spacious bathroom and a disturbing number of mirrors on the walls. It was only as she signed in and noticed that the rooms were also available by the hour, or the afternoon, that she realized just why it was so reasonable. She'd get back late at night, run herself a deep bath and fall asleep to the sound of shy giggles and footsteps down the corridor, and laugh at the improbability of ever staying in such a place.

What was important now was that she prove herself to Max. Normally she would have held back from making any definitive changes to the system until she was better established. But it didn't take her long to realize that at Frontier there *was* no system, and that each department looked after itself, rarely interacting with the others. What the channel needed was overall management, someone to pull together all the loose threads.

She discovered she had two Kiwi promo producers, Darrell and Eddie, who had been poached from the local terrestrial channel, and who would turn up randomly to hover at her desk until she gave them something to do. She created a system for them, assigning them specific tasks rather than gratefully accepting their offerings, as they seemed to expect.

But it was never enough for Max. He would sit at his oversized desk studying the channel, and complain bitterly about the repetition of promos, demanding to see fresh new material every day. In principle Cat agreed with him, but her producers chose to spend days laboring over a thirty-second spot. She tried to bully, beg and even bribe them into increasing their output, but they would just complain that she was "undermining their creative integrity."

"Much as I'd love for you to go off and spend six weeks creating a masterpiece," she tried one evening in the edit suite, "right now I need bulk. I have a pool of about a dozen promos available to me, a twenty-four-hour schedule, three breaks an hour and no commercials. We're on a ridiculous level of rotation here and Max is watching religiously. Please, just get into that suite and knock up a dozen quick, simple promos I can use for now. Then go off and start creating masterpieces."

"We have edit time over the weekend," said Eddie, who was somewhere in his late thirties and wore thick glasses and stone-washed jeans. "I dare say we could knock up a couple for yous then."

"A couple? In one day? Come on, I used to do this job, you could churn out five or six if you tried."

"You kidding? If you want to see crap on the air you might be able to but—"

"But that *is* what I'm seeing. Because no matter how stunning your promos, if they're on twice an hour every hour they become crap. I need choice, flexibility. I need simple, direct, no-nonsense promos, that's all."

Clearly this was beneath them. Throughout the encounter Cat noticed the editor, Declan Moran, was keeping a distinctly low profile.

"Declan, how many trails do you think you could cut in one session, just good opening shots, bit of dialogue, an explosion here, the odd smooch there, good closer?"

"Oh well, if you're after a formula approach," Darrell started. He wore a lumberjack-style shirt and a thick scowl.

"I could do five or six in a session," the Irish editor replied quietly.

"I don't need elaborate graphics, I don't need multi-layered images, just well-cut shots with a tight script."

"Well, you're welcome to try your hand if you like," Eddie suggested bitterly.

"All right I will," Cat snapped. "Not every trail has to be worthy of a show-reel, you know. I just need to get new stuff on air. When's our next decent edit session?"

"Saturday overnight," Darrell told her triumphantly, clearly relieved to be offloading it. "Eight till eight with Mr. Moran here." He nodded toward the editor.

"Great," Cat groaned. "There goes my house-hunting again. Show me the outstanding stuff on this list." Her promotions request sheet lay virtually untouched. "A drama, three sitcoms, a documentary and a soap opera. Fine," she said defiantly, wondering how she would ever find time to prepare. "I'll show you it can be done. And then maybe you can rethink your creative strategy and add quantity to the quality. See you Saturday, Declan."

Dutifully she spent Friday and Saturday preparing for her edit—logging shots, writing scripts and working out rough paper edits, trying to visualize which shots might work well next to each other. It was always satisfying when she got it right and each cut flowed seamlessly into the other, and challenging if she were wrong and would have to think on her feet to correct it.

That night she and Declan Moran worked well together. He appreciated the fact that, unlike her producers, she had her tapes ready and in the right order, she'd logged the time codes for each shot and there was no last-minute dashing around to find materials. She had written her scripts already and could judge the length of mute shots needed before a piece of dialogue. She appreciated that he was a creative editor, suggesting alternative shots and trimming off frames here and there to make the perfect cut. Together they laughed, enthused, drank coffee and Coke, ate greasy take-out noodles and bullied each other into staying awake. By four in the morning, Declan was working on a piece of audio and Cat lay down, exhausted, on the sofa.

"Catherine, don't," he urged. "Go and get some coffee and a snack, but don't go to sleep now. If you do you'll lose it completely."

"I know, I know, you're right." She yawned. "How do you manage this?"

"It's easier on shift, you fall into a pattern. It's the one-offs that are tough. I got some sleep this afternoon—that's what you should have done."

"I was bloody well working all day," she groaned. "One of Monday's shows was rejected because of tape damage, and I had to rework the schedule, not to mention finish preparing for this lot." She yawned and stretched. "I've never worked so hard in all my life."

"You're doing a good job," he said quietly. "You've transformed the channel. Everyone's saying so. It actually makes sense now; it's starting to look like a proper station. And you're right about getting more stuff on air."

"Try telling Cecil B. De Mille and Alfred Hitchcock out there." She hauled herself back into the chair beside his, quietly thrilled by what he had just said.

By seven-thirty they had produced six thirty-second trailers which were dramatic, funny, direct and to the point. Despite her exhaustion Cat felt a huge sense of pride.

"Thank you, Declan, I really enjoyed working with you."

"Go and get some sleep in the sun," he suggested. "It'll do you good."

"I haven't got any sun. All I've got is a room in a love motel full of mirrors."

He looked shocked. "What the fuck are you doing there, can that be safe?" They had started walking out of the building now, and were immediately smothered by the heat and humidity outside. "What kind of people use those places anyway? Let me ask around for you, see if anyone's heard of anything else."

She couldn't help but feel touched—he seemed genuinely concerned. After six months of being strong and independent and brave, someone else was actually concerned about her welfare. She hadn't realized she'd missed it until that point. She looked at his face in the light for the first time. His grey-blue eyes were squinting slightly, revealing a spread of lines she suddenly wanted to touch. His hair was a tousled dirty blonde and she could see a triangle of darker blonde hairs creeping up from his chest toward his throat. He really had become better-looking as the night wore on.

"Look." He paused, as if not sure whether to say what he wanted to or not. "I've got a place in Sai Kung with a roof terrace. I was going to sleep for a bit and then do a late roast lunch. You're very welcome to join me."

"Declan, are you sure?" Nothing could have sounded nicer. He had his motorbike with him but hailed her a taxi, giving the driver his address in a faltering but impressive Cantonese. She snoozed in the back, wrapping her arms around herself against the fierce air conditioning, and found herself fantasizing that they were his arms, and that she could feel the warmth of his breath on her neck.

Declan Moran's apartment was on a leafy road overlooking Sai Kung and its sweeping bay, surrounded by hills. This was Cat's first visit to the New Territories, the mass of land north of Kowloon that bordered on China, and she had no idea that Hong Kong could be so beautiful, or so quiet. It was about as far removed from the harsh grey of Frontier's neighborhood as it could have been, and in Declan's presence, it seemed like paradise.

She showered and dressed again before joining him on the roof terrace, where he had laid out a sun-bed for her.

"I'm setting my alarm for three," he said. "Then I'm roasting a chicken and will aim to be out of here by seven for tonight's edit. Oh and I've got strawberries, too." His face brightened at the prospect.

"Declan Moran, I think I've just fallen in love with you," Cat gushed as she clambered on to the canvas sun-bed, hoping it wouldn't topple over under her weight. And then it struck her.

"Oh bloody hell," she murmured after he'd gone. "I think I have, too."

Six

"Catherine, will you come into Mr. Carnegie's office, please?" Lacy Fok had been Max's secretary since Frontier had started. She had the frame of a twelve-year-old, with the tiniest waist Cat had ever seen and the skinniest legs, which today were encased in a pair of white nylon tights, despite the soaring temperature outside. She had a straight dark bob and a greyish complexion, and was wearing a neat black skirt and white synthetic blouse. Her breath smelled of the pork bun she had just eaten.

Max's office was twice the size of any other, and overlooked the main floor where the programming department was based. In one corner stood a grey meeting table with four matching chairs, and in the other a black leather sofa behind a chrome and glass coffee table. Above them five television monitors were mounted—each dedicated to a different Frontier channel. A panoramic night view of Hong Kong's Victoria Harbor hung on one wall, next to a selection of framed photos of Max with people Cat supposed were local celebrities and VIPs. One showed Max and Desmond Tang shaking hands in front of a large satellite, taken as the service was announced. Next to that was a copy of Max on the cover of the *Asian News Weekly*, the word PIONEER emblazoned across his chest.

Visitors were clearly meant to feel awed in his presence. Max himself was sitting at his oversized black desk, reading a document.

"Been shopping?" He gave her a vague look of approval before nodding to the chair opposite his. She was wearing a soft beige pantsuit with a Mandarin style jacket and a pair of oyster-colored mules from which ten rouge-noir painted toenails peeped. It was amazing how efficiently she could shop in the last minutes of Sunday's opening hours—she never ceased to impress herself.

"So you sent those two assholes a rocket, I see."

"I'm sorry?"

"The new promos." He looked up, irritated. "It was about time."

"I'm glad you approve," Cat beamed. "Something I knocked up at the weekend."

"You made them?" He put his papers down in surprise.

"I wanted to keep my hand in."

He studied her for a second before returning to his reading, as if embarrassed. "In any event, I have a board meeting in Taiwan coming up this week and will need a list of all your available programming. When can you have it ready by?"

"Oh, I'll just print it out," she said simply. "I've created a log with everything listed, including all the dates they've been scheduled. Is that the kind of thing you were after?"

He frowned, as if disappointed that this request wasn't going to create hours of work. "Yes, well, that'll be all. Good work," he half mumbled as she left.

Cat returned to her desk, printed out the inventory and gave it to Lacy. "How long will Mr. Carnegie be away for?" she asked.

"Until the weekend," she replied in her faltering English. "He'll be back in the office on Saturday."

"Good. Some peace and quiet for everyone," she whispered to Lacy's delighted giggles.

In Max's absence the atmosphere in the building seemed to lighten. Cat was aware of laughter, of people chatting, taking time out to get to know each other. It was as if a collective sense of relief had descended on the premises. For her part she took a couple of afternoons off to house-hunt, and found a tiny place in Wanchai on Hong Kong Island, close to the ferry that took her to work. It had two bedrooms that faced on to a busy road and a tiny kitchen with a view of a building site. The bathroom was covered in mustard yellow tiles and there were few windows, but the rent was cheap and the contract ran on a month-to-month basis, allowing her to look out for something better in the meantime. Having spent the last seven months in beach huts, backpacker haunts and a room that was available by the hour, Cat thought it was wonderful.

The day she moved in she found her nearest supermarket and bought groceries, vodka, tonic water and some Australian wine, and enjoyed the pleasure of cooking herself a meal for the first time in months. She unpacked her belongings, throwing a Thai silk sarong over the Formica dining table and hanging some Indian prints on the walls. She color co-ordinated her clothes in the wardrobe and placed her toiletries in descending order in the bathroom, aiming to cover up as much of the mustard as was possible. Then she sipped her Chablis and surveyed her property with a sense of satisfaction. In less than two months she'd found a job, a home and even a potential love interest. People weren't exaggerating when they said things moved fast out east.

Although seedy in parts, Wanchai was a fascinating location, and Cat felt she had moved into the heart of the real Hong Kong. As well as the numerous bars and strip joints she had at her disposal, she quickly found everything she needed, from Asian restaurants of all varieties, to dry cleaners, furniture stores, a video rental place and several markets. These she decided to browse one Saturday afternoon, fighting her way through the hordes that made Oxford Street look like a country lane.

One market sold mostly household wares and cheap electronics, and Cat stocked up on useful items for the kitchen and bathroom. Lugging home a dishwashing bowl and sink-tidy, she passed a narrow alleyway selling songbirds in intricately carved bamboo cages. At the far end a group of wizened old men had gathered, each clutching his own cage. She stopped to watch, thrilled by her discovery, before turning a corner to find that a crowd had gathered. She joined them to see a man waving a writhing snake in his arms, making loud whooping noises as he did so. When satisfied that he had a large enough audience, he bit its head off with a roar and spat it to the ground. Cat watched in disgust as he then threw the headless snake on to a pile of others still wriggling in a mass at his feet.

It was another Hong Kong story to tell her parents—there

were so many of them. She enjoyed the fact that as her mother spoke of bridge and tennis evenings and the odd theatre trip to Bath, Cat could describe love motels, cockroaches and men who bit the heads off snakes. She felt as if she had never really lived before, as if her life until this point had been nothing but a dull and vapid existence, and that now it had become something vibrant, something colorful and intense.

Intense was the right word for work, too. Max watched over his staff as if he expected them to let him down at any moment. And when they didn't—when they worked fifteen-hour days to deliver the shows, graphics and schedule changes that he routinely demanded—they received not gratitude, but just an even harder push.

He introduced weekly department heads meetings, which in theory were a chance to exchange information but in practice gave Max the opportunity to hold court, make either sexist or racist remarks and hand out ritual beatings. Cat sometimes felt she was on the set of *The Untouchables*, and half expected him to produce a baseball bat and slam it down on to some unsuspecting skull at any time.

The department heads included Trent Davies, the American in charge of Vibe who was cocaine-thin and had dyed black hair and a permanent sprinkling of dandruff on his shoulders; Greg Sharp, the Australian head of Score whose passions, Cat learned, included fly fishing and computer games; Lorna Cardelli, a petite New Yorker with a quick wit and the longest fingernails Cat had ever seen, who ran the press office; Brandon Miller, who headed up program acquisitions and Jerry Greenberg, who was responsible for sales and distribution.

"Catherine." Max rounded on her at one meeting. "What exactly are your promo makers doing? I walked past Eddie yesterday and he had his feet on the table and he was watching TV." He spat out the words in disgust.

"He does have to watch quite a lot for his job," she replied. Max seemed to forget that watching television could no longer be considered a leisure activity. She added quickly before he could erupt, "He was probably logging shots for a promo."

"Well, will you read him the riot act and tell him to get his fat ugly feet off of the furniture? And why all the repeats on your channel? Do we have a problem with programming here?"

"I agree that we'll always need new programming, Max." She

looked nervously at Brandon Miller, whose team she knew was concentrating on a forthcoming movie channel deal. "I've been wondering lately why we don't go after British material—is there any particular reason for that?"

Max shrugged. "I wasn't that crazy about it, but I guess we could see how it works."

"We're broadcasting to several old colonies, aren't we? Hong Kong, Singapore, India, Malaysia—these people might well relate to British product. Many of our viewers may have been educated in Britain, after all. A handful of quality period dramas would make perfect, safe viewing and really embellish what is very much an action-oriented schedule right now." Cat had to laugh at her own grasp of the required language.

"You might have a point there. Brandon, do you have a problem with this?"

Cat hadn't quite worked Brandon Miller out yet. He was tall and balding, and she guessed in his mid thirties, though he looked like he'd always been forty-five. Originally from Chicago, he wore slick suits and a chunky fraternity ring on one finger. His sentences were as carefully co-ordinated as his shirts and ties, and he gave little away of himself.

"No, I don't. I think it's a great idea. I'd be happy for Cat to help out with the selection process."

"Well then, you go ahead and get it. You know the product, you talk the same language as the suppliers, and you know the deal terms we require. See what you can come up with."

Cat stopped, not quite sure of herself. "You want me to do the deals?" She looked awkwardly at Brandon, whose face was emotionless.

"You saying you're not up to it?"

"Oh, not at all, I'd love to do it." Brandon, she realized, was holding his pen so tight it might snap.

"Good, go get me some decent Brit series. I won't be satisfied until I see *Upstairs, Downstairs* and *Brideshead Requested* in the schedule." He smiled, pleased with his knowledge of British programming, and Cat didn't have the heart to correct him.

She left the meeting in shock. It seemed that just as she thought she was on top of all her responsibilities, she was given yet another huge project to cope with. And it wasn't just happening to her—Trent was under constant pressure to devise new music shows, with new presenters; Greg was forever being pushed to acquire some little-known sporting event in China and Lorna was supposed to turn their every move into front-page news.

Cat was presenting her program selections to Max a couple of weeks later when he stopped her.

"You know, Catherine, I've decided to restructure the department. Movies Galore launches next week and so your channel can morph into Variety. I've hired someone else to head up promotions and corporate services—she'll be starting at the end of the year. A Brit, Joanna Kindly Word, or something like that, some double-barrelled name." He said it as if that fact alone guaranteed her ability to do the job.

"I need Brandon's department to focus on long-range strategy, the second phase of channels, joint-venture partnerships, interactivity. So I'm making you program director of Variety, with immediate effect. You can have that corner office. I'll give you a fifteen per cent raise and expect you to fill your channel with excellent Brit programming. I'm currently looking around for a general manager, but in the meantime, you can build your own team. Can you handle it?"

"Max, I don't know what to say but, yes I can, and thank you."

Slightly dazed, she made her way back to her work station. Things were falling into place so quickly that she couldn't quite believe it herself. But instead of wanting to get back to work and prepare for her new role, Cat felt this terrible urge to open a bottle of wine and discuss it with a friend. She smiled to herself—she wasn't growing that quickly, then.

The route led her past the press office, and Lorna Cardelli's area. Lorna hailed from Brooklyn but had lived in Hong Kong for six years with her investment banker boyfriend Andrew. Cat didn't know her well but suspected that they could become great friends, given the chance. She was immensely popular amongst both the Chinese and Western staff. Cat sometimes heard her in the mornings, learning her Cantonese word of the day and trying to create pigeon sentences with the few she could remember, much to the amusement of her Chinese team. She would answer her phone in an exaggerated Cantonese "Wei" and greet everyone she passed with "jo san, jo san"—or good morning—as she arrived each day.

Her partition walls were cluttered with a selection of headlines, cartoons and photos, each of which she had wittily cap-
tioned herself, and Cat noticed how passers-by were instinctively
drawn to her, as if she guaranteed them a rare moment of fun.
Whenever Cat looked up it seemed that yet another adoring
graphic designer or editor was in her midst, laughing at her jokes,
her wickedly accurate impressions and the funny stories of her
day.

Today Lorna was surrounded by a group of giggling Chinese
secretaries who were tearing pages out of a huge pile of magazines. Lorna, who wasn't much taller than they were, stood out
with her auburn bobbed hair, orange T-shirt and olive-green
pantsuit.

"Having fun?" Cat asked.

Lorna looked up, raising an eyebrow. "Bliss. Want to join us?"

"What are you doing?"

"Frontier's first ever listings magazine, imaginatively called
Frontier. Issue one, volume one. This page is the Message from
our President, Maximilian Carnegie. Spot the deliberate mistake."

Cat picked up one of the torn-out sheets. There was a photo of
Max, smiling proudly. The message spoke of Frontier's aims, its
channels and the highlights of the month.

"I don't get it. What's wrong?"

"Max Carnegie is President and CEO," Lorna hissed. "We left
the CEO bit off."

"And would our esteemed viewers care?"

Lorna looked around her, clearly not wanting her staff to
overhear. "You wanna take a walk? I doubt they could give a flying
fuck," she added once they were out of earshot. "But Max cares."

"So subscribers are going to be sent a listings magazine with a
page torn out?"

"Honey, there's even an ad on the other side. Jerry Greenberg
has *so* got to kiss their asses right now."

"It's crazy," Cat whispered guiltily as they reached her desk.
This was the same madman who'd just offered her a huge promotion after all. "What's Max's story? I mean, how did he get here
anyway?"

"He's been in Hong Kong a while. The story goes he was involved in production many years ago, and even had his own company at one point. But the last few years he's been working directly for Desmond Tang."

"Doing what?"

"Right-hand man, dogsbody, bearer of bad tidings. Tang's dirty work mostly. But I guess it incorporated an element of strategy, and he was the one who pushed for the move into broadcasting. Tang trusts him."

"But he has no real TV experience?"

"Can't you tell?" Suddenly things were beginning to fall into place.

"And how long have you worked here?" Cat asked.

"Since the beginning, I was in PR at Tang Bauhinia Holdings, and Max asked me to cross over. So I knew what I was letting myself in for."

"So you've known Max for years, then?"

"Oh yes." Lorna smiled secretively. "The stories I could tell about our Maximum Carnage. Run Carnegie through spell check." She added, seeing the puzzled look on Cat's face. "It's kind of appropriate."

"Is he married?"

"Why? You interested? Twice divorced. Kids in the U.S. Dates around these days—mostly Asian. I always figured Frontier was a useful ruse, you know, to meet women. That black leather casting couch of his."

She wanted to find out more, but Cat was suddenly distracted as Declan Moran walked past. It had been over two months since they'd worked together. She'd meant to stay in touch, but somehow her work never finished and it was easier to slip home to a large vodka than it was to slip around to the edit suites to find him.

Lorna followed Cat's gaze. "Ah, dreamboat Declan?" she teased.

"You think so?" Cat pretended to look as if she couldn't see it, but felt her cheeks redden.

"Oh God yes, he's got a bunch of fans."

"He has?"

Lorna tutted. "Come on, look at the competition around here."

"And there I was, thinking I was special." Cat told her about their edit and the subsequent afternoon.

"Sounds special to me, my dear, silly girl to let that one slip away." She sighed and lifted herself off Cat's desk, pausing to pick up a stapler and run her red-tipped fingers over it. "Better get back to the madhouse."

Cat watched as she sauntered back to her own department, pausing to say a few words in Cantonese to one of the IT assistants, whose face lit up as she did so.

So Declan was in demand. He was popular—a catch. And she, Cat Wellesley, had spent the night with him, albeit in an edit, had had lunch on his terrace and then failed to do a single thing about it. She hadn't even called to thank him. Suddenly there were others after his affections, and Cat felt threatened. She had let their friendship drift, unaware of the competition she faced.

She had no real excuse to go to the operations area, but her producers were editing and she decided it was time to pay them a visit. She was still on a high from her meeting with Max, and felt capable of anything. As she approached, she saw that Declan was in the opposite suite with a producer from Vibe.

Eddie jumped up as she entered, greeting her defensively as if he'd narrowly missed being caught dubbing pornography. "Can we show the boss here what we've done so far?" he asked his editor, who duly rolled back the master tape and ran through the thirty-second cut pieces they had just finished. Cat watched with disinterest, noticing out of the corner of her eye that the Vibe producer had just stood up.

"They were great, thanks everyone." She made for the door.

"Hang on a sec, we did that new comedy series you can take a look at."

She could see Declan's producer leafing through a file as if he needed to fetch something. The promo lasted thirty seconds, but felt like thirty hours.

"Well done, great," she said weakly.

"There are some others on the tape if you like," Darrell added. "It's such a rare treat to see you over here, let's make the most of it." Cat flinched but decided her best defense was to ignore him. "I cut a game show compilation yesterday, too," he continued.

In the other suite the producer was leaving. Declan had pushed back his chair and was stretching his arms behind his head. Another thirty seconds went by.

"Thanks guys, great job," she said as quickly as she could, moving to the door. She had paid little attention. If the promos looked terrible on air and Max complained, she only had herself to blame. She headed toward Declan's suite, pausing for a second. What if he were angry with her? Or thought her rude? Worse still, what if he couldn't remember who she was?

"Declan, hi," she started brightly. "So you're on shift today?"

"Catherine. This is a nice surprise." He lowered his arms, smiling warmly. Her legs nearly caved in.

"Look, I feel terrible, I've still never thanked you for that lovely day in Sai Kung."

"There's nothing to thank me for. It was a pleasure. Have you got yourself out of that brothel yet?"

"Yes I have." She laughed. "It's not much, but it's home." For a second she could picture him there, inside the flat with her. He smiled and there was a slight pause.

"So anyway," she continued. She'd forgotten how dreamy his voice was, and how kind his eyes. She stumbled over her words.

"Well it meant, it meant a lot to me, and I'd like to thank you properly. Would you let me buy you supper, or lunch or something?"

"It's not necessary, Cat, but that would be very nice." His smile was warm and the mood in the darkened suite seemed to lighten. "I'll be off shift in a couple of days."

"Friday perhaps? Drink and dinner?"

"Friday'd be great. What's your extension number?" He wrote it down and promised to call her during the day.

"Still here, boss?" Eddie appeared in the doorway. "I found another trail for you to take a look at."

"Thanks, Eddie, I can't wait." She turned to Declan, a glow in her cheeks. "Better dash." He smiled back, clearly pleased at her invitation. She returned to Eddie's suite and endured another thirty seconds of mediocrity before escaping to her cubicle, and thoughts of restaurants, bars and what on earth she should wear that Friday.

Seven

Cat emerged from the ladies' room with retouched makeup and freshly applied lipstick and could feel the cold steely glare of Max Carnegie upon her. It was just seven o'clock as self-consciously she gathered her bags and logged off her computer, knowing that her every move was being watched. She might have just been promoted, but all that her new-found favor meant was that she felt obliged to work even longer hours.

As she walked past Max's office, she popped her head in. "Half day today," she joked, before he could say anything, secure in the knowledge that he could hardly accuse her of being a slouch.

"So it would seem," he replied curtly. "You got a date?"

"Yes, imagine!" she beamed, refusing to apologize for it.

Max went slightly red and turned away. "Have a good evening, Catherine," he muttered, and she knew she would be punished for it in the morning.

"I know what you're up to," Lorna trilled as she walked past. "Be a good girl, my dear, and be sure to tell me all about it."

As she approached the ferry Cat felt heady with excitement, like a child before Christmas. In Declan and Lorna she would have two wonderful new friends, and life would be funny and sexy and exciting. Her career would settle, her working hours become more reasonable and she'd hopefully have the support and companionship of a wonderful man.

She checked her appearance in the mirror. The early November breeze was doing nothing for her hair. It had taken a long time to dress that morning. She hadn't wanted to look too corporate, so had settled on a simple white T-shirt under her pale blue suit with its extremely short skirt. Her jewelry and makeup were discreet and her heels high. She had given her nails a French polish the previous evening, and from a distance they looked all right. As the ferry docked she sprayed a little Cristalle onto her wrists and through her hair.

He was waiting for her in Lan Kwai Fong, a tiny area in Central full of bars and restaurants. Cat suspected that many expats simply migrated there every evening from their offices, before heading up to their apartments in Mid Levels, and rarely went anywhere else.

For a moment she'd forgotten what he looked like, but was reassured by his pale tousled hair, sloppy sweater and black jeans. Should she kiss him hello? She decided to follow his lead. His face lit up as he saw her, and he gave her a quick peck on each cheek.

"You managed to get away then?"

"Something tells me I'll pay for it in the morning."

They chose a bottle of wine and Cat took her first sip gratefully, enjoying the instant buzz it gave her. At the next table a forty-something European was stroking his Chinese girlfriend's thigh. He was old enough to be her father, and about twice her weight. She was chatting animatedly, wearing a lime green suit with black accessories and white tights.

"You know the expression, FILTH?" Declan was frowning at them. "Failed-in-London-try-Hong Kong. I wonder what he failed at."

"Why do the girls all wear white tights?" Cat asked, wondering if she, too, could be considered a failure.

"You know they wear them throughout the summer?" Declan continued, a puzzled look on his face, "I pity the gynecologists around here."

Cat quickly discovered that Declan didn't take things seriously, which she found madly attractive. He had a wry sense of humor and the ability to sum up in an instant everything she was thinking and feeling about Frontier, or Hong Kong. And he had that soft Irish accent and twinkly come-to-bed eyes that made her feel like the most desirable woman on the planet. But best of all he was normal—gloriously, refreshingly normal. When he joked about Max Carnegie he clearly didn't think for a second that she might use it against him. And had she said anything herself, she knew Declan would never betray her, either.

"You know what I really feel like?" she asked as they were wondering where to eat. "Peking duck. I haven't had any here yet, and that was always my favorite."

"There's a big place a couple of blocks away that specializes in it, though I haven't been. Shall we give it a go?"

The restaurant, like so many, was low on style and ambience, but high on clientele and noise. They ordered and to Cat's delight, a huge roast duck was wheeled toward their table. As much as she wanted to stay and watch the waiter break up the pieces of meat with his chopsticks, as they did in London, she excused herself and went to the loo quickly. On her return, the duck was gone, and all that was left was a plate full of skin and fat.

"Declan?" she cried. "Where's the duck gone?"

"I don't know." He shrugged, looking faintly embarrassed. "They carved all this stuff off and took the rest away."

They looked at each other in surprise before bursting into laughter. It didn't really matter. There would be other meals, she told herself dreamily, other meals, other dates and more shared experiences. Stories they'd laugh about and private jokes. Her career was looking after itself, and Declan would make life complete.

When they had finished, he offered to walk her home. Her place was only fifteen minutes away along Queens Road Central, one of the many streets that ran from east to west, parallel with the harbor front. Once it might even have been the harbor front, Cat mused, as so much land had been reclaimed, and endless skyscrapers built.

"Is it me or is it getting cooler?" she asked awkwardly after a brief silence.

"No, it's getting cooler," he agreed. "Quite pleasant now really."

"I can't believe I've been here almost four months," she told him. "Sometimes it feels like everything is still so new, and then other times, like at work, it feels like I've been here a lifetime."

He didn't say anything, and she wondered what was going on in his mind. It was curious how their easy conversation at the table could falter into awkward silence now they were walking home. Did he share her feeling of inevitability, the unspoken understanding that they were only going to her place for one reason, and it certainly wasn't coffee?

Passing the Bank of China Tower she arched her neck to look up. "I just love the architecture in this place, you know? It's so bold and interesting. I've never seen anything like it before."

She lowered her face and smiled at him, trying to lighten the moment. He took her arm and allowed his hand to drop into hers. It was an easy, natural movement. At the Pacific Place cinema complex they paused to look at the posters.

"There are some great movies on," she said. "Can you believe I haven't seen a thing since I've been here?"

"We could go to one tomorrow if you like," he suggested quietly.

"I'd love to." Thrilled, she began talking about movies, actors, British television and the programs she was trying to acquire. She was just describing a detective series she had been offered when he pulled her toward him, one arm around her back and the other drawing her head in toward his, and kissed her.

"What are you doing to me, woman?" he whispered as he kissed her face and neck, breathing in the scent of her skin. "That day you were at my place, I couldn't sleep for thinking about you. I just wanted to call you into my bedroom and make love to you all day." He kissed her harder, forcing her against the wall.

Cat knew the street they had reached for its market; for the dead pigs she'd watched being delivered early every morning and the rivers of blood which would flow down toward the tramline. It was hardly the most romantic spot to start their affair.

"Let's go home before we get arrested." She fumbled with her keys and he took them from her authoritatively, opening the main door. In the elevator he grabbed her, kissing her deeply until the doors slid open. Then, inside her apartment they tore at each other's clothes, laughing as they were strewn over the floor. He fell on to her bed first, naked but for his boxer shorts, and softly she climbed on top of him, kissing his chest and neck. Suddenly he pulled away and groaned.

"Oh God, I can't do this, Cat, I'm sorry, but I can't."

"What?" She felt a sharp pang in her chest. "Why not?"

He took a deep, troubled breath. "I have a girlfriend. Back in London. I'm sorry."

Cat tried hard to keep her composure. "You wait until you're in my bed to tell me?"

"I'm sorry. I'm not good at this. I've never had to do it before. I've never wanted anyone else."

Cat slumped on the bed beside him, self-conscious in her underwear. "How long have you been with her?" She had to ask something.

"A few years. Three, four?"

It was gratifying that at least he couldn't remember. Three years, four months and two weeks would have been way too eager. "So why doesn't she join you here?"

"She might one day, but she's got her own career. She's pretty ambitious."

She sat back, deflated, and studied her nails. The French polish effect suddenly looked blotchy and unnatural. "What does she do?" She wanted to find out as much as possible, give herself plenty of ammunition for self-torture.

"Cat, please, don't." He turned to look her in the eye for the first time. "Let's not talk about her." He stroked her cheek as she focused miserably on a spot on the window.

He took her in his arms and she lay her head on his shoulder. "So what shall we talk about then, the weather?"

"No, I don't want to talk about the fucking weather." He laughed gently. "God, I want you so much."

She ran her fingers through the pale hairs on his chest, tracing their line down his stomach to his shorts, noting the fading bulge within them.

"I'm not stopping you," she tried. He'd gone this far after all. He'd kissed her in the street, come back to her place and torn off most of her clothes, hadn't he? And he'd done all those things without any persuasion from her.

"And I'm not going to tell her—are you?" She ran her hand over the bulge, and he groaned half-heartedly. "Look, Declan, how would she ever find out?"

She had made up her mind to have him, and wasn't about to

let a woman six thousand miles away stop her. But as she gently lowered his shorts and started persuading him the best way she knew how, some nagging doubts surfaced in the back of her mind. What if there really was no future for them? What if this girl did actually join him? She pushed them away and focused on giving him as much pleasure as she could, and resolved to make herself the most desirable and irresistible woman Declan Moran had ever come across in his life.

Eight

"You are a bad girl, Cat Wellesley, and I don't know what I'm going to do with you."

"I can think of a few things," she teased, kissing him on the mouth.

They had arrived at the tram stop nearest to her place, and Declan was to jump on the next one, while Cat made her way down to the Wanchai ferry. She couldn't bear to leave him, finding it hard to say goodbye, as if the fragile beginnings of their relationship might shatter if she did. Beside them a young Chinese couple were waiting, whispering and giggling to each other. Declan nudged Cat as the girl, who could only have been in her teens, playfully leaned forward and squeezed a large zit on the boy's chin.

"Oh fuck, now I've seen everything," Cat muttered into Declan's neck, trying not to watch the results.

He pulled her away, laughing, as the tram approached. "Do you still fancy a movie tonight? I'll meet you at the cinema if you like and we can get some tickets."

He promised to call her and with a quick kiss goodbye jumped on the tram, along with the teenage girl and the boy, who was now wiping his chin with a tissue.

She was still laughing in disgust as she arrived at her desk. The last thing she felt like doing was working on a Saturday morning, but she was getting used to it. It was a good time for paperwork, and for catching up on her viewing. She shuffled a few papers and tried to watch some tapes, but her heart wasn't in it. She was too full of the events of last night, Declan's admission that he had a girlfriend, and the feeling of his warm body next to hers when she woke up. How could he have another girlfriend when she wanted him so badly? She sighed. Life could be so unfair.

She wondered whether to stop off at the supermarket on her way home and buy champagne and smoked salmon, some eggs perhaps for breakfast? Would she have time to change the sheets, or should she even buy one of the ivory silk sets she had seen in a market? They would be seductive, all right. And what about some new underwear? The only time she ever bought any was when she had a new love. She was just wondering whether she'd find anything in her size when Lacy Fok appeared at her office, bringing her back to earth with the faint smell of her breakfast noodles. Max wanted to see her.

He was frowning at his monitors when she walked into his office. "So. How was your evening?" he began, not bothering to look at her.

"Great, thank you."

He rubbed the back of his neck, flinching. "Desmond Tang called me this morning."

Cat's stomach tightened. She felt like an imposter who was about to be found out. They had realized she was incompetent, naive and not up to the job. Desmond Tang personally wanted her to be let go, effective immediately. She braced herself for the worst.

"You ran a cooking show last night where an American was making stir fry and noodles." He said it as if it were a crime. "How dare an American tell the Chinese how to make noodles?"

"Oh, you're talking about *The Cheaper Chef*, it's an American series. I must say I haven't watched every episode, but it was cleared by the Standards department, who didn't seem to find it offensive."

"Well, Desmond Tang did, so get it off the air right now."

Cat nodded, relieved that that was the best he could come up with.

"Now this new girl, Joanna, she starts next week," he continued. "Are you ready to hand over to her?"

"Yes, of course I am, Max."

"Good. That's about all for now, you can go."

She turned to leave.

"Oh and one more thing," he said quickly, and Cat knew instantly that this would be the real reason he had called her in. He shook his head, as if there was something he truly didn't understand.

"You know, Catherine, you're in a management position now. I know it's all new to you but you have a whole new set of responsibilities. You gotta keep your distance from the other staff. Don't let them get too close, because you never know when you're going to have to rattle their cages. You understand me?"

"I think so, Max, but, you know, I want to make friends here as well. Hong Kong can be a lonely—"

"Catherine, Catherine," he interrupted, shaking his head in disbelief. "Are we in this business to be liked or to be respected?"

To her relief Lacy Fok put her head around the door to warn Max that Desmond Tang was on the line again, and silently Cat escaped.

She did some more viewing, toyed a little with her schedule and caught up on the trade magazines. By a quarter to two she was beginning to think the worst when the phone rang, making her jump.

"I was wondering when you were going to call," she said on hearing Declan's voice. "I'm leaving any minute now."

"I'm sorry." Was he apologizing for leaving it so late, or was there more on his mind? In the brief pause, Cat knew instinctively it was the latter. "I'm not going to be able to make it tonight."

"Oh no, why?" It felt like her world, at least for the weekend, had just fallen apart.

"I'm sorry, Cat, I just can't. You know what would happen. We'd only be starting something we couldn't finish, and I can't do it. I've been thinking about it all morning. I think we should leave things the way they are."

"Oh, Declan, come on." Cat felt herself panic. She had to talk him out of it. "Let's have a drink at least and talk about it."

"I can't, Cat. If I see you I'm just going to want to fuck you."

Fuck. The word sounded so brutal.

She tried to hide her irritation, but knew she was failing. "So what about when we see each other at work, then? Am I going to have to sneak around avoiding you?"

"Of course not. We hardly ever see each other anyway. Look, I'm sorry, I'm only trying to do what's right. If anything developed it would be unfair on you as well as her. Last night shouldn't have happened."

"I don't believe this. A man with a conscience."

"I'm sorry, Cat." His voice began to trail off. "Have a good weekend, now."

She paused, not sure whether she wanted to scream something sarcastic down the phone or just burst into tears. There was little chance of her having a good weekend now. If anything she wished she could take a pill and just sleep right through it, only to wake up on Monday morning and go straight back to work. At least there she would feel closer to him. She put off saying goodbye in the hope he might change his mind.

"Cat, are you still there?" He sounded concerned.

"Yes of course I am," she snapped. "Have a good weekend yourself." She slammed the phone down bitterly. What had promised to be a perfect weekend had just turned into a disaster. There were to be no more fantasies, no more sexy underwear, no more plans of champagne and smoked salmon—no more anything. She had made herself too available too quickly, and now had all the allure of a used condom.

As she walked to the ferry she wondered how he would feel if something were to happen to her over the weekend. She imagined word spreading around the company that she had been killed somehow. What would be a good way? A freak accident on the ferry—a bit undignified, that. Knocked down by a tram? Too messy. Perhaps she could get caught up in the crossfire of some triad gang or other? That would be pretty good—glamorous but so utterly unnecessary, exciting but tragic.

Her picture would appear in the *South China Morning Post* and Declan would tear it out and keep it in his wallet. Then one day his girlfriend might find it, and it would be her turn to get jealous; her turn to go through what Cat was right now, only her pain would be tinged with the strange guilt that she was resenting a dead woman. And as she'd try to come to terms with her feelings, so their relationship would be torn apart, and Cat ultimately would have won, albeit from the grave.

The fantasy cheered her up a bit and she decided to go shopping. At the ferry terminal she bought a two-day-old English paper, then made her way to her favorite shopping mall. The sun was shining through the pollution as she walked through the passages that wove from one building to the next. However bad she felt, this was still an incredible city, and she was lucky to be living in it. She made her way through the hordes into the mall and stopped off at her favorite pasta place for some lunch and a glass of wine.

They could have come here this evening, she mused, Declan and her. Got tickets for the cinema, had a quick supper, and then gone to see a film. Would they have sat hand-in-hand through the movie? Might she have rested her head on his shoulder? She would never know now, she thought sadly, taking a large sip. And what was he doing now? Reading a book on his terrace, not giving her a second thought? Or would he be cursing himself and regretting the call? She smiled as the wine began to make life tolerable again. It didn't really matter what he was thinking, it was over now. Those sudden and wonderful dreams were over, and life was back to normal.

She had another glass. It wouldn't hurt to buy something drop-dead gorgeous for the next time she saw him, though. He would be back on day shift in a couple of weeks. She could still get him back. She would make him miss her so badly that he'd be begging her to take him back. That was more like it. She drained her glass, thankful for its reviving qualities, and made her way to the shops on the third floor.

Nine

Cat was handing over many of her responsibilities to Jo, who started that week, and it felt like she was shedding a skin. No longer would she have to worry about placing a sports promo on Vibe, or whether an action-packed movie trailer would be suitable for kids; she could finally concentrate solely on Variety, *her* channel. She would acquire decent programs, create an attractive schedule and make it all look sexy and watchable. She was beginning to feel lighter, and to see the hours she worked shrinking down to a near normal day.

It was mid week, Max had left for a board meeting and she had decided to take Jo out to lunch to meet Lorna properly. They were waiting for her in the reception area when Declan walked by, clutching a Kit-Kat from the chocolate machine. Cat's heart jumped like an over-enthusiastic puppy and she could feel her cheeks redden.

"What are you doing here?" she asked him. "This isn't your shift."

She must have rehearsed their next meeting a million times, and had told herself that whatever she said, she should keep it brief and breezy. But irritatingly he had caught her off-guard. She was looking elegant, or so she hoped, in the charcoal-grey pantsuit she had acquired at the weekend. It flattered her long slim legs and was business-like without being austere. She had finished it off with a skinny-fitting pink T-shirt.

"One of the boys is off sick, so I'm standing in." He hovered, a look of boyish delight on his face.

"Sorry, Jo." Cat caught herself. "This is Declan Moran, one of the editors." She tried to make him sound like a passing acquaintance. They shook hands.

"How was your weekend?" he asked, paying little attention to Jo.

"Fine, thanks," she replied crisply, as if irritated that he should ask. "Yours?"

"Oh, you know, pretty much the same as ever. You going out to lunch?"

"That's right, yes." She spotted Lorna walking toward them.

"Oh well. Have a good one."

"You too." She turned and beamed at Lorna. Slightly dejected, Declan shuffled back toward the operations area.

"Oh God, am I relieved the last couple of days are over," Lorna had started as she burst through the swing doors. "You would never believe the amount of work Carnage can generate when he has a board meeting. I finally packed him off to Macau a few minutes ago." She paused. "Was that Declan I just saw?"

"Yeah, he's standing in for someone." Cat had begun to feel slightly guilty.

They pushed their way through the main doors and into the mild Kowloon sunshine.

"He was quite good-looking, wasn't he?" Jo started.

"Join the queue. Dreamboat Declan," Lorna cut in.

"More-ish Moran," Cat added. "Has a girlfriend and a conscience, I'm afraid. Dim sum?"

The River Seafood restaurant was a bit like the Tardis. Outside stood a couple of tanks containing some of the biggest crabs Cat had ever seen, while downstairs one room led to another, each apparently larger and more cavernous than the last. It was so huge that girls carrying walkie-talkies would meet customers at the entrance, take instructions on where there was a free table and then guide them through the labyrinth to find it. It felt like half of China was eating there today, and amongst them Cat, Jo and Lorna were the only Westerners. There were a few surprised glances, but mostly the other diners just ignored them, concentrating rather on shovelling rice into their mouths and holding conversations of great urgency. The sound was deafening.

They selected the seven or so dishes they could eat out of a menu of around one hundred, avoiding such delicacies as chicken's feet, birds' tongues, sea blubber and crispy fried intestines.

"Can we get a beer?" Jo asked hopefully and Cat knew in that instant that they would be friends.

"Sure, while the cat's away," Lorna trilled, visibly relieved about Max's departure. She began to paint a clearer picture of the company for Jo—the different departments, the company background and the people to watch.

"The best way of getting to know the operations guys," she suggested, "is to go to Sam's in the evening."

"Sam's?" Jo asked, and Cat became more attentive. She'd never been there herself.

"A sleazy working men's bar on the way to the station. It's filthy and a total dump but the beer's cheap, and that's where they all go. You should come too, Catherine." She turned to her. "You know, everyone goes."

"Everyone?" Cat knew what she was getting at.

"I'll be there tonight, you guys should join me."

"Damn, I can't." Jo sighed. "I'm house-hunting."

"I'll come," Cat said, rather too quickly. She was beginning to feel heady, and wasn't sure whether it was just the beer or the thought of seeing Declan again if she did. With Max away she felt like she'd just been given the keys to the jail. "I could even leave early, like sevenish?"

"Make it six and you've got a date."

"You are a bad influence, Lorna Cardelli," Cat laughed. "And you are definitely on."

Ten

"So they call you Cat, do they? Well, I'm going to call you Pussy." Derek MacDonald was the sort of man who'd fart in bed and hold his girlfriend's head under the covers. In the course of a working day he thought nothing of groping balls, tweaking nipples and poking his beery tongue into the unsuspecting ear of any of his Western operations staff.

He had a quick temper, an ever-expanding beer belly and an inability to sit still for long. He was known to flick rubber bands at participants of meetings or to send them flying the length of the operations area in their chairs. But beneath the joking lurked the deceptively sharp mind that had built Frontier's state-of-the-art operations, brought in key Western personnel and overseen the training of some sixty-odd Chinese junior staff.

Cat, who had had little contact with him since their introduction months ago, was slightly in awe of him. She had no wish to get on his wrong side, but was equally wary of becoming too close either. While his physical attacks were kept strictly for the boys, his mocking tone and ability to discover and exploit a carefully hidden vulnerability could reduce even the toughest of women to tears.

"You can call me anything you like, Derek," she answered self-consciously as he pulled out a chair for her. She brushed off some chip crumbs before sitting down and worried about her new pants.

"So what are you drinking, ladies?"

"Derek, you're buying a drink?" Lorna acted shocked. "That has to be a first."

"Now, now, you, that's how rumors get started. Not all Scots are cheap. Pussy, what will you be having?"

Cat followed Lorna's lead and asked for a beer. In the corner of the bar a Chinese drinking game was reaching its noisy climax, and Cat paused to take in her new suraroundings. Sam's bar was in fact called the Mayflower, but as it was run by a local called Sam the name had just stuck. It was tucked down a tiny alleyway between a shoe repair shop and a hardware store, and was dimly lit with grimy walls and seats covered in a dirty red velvet. Derek had found it months ago during his first week at Frontier, and with its shabby décor and generous happy hour it had become an instant hit with the technicians.

"So which is better, Pussy?" Derek settled down with their drinks. "Male masturbation or female?"

"No idea, Derek, which?" She caught the knowing smile of Phil Tucker, who as a duty manager was responsible for the day-to-day operations, from the dubbing of incoming material to actual transmission itself. Tall and thin, with a mop of red hair, he seemed to live off nervous energy. Hard not to, Cat thought, with Derek around.

"Female, because it's digital." Derek said triumphantly as Cat laughed into her pint. It was six-thirty, and Declan would be off shift at eight. Life began to feel good as the cold beer hit the spot.

"Have you heard about my new secretary, Pussy?"

"No, Derek, tell me?"

"She's a lovely young girl who goes by the name of Fanny Chu."

"There's a girl in our electrical supply store called Fanny Pong," Phil Tucker added. "You'd think someone would say something."

"I'm very fond of Lazy Fuck myself," Lorna pronounced with relish. "Max chose well there."

"So how has Mad Max been treating you then?" Derek turned to Cat.

"Probably no differently from anyone else."

"Have you learned the three Rs yet?" Phil asked her excitedly. "Read them the riot act."

"Send them a rocket," Derek continued.

"And rattle their cages!" Cat laughed delightedly as a few more technical staff and engineers joined them.

She gulped back her beer, happy to be on drinking terms with these guys. These were the people Cat respected the most at Frontier, the people who made it all happen. Her fortune was held in their hands, after all. If she needed an urgent dub, these were the ones she turned to. If she found an unsuitable shot in a program at the last minute—these were the people to edit it out. Experience had taught her that technicians and engineers were far too powerful even to think about alienating. Should you be foolish enough to do so, machines would be tied up, the editor on his break or they'd have run out of blacked tape stock.

"Well, he's given me a big break so I should be grateful, I suppose." Cat tried to be fair.

"And that's exactly where he gets you." Derek turned serious for once. "He put his faith in you, and he's no doubt paid you more than you ever thought you were worth. And so you work yourself to the bone out of gratitude. And you accept all his demands. And you say yes to everything he wants. And that—" Derek raised his glass triumphantly, "Is how he gets you."

Cat didn't like to feel singled out. "I guess that's what he's done with everybody."

"Max will always be all-powerful, as long as he's surrounded by grateful sycophants. Not that I'm saying you're one of course, Pussy. Rumor has it you've stood up to him a couple of times."

"I've had a go. And you?" she asked. "Are you a grateful sycophant?"

"Fuck me, yes. For as long as it suits. I'm making three times what I was in the UK and as Max doesn't understand technology he leaves me alone. I'm not rocking the boat."

"But what if he asked you to do something that made no sense at all?"

"The glorious thing about technology, Pussy," Derek drained his glass, "is that the cunt doesn't understand it. So whatever he asks I can deliver on my own terms."

Lorna started one of her many stories, distracting them. She proved to be an inspired raconteuse, a talented mimic and fantastically indiscreet with it.

"So anyway, I'm wondering why we never get sandwiches at meetings. The girls are bringing in rice and noodles and you know it's so hard to eat that shit when you're trying to work. So I suggest to Lazy Fuck that in future we just order an assortment of sandwiches and her face practically turns white. '*Mr. Carnegie insists.*' " She put on a highly exaggerated Chinese accent. " '*No blead arrowed.*' Turns out he suffers from chronic fucking constipation, and is convinced that bread only exacerbates it."

She looked around, enjoying the delight of her audience.

"He can't even watch other people eating it, he's totally paranoid. So every morning Lacy has to bring him orange juice and laxatives, and then he takes his paper to the executive john. Oh, and you know those stupid fucking key rings I had to get made? They were because the original one for the bathroom was so big he hated being seen with it every time he went to the loo." She pronounced her new English word with relish.

"God, this is the Max I fortunately never get to see," Cat said.

"Oh, that's because he's trying to impress you," Lorna said pointedly. "He has a little crush on you, my dear, hadn't you noticed?"

"No!" Cat was incredulous, and felt herself blush as all eyes were suddenly on her. "What on earth makes you say that?"

"Because it's true. I can tell by the way he looks at you. Clear as day."

"Well, well, Pussy, what it is to have friends in high places. More drinks?"

As Cat looked up to watch Derek make his way to the bar, Declan Moran appeared at the entrance. His face brightened as he saw her.

"This is a surprise, you don't normally come here." He moved straight toward her.

"I'm being led astray by my friend Lorna here." Cat could feel she was a little giddy. This was the nicest stage of drunkenness, when all her inhibitions had melted and she could laugh easily. If only she could stop at this level and switch to water. Of course, though, she never did. Life would be far too uneventful that way.

As Derek returned with more drinks, Lorna turned to him, allowing Declan to sit next to Cat. "Is that a real Rolex you're wearing there?" she asked him, pulling up his shirtsleeve for a closer look.

"It's as fake as your orgasms, Lorna," he replied as the table dissolved into laughter.

Suddenly alone, Cat found it hard to talk to Declan, to make the conversation flow like Lorna could. He had humiliated her, after all. Eventually he broke the awkwardness with a lame query about her weekend.

"Oh, you know. The usual. Went shopping, had some lunch." Suddenly Cat felt inspired. "Bought some champagne and smoked salmon, some saucy underwear. Then I had a date with this guy, and we met at the cinema." He started to smile. "We bought our tickets and then went to this Italian place for a drink." She got into her stride. "But you know, my leg kept brushing against his and he started getting all distracted."

"Oh did he now?" Declan shifted in his seat.

"So we went to the cinema but really, the film wasn't up to much. I had my hand on his thigh, you know, and as I was getting bored I started stroking it gently."

"And what did he make of that?" Declan's eyes darted around the group, making sure that no one was listening.

"He wasn't complaining. So then I undid his fly." She lowered her voice but knew that all attention was focused on Lorna and Derek and their easy banter. "And I started to stroke him there."

"And how did he respond?"

"Well, he seemed to enjoy it," she answered. "I think he was a little nervous at first, but it grew on him."

"I bet it did. And how long did this go on for?"

"Well, you know, till it got a little difficult to concentrate. Then we snuck out and started to walk home. But you know? He couldn't wait. He thrust me up against a wall in this dark alley and thrust his hand up my skirt."

"You weren't wearing jeans, then?"

"No, no, I can do better than that. I was wearing this short black skirt, quite tight." Declan shifted uncomfortably again, taking a large swig of his beer.

"So he puts his hand up and pulls my panties down to my knees."

"I think people are beginning to listen, Cat."

"Oh are they?" She threw her head back and laughed. "So how was your weekend then?"

Eleven

Cat could hear the phone ringing as she tried yet again to get the key in the lock. Once inside, she raced to the receiver.

"Cat? You're back." It was Declan. She wandered into her bedroom and sat down heavily on the bed.

"Just got in," she told him breathlessly.

"I've been trying a few times, I wanted to make sure you got home safely."

"Yes, of course I did, thanks."

There was a brief pause. "You are such a bad girl."

"Me? Whatever makes you say that?"

"For making me feel uncomfortable all evening, that's what."

"Oh dear. And do you still have that painful swelling?"

"Yes I do. I'm going to have to do something about it."

"Do you want me to help you?"

There was a groan. "Oh, I can't do this. I've never been unfaithful before, never. I can't start now."

"Well, what do you want me to do about it, then?"

"I don't know. Just talking to you is helping."

"You know there are numbers you can ring for that sort of thing." She had slumped on to her bed and was kicking off her shoes.

"It wouldn't be the same. It's you I need to speak to."

"Well look, Declan, you can't have it both ways, you know."

"I know, I know that. I don't know what to do."

"Well, like I said, I won't tell anyone if you don't."

"Cat, it's not as easy as that. I have to live with it. I talk to her more or less every day."

Every day? Cat wasn't prepared for that, and she felt a pang of hopeless jealousy. What could they possibly find to talk about every day?

"Do you?" she managed. She was burning to know more. "What's her name anyway?"

"Harriet," Declan told her.

"Harriet?" Cat repeated, trying to picture what a Harriet might look like. The last few days she had persuaded herself that Declan's girlfriend had the body of Elle MacPherson and the face of Claudia Schiffer, but a Harriet was more suited to the cover of *Horse and Hounds* than *Vogue*.

"You should know she's coming over for Christmas," he said almost apologetically and Cat felt her chest tighten. "She arrives Friday. We're going to Thailand for a couple of weeks."

She couldn't speak, just managed a quiet "Ah."

"I'll be back for New Year's." She said nothing. "So you understand how difficult this is for me. I'm sorry to let you down, but—"

"Look, Declan, it's no big deal," she snapped. "Really, I just thought that you and I could have some fun. I'm not looking for marriage or life-long commitment or anything like that."

Just friendship, she thought. Company. Someone to spend time with, to flirt with, laugh with. "But if you can't handle it that's fine. There are plenty of other men around."

"OK." He sounded a little taken aback, and immediately she hated herself for it.

She took a deep breath, and added more softly, "So goodnight then. Sweet dreams and have a lovely holiday. I'll see you when you get back."

"All right then. Sleep well."

She hung up, bitterly disappointed. "Fuck you, Declan Moran," she said aloud as she stumbled up off the bed. "Fuck you." It felt like every time they talked they took one step forward and two back.

Shaking her head she made her way to the bathroom, where she tripped in the doorway and, in trying to regain her balance, threw up into her mustard-colored toilet bowl.

Twelve

The room was of warm terracotta and turquoise and bathed in a pale gold light. Cat sank into the deepest, most comforting chair she had ever known and let her head fall back into the oversized basin. A Filipina called Elsie started to wash her hair, her fingertips soothing away any thoughts of schedules or missing tapes or episodes run in the wrong order. Gentle, New Age music was playing in the background and for the first time in months Cat began to feel incredibly, deeply relaxed.

With Max still away she had left the office at three that Saturday afternoon and headed straight for the hairdressers at the Shangri-La hotel. In London she would have resisted visiting and paying the price of a top salon, but in Hong Kong she needed this luxury, needed this pampering, and resolved to treat herself every month or so. Elsie washed her hair in a shampoo that smelled so delicious Cat instantly wanted to buy it, and then began the best head massage she had ever experienced. Silently she worked the conditioner into Cat's hair, rubbing her temples, working pressure points and using deep, circular movements that made Cat wonder if massage was perhaps even better than sex. She wanted it to last for ever. She would come back every week, every evening if she could, just to experience it again.

In the distant background she could hear the voices of other stylists and clients. They faded in and out of her consciousness as she floated, somewhere, way above even her own existence, somewhere light and graceful and trouble-free.

"You staying in this hotel?" A grating male voice asked a client nearby. Cat wanted to tut out loud as she fell right back to earth.

"No, with my boyfriend," a quiet, faintly embarrassed-sounding English voice answered.

"He Chinese?" The man asked with a giggle.

"No, Irish actually."

Cat's chest tightened and she was suddenly alert.

"You staying here for Christmas?"

Suddenly there was a loud whooshing noise as Elsie turned on the spray and started to rinse the conditioner out of Cat's hair. Like a fidgety schoolgirl she tried to lean forward to hear better, but with surprising force Elsie just yanked her back, filling her ears with water as she did so. When the rinsing was over Cat could just make out something about Thailand before Elsie wrapped her head up in two thick towels that acted infuriatingly like sound-proofing. As she was ushered into the next room Cat glanced over at the girl sitting by the mirror. She had a mousy-colored bob that needed a trim, and she wore no makeup. Her cheeks were flushed pink and she looked as though she was suffering from the heat. Under her robe she wore a voluminous beige skirt and some plain brown sandals.

From her new seat Cat could barely see let alone hear her. Whenever she did crane her neck to get a glimpse she was pulled back sharply by her stylist Wendy, who had choppy red streaks and wore thick-rimmed glasses, and who looked like she'd only eaten a couple of wantons in the last six months.

That was Harriet? Cat thought in awe. That was her? Her mind began to race—could she get talking to her, befriend her perhaps? Pump her with questions, more like. She turned to get another look and Wendy pulled her back smartly. Could she follow her, even? Watch her movements, see where she went, get an idea of who the real Harriet was? She tried to picture herself waiting outside the salon, only to follow her straight into Declan's arms, and knew she couldn't do it.

Wendy finished cutting and began to blow-dry Cat's hair. What if Declan was waiting outside when she left? Who would be the more embarrassed she wondered. She could picture the look of horror on his face at the sight of her. She could tease him, perhaps, pretend to have had a nice long chat with Harriet, hint about all the things they'd discussed over the din of the blow-dryer.

Wendy took an age to finish her hair, determined to make it curl under at the shoulders. Cat just wanted to escape, to leave before Declan arrived, to get out, run, to pretend she was in a movie and being chased through the hotel foyer and into the shopping mall beyond. She couldn't face him. Couldn't face knowing for certain that this was his girlfriend, his future wife even, the mother of his children.

She fled the hotel but couldn't bear to go home. It was too early and she needed time to calm down. She turned left into Queensway and headed toward Central, wandering down its many narrow streets with their oh-so-English-sounding names: Duddell Street, Wyndham Street, Old Bailey Street, Staunton Street, and wondered whether Hong Kong had ever really been as refined as they implied.

She needed a chat and a drink, but there was no one she could contact. Lorna would be with Andrew, she didn't know Jo's number and the only other person she could talk to was the source of all her troubles. Why did Declan have to love Harriet? Why? Why couldn't he just be there for Cat, why couldn't they just have a normal relationship like everyone else? She felt rather like a lost child—so far from home, so far from anyone she knew, and so terribly alone.

She stopped to look at a gallery, and idly studied the menu of a Sri Lankan restaurant she'd never come across, before slowly meandering down one narrow street after the other. She took in a display of Chinese medicines in one shop, admired some pale jade trinkets in another and paused at a stand selling old black and white photos of a Hong Kong she hardly recognized. The sight of some crystals hanging in a window made her stop, and she found herself in front of the so-called New Age Centre, an emporium of books, CDs, chimes, incense sticks, candles and tarot decks. Gratefully Cat wandered inside, pleasantly surprised by her discovery. It almost felt like she'd been meant to find it.

She was choosing a scented candle when she overheard someone book an appointment for a psychic reading for the following week. A reading! That was what she needed right now—some clarity on her life. A hint that Declan might still be hers, or if not him, someone more handsome, more sophisticated and more worldly. Someone who lived on The Peak and took junk trips to the islands and who would whisk her off to Bali for the weekend. Someone who'd make her laugh, who'd lend her support and love her exclusively, with no other attachments.

Fat chance of ever meeting him, she told herself glumly, as her heart tugged back to Declan. *And fat chance that he'd want me.* But something *had* to happen, surely?

"You do readings?" she asked the woman behind the counter, hoping not to look too desperate. "Can I make an appointment?"

Thirteen

Cat was surreptitiously studying the newly released production rota, looking for Declan's name, when Lorna burst into her office.

"Urgent, department heads," she told her. "Max just flew into a rage. You coming?"

Cat felt her stomach churn as if whatever the problem was, it had to be her fault. She followed Lorna into the meeting room where the others were assembling, and chose a chair that overlooked the window halfway down the table, where Max wouldn't be able to see her without leaning forward.

Regally he entered the room, sat at the head of the table, and leaned forward.

"So." He paused for dramatic effect. "We're all here? You're probably wondering why I've called this meeting." He studied the anxious faces of his team, and then swept around in fury as the door opened and Jo crept in. He took a long-suffering breath as she shrank down in a seat next to Greg Sharp's.

"We failed to meet our advertising revenue projections for the first quarter of broadcast, and I want to know what we're going to do about it." He glowered at each member of his team in turn. "I'll let Jerry do the explaining."

Jerry Greenberg shuffled in his seat nervously. What he lacked in style he usually made up for in enthusiasm, but today he looked like a man who'd got caught walking around the supermarket with his zipper undone, his mind firmly elsewhere. Wearing grey slacks, an off-white shirt and a moss green tank top, he seemed out of place in Max's polished company.

In truth Frontier had reached the projections he had originally drawn up, but these had been arbitrarily increased by Max to impress Desmond Tang and the board. Jerry, who had lived in Asia for over fifteen years and knew the region intimately, was feeling slighted and on edge. Quietly he talked the team through the results, being careful not to implicate his boss.

"So in short, things have fallen between the bar stools," Max interrupted him, and Cat wondered what that meant. "So what's the solution?"

"The long-term solution is that we keep on improving the programming and Frontier's profile. We've only been on the air a few months, and we have to look to strengthen our branding, our image and our presence in the market."

Cat's gaze left Jerry and wandered toward Lorna, who was in a fitted black suit and tapped her pen nervously on a notepad. Her nails were long and thick and that deep, deep red but, as she turned her hand, Cat could see her left thumbnail was missing, or rather, what was left of it was bitten, ragged and unpolished. Cat was so surprised she barely heard what Jerry was saying. She'd never known anyone to wear fake nails before—it felt faintly thrilling and secretive, as if she had caught Lorna out in a lie.

"We need to earn our advertisers' confidence," Jerry continued. "And that kind of thing doesn't happen in a day."

"So that's your long-term strategy, now what about the short term?"

Jerry shuffled unconvincingly. "Well, Max. I would suggest that each channel comes out with a special event in February or March that we can promote effectively. We get maximum press coverage and we aggressively target our main advertisers."

"I like that. But it's got to happen in January. Let's start the year off as we mean to go on. So what can we all come up with?" He surveyed his team, enjoying their discomfort. "Trent, you go first."

"Can I just say something here?" Lorna broke in and all faces turned to her. "I have to agree with Jerry on the timing. The channels all gave me their January schedules three weeks ago and they're being released to the press later this week. There will be no time for changes. The listings magazine is almost ready to print and needs to be sent out at the end of the month. It makes a lot more sense to give ourselves a little more time and make a big splash in February."

"It does, does it?" The look he threw her was of pure contempt. "Well, to the board it makes more sense to try and recoup our losses as soon as possible, and that, to me, makes it January."

"But Max, the printers—"

"Lorna, the business we give them, you can tell them to put their printer where the sun don't shine. Trent. What have you got for me?"

In turn, each department head came up with suggestions which were either ridiculed or induced a fit of fury. Cat waited nervously for her time to speak, knowing that she'd fare no better.

"I have a couple of new series starting," she tried. "And some good TV movies—"

"Not good enough," Max snarled. "We need an event. Can't you get a big award show, or a beauty pageant or something?"

"I'm not sure anyone would hold a pageant just to help us out like that." The words were out before she could stop herself, and she bit her lip, waiting for the attack.

"There's always the Golden Orbs, but I don't know their position on satellite rights," Brandon Miller suggested, neatly avoiding Max's eruption.

"Now you're talking!" The Golden Orbs ceremony was a forerunner to the Oscars, and often seen as an indication of how the prizes might be awarded. He turned back to Cat. "Get me the Golden Orbs, Catherine. Now *that* you should be able to sell?" He sneered at Jerry.

"OK," Cat said warily, not knowing where to start. "I'll see what I can do."

"You'll see what you can do, will you? How very kind!" He shot her a look capable of dispersing a high category typhoon.

"OK, Max," she replied quickly. "I'll get them."

"OK, all of you." Max concluded. "Work on your specials for January and Lorna, make sure they get plenty of press attention.

And I don't want any of this bull about longer deadlines, you hear me? Jo, we'll need a sales tape—something upbeat and dynamic that reflects positively on each channel. We'll talk about it in a separate meeting. Jerry, when does Melanie Chan start?"

"First week of January."

"Good, it'll be a good project for her to get her teeth into. For those of you who don't know, I've hired Jerry some help. Melanie's a Harvard graduate, Chinese American and will be supporting Jerry in all sales and marketing activities. I want you all to make her feel welcome."

Cat could tell from the expression on his face that Melanie was also very attractive. She had a sense of foreboding for Jerry.

"OK, all of you, I'm out of here. Adios." Max left and the mood lightened.

"I've got gossip," Cat whispered to Lorna as they headed for her office. "You know I was at the hairdressers on Saturday?"

"I can tell, you look great."

"Guess who should be there getting a very mousy-colored bob trimmed? Declan's girlfriend." Cat loathed using those words. "Harriet."

"Harriet? That's her name, Harriet?"

"Lorna, if you saw her you'd be even more confused. She's nothing. I can't believe they're off to Thailand this week."

"She'll get sunburned."

"Yes, she will, she's got that kind of skin."

"And maybe diarrhea?"

"Hopefully. Not to mention mosquito bites."

"He'll be back," Lorna assured her. "Don't give up on him yet. That relationship has so run its course."

"I hope so. I've been killing myself about it all weekend. You know I even fixed up to have a psychic reading soon?"

Lorna laughed. "Oh you did? Very cool. He'll be back."

"Yes I think he will," Cat agreed, as if Lorna's opinion might force the issue. "I just wish I could stop thinking about him screwing her, that's all."

"Honey, who do you think he's thinking about when he's doing it with her?"

"Oh come on." Cat frowned, but she loved the idea.

"Seriously. And you know what they say, which would you rather, that someone was having sex with you and thinking about someone else, or sex with someone else and thinking about you?"

Cat stopped, taking this in. "That's very good, Lorna, I'd never heard that one before." She paused for a second to think about it, as if it shed a whole new light on matters.

"I like that."

Fourteen

"**B**randon, d'you mind if we go through this Golden Orb thing now?" She hated disturbing the tall American. He looked up at her with irritation, as though he had finally come up with the solution to a puzzle and because of her, just lost it again.

"Sure, Cat, come on in." He barely looked at her.

There had been days when she found herself wondering if she could ever fancy Brandon Miller. He was, after all, intelligent and presentable with a fit, strong body, even if his curly hair was receding and his face looked a bit like a Martian had thrown it together. But sitting opposite him now, his skin pale and blotchy and his nose streaming, she decided not.

"Hong Kong is terrible for my allergies," he snuffled, grabbing a tissue.

"Must be tough." She flinched as he blew his nose.

"The air con," he wheezed. "I swear it all comes through the air con. Now what can I do for you?"

"The Golden Orbs. Do you really think I stand a chance of getting them?"

"Nope, but you have no choice but to try."

"I'm a bit out of my depth here," she told him honestly. "I mean, do I pay for satellite delivery, that sort of stuff?" She would have liked a mentor, someone to guide and advise her, give her confidence in what she was doing. Instead Brandon just popped some vitamin pills in his mouth.

"Yeah, we'd probably have to pay for that." He gave her some contact information and a few pointers, but Cat got the distinct impression that he resented her handling it at all. As it had been his suggestion in the first place, she wondered if he might even be setting her up somehow.

"How are you getting on otherwise?" he asked. "The Brit stuff?"

"Slowly. One company, Midland, seems a possibility. My gut feeling is that if I can just pull one in, the others will follow."

"Well, good luck, Max is getting impatient." He made a funny snorting noise and Cat's stomach churned.

"Thanks a lot." She left him to his antihistamines.

She spoke to Derek about satellite delivery, worked through a payment plan and some presentation ideas, and made the call. A few days later, to her astonishment, a fax had arrived confirming the deal.

She rushed to Max's office, thrilled with the news. On his desk stood a small jug of orange juice, and she flinched. He was wearing some kind of headset that linked into his phone, and Cat couldn't decide whether he looked more like an airline pilot or Madonna on tour.

"So? Did we get the Orbs yet?" He looked up at her expectantly.

"We certainly did." She showed him the fax.

"A little on the high side," he muttered as he read it through.

Cat was not to be put off. "The feed's coming in at 11 a.m. our time so I think it's best to tape delay it, and run it in prime time," she continued. "And then I was thinking about wrapping the commercial breaks with a series of vox pops—you know, like asking people on the street who they think might win which award, that sort of thing."

Suddenly the show had come to life for her. It could involve shooting and editing, and that might mean working with Declan again. A project that had hung over her like a monsoon cloud had suddenly become exciting.

"Wait a minute, I want it to go out live," he growled, ignoring her enthusiasm.

"But Max, it's at eleven in the morning, there'll be no one watching. And what if there's a problem with the feed? If it went down for any reason we'd be in trouble. If we're just recording it we can patch it up in edit. I recommend scheduling it around nine pm so we have a good six hours to work with the material before transmission."

He pulled off his headset. "You do, do you? Well, whatever you say, Catherine. Clearly you're the expert, and I'm only the President and CEO around here."

Cat stopped, suddenly deflated. "You don't think that makes sense?"

"Catherine," he sighed. "I have a mountain of work to do here. This is just one minor awards show on one of my lesser-watched channels. Just take care of it, OK? And what is happening with that Midland deal? I thought you told them what you wanted weeks ago?"

"I did, but they're having to check rights clearance. These things take time, apparently."

"Well, I don't have time, you hear me? Desmond Tang was complaining just yesterday about the repeats on your channel. It's got to get better, Catherine."

Outside his office, Cat ran into Jo.

"What kind of a mood is he in?" she asked nervously.

"Irrational, impatient—the usual."

"He wants to talk to me about this sales tape thing, something I can work on with Melanie. Why do I hate this girl already?" She disappeared into Max's office.

"Pussy?" Derek called out behind her. "What're you doing for Christmas?"

"Nothing special," she told him as they walked toward her office.

"Then come to a barbecue at my new place on The Peak."

"You have a place on The Peak?" she repeated incredulously as they walked inside.

"That's right." He handed her a card with the address, clearly pleased with himself. "I met a chap in a bar, a real estate agent, and he put me on to it. Fully furnished, magnificent views and about a third of the going rate. Moved in last week."

"You have a place on The Peak?" Cat said again.

"Something to impress the girls with," Derek beamed. "And I can see it's working."

At Christmas she was surprized to find that little changed in her neighborhood. Shops were still open, public transport operating and the place was only marginally less crowded than usual. She caught the Peak tram, which climbed up the mountainside, and had time to explore a little before finding Derek's address.

This was the Hong Kong that everyone aspired to—the place that said you'd made it. Cat imagined that there were teenagers living in tenement blocks with their extended families who would look up at this view, determined that one day hard work and wise investment would finally get them there. Cat eyed the villas and luxurious cars and stopped every now and then to admire the views that stretched out across the skyscrapers of Central, over the harbor and right out to Kowloon and the New Territories beyond.

Derek's apartment was in a small block on a leafy, pleasant road, and could have been a million miles from the noise and bustle of her own locality. She envied Derek his luck, and couldn't help wondering what his neighbors made of him. The place was light and spacious and furnished with ornate Chinese antiques and delicately colored silk rugs. It was hard to imagine him living there, sitting on the elegant sofa drinking beer out of a can. It was too delicate, too sophisticated, and there was too much that could be crushed with one kick of his size twelve boots. Cat couldn't help but hope that the owner had taken out decent insurance coverage.

The party was gathered on the wrap-around terrace outside, where he had lit a barbecue and, wearing a naked woman apron, was beginning to grill chicken pieces, lamb chops and a couple of pounds of fat pink sausages.

In one corner two graphic designers were smoking a joint, and every now and then Derek would turn around and take a large puff. Cat poured herself a glass of wine and chatted with Simone, a makeup artist from Chingford who had cropped peroxide hair, and Tony, a producer at Vibe with a pierced eyebrow and a tattoo of a rose on one arm. He had been busy auditioning would-be presenters for his channel, and was clearly tiring of the task.

"Carnage gets 'em off the street," he complained. "I swear he just picks these girls up in bars and gets them to come over."

"I know that's what he does," Simone added. "I get to talk to them. One girl told me he invited her sister to a party on Desmond Tang's yacht, and when she got there it was like a brothel, with the old man trying to get off with everyone."

"They're useless, fucking useless," Tony went on passionately. "And I have to waste my time giving them direction just so's we can tell him we did."

Cat drifted in and out of different conversations, never really feeling at ease. It felt strangely surreal, watching Derek in his opulent surroundings, and chatting with people who'd be more at home in a Soho pub, or a Chinese restaurant at closing time. She drank more wine, munched on a couple of drumsticks, and joined a group who were identifying landmarks they could see through the hazy afternoon sun. One tape operator was convinced he could make out the Frontier premises, all the way over in Kowloon, and Cat pointed out her own block, or at least the road it was on. They watched the boats sailing in the harbor, and she wondered if Desmond Tang's might be out there too, and whether he'd be enjoying a Christmas party with yet more wannabe presenters.

She was getting ready to say her goodbyes, when she heard a key in the lock. The front door opened and in it stood a middle-aged man in a grey suit, his hair swept over on one side to disguise a bald patch. His face had turned white with fury.

"What the fuck are you all doing in my apartment?" he yelled as the party fell suddenly silent. "Out. Now. The lot of you."

Fifteen

Declan Moran was back on shift by the end of December. The first glimpse Cat caught of him was in the kitchen, where he was deep in conversation with Derek and helping himself to a coffee. Not wanting to interrupt, and certainly not wanting to speak to Derek just yet, she retreated to her office and checked her appearance in a hand mirror. Satisfied, she tried to kill time, willing him to come to her. She switched on her computer and rearranged some paperwork in her in-tray before shuffling through a pile of videos to watch.

"So how's it been going then?" he peered around her door.

She smiled with relief. He looked tanned and relaxed and his hair was slightly blonder, showing off his pale blue eyes. She thought she had never seen anyone more handsome.

"Really, it's been OK. A little insanity over some January specials, but otherwise it's been fine. So how was Derek just then?"

Declan smirked. "Mightily pissed off. You were there, were you?" Cat nodded. "He's been in touch with the agency. Seems the guy he spoke to got fired a few weeks ago. They were supposed to be managing that property while the owner was in Bangkok. He had access to the key and needed to make a quick buck."

"So he's run off with all Derek's money?"

"His deposit and two months' rent. Painful."

"I can't believe it happened."

"Neither can Derek. All his dealings with this guy were on his cell, which of course is no longer working, so he has no way of tracing him. But he'll have skipped town anyway. He's probably sunning himself on some Thai beach at Derek's expense as we speak."

Cat shook her head. "Only in Hong Kong, eh?"

"Declan, how are you?" Lorna breezed in, kissing him on both cheeks. "So how was Thailand?"

"Fantastic, thanks, we had a great time."

We. Cat cringed as he described their island-hopping and elephant trek.

"Do you get many mosquitoes there?" Lorna asked, maybe a little too deliberately, and Cat had to cover her mouth with her hand.

"Yes you do. Harriet got quite badly bitten."

"That's too bad." Lorna's eye caught Cat's. "You're looking a great color, I hope you used a high SPF?"

"No, not really. Harriet got a bit burned but my skin's quite tough. Surprising, really." Suddenly he knew he was being set up, he just didn't understand how.

"And has she gone back now?" Lorna asked.

"Tomorrow. In fact, she's coming down to Sam's tonight." He looked at Cat awkwardly, as if to warn her.

"Oh, I can't wait to meet her," she immediately enthused.

"Good. Well, I'd better get back and see if these producers have got their acts together yet." Declan started to leave, slightly unsure of himself, as the two women turned to each other triumphantly.

"Sure as hell going to make that a date," Lorna said.

"Wouldn't miss it for the world."

That evening, Lorna excelled herself at Sam's, "So was it wonderfully romantic? Cocktails at sunset as the waves rolled in?"

Cat found herself flushing, but was enjoying her friend's performance. Harriet smelled of mosquito repellent and calamine lotion, her nose was peeling and there was a line of swollen bites running the length of her pink calf. Her plump hands clutched half a lager, the stain of a discontinued lipstick patterning the rim of her glass.

"So how are you enjoying Hong Kong?" Cat asked her. "Do you think you might join Declan out here?"

"He keeps suggesting it," Harriet said shyly as Declan stared awkwardly at his feet. "But I'm not sure, it's a big move."

Cat froze, a smile set on her face. So he was actually encouraging her! Nervously Declan guided Harriet toward Simone, and shaking inside, Cat excused herself and went to the loo. Lorna joined her.

"There has to be a reason he stays with her." She shook her head, bewildered. "I mean why pick *her* over me?"

"D'you think she's got money?" Expertly Lorna started touching up her makeup in the grimy mirror.

"With clothes like that? I don't know, I'm so depressed." She sat down heavily on the loo seat. "Why does this have to happen to me? I know he likes me."

Lorna turned sharply. "He's crazy about you. That's what I keep telling you. Don't give up. He'll lose interest in her, probably already has. Have patience, my dear."

"I don't know. Why can't I just meet someone else?"

"Because you don't want to." Lorna scrutinized her foundation cover. "Because if you did you'd forever be thinking about what could have been with this one."

"Maybe. But what the fuck does he see in her?" Cat was suddenly feeling very despondent, and very drunk.

Lorna took a deep breath. "She must have come in at a time in his life when he was vulnerable, when he needed someone who would love him unconditionally. Maybe he was on the rebound? Men aren't good at handling rejection, you know."

"Maybe." Cat sighed, fascinated as Lorna's purple fingernails rummaged in her makeup bag. "Or maybe it's some past life connection. Like he was responsible for her before and something happened, you know? He was her dad or something." She wasn't sure if she could get up any more, and sighed heavily.

Lorna produced a travel bottle of Visine and dotted it in both her eyes. "Or he was her lover and broke her heart with a girl like you?"

"Or maybe he just ran her over or something?" Cat tried, warming to the theme.

Lorna shrugged and blotted her deep mauve lipstick. "That would certainly explain the state of her face."

Sixteen

Cat hated New Year's Eve almost as much as she hated weddings. All the false joviality, the chatting to people she hardly knew and the wasted hours spent waiting for something to happen. It was unnatural to have to stay up until midnight just to hear a clock chime and kiss a few drunks. The New Year rarely brought more than a hangover and some unlikely resolutions. But every year she'd tell herself that this time it would be different; that this time she would meet interesting and entertaining people, that she herself would shine and enhance the proceedings, and that she'd go home with a warm glow and a healthy air of optimism.

Jo had invited her to a dinner party held by some friends of friends of hers from university. Nigel was a lawyer, Martin a banker and Simon a management consultant. Together they had assembled around twenty guests—Brits, Americans, Chinese Americans and one Australian couple—and brought in a catering company to cook and serve dinner. Cat found herself sandwiched between two friends who had recently been diving together in the Philippines, and who spoke of little else. When the conversation finally did move on it was to rugby, and an in-depth discussion of the upcoming Rugby Sevens event.

By the dessert course she was having fantasies that Declan might turn up and drag her off. If she weren't so hung up on him, she mused, would she find any of these men attractive? They hadn't particularly bothered to speak to her, let alone make her laugh.

None of them had his warmth. She looked across at Jo, who was stifling a yawn. It was eleven o'clock. She could sit with these people for one more hour, kiss and hug them as if they were old friends and then leave, or she could escape now, and go in search of fun? She threw Jo a *get me out of here* look, and to her relief, Jo returned it with one of her own.

"I hate to be anti-social," Cat said suddenly. "But I'm afraid I'm getting a terrible migraine." She rubbed her temples with her thumbs, as if to prove it. "I hope no one's offended if I leave?"

"Oh you poor thing, let me come with you." Jo jumped up, following her lead. "There's nothing worse than feeling ill and trying to get home on your own."

Gratefully, they extricated themselves from the dinner table, as the conversation resumed.

"Well, I'm sorry you have to leave so early," Nigel the lawyer said, kissing Jo goodbye. Plump and pasty, he had the type of hair that could scrub a frying pan clean. "By the way." He lowered his voice as if discussing a delicate case. "There's the small matter of the caterers. I think four hundred dollars each is reasonable."

Jo faltered for a second, as if not understanding. "Oh I'm sorry, I didn't bring any cash, may I send you a check?"

"Yes, me too." Cat managed, hoping her illness might excuse her.

"That would be fine," Nigel assured them both and ushered them to the elevator. Once out in the open, they burst into shocked laughter.

"Who were those people, Jo? Friends of yours?"

"Hardly, I just stayed there when I first arrived. Bloody hell, I'm sorry, I had no idea they were going to pull a stunt like that. Four hundred Hong Kong dollars to get bored out of my brains? It would have been one thing if they'd bothered to mention it from the start. Thank God we left, this woman talked non-stop about her labor, and her water breaking. I thought any minute now she was going to bring out the birth video."

They launched themselves on the escalator leading down from Mid Levels to Central, and decided to head for the bars in Lan Kwai Fong.

"There's bound to be someone we know there," Jo assured

Cat, who for her part was just relieved to have escaped. As they approached she felt a mixture of heady excitement and nerves. Earlier that week she had read of the twenty people who had died on those same streets one New Year's Eve, crushed under the weight of the crowds. And the closer she got, the thicker they became, an impenetrable wall between her and the one person she was hoping to find. Most were clutching glasses, and the entire area had become one big street party.

"Come on." Jo sounded like a hockey mistress. "We can do this."

With impressive force she pushed her way through, knocking people's glasses and sending several off-balance. Cat gazed at her in awe as another group blocked her own way. Jo stormed on ahead but in the distance Cat saw her signalling a certain bar, as if she'd seen someone she recognized, and then disappearing inside.

Taking a deep breath, Cat fought her way through. Once finally there she looked around at all the unfamiliar faces. What did all these people do every other night of the year? Where had they all come from? She recognized a couple of sound engineers and her heart leaped. Jo had already reached the bar and was chatting to Simone, who was clutching a waiter like he was her long lost brother. Cat spotted Derek in deep conversation with a wire-man at the other end, and was sure that Declan had to be there somewhere.

She found a tiny opening in the queue and forced her way to it. The staff were frantic, but she didn't mind waiting. Until she got a drink she had a mission, a reason to be there. Once she had a glass in her hand she would have to find someone to talk to, and she wasn't even sure that that person was there.

She was almost at the head of the queue when a clock chimed and the lights dimmed to a roar from the crowd. Suddenly she was jostled as everyone hugged and beer was slopped from swaying glasses. She pushed herself forward, convinced that the back of her jacket was splattered. Someone trod clumsily on her feet and she kicked out, then ducked down in case they saw her.

Once the bar staff had stopped hugging each other she ordered a glass of white wine. Farther along Jo and Simone raised their glasses to toast her. She would go and join them, she told herself, she would struggle through. But in reality there was only one person she wanted to see that night, and no sign of him whatsoever.

Derek caught her eye and raised his glass with a wink, and she smiled back. She could always make her way toward him, she thought, see how he was doing. As she started to push back from the queue she caught her breath. There, just behind her, looking decidedly unmoved by the festivities, stood Declan Moran. He was wearing a denim shirt with a white T-shirt underneath, and was looking tanned and bored.

"I wasn't expecting you tonight." His face lit up and he leaned forward to kiss her, first on one cheek, and then on the other. "I was on my way out."

"What now?" Cat was appalled. She hadn't gone through all that for nothing.

He nodded. "I was just going to say goodbye to a few people. I've done my bit, now it's time to go back to being a miserable bastard again. What have you been up to?"

"The dinner party from hell," she gushed. "Why don't you stay and have another drink?"

"No I can't, I'm working tomorrow, I have to be in by eight."

"That's too bad," she said lamely, her mind going blank. A mass of people forming a human chain bumped into them, knocking most of her wine out of her glass.

"Oh fuck it, I hate crowds," she shouted. "I don't know why I came."

"So let's get out of here," he said simply, taking her hand in his. "We can be first in line for a taxi."

He pulled her authoritatively through the crowd, his grip strong and warm, making her feel feminine and protected.

"I can't tempt you to a coffee, can I?" she tried hopefully, once they were clear.

He shook his head. "I've really got to get back."

They walked in silence, and to her disappointment he let her hand drop.

"You know something, I think I'll walk home, it's not that far," she told him. "I still feel a bit claustrophobic."

"Are you sure? I wouldn't want to leave you alone on a night like this."

"Come on, Declan, it's safe enough. I'll be fine." She didn't want to say goodbye at all, but couldn't bear to cling on to him either. "Happy New Year, by the way," she said finally.

"Happy New Year, Catherine." He drew her in closer and kissed her, hesitantly at first before sinking into it, oblivious of the traffic, passers-by and of his own guilt. "God, you drive me crazy, you know that?" He took a deep breath, as if controlling himself.

"Why don't you come back with me?" she asked quietly, as they reached the taxis.

He sighed, a deep, heavy, resigned sigh. "I can't." He opened the taxi door.

"Yes, you can. I'll get you up early in the morning."

He shook his head. "It's not that, and you know it. Jump in, I'll drop you off."

She climbed in, her walk suddenly seeming unbearably long. "For some reason, I got the feeling you'd started pulling away from her."

"I haven't," he said simply.

"Oh well." She tried to smile. "Better make it a New Year's resolution. To stop trying to tempt you."

"Would you do that for me?"

"Don't have much choice, do I?" She felt herself retreat into her corner of the cab, watching the view rather than his face. Part of her wanted to cry and another to yell at him, but mostly she was so tired she just wanted to crawl into her bed and forget. The taxi stopped outside her block.

"Don't work too hard tomorrow," she told him, getting out without bothering to say goodbye. She listened as the cab sped off, willing him to have jumped out of his side, and to be standing there behind her. But she turned around and he'd gone, and heavily she pushed the door open, and made her way toward the elevator.

Seventeen

Cat enjoyed her strolls down Hollywood Road. It was full of cheap Sri Lankan restaurants and expensive antique shops, and she loved to peer into the windows and fantasize about the chests and paintings and rugs she'd buy if she had the money. Life in Hong Kong must be wonderful for some people, she thought, a constant round of shopping, parties and junk trips. For her it was hard work, a difficult boss and a relationship that was over before it had even started. Enough money to survive, but not enough to buy antique chests and sideboards.

Maybe it was just the mood she was in, but all the things Cat had found so fascinating when she first arrived were beginning to irritate her now. She held her breath as she walked past a window full of flattened ducks and chickens, and her stomach lurched at the sight of the one-hundred-year-old eggs that were considered such a delicacy. Turning the corner, she cringed as a builder high up on a bamboo scaffold spat on the pavement in front of her.

She made her way past a noisy teashop. A group of ancient-looking Chinese men stared at her, but none of them smiled. She caught the eye of one of them, determined to make some form of contact, but he looked away, slurping his tea. There was no sense of flirtation or fun. To them she was just another foreign ghost, not to be trusted and about as welcome as a lost bet.

What was she doing there, she asked herself. In a place that could be so exhilarating one moment, and yet make her feel so small the next? Maybe today she'd get some idea.

She found the New Age Centre again and being a little early, had another look around, flipping through books with titles like *Heal Yourself from Within* and *Letting Go of Bad Luck*. It was another world, and again one she wasn't convinced she belonged to. She imagined her mortification had Declan seen her there. It felt like an admission of failure, an admission that all was not well in her world. Happy, confident, adjusted people never went to clairvoyants, after all.

She studied the rows of New Age CDs, pondered over the guided meditation tapes and admired an assortment of tarot decks. The walls were covered in posters showing palmistry, chakras and auric fields, and Cat felt terribly conservative in her Saturday casuals. The assistants spoke quietly and in almost evangelical tones. They looked like they'd been cleansed by some sparkling waterfall, and Cat felt grimy and full of office hostility amongst them.

As she was figuring out where her chakras were, and expecting a vision in a kaftan to appear at any moment, Tiffany Cheung called out her name. She was younger than Cat was expecting and, dressed in a pale grey suit with a simple strand of pearls around her neck, looked even more conservative than Cat.

She showed her into a small room at the back that was draped in purple silk. Cat couldn't help staring at Tiffany's skin. It seemed to glow—it had a kind of luminescence she had only ever seen in commercials. For a moment she wondered if it was some genuine inner beauty radiating through, but then put it down to the mineral water Tiffany sipped frequently.

Tiffany set her tape recorder and Cat noticed her bare, elegantly natural nails. Earlier that day she had been admiring her own, freshly painted in deep mulberry. Suddenly they looked vulgar and slutty, and Cat curled them in toward her palms.

"Just to explain, I receive visual and audio messages and use the cards to support these. I'll just go along and tell you what I'm getting, and then there'll be time at the end for any questions. Is that OK?" Her accent was American midwest, and she ended every sentence as if it were a question.

"I should also tell you that sometimes I can see past or even future lives, especially if some aspect of them is relevant or influential in the present life."

"You're talking about reincarnation?" Cat asked incredulously as Tiffany unwrapped her deck of tarot cards. It was a theory she'd always been open to, but had never really given much thought before.

"Yes that's right," Tiffany said matter-of-factly, shuffling the cards. "You understand the principles? That we reincarnate many times, and that each life brings us specific teachings. And all our lives are bound together by karma, and the forces we have created ourselves. Now many people assume that karma is bad, and linked to punishment of some kind, but that's really not the case; it can be positive as well."

She cut the deck into three and indicated that Cat should choose one pile, and then began spreading the cards out, pausing to smile knowingly from time to time. Cat would have liked to ask more questions, but worried that she might break Tiffany's concentration.

"Do you work in communications of some form?" she asked.

Cat nodded, wary of giving too much away.

"There's someone in the company who has strong feelings for you." *Declan?* "It could cause problems in the future, but it's nothing you can't deal with. You're not seeing anyone at the moment, are you?"

"No, not really," she said reluctantly, hating to admit the truth.

"Someone's coming in in the next few months. Through your work. It might take a while for you guys to get together, but it's a good relationship, and a possible marriage partner. I really see a karmic bond with him."

"Could it be someone I know already?"

Tiffany shook her head. "I don't think so."

Cat found it hard to imagine falling in love with anyone other than Declan.

"You've had a lot of bad luck in relationships, haven't you? Nothing's ever quite worked out the way you'd hoped? It's a shame, because when you're with a man, the right man, you feel you can conquer the world, don't you?"

Cat smiled in agreement, remembering the all too brief but heady periods when she had been in love, and it was reciprocated. The days when she could run companies, climb Mount Everest, cook exquisitely and make everyone around her laugh. The days when she was alive, alert and enthusiastic. But invariably something would happen and off he'd go, either with another woman or to another country, taking her confidence and her sense of adventure with him.

"This man you're going to meet, he makes good money," Tiffany continued encouragingly, snapping over a few more cards. "He has a high level of education, and a good brain. He wears suits on the outside, but he's not a suit man. He travels a lot."

"And when do you think I might meet him?" she asked.

Tiffany shook her head. "In the spiritual dimension time is not as we recognize it," she said mysteriously. "And of course we're given free will, so the time it takes the Universe to pull things together can vary. So that's one thing we can never be clear on."

"I'm sorry, the Universe?"

"That's what I like to call it," Tiffany trilled. "You know we all have spirit guides, don't you? Well, I believe they harmonize together, planning a route for you to take. But as mortals we're not necessarily attuned to that route, and I guess we make life hard for them!" She laughed.

"So you're saying everything's fixed?"

"Not fixed, like, set in concrete. Your soul chooses the experiences it needs to grow, and your spirit guides, or the Universe, make it all happen. But as everyone has free will, a person you're meant to meet might take a different route and make you wait a bit."

"But if you can't judge time," Cat tried, getting confused, "then how do you know that I haven't met him already? Maybe it's just that the time isn't right for him yet, that he needs a bit longer?"

Tiffany shook her head with an apologetic smile. "I'm sorry. He hasn't arrived yet, I'm getting that quite strongly."

The reading continued, with Tiffany making comments on Cat's work, an imminent move and a health scare within the family. But she ended on a positive note.

"Your life gets more exciting the older you become," she told her. "You're about to shrug off this bad karma in relationships, and you will find great happiness."

Cat left Tiffany's room feeling exhilarated, like she'd taken some new drug, and wondered how long the effects would last. There was so much to think about, so much to try and understand. A book called *Follow the Signs* attracted her, and she decided to buy it, and to devote the rest of her weekend to being spiritual and reading. She paused, intrigued, at a set of tarot cards, full of romantic figures like the Empress or the Magician, each with its distinct spiritual interpretation. She flipped through the accompanying book and read gentle, mystical phrases like *wait on the guidance of your soul* and *leap, fearlessly, into the unkown*, and decided to buy a set. Then she stopped at a cabinet full of crystals.

"I'd recommend a rose quartz." Cat swung around to see Tiffany behind her. "One of these." She indicated a group of pink rocks. "Choose which one feels right for you. Hold it as you meditate. Rose quartz has healing properties for relationships as well. There are some pamphlets over there on the various courses we run here at the center," she continued. "There's one coming up on crystals. You should take a look, and maybe think about signing up?"

Cat smiled appreciatively, but was a little disappointed at this last-minute sell. She tried a couple of crystals. They felt cold and awkward in her hand, but a third filled her palm, and had an interesting pattern of grooves along one side. This was to be hers, she decided, and she'd learn to meditate with it.

As she paid she picked up Tiffany's leaflets. Skimming through the list of workshops with titles like *Manifesting your Desires* and *Creating Love and Harmony* Cat began to see a new lifestyle ahead. She would take these courses and become a new person: a squeaky clean, centerd, harmonious person who would drink less alcohol, eat more vegetables and become less reliant on the affections of another person.

She walked toward the shopping mall, trying to sift through the tangle of new ideas and theories. It was fascinating to think that people kept coming back until they had learned all of life's lessons, and it made sense too. After all, if everyone ended up in heaven, then wouldn't heaven be a bit like Lan Kwai Fong on a New Year's Eve?

And if heaven was so great, then what right did anyone have to expect to get there after a mere seventy, eighty years, and sometimes a lot less? Surely it took more work than that? And as man had been around for some 200,000 years, wouldn't heaven be full of cavemen and Vikings?

Reincarnation was actually logical, which was strange given that most people thought it far-fetched. Why were some people born rich, and others poor? Why were some dogged with bad luck or ill health, while others flowed through life with apparent ease? Reincarnation was fairer; it created more chances for everyone.

And didn't it also make sense that one person could be attracted to another because of a shared past life? That their backgrounds didn't matter—that theirs was a deeper love, born out of another relationship, in another life, which was perhaps not yet concluded? A love that no one else might understand, but that no one else could break, either.

That must be what Declan and Harriet had, she told herself. He *had* to love her; it was beyond his earthly control. He and Harriet had a past, a soul connection, and there was nothing Cat or anyone else could do about it.

Suddenly enlightened, she bought her groceries and hurried back for a night of reading and meditation. She couldn't blame herself for not winning Declan over; it was beyond her control. Instead, perhaps this situation had arisen so that she could learn exactly that? Maybe the Universe had specifically created this experience for her? Perhaps it had even forced her to flee the hairdressers, so that she would be drawn to Tiffany and her message?

How exciting to think that she was being moved farther along a spiritual path, and that with each day, and each new event, she would make another discovery.

So where was the man she had a karmic connection with, what was happening to him?

He was coming, Tiffany had told her so. He was on his way. And when he arrived, Cat would feel complete. There would be no more loneliness, and no more pain. She just had to keep her head down, get on with her life, and wait on the will of the Universe.

Eighteen

It was Cat's first winter in Hong Kong, and the cold took her by surprise. It was a damp, dank, inhospitable cold, not helped by the fact that the shops and ferries kept their air conditioning on high, as if no one else had noticed. Cat lived in a black woollen jacket and caught herself eyeing thermal underwear in clothing stores.

Melanie Chan arrived and showed a bewildering interest in the Golden Orbs event. She had the straightest, shiniest hair Cat had ever seen outside a shampoo commercial, high cheekbones which were a deep pink and the fullest and poutiest of lips. They pouted when she was happy, they pouted when she was concentrating and they pouted when she wasn't getting her own way. But that, Cat got the impression, rarely happened in Melanie Chan's life.

Cat was instinctively wary of her, despite the fact that she helped talk Max around to her ideas about the show's timing and presentation. He even agreed to a small production budget, and Cat sent her team out to ask passers-by who might win which award. But since not many of the locals knew, cared, or even spoke English, they ended up dragging colleagues from their desks instead. Melanie volunteered, and to everyone's surprise was a natural on camera: funny, warm and unselfconscious. Cat, who couldn't bear having a lens trained on herself, envied her poise and confidence.

Melanie attended the following department heads meeting, and Cat noticed how she sat directly next to Max, making notes and nodding in agreement at everything he said. Max, in a blue shirt with white collar and cuffs that was teamed up with a surprisingly stylish tie, was clearly enjoying the attention.

"So, how are we all doing with those specials? Let's start with Score."

"We're getting close on that one," Jerry stepped in.

"Close?" Max roared. "Don't give me close. I want a signed deal!"

"Max these things take time. But we have one very interested sponsor and I hope to have a signature by the end of the week."

"That's not good enough, Jerry. I want it today. Now, Catherine? What's happening with the Orbs?"

Melanie broke in. "I have two companies interested at the moment, and I'd say we were nearing a signed deal."

"Excellent work," Max beamed. "Keep it up, Melanie."

Cat shared an amused glance with Lorna and then looked quickly at Jerry, who was studying the stitching on his tank top.

"Who's next?" Max took a deep breath. "Ah, Miss Kindly Word. How's the sales tape coming along?"

Jo tried to contain her irritation. "Well, we finished shooting last week and are on the second draft of the script, having made the amendments you suggested."

"I took a look at the script myself," Melanie added. "And made a couple of suggestions. There were some things in the running order that didn't make sense to me, and I changed some of the programs Jo had selected to make it stronger."

"Good work. When do I get to see it?"

"At the beginning of next week, I'd say," Jo told him.

"Excellent," Max said. It was directed at Melanie.

The meeting over, Jo accompanied Cat back to her office.

"If he calls me Miss Kindly Word one more time," she started angrily, "I'll send him a kindly word where the sun don't shine." She affected Max's accent. "And just who the fuck does Melanie think she is?"

"It won't last," Cat said confidently. "She's trying to impress him because she still thinks he knows what he's doing. I was like that at the beginning, everyone is."

"She's flying way too close to the sun." Lorna joined them. "I've known Max for years. He has his little favorites, and then he tires of them. So anyway?" She brightened with obvious delight. "Did you hear today's big story? Phil Tucker was caught masturbating in edit two last night."

Despite her shock, Cat could almost picture the scene—a long overnight, a long way from home, an empty edit suite . . .

"Oh my God," Jo exclaimed. "And I thought I had problems."

Nineteen

The Golden Orbs event, with the lucrative sponsorship deal Melanie had tied up, was a great success. Cat watched the incoming feed that morning and oversaw its edit with the pieces they had recorded. It was a slick show with an Asian twist, and even Max had to admit he was pleased.

"It looked great, Cat, I watched it last night," Jo told her.

"Thanks. How's your epic coming along?"

Jo sighed. "We're on the fifth draft of the script now. Melanie keeps changing things, and then Max changes them back. Then she feels she has to change something else. It's a complete nightmare." She took a deep breath. "So we're rerecording the voice-over tomorrow, and in final edit the next day. And then it'll all be over. Unless Max comes up with another crisis to bugger up Chinese New Year."

"Oh, you haven't heard?" Lorna joined them. "He wants a whole new look for Variety. He's decided he hates the name and wants a whole new ID. Just kidding," she added, enjoying the horrified look on their faces. "Max is heading for Bangkok tomorrow, don't worry."

"I still can't believe we get four days off," Cat said.

"Use it or lose it, that's what he said. That's the best thing about Hong Kong, the vacations. You start to live for them."

"Where are you going?" Jo asked her.

"Off to Hawaii with Corporate Wonderboy. Trying to breathe new life into our relationship. You?"

"Thailand," Jo beamed. "I cannot wait."

"And I have just booked a trip to the Philippines," Cat announced, feeling herself relax already. "I am going to lie on the beach, screw some Australian surfer and forget all about this place."

She had no intention of meeting a surfer, but went instead armed with her runes, her book and her crystal, determined to make the trip a kind of spiritual retreat. Four days of meditation, reading, eating healthily and drinking no alcohol, she told herself. But once she had settled into her beach hut and wandered down to the sunset bar serving ice-cold beers, she thought perhaps that was asking too much.

She'd wake early and try to meditate in the sunrise, holding her rose quartz crystal in the palm of her right hand. She didn't know if that was what she was meant to do or not, but it felt right. She'd clear her mind of all thoughts and just relax, listening to the sound of the waves and of the island coming to life.

Then she'd wander along the white beach to have breakfast in a little café—some granola, orange juice and coffee. For the rest of the morning she'd look at the shops, buying more sarongs and T-shirts than she really needed, and have a massage. After a light lunch she'd lie on the sand and read, breaking only for the occasional dip in the sea.

Follow the Signs was about learning to pay attention to the coincidences that propel life forward, and the blocks which hold it back. Nothing happened without reason, according to the author, and the key to happiness was to relax, have patience, and wait for the Universe to provide. By following the coincidences you were following your soul's path, whilst inexplicable blocks and delays happened merely to bring something, or someone new in. Trying to control events was futile, and would only result in upsetting the Universe's will.

As Cat read she pictured herself on some esoteric game of Chutes and Ladders, climbing up as she followed the signs and then slithering down if she ignored or tried to change them. There had been coincidences—finding herself in edit with Declan in the first place, running into Harriet in the hair salon—but what did any of them mean? Where were they actually taking her?

One evening as she returned to her room, she impulsively drew a tarot card. It was the twelfth card: the Hanged Man, who, as depicted in the picture, dangled upside down, tied to a tree by his left foot. *He looks happy enough*, she thought, *but he can't move.* Was that the key? Puzzled, she turned to the book. *Like the Hanged Man you wait, motionless, unable to move forward until the issues which are holding you back are resolved. Accept the past with thanks and then release it, for only when you do so can you finally reclaim your future.*

Cat analyzed the interpretation with a sinking heart. She didn't feel ready to release Declan from her life just yet, but that seemed to be the message. He was becoming fainter, though: it was only at night, as she'd watch the orange sunset fade to black and have a meal and a beer by herself that she'd think of him. He and Harriet would have enjoyed beaches like this in Thailand. She tried not to imagine them together, but everywhere she looked there was yet another couple laughing and holding hands, reminding her.

Maybe she was growing spiritually, she mused one evening, sipping her beer. Maybe that was one way of looking at a period in her life when nothing much seemed to be happening. Maybe all sorts of exciting things were in fact happening, but on a deeper, subconscious level. Maybe the Universe was sorting stuff out in the background, creating the events that would speed her soul mate into her life?

But what was she thinking of, anyway? Nothing happening? She could look back on the Golden Orbs with pride—she had achieved something she'd never previously thought herself capable of. She was being given huge opportunities at work—the chance to run her own channel, buy her own programs. So what if her love life was a non-event, she couldn't expect all things, all of the time, surely? Now was a time to focus on the opportunities the Universe was giving her, and not on the ones she was still missing.

And maybe if she let Declan go, if she could release him from her thoughts for ever, that someone new and unattached would come in? She took a deep breath.

Or maybe she could just try another card?

Twenty

For the next few weeks Cat concentrated on pulling together her channel. She hired more staff until she had a team of sixteen—three schedulers, a promotions group, two marketing representatives, a program management team and a secretary, Winnie—and her time became a delicate balance between overseeing them and keeping Max happy. His programming strategy changed according to the latest whim of Desmond Tang: on his return from Malaysia it was decreed that any cooking shows using pork be withdrawn; after a trip to India the same went for beef. Deciding the rest of Asia probably wasn't that interested in cake making, Cat withdrew the whole strand.

One week the emphasis was on detective shows and another it was murder mysteries, and one week Max even had Cat research any series featuring a certain actress Desmond Tang had developed a crush on. Instead of fielding these requests, Max simply complied with them, leaving Cat to deal with the numerous half-finished agreements over programs they had lost interest in. Then there were the strange, mystery deals that Max would suddenly present her with. A random package of 1970s TV movies; the occasional concert by some fading artist; a package of game shows with no relevance to the region whatsoever. Cat knew better than to ask the background of any of them, and would just shake her head and pray that sanity might one day prevail.

She moved, finding a more spacious apartment in Happy Valley, near the race course on Hong Kong Island. It was just a tram ride away from the ferry, and although it meant getting up half an hour earlier each morning, it was lighter and quieter than Wanchai and more importantly, it held no memories. The rent was twice as high, however, but it was worth it.

Derek also found a new home, a small villa on the Shek O Peninsula, southeast of Hong Kong Island, where he promptly rescued two stray dogs and threw a water-pistol party. Cat got drenched before she'd even made it through the garden and the entire ground floor quickly became a lake. When Jo slipped badly in the kitchen, hurting her back, they decided it was time to leave.

During these weeks she forced herself not to think about Declan. It wasn't easy, as he was always there, lurking somewhere, waiting to pop into her thoughts when she was least expecting him. His memories were everywhere—the edit suites, the places he'd kissed her, even the hairdressers reminded her of him. The jealousy was still there, struggling to assume pole position in her mind, but she tried not to let it. There were days, especially on the weekends she knew he was free, that she would have enjoyed that misery; she would have enjoyed her martyrdom and all it brought. But she was growing up, or so she told herself, and would find distraction in massages, or hair treatments or buying clothes she rarely got to wear.

Occasionally she caught a glimpse of him in the building, either heading toward the kitchen or collecting tapes from the library. His face always lit up when he saw her, she noticed, and there was always that big, twinkling smile.

She had seen him briefly that morning, stopping off for a chat with Lorna. She saw him laughing as he walked away, and felt a pang of jealousy. Lorna, who had neither got so close nor become so distant, could still chat easily about everything and nothing. She envied her friend that.

She was giving Winnie some filing when she noticed the closing credits of an afternoon movie had started rolling. Max had heard that Friday afternoons were the start of the weekend in the Middle East, and had suddenly demanded that she incorporate a movie or a special event for their viewers there. Was it as late as that already? She checked her watch. The matinée wasn't due to finish until five o'clock, four-thirty at the earliest. But it was only three forty-five, and something must have gone wrong.

A sense of dread creeping over her, Cat watched as the commercial break finished. Then up came the opening titles of the very same movie that had just finished.

Quickly she made her way to the operations area, glancing in Max's office as she did so. He was at the meeting table castigating Trent Davies and was clearly paying no attention to the monitors. Cat wasn't sure which bothered her the most, upsetting her viewers or infuriating her boss.

Phil Tucker was checking a damaged tape when she arrived.

"Phil, the movie we're showing. We just ran part two before part one."

"Oh we did? Whoops." Phil ushered her into Variety's transmission suite. "Terry, this movie," he began.

"Er, yes, I know, this is the first part. This was how it was printed in the log." Terry pointed it out to them.

"Oh there, you see?" Phil showed Cat. "It was scheduled this way."

"Oh OK." Cat smiled to Terry, beckoning Phil out. She began to whisper. "But Phil, aren't the tapes clearly marked part one and two? And I thought your guys always checked the first few seconds beforehand, just in case of something like this?"

"Cat, at the end of the day they're going to follow the running order they're given," Phil said defensively, folding his arms.

"When they can see that they're about to run the wrong tape?"

"What can I tell you? My guys aren't here to make editorial decisions. If we started mucking about with running orders you'd get pretty pissed off, wouldn't you?"

In the distance an edit suite door opened, and Declan walked out.

"We're here to make sure the tapes, and more importantly commercials, go out in the order we're given," Phil continued. "But we're not here to take editorial control."

"Even when you can see quite plainly that you're about to play part two of a movie before part one. Great. Very constructive. Thanks a lot."

She turned and stalked out, frustrated by his defense and

angry with herself for not getting her point across strongly enough. Immediately she began mentally constructing a superior argument, better sentences, a more compelling case for working for the greater good of the channel. And in the back of her mind she was praying that Max wouldn't notice.

"Catherine. Long time no see."

It was Declan. She could barely bring herself to look at him. Once he would have been an ally, someone she could have turned to. Now he was just someone else who made her life more difficult.

"Whatever." She frowned, walking past him.

"Hey, Cat." He called her back, a puzzled look on his face. "What's up?"

"I don't want to talk about it." She took a deep breath. "It's just a stupid thing with a movie. They ran part two before part one." Despite herself she broke into a slight laugh.

"Was that such a terrible thing now?" He smiled, the lines around his eyes beckoning her, calling her closer.

"Well yes." She began to melt. "Who knows, someone in Abu Dhabi might have really been looking forward to it." She took another deep breath, knowing this was futile. "I know, no one died. But I might if Max catches it."

"We'll have to distract him. When's it due to finish?"

"Oh I don't know, four-thirty?"

"Maybe we can call him up about something," Declan tried helpfully. "Or set off the fire alarm?"

Despite herself she had to laugh.

"Were any commercials affected?"

"I doubt it."

"Then you don't have a problem."

"In the real world it would have been a problem."

"But this isn't the real world, it's Hong Kong."

"Well thanks for that. I keep forgetting to lower my standards, silly me." She started to walk away but stopped as someone opened the studio door. There, right in front of her, was a camera trained on Melanie Chan, looking coquettish in a simple strappy dress and reading from autocue.

Cat turned to Declan. "Now I've seen everything. Is she becoming a presenter?"

"Pretty girl. Is Max boffing her?"

"If he isn't he will be soon. What are we doing here, Declan?"

He smiled. "I'm in it for the money, I don't know about you." His voice softened. "It's good to see you, you know that?"

Immediately she felt the blood rush to her cheeks. He was wearing a worn blue and white checked shirt, the first couple of buttons of which were open to reveal the soft blonde hair down his throat, a v-necked fawn sweater and a pair of navy chinos. His hair looked like it hadn't been brushed for a couple of days. Cat thought he looked wonderful. She nodded and walked away, as if escaping danger.

Back in the programming area, she made a quick detour to see Lorna.

"Any idea what Max is up to in about forty minutes' time?"

"I think he has cocktails on Desmond Tang's yacht, why?"

Cat smiled in relief. "I'll explain later."

"Hey," Lorna called out. "Wanna hear the latest?"

"Melanie Chan, auditioning for Vibe?"

"Damn, how did you know that?"

By the time she got to her office Cat's phone was ringing, and she knew instinctively that it was Declan.

"I know you must hate me, but—"

"I don't hate you."

"Do you fancy a drink later?"

"Why not?" She sank back into her chair, thanking the Universe for her sudden good fortune. Max would know nothing of the mistake and Declan still wanted her.

"But not Sam's. Let's go somewhere else, say, Dan Ryan's, Pacific Place?"

Deep inside a distant voice yelled at Cat, trying its hardest to stop her from saying yes. But like a Stepford Wife she heard herself agreeing to meet him, took childish delight in being wanted and knew that yet again, having climbed so far, she had started to slither down that esoteric ladder.

Twenty-One

Inside her new flat Cat kicked off her shoes and unzipped her skirt, throwing it over the back of a chair. She allowed her jacket to drop from her shoulders and hung it inside her wardrobe. She had spent the ferry ride home planning what to wear. Declan was certainly looking casual and she didn't want to look out of place beside him. She was veering toward her new jeans with her black, toeless high heels. A plain white T-shirt, similar to those she wore under her suits, and perhaps a jacket. Or would that be too dressy? A shawl perhaps, or a baggy sweater thrown over her shoulders?

She showered and retouched her makeup and then stood in front of her wardrobe, searching for ideas. What did people wear in the evenings? What was it she was trying to convey? She didn't want to look vampish, that might frighten him off. Nor did she want to look like she was expecting sex that night, though she could always hope. She wanted to be approachable—casual yet stylish. Soft and feminine, but not too vulnerable. She had a pale blue cardigan that fastened with just one button, that might do it. That, the jeans, the sexy shoes and a simple black evening bag. Lots of fresh Cristalle perfume. Extra shine on her hair and some lipgloss over her dusky pink lipstick.

She tidied her room quickly, just in case, and took the elevator down to the lobby, where a security guard, if he could have been called that, sat in his vest eating a bowl of noodles.

"Leh ho ma?" Cat tried. *How are you?* The man ignored her.

A quick cab ride later and she was in the shopping mall, feeling the sudden cold of the air conditioning against her skin. She took the escalator up and wandered toward Dan Ryan's, peering at shop windows on the way. The bar was some three people deep, and there were monitors in all corners showing a rugby match. By the time she'd ordered a glass of wine, Declan had appeared.

"So did Carnage find you out?" he asked once they'd bought their drinks. "The movie?" he added, seeing the puzzled look on her face. "Part two first?"

"Oh that." She laughed. She'd practically forgotten all about it. "No, he didn't. I think he was distracted by Melanie doing her rock'n'roll act."

"You see, if no one dies, there's not a problem."

"Yes, yes," Cat sighed, not entirely agreeing but not wanting to get into it either. Then she remembered something. "I thought Phil was going to be suspended?"

"What on earth for?"

"You know, his nocturnal activities in edit two."

Declan threw his head back and laughed. "Oh that. That was all a lie. He tried to start a rumor that Derek had genital warts."

Cat shook her head. "Never heard it."

"I know, feeble attempt." He swigged back his beer. "So Derek set up the masturbation rumor."

"Which went everywhere."

"Yes it did, Phil was mightily pissed off."

As Cat laughed, a man carrying three pints of lager knocked into her, and Declan reached out protectively. That really was a terrible shirt he was wearing, she thought. But how wonderful it was to see him again after all those weeks.

"What made you ask me out today?"

He smiled affectionately. "You think I haven't wanted to before? But seeing you this afternoon, in that short little skirt and your high heels—you just wanted to come over and torment me, didn't you?"

"And did it work? Were you suitably tormented?"

"Catherine." He leaned so close she could smell the lager on his breath. It smelled sweet and sexy and made her want to kiss him. "I'm always tormented over you."

"So what are we going to do? Every time I try to relieve your suffering you turn me away."

"I know I do," he said quietly, pushing a stray hair out of her eyes. "I don't know. My life used to be so straightforward, you know? A regular job, a steady girlfriend—"

"Who's thousands of miles away and doesn't want to join you out here," Cat jumped in, regretting it instantly.

"Catherine. She has commitments."

"But no sense of adventure." She said it before she could stop herself, resenting the way he defended Harriet. "I mean, who would turn down the opportunity to experience all this? What kind of a person gives that up to stay in Peckham or somewhere?"

"She does not live in Peckham." He laughed, pulling her toward him and planting a kiss on her forehead.

"So where does she live then?"

Cat knew perfectly well that she was pushing it, but suddenly she *had* to know where Harriet lived, she *had* to picture her flat— whether it had a garden or not, how her commute was, where she would have done her shopping.

"It doesn't matter. Can we keep her out of it?"

"Pretend she doesn't exist?" Cat went to drink and found her glass empty. "That's what I keep suggesting, remember?"

"Let's get another drink," he said quickly. "And maybe something to eat?"

They had a bottle of wine and ate in the American-style restaurant in the back. It wouldn't have been Cat's usual choice, but that didn't matter. All that mattered was that she was with him. She had a Caesar salad and some buffalo wings and he ordered a cheeseburger and fries. She watched with affection as he squeezed tomato ketchup on the side of his plate and bit into the burger, holding it in both hands. She had never imagined herself dating a man who ate burgers, and she enjoyed the raw manliness of it. She fed him a piece of her buffalo wing and he sucked the barbecue sauce off her finger, a smile on his face.

"Coffee?" he asked as a waitress called Kim cleared their plates.

"No," she said simply. "I should go home. What do you want to do?"

"Let's have another drink. What about upstairs, one of the hotels?"

Attached to the shopping mall were three hotels, and they chose the bar on the top floor of the Marriott. Cat knew she should have gone home, but it had become one of those evenings she didn't want to end. She had forgotten how much fun he could be, and how exciting it was just to sit close to him, and to feel his leg brush against hers. There was something about the Hong Kong night sky, she thought staring out at the view, something sexy and hedonistic, urging her to misbehave. There was nothing she wanted more than to take Declan to her bed.

In the elevator going down he lunged at her, pressing her up against the wall and running his hand over her breasts. It felt so right to hold him in her arms, their bodies a perfect match, that Cat was barely aware when several floors later an elderly American couple joined them. They were wearing matching outfits, so she assumed they were Americans.

Declan pulled away sheepishly, and she suppressed her laughter until they left a few floors later. Then he pounced again and they were undisturbed until the lobby.

They jumped in a taxi and were inside her place within minutes. She pulled him toward her bedroom and unbuttoned her blue cardigan. He pulled it off her shoulders and threw it on the chair beside her bed, and then took off his own shirt. She stepped out of her shoes and jeans as he undid his belt and let his own drop to the floor. She pulled off her T-shirt and stood there in her new white underwear, before pulling back the sheets.

"Cat, there's something I have to ask." She took a deep breath. "Can we do everything but?"

"What?" she cried, exasperated. "But what?"

"I know it sounds stupid." His face was wracked with guilt again. "But if I don't go inside you it feels less unfaithful, somehow."

"Oh Declan." She despaired. She was too tired to fight. "If that's what you want."

"Thank you." He climbed into bed, folded her into his arms and kissed her. "Thank you."

Later, as she watched him sleep, she resolved never to lose her temper, never to get upset or bitter or jealous, but to be the perfect, dreamy, smooth girlfriend for him; the one who'd make him feel secure and warm and loved.

It would take time, she knew. But she hadn't invested in all these months for nothing. He would be hers, she told herself. He was weakening.

Twenty-Two

Cat made coffee, humming to herself as Declan showered. She felt like an American housewife in the 1950s, looking after her man. She wiped down surfaces and watered the plants as the kettle boiled, and fantasized that this might become a regular routine. Of course that only led her to think about Harriet, and she quickly pushed those thoughts away. She had to be bright, fluffy and sweet for him early in the morning. He couldn't go into the shower with an American housewife making coffee and come out again, all wet and clean, to find *Fatal Attraction* waiting for him in the kitchen.

"How the hell do I get to work from here?" he asked, slurping coffee and trying to towel dry his hair at the same time.

"You have plenty of time." She tried to soothe him.

"I'd better be off, just to be on the safe side. I'll get enough flak as it is for wearing this shirt again."

"I'm surprised you didn't get flak for wearing it anyway."

He threw her a resigned look and smiled. "What am I doing with you, woman?" He leaned forward and kissed her. "Look, I have to go." He reached for his jacket. "Thank you for, for—"

"Having you? Any time." She put her arms around his neck and kissed him.

"Yes, thank you for having me." He kissed her. "And for kissing me." He kissed her again. "And for letting me touch you."

Again. "And for being so fucking beautiful." And again. "And for the best blowjob of my life."

"That is a compliment," she giggled.

"I'd say so. I'm off work tomorrow. Can I see you tonight?"

"Of course you can." Instant happiness. If she could bottle that feeling she'd make a fortune.

"Do you want to come to my place? I'll call you later. We could get something to eat in Sai Kung if you like."

"Sounds wonderful."

"I'd better go." He gave her three big kisses on the mouth.

"OK. Have a nice day at the office, dear."

She held the front door open and watched as he waited for the elevator, then closed it dreamily, ignoring the fact that she was now running about half an hour late herself. What did she care? She had Declan, and this time he'd be there to stay. How good life was going to be.

It was only as she showered that she began to feel some irritation that they hadn't yet had full sex. It was as if she wasn't good enough to have him inside her, that it was a privilege only to be enjoyed by Harriet. By the time she left for work she was beginning to feel angry. Had she run into him she would have felt like shouting. As she reached the tram stop the sky seemed to reflect her anger, and by the time she'd got to the ferry, the rain was pouring down, splashing her ankles and ruining her hair.

She had barely sat at her desk when there was a call from Lacy Fok, asking her to see Max. Had he found out about yesterday's movie fiasco? She grabbed a pen and pad and made her way to his office.

"Sit down." He was studying his immaculately manicured fingernails. "What are your plans next week?"

The question caught her by surprise.

"You want a trip to France? I've booked you into MIP, the programming market in Cannes." He threw a form at her. "I think you should be there. Lacy's organizing your hotel and travel arrangements."

"Max, thank you!"

"It'll be hard work," he said, as if wanting to deflate her enthusiasm.

"Of course it will," she agreed, hoping her expression was suitably serious. "But it'll make a big difference meeting some of these people face to face."

"Take this book." He handed her a guide, collected at the previous event. "It'll help you make your appointments. Did Midland sign yet?"

"We're on the verge—" she began.

"Catherine—this deal's gone on long enough." He started raising his voice. "I want you two to have sex, now, and I want to come."

Cat shrank back as Brandon Miller appeared at the door, clearly imagining the sexual harassment suit that would be filed if they were in the States.

"Don't rush me, Max." She managed to keep a straight face. "We're barely at the heavy petting stage." With a nod to Brandon she escaped the office.

At two, Cat and Lorna took a taxi to the Pacific Place shopping mall.

"So he's given me a week to prepare," Cat told her. "A week! Why couldn't he have said anything earlier?"

"Not his style, honey. He likes to keep you on your toes."

"Funny how everything happens at once—Declan comes back and then I get a trip. Typical."

She watched, fascinated, as Lorna retouched her eyeliner in her hand mirror, pausing instinctively whenever the car jolted.

"So I've been thinking all morning about how to get him to do it properly and it suddenly occurred to me about an hour ago. Stockings! I mean, have you ever known a man to resist? So this afternoon I'm buying stockings and a garter belt. He won't be able to say no after that."

"Honey, he'll be worshipping you for the goddess you are." Lorna turned to her, her eyes a triumph of concentration.

The taxi dropped them off at the mall and they made their way to Dan Ryan's. An hour later, rifling through the underwear section, fortified by Margaritas, Cat was disappointed, but not surprised, to find very little in her size. Shopping had become an exercise in frustration, where even a size 8 was considered large.

"Excuse me, do you have these in grown-up sizes?" she said to no one in particular and they giggled. Lorna was admiring a lacy black all-in-one piece.

"You know I used to have something like this in New York—it would have been perfect for you, because it was—" As she said the words her fingers popped through a gap between the legs. "Crotchless."

"Oh my." Cat was beside her immediately.

"This, darling, a little Chanel No. 5 and a pair of high black heels."

"And then what?" Cat asked, faking naivete.

Lorna lowered her voice. "And then you bend over."

Twenty-Three

The stockings felt strange on her legs as Cat sat in the back of the taxi heading for Sai Kung. With her she had two bags—one contained her jeans, a light sweater and a change of underwear for tomorrow, along with all her skin care stuff. The other had two bottles of champagne, some smoked salmon, fresh eggs, a punnet of strawberries and some thick double cream.

She could barely remember the directions to his place, and the taxi made a couple of false turns as they descended into Sai Kung village. The streets were narrow and steep and the houses white-washed and in a way Mediterranean-looking. She felt she could almost have been in a Greek village. Finally she recognized his first-floor apartment and asked the driver to stop.

She stepped out in her kitten heels, rang the bell and listened to the sound of his feet on the stairs. Then he was there, admiring her. She was wearing a slim-fitting cashmere T-shirt and a floaty floral knee-length skirt. As if she were in a romantic drama, she dropped her bags to the ground, threw her arms around his neck and kissed him.

"You look incredible," he said. "Come in."

He took her bags and showed her upstairs. He had obviously just showered and had changed into a pair of beige jeans with a faded blue shirt, unbuttoned at the top.

"I brought champagne and breakfast," she beamed.

"Good girl."

She found places for her provisions in the fridge as he opened a bottle. She admired the view from his little kitchen, enjoying this simple act of domesticity, and had a quick fantasy that she lived there with him, and that he was all hers.

He didn't have any champagne glasses, so he poured it into some cheap white wine glasses instead, and Cat made a note that they would make an ideal birthday present. He would be touched, she thought, and Harriet would wonder where they had come from.

They moved out on to his terrace, where he stood behind her, brushing her hair to one side, and nuzzled her neck. Could life get more beautiful? She held on to his arm with her free hand, examining the hairs, pulling at them playfully. He moved his hand up and cupped her breast, gently squeezing the nipple through her top. She turned her head to meet his, and he pulled her to face him, kissing her.

"God, you're gorgeous," he whispered.

She smiled triumphantly, staring out at the bay, thinking how much the twinkling lights resembled the sparkles in her champagne.

"What do you want to eat tonight? There are some good seafood places in the village, but they're a bit basic." He looked hesitantly at her clothes.

"That's OK."

"Well, let's do that then. It's a nice walk along the front. Better finish this bottle first."

"Silly not to." She wondered when to let him know about the stockings. Whether to torment him with them now or to wait until supper, or maybe even to let them come as a delicious surprise when they went to bed?

Life was too short, she decided. She moved over to a white plastic chair and sat on it sideways, letting her legs lie on the armrest. Her skirt rode up her thighs, and she made no attempt to cover herself.

"Cat, what are you wearing?" He was incredulous. "Oh my God, woman." He came closer to examine them. He stroked her thigh, fingering her garter belt as if he'd never seen anything like it before. "I don't believe you."

"What's the matter? Don't you like them?"

"Well, of course I like them, it's just, well, unexpected, that's all."

"Declan, hasn't anyone ever worn stockings for you?" she teased, and he gave her a stern look.

"Not for a long time."

"You poor, deprived love." She ran her fingers through his hair, and he kissed the palm of her hand.

"I can't go anywhere now." He shifted uncomfortably in his jeans.

"Do you want me to help you?" She unzipped his fly. He groaned as she lifted him out and, leaning forward, took him in her mouth. He held her closely, until with a giggle she pulled away, took a sip of her glass, and then scooped him back inside, sloshing the cold champagne over him.

"Fucking hell, woman, what are you doing to me?" he moaned, and she began to wonder if he wasn't very deprived indeed.

They had dinner in a brightly lit restaurant full of local families. They chose steamed fish with peppers, some rice, noodles and stir-fried vegetables. She spent most of the evening not bothering to eat but playfully running her foot up his leg instead. By the time they'd finished they had to wait several minutes before they could leave, as Declan was unable to stand up in public without being arrested. Then they walked along the bay, hand in hand, stopping only to kiss and laugh.

Inside his apartment he pushed her against the sitting room wall, running his hand the length of her stockings. He pulled back, shocked.

"Cat! You're not wearing any panties?"

"Is that a problem?"

"I don't believe you." He sighed. "Oh God, let's go to bed."

She knew then that if she kept the stockings on all night, she'd be sure to get her way.

Twenty-Four

Cat woke dreamily the next morning and turned to look at the body beside her. Declan slept soundly, his soft wavy hair falling haphazardly on the pillow. She thought he looked beautiful. Carefully she got up to retrieve her makeup bag, noting with satisfaction the condom he'd wrapped up in a tissue and left on the bedside unit. She always got what she wanted in the end.

When she had removed all traces of last night's makeup she returned to his side, snuggling up next to him, and made sure that every part of their bodies was touching. He stroked her, and they lay like spoons, breathing softly. She was wide awake now, and would have liked to make love again, but he seemed content to sleep a while longer.

She studied his room instead, taking in the pile of dirty clothes in one corner, and how the light, which shone through some dusty venetian blinds only a man would keep, fell in patterns on the floorboards. A few battered paperbacks lay on the floor along with a couple of motorbike magazines. Then she spotted a wallet containing photographs, and longed to peek through them. She wondered if they were from Thailand, and if so, how many would be of Harriet? Maybe when he went to the bathroom, she thought, maybe then she would have a quick look.

She tried to memorize exactly how it was positioned, at a slight angle, poking out under a couple of socks. They couldn't have meant much to him surely, if he could just leave them lying around like that, just tossed on the floor? She thought of her own photograph collection, which was neatly arranged in albums and filed on a bookshelf. She could no sooner allow them to lie on the floor like that than she could her clothes, or have shampoo bottles randomly scattered about the bathroom.

She began to tire of lying like that, began to get fidgety. The sun was shining, it looked like another beautiful day and she wanted either to be out on the terrace having breakfast or to be made love to again. But now Declan was fast asleep. Carefully she rolled on to her back. She could always get up, make some coffee and get some sun. But then what if she missed an opportunity, and they didn't go back to bed? His breathing was hard. If she were alone right now she would make fresh coffee, pinch the photo album and sit on the terrace, studying it.

She couldn't stand it, got up carefully, pulled on her clothes and tiptoed into the sitting room. She desperately wanted to go through the photos, but knew they would only make her depressed and angry. And why spoil a beautiful weekend? She had to distract herself, and a fax sheet on his coffee table caught her eye.

She made some instant coffee and pulled it out from under the book where it lay. It was a photocopied newspaper article about Thailand, but what caught her eye was the fax number at the top of the sheet. Only Harriet would have sent him this, she was certain, and so the fax number had to belong to her company. Feeling like a private detective, her pulse racing in case he woke up and caught her, she found a pen and bit of paper and scribbled the central London number down.

"Cat?" She heard him call, slipped the paper into her bag and returned to the bedroom. He had woken up and was stretching. She stroked his hair again, pushing it gently out of his eyes. Suddenly he grabbed her and pulled her on top of him. In delight she kissed him, ignoring the taste of stale alcohol on his breath. He hardened straight away and threw her on to her back, reaching for the condoms. He said nothing, just tore open the square packet, and Cat thought that she had never been happier.

Twenty-Five

"**W**anna hear some gossip?" Lorna's head appeared around Cat's door.

"Is the pope Catholic?"

"Corporate Wonderboy suggests dinner Saturday night. So we go to the Veranda on Repulse Bay. Stunning, you should go there some time. So we're just starting when guess who sits down, right at the next table?"

"Thrill me."

"Mad Max and—"

"Melanie Chan."

"In one." Lorna said triumphantly. "So Max is, like, appalled. Horrified to see us. Says hello and tries to make out like there's nothing going on, but you could see he was trying so hard to come up with some excuse. Gets talking to Corporate Wonderboy and I chat briefly with Melanie, tell her how great her tapes looked, that kind of thing. So anyway they order and Melanie goes to the bathroom, and Max turns to me all serious and says 'this isn't what it looks like.' " She mimicked his voice. " 'This is confidential but as you're the press officer you'll know sooner or later. Melanie is to become our new chart show presenter, and I'm just going through a few details with her. Like, how to perform in front of the camera, how to deal with media attention, life in the public eye, that kind of thing.' "

"Oh my God." Cat laughed into her hands. "Did Trent have

any say in the matter? I saw him getting a talking-to just before the screen test. She's good on camera, but I thought she was supposed to be the goddess of air-time sales?"

"Who knows? He must be fucking her by now, though," Lorna added knowingly. "So how was your weekend?"

"Good morning, ladies." Lorna jumped as Max was suddenly behind her. "I have a new show for you, Catherine. *The Pride and the Passion*, know it?"

Cat shook her head as Lorna quickly excused herself.

"One of the U.S.'s leading daytime soaps, seen in over fifty countries world-wide. Set on a Beverly Hills health farm."

"Sounds fabulous."

"Just to show you how quickly deals can be struck." He walked out again, leaving a faint smell of aftershave behind him.

She began to prepare for her French trip, e-mailing distributors and setting up her appointments. Once she had contacted all the main suppliers, she started on the job that was really on her mind. She reached for the guide Max had given her. In it were the contact details of every buyer and distributor to attend the market. She took the scrunched-up bit of paper out of her bag, and turning to the UK pages, began at the first entry. Determined to find Harriet, she checked every single company listed, trying to match the fax number.

By the F's she was beginning to tire, but carried on anyway. She had no idea what she was going to do when she found it, but that wasn't the point. Until she did, it gnawed at her, and she felt restless and incomplete. By the R's she was beginning to feel disheartened, and that she was wasting her time, and by the T's she felt a bit like a stalker.

Suddenly she got it—the exact number. She laughed in disbelief, as if she hadn't seriously expected to at all. She laughed at her discovery, and then at Declan for leaving such incriminating evidence around the place. Had he really thought she wouldn't see it? World Daytime Network—she had had to wait till the bloody Ws to find it! They made lifestyle programming for both the BBC and ITV, from chat and talk shows to gardening and cooking.

And why couldn't any of those programs be good for Frontier? She suspected that Max wouldn't be interested, but what was to stop her from talking to them anyway? Her imagination began to race. If she could just meet with their sales person in Cannes, maybe go on to make friends with them, then one day mention her lover in Hong Kong—well, word might surely get back to Harriet? It was worth a shot. She checked her watch—in two hours she could ring them and set up an appointment. She was flushed with excitement, and deeply proud of her achievements.

The little white envelope popped up in the bottom right corner of her screen, taking her out of her fantasy, and Cat clicked it open. It was an e-mail from Midland, and they were agreeing to her revised offer on a package of dramas, sitcoms, documentaries and several TV movies. All final queries in the contract had been agreed, and it was ready for signature. There was also an invitation to a celebratory dinner with the sales rep, Terry Johnston, and his boss Mark Gilmore.

She printed it out and rushed around to Max's office. Seeing Jerry Greenberg was inside, she left it with Lacy, thankful not to have to speak with him and delay her phone call any longer. Back in her office she dialled World Daytime Network's number and asked for one of the names in the book. Eventually she was put through to a man who sounded seriously harassed.

"I'm acquiring pan-Asian satellite rights and was interested in some of your product," she began.

"Well, let me stop you right there," he interrupted. "We don't own any of the rights, they're retained by the broadcasters we work for. We have format rights if you're interested in original production, but otherwise I'm afraid I can't help you."

"Oh, I hadn't realized," Cat said awkwardly. He didn't sound too friendly. "That might be something we get into in the future, but not just yet. But will you be at MIP?"

"Yes, we'll have a stand there."

"Well, maybe I'll visit you then?"

"Why don't you do that? Now if you'll excuse me."

Cat put the phone down, feeling slightly foolish. It was hardly the big impact she'd been hoping to make.

She turned to the document and video Max had given her. *The Pride and the Passion*, so the marketing blurb stated, had quickly become one of America's favorite soap operas, regularly achieving an above-average market share in its daytime slot. Set around the

Dolores Leigh health club, it focused on the lives of Dolores, a former actress and the health club founder and her two children, Lake and Fire. Fire was the handsome business brain behind the enterprise, whilst Lake managed the health and beauty side. Quite what Dolores did, other than interfere with everyone else's lives, Cat couldn't make out. The show had actually won a couple of Emmy awards, even if they were just for makeup.

Cat loved it. Everyone was beautiful, the story-lines were as improbable as the characters' names and it was full of dramatic pauses and quivering collagen implants. She was looking for a suitable gap in her schedule when another e-mail popped up. It was from Declan, his private account. Her stomach jumped, anticipating a joke, or something sentimental and romantic, or a dinner invitation for later in the week. Instead it read:

When are you back from Cannes? I'll be in London for Easter, leaving this week, so I won't see you for a while.

She slumped in front of the screen in disbelief, before writing back:

Now you tell me? You didn't think to mention this at the weekend?

A few minutes later he replied:

I'm sorry, but it's never a good time, you know? I didn't want to spoil things. I'm sorry. I'll be back in May.

She sat, motionless, staring at the screen. She was too numb even to work out how she felt. In the corner of her office Lake was dithering over whether to marry her reliable but dull senior accountant or to run off with the dangerously handsome actor who was being treated for his addiction to prescription drugs. Both were proclaiming their love for her.

"Some girls have all the luck." Cat shook her head bitterly.

Twenty-Six

The French Riviera—she'd never been there before. Cat breathed in the fresh April air and delighted in everything she saw—in the brilliant golden sunshine, the turquoise sea, even in reading the shop signs in her schoolgirl French. She sank back in the taxi that took her from Nice to Cannes and felt like a movie star. To think she had left Europe some eighteen months earlier an out-of-work producer, and was now returning as a buyer with a multi-million-dollar budget.

She breathed in the sea air. Life was good. She had half-hourly appointments with distributors from all over the world, all kinds of dinner and lunch invites, a suitcase full of designer suits and a free day in which to add to them. Max had made no attempt to check her schedule or to arrange any meetings, so it looked like she would be left to her own devices. And he and Brandon were on a later flight—how lucky could she get?

She checked into her hotel on the Croisette, showered and changed and made her way to the Palais, the venue for the market. There she registered and picked up a vivid pink promotional bag full of flyers and leaflets and the all-important guide book.

Her only duty of the day done, she was now free to go shopping. She strolled along the Rue d' Antibes, pausing to sip a *café au lait* on a street corner. Bliss. The sun warmed her face but the air was fresh—she had forgotten quite how clear air should be—

and it felt like she was seeing things in sharp focus again after months of fuzz.

She bought some Capri pants and felt terribly European. She found a pair of cream kitten-heeled shoes and bought them without even checking the price. Things seemed cheap anyway, and it was refreshing just to find plenty in her size, and not to be made to feel like some ungainly giant, after all this time.

Was Declan in London yet, she caught herself wondering. Would Harriet have picked him up from the airport, and would they have made plans for the weekend? It was strange to think of him making plans with another woman, to think of his belongings strewn over someone else's floor. But as a cool breeze whipped through her hair she began to let go, began to feel cleansed of him.

By six-thirty she was tired, and had a helping of *moules marinières* in a bistro near her hotel, washed down with a carafe of red wine. Once back in her room she fell into bed, sleeping soundly until four, when she woke up a different person, and spent the next few hours torturing herself over where exactly Declan was right now.

When it felt like she had just got back to sleep, the phone started ringing.

"Ready for breakfast yet?" It was Max.

"Oh gosh, already?" She panicked. It was only seven.

"See you at the Carlton in an hour." He hung up before she could ask why they would meet there and not in their own restaurant. How was she going to brush her teeth? Irritated, she showered and dressed, packing her toothpaste and brush into her already overloaded bag. In just one short sentence he had spoiled the start of her day. Vintage Max.

When she finally arrived he was sitting alone.

"You look well." He looked her up and down admiringly. "Good to be back in Europe?"

"Fantastic," she enthused before remembering that Max would hate anyone to have a good time at his expense. "I mean, I've registered and I've been preparing for my meetings and—"

He was eating scrambled eggs, and dabbed his mouth with his napkin, hardly paying attention. "Get yourself some food. You want coffee?"

"Please." She smiled, slightly awkward at the intimacy having breakfast together implied. It was silly, she told herself, as she headed for the juice and yogurts. Americans had breakfast meetings all the time, it didn't mean anything.

"Are you expecting someone, is that why we're here?" she asked on her return.

He looked at her scornfully. "Catherine, you can be so naive. The Carlton is *the* hotel of the festival. This is where the major players stay, the heads of Disney, Fox, the studios, everyone. Now, you want to be seen with the big boys or the bit-part players?"

She leaned forward. "You want people to think we're staying here too?"

"It'll open doors, create opportunities, give the right impression."

She nodded, understanding but finding it ridiculous. It would have been a funny story for Declan, she kept thinking, only to remember that there were to be no more funny stories for him.

"So how's your schedule today?" he asked. Ignoring her food, she reached for her itinerary and went through it with him.

"Shall we have dinner this evening?" he asked.

"I'm sorry Max, I have something planned already."

He looked put out. "Well, maybe Thursday then."

"Oh no, I have dinner with Midland," she told him guiltily, remembering how Max had been invited, but that she had told them he had other plans. "If you like I'm sure I could change something," she tried.

"No, Catherine, I'd hate to disturb your busy schedule." He drank his coffee stonily. She tried to make conversation, asking where Brandon was, and about the major deals they were hoping to strike, but he replied in monosyllables until he saw someone he recognized in the distance. Without excusing himself he went over to greet them.

She swore under her breath. Dealing with Max was like living under a volcano. Without knowing how she had just caused it to rumble, and had no way of knowing whether the rumbling would last a few minutes and fade away, or whether it would spark a major eruption.

She left the dining room without disturbing him, and went in search of the ladies' room. Inside, she joined two others brushing their teeth. So everyone had to be at the Carlton, she laughed, and everyone had to make the right impression.

She had three appointments, one after the other, and then a spare half-hour to explore. Without even trying, she found herself by the World Daytime Network stand. It was covered with posters of the various shows they produced. *The Everyday Chef, Cooking with Clint, Extreme Interiors, Authentic Antiques.* She wondered which shows Harriet had worked on, and in what capacity? She picked up a couple of leaflets, hoping to catch someone's attention, but was ignored by the small group in a corner, and felt like an outsider. She was wasting her time, she told herself. It was time to let go.

Thursday night she had dinner with Terry Johnston and his boss Mark Gilmore of Midland Television to celebrate their landmark deal. She'd had three nights of socializing and networking at the Martinez bar, and was enjoying her routine, and the adrenalin that kept her going. She was working hard and playing hard—doing deals, having lunches, wearing cute shift dresses and heavy sunglasses and being fancied by French waiters. She felt rebellious, giddy, high on the excitement and atmosphere. And now she was sitting in a cab, heading for the hills, chatting easily with the head of sales for one of the UK's largest distributors. And she was his client, and he was kissing her ass.

They drank champagne as the sun set over the pretty French countryside and Cat listened politely as Terry highlighted new offerings in the Midland catalog. Mark Gilmore sat quietly, downing his champagne and watching Cat, and she enjoyed the attention. He couldn't have been much older than she was, she thought, but he had something, a presence, making her aware of him the whole time, even when he said nothing.

And when he did speak she found him compelling, a natural salesman. He had a rough charm, an easy-going manner and was so laid back that at first she couldn't see him running a huge department. But the more they talked, the more she could tell how sharp he was, remembering small things she'd said and prying details out of her that she might otherwise have kept to herself.

"We've just signed a deal to represent Beauman Franks in Europe," he told her. "D'you know them?"

"They're the makers of *The Pride and the Passion*, aren't they?" Cat replied, relieved that she did. "My boss just did a deal with them. Five glorious episodes a week, fifty-two weeks a year."

"How much did he pay?"

Cat smiled. "I'm not telling you that."

He pulled a face, as if he couldn't see why. "Two thou? Fifteen hundred?"

Cat imagined the figure was more like three. "I don't know," she said. "He just did the deal and handed me a preview cassette. I wasn't in any position to ask."

"If he paid any more than two he was screwed." Gilmore drained his glass. "Which episodes are you starting from?"

"The beginning, I think."

"It gets better in a couple of years."

"I don't know about that, Lake's love triangle has got me riveted already."

"Ah, it's when Dolores is framed for murder that things really heat up."

Terry Johnston looked vaguely baffled. "I had no idea you knew so much about the show," he told his boss.

"Be a salesman, you got to know your product," Gilmore replied. He turned back to Cat. "You know there's a website?"

"I didn't but now I do I'm going to check it faithfully."

Terry was shaking his head. Gilmore looked at his watch and began to stand up. "Well, now we've got the serious business out of the way, time for dinner, I think."

He escorted Cat to the dining room, where Picassos vied for space with Chagalls and the odd Matisse. Cat had never seen anything more lovely, and had never felt more sophisticated. She had white wine with her smoked salmon roulade and she felt in cool control like Grace Kelly. With the red wine over her noisettes of lamb she could feel his leg pressing against hers and she felt kittenish, like Meg Ryan. But by the dessert wine she knew she wanted him, and was pretty sure he felt the same. When they got to the brandies in the sitting area she had turned into Sharon Stone, crossing her legs and wishing she'd removed her underwear. With a giggle, she went to the ladies' room and did just that. The next time his hand slid up her dress he was in for a bit of a surprise.

They finished their brandies and stumbled into a taxi back to Cannes. Terry sat in the front leaving them together in the back. She couldn't remember much of the conversation, couldn't really remember much at all. She could remember kissing Terry goodbye on the cheek before tripping through the swing doors of the hotel lobby. She could remember telling Mark her room number, over and over again, until he assured her that yes, he would come. She vaguely remembered raiding the mini bar, for, oh God yet more drinks, and then his knock at the door.

She remembered him standing there, hair a mess and his shirt-tails falling out, and how she quickly pulled him in by his tie, in case Max walked past. And then sitting on the edge of her bed with a bump, and undoing his fly. She could remember taking him in her mouth, looking forward to feeling him inside her, and then the surprise and disappointment when he suddenly squirted that sticky salty goo down the back of her throat.

And then she could remember nothing else, just waking up at four in the morning, fully dressed and slumped on her bed in an otherwise empty room. He had gone, and she could remember no more.

Twenty-Seven

Cat lugged her heavy suitcase into the apartment, the smell of stale air hitting her the minute she walked in. Hong Kong had warmed up noticeably in the week she'd been away, and the lightweight jacket she wore was beginning to stick to her back. She showered and had a cup of black coffee. It was a Sunday morning, so at least she had all day to shop and prepare for the next week. She unpacked and sorted out some laundry, trying to get her life straightened out, but already a thick grey lining of depression was smothering her, like the blanket of Hong Kong smog which hung over the hills behind her.

She would not see Declan again. It was too hard. There would always be holidays, always another trip, always Harriet. But without him what did she have? Six working days a week and a boss from hell. A handful of friends with whom she discussed work the whole time. There was no variety. In London she had distractions, friends from different backgrounds, so much more than work to talk about; her parents in the southwest, a brother in Kent. There was always somewhere to go, something to do, someone new to see. She had become overly reliant on Declan, that was her problem. Now she just had to find something or someone else to replace him with.

But in pushing Declan out of her mind she just made space for Mark Gilmore to pop in. She had lurched from hungover amusement at the memory to sober mortification. She knew that one day she would have to do another deal with Midland and the idea appalled her. She had seen him again, the following afternoon, in the Palais. She had been rushing to another appointment and caught sight of him further down the aisle, laughing with a couple of others. Quickly she had diverted into another stand and pretended to be fascinated with some Japanese animation.

What had she been thinking of? Drunken sex with a virtual stranger, very clever. It was pitiful, really. She'd just wanted to feel attractive and desirable again, that was all. She'd wanted to prove to herself that someone intelligent, funny and successful would want her, even if Declan didn't. But in trying to boost her self-esteem, all she had achieved was self-hate.

If anything it felt like a warning. Her life was being swept out of control and she was allowing it to happen, while the amount of wine she drank was positively encouraging it.

It was time to change.

Idly she turned to her cards, shuffling them until one silently contacted her—it was the Death card, the number thirteen, and the one she least liked or understood. Its depiction was of a skull in a black cloak, clutching a scythe and a white rose, a row of ominous-looking fir trees in the background. It was too gruesome to even try and intuit. She turned to the book: *For Death read change, a change of circumstances, a shedding of the old ways, a traumatic start to a brand new life. Sometimes, a karmic connection with your past and your future is indicated here. Cut yourself free and close the door firmly behind you—the Death card represents a vision of your new life, the life that fate has determined and that you have long deserved.*

Vaguely encouraged, Cat made her way to the shopping mall, where she went to her favorite food hall. She decided to treat herself to anything she wanted, and bought smoked chicken, an avocado, Parma ham and some crusty French bread, some eggs, milk and filter coffee. Comfort food, she laughed at herself, something to fill the gaps.

She bought Linda Goodman's book *Star Signs* and sank into it, loving its directness and honesty. She would work hard during the week, she decided, planning her new life. She would put her all into her job, drink no alcohol on weekdays and focus on her spiritual life at weekends. She would attend one of Tiffany's courses. She would turn herself around, turn a negative event into something positive. Mark Gilmore had been a wake-up call, and if that was what it took to sort herself out, then one day she'd be grateful for it.

She was feeling better already. She would call Declan when he got back and end it. It would be better to finish the relationship herself than let it limp on. By releasing him she would surely open the door for someone else. Or perhaps, a little hope urged from somewhere deep inside, for him to walk right back through it.

She rehearsed calling him a thousand times, but the reality of it terrified her, and she started to back down. Wasn't it better to stop trying to influence him and learn to go with the flow? Surely the more she worked at him, the more she deviated from her own path? If the Universe supported their relationship, it would happen. If it didn't, it would create blocks. It was not for her to decide. All she could do, the *spiritual* solution, was to let him choose what was right for him. She didn't need to take such a bold step.

Comforted, she sat back and read some more. She would do nothing, just have faith that the Universe was working its magic.

At least it absolved her of the responsibility.

Twenty-Eight

It was summer before Cat knew it. May rolled into June, and June into July. Desmond Tang tired of murder mysteries, and put the emphasis on period dramas instead. The first consignment of *The Pride and The Passion* tapes arrived, and Cat put them in the schedule, then three weeks after they started airing, she received her first fan mail from India. She stuck it on her channel notice board, where it was soon to be joined by several others.

Declan had long returned from London, but neither of them spoke. Occasionally he would forward her a joke, but she never bothered to respond. It was better to pretend he no longer existed. She saw more and more of Jo, and on Saturday afternoons they'd share a bottle of wine at the pool of the Conrad hotel and swim and read books. Then Jo started to see someone, a lawyer friend of Nigel's called Malcolm, and would disappear in the evenings to meet him, leaving Cat to rent a video and find a good book to read.

Max began concentrating on the second phase of Frontier's launch—a new range of channels, interactivity and the Internet. Cat found it hard to believe the company could ever get that professional. She tried to feel more enthusiastic, but when Max warned her that Desmond Tang didn't like a new story-line in *The Pride and The Passion*, and what was she going to do about it, she began to wonder why she bothered at all.

She booked herself on to one of Tiffany's courses, thinking

that might help. It wasn't for a few months, but according to the blurb, just the act of booking, of making that decision, would trigger some kind of Universal reaction. Cat felt slightly bribed, like she did whenever she received a chain e-mail which assured her seven years of bad luck if she didn't forward it, but went ahead and booked anyway.

The course was called *Divine Communication: befriending the soul.* The blurb said that it would show her how to interpret everyday messages in order to follow the chosen path of her spirit. What secret messages had she been getting lately? she wondered. Whatever they were, she kept missing them.

"Cat?" Jo was at her door, pulling a guilty face. "I can't go to the pool this afternoon, I'm sorry."

"Oh, not to worry." Cat tried not to sound too upset. "Doing something nice?"

"Malcolm's organized a surprise weekend to Macau." She could no longer disguise her excitement. "We're going by helicopter."

"Fantastic, lucky you," Cat said enviously. "I want to hear all about it on Monday."

She didn't feel like going to the pool by herself, she wanted company. As one o'clock approached, she tried Lorna. "Shopping? Lunch?"

"Can't, I'm afraid. I have this stupid junk trip with Andrew's company. A bunch of corporate wives, some arrogant bankers and bad seafood on Lamma Island. I've had more fun at the hair salon."

It was typical of Lorna to look on the bright side, Cat laughed. Oh to have something like that to do, and a partner to do it with. She left the office, made her way through the sticky Kowloon streets and caught the ferry to Central. There were some junks waiting to pull out near the terminal, and Cat watched as a group clambered aboard. She would have loved to be in their position, to sail around the islands, drinking and meeting new people. She felt unconnected, somehow, that there was a great life to be had in Hong Kong, but that somehow it was passing her by.

She made her way to the mall and trawled through the shops on the second level. There were only a couple of things she liked but typically they weren't in her size. She began walking to the escalator but stopped. Why was she doing this? Could she really be bothered to fight her way through these stores only to find rows of size four skirts?

She paused—what else was there to do? What did other people do with their time? She made her way to the ground floor, deciding to look at the makeup. She visited the department stores, but quickly tired of the glitzy displays and vast ranges of cosmetics. Did any of this really matter? What did anyone really care what type of mascara she used? How many hundreds, thousands of dollars even, had she spent on lipsticks which were going to change her life, only to find the same old Cat wearing them? What was the point of it all? Superficial, everything around her felt superficial.

She wandered into a drugstore to look at the cheaper ranges. To her intense irritation the lipsticks were all out of sync, number 207 was where 304 should have been, and 304 was in the compartment for number 116. She began rearranging them, sorting them into their correct compartments, determined to get them all in the right order.

It was only after a highly satisfying twenty minutes that she noticed a pair of shop assistants were giggling at her, and realizing that this was not the behavior of a sane person, left the mall for home.

Twenty-Nine

And then, the following week, he was standing there, in her office.

"Did you hear what happened to Derek?"

"No?" she replied, her heart choking her somewhere in her throat.

"He went home early the other day with a migraine. Discovered his maid was running a brothel from his house."

"What?" She burst out laughing, her heart having shot back in its rightful place.

"There were four men lined up waiting their turn."

"Poor Derek, I don't believe it. He doesn't have much luck, does he?"

"Must have been a wicked landlord in a past life," Declan suggested and Cat thought it was an odd, but perhaps significant, thing for him to say.

There was an awkward pause. She couldn't bear the thought of him leaving her office, but didn't know what to do with him either.

"Mad place," she said feebly.

"I can't believe I've been here a year already."

"Yes, me too. It's my anniversary next week."

"We should celebrate, go out for a drink?"

"No Declan, we should not," she sighed, knowing it was the

right thing to say. Inside her a voice screamed out for her to say yes and stop being such a dope.

"Oh well. It was a nice thought." He seemed to slump, to look smaller somehow, and made for the door.

"Declan," she started, desperately. She couldn't let him go now, not after all this time. "You could at least try and talk me around!" The words were out, she had pulled the trigger and released them without even thinking about the consequences.

He brightened. "Let's have a drink, Catherine? To celebrate your first anniversary. And maybe dinner?"

She could do this, she told herself. She could have a drink with him, have a bit of dinner, and then walk away. She could do it, she urged herself. It was possible.

They met in a bar, tucked away beside the Mid Levels escalator. It looked like something out of a pre-war Berlin, complete with chandeliers, oversized paintings depicting *Cabaret*-style scenes and a small, gilded room at the back for private dinners. They sat outside under a tree decked with fairy lights and Declan ordered a bottle.

"Where else in the world would you get something like this?" she asked him. "I mean, here we are, drinking a very civilized Australian white, sitting outside a bar more decadent than anything you'd find in Europe, and just up the road there's an open-air escalator taking people up to their homes. And on my right is the makings of a great big skyscraper covered in bamboo scaffolding. Where else would you get all this?"

He smiled at her, and she went on. "I mean it feels like some secret club or something. You never know what you might find when you turn into a new street, or what ridiculous story you might hear when you come into work. There are days when the place drives me nuts, when work drives me nuts, when I dream of being somewhere normal, and then there are days when I can't believe how lucky I am to be here, how privileged."

"I don't know, I've had enough." He looked amused but unmoved. "I'm giving it till Christmas."

Irrationally, Cat felt herself panic. "That's only another six months, that's not long. I mean, what about all the new developments, the new channels, all the digital stuff?"

He gave her a despairing look. "Do you really believe all that's going to happen? I don't see it, somehow. And I know things have been delayed. Derek's put in proposals for new transmission suites, edit facilities, all the stuff we'd need for the second phase, and either he's told to reduce costs, or that it's not going to happen for a few more months."

Cat had a sip of wine, chastened. All she had in Hong Kong was her job, and now suddenly even that was sounding less secure.

"How is Derek by the way?"

"Pissed off." Declan laughed. "Fired his maid and got another who stole from him."

"Perhaps it's a sign? That he should do his own ironing in the future?"

Declan laughed. "Let's eat something. But not Peking duck."

They went to the Sri Lankan restaurant Cat had once seen on Hollywood Road and helped themselves to a buffet of chicken and vegetarian dishes. It was appropriately low key, serving only beers, and the lighting was terrible. It was the sort of place you'd go to with an acquaintance, someone you didn't know very well, or with a good friend you didn't need to impress, but it wasn't the sort of a place for a date.

As they finished he asked what she wanted to do next. She had a brief fantasy about brandies in the Marriott, or a taxi to her place—situations which would only lead to her downfall, and smiled.

"I'll go home." She pecked him on the cheek. "Thanks for a lovely evening."

Thirty

"**B**ravo, my dear, leave him wanting more." Lorna obviously approved. "Didn't that feel good?"

"Well, sex would have felt better, but yes, there was a certain, I don't know, power, in walking away, I must say."

"He will *so* be wanting you now, I bet you find a voice mail waiting when you get back."

They were walking back to the offices from lunch, sluggish in the afternoon heat. As they reached the reception an elaborate bouquet of flowers was being delivered, much to the delight of the receptionist, Tina Lam, and a small gathering of Chinese girls.

"For me?" Lorna played up to them.

"No, er, for Melanie Chan," Tina read out.

Lorna lowered her voice. "Fifty bucks says they're from Max. It's his favorite florist."

"It'll end in tears," Cat whispered as Melanie arrived to pick them up.

"A secret admirer?" Lorna asked her.

"No, I don't think it's anything like that." Blushing, Melanie smiled and took them back to her office.

"Another fifty says Jerry Greenberg's not long for this world," Cat whispered.

As she entered her office she could see the voice mail light on her phone flashing. Declan! It was working—he really did want to see her again! She flung herself on her chair and picked up the receiver. To her disappointment it was Lacy Fok's voice, asking her to see Max on her return.

"Nice lunch?" he asked as if eating were a crime. "I have a new project for you." He looked up. "You know the pianist Jimmy Chancellor?"

"I've heard of him vaguely."

"I bought the rights to his live concert, here in Hong Kong. It's on Saturday."

"Saturday?" Cat leaped forward. "You want it to go out then?"

"He's not going to delay it on our behalf," he said sarcastically.

"But Max, the schedule. We won't have time to promote it, it's missed all the listings, we've already got trailers on air promoting the existing weekend line-up, and, what about all the production involved?"

"Catherine, Catherine. Do I want to hear your problems? No. Do I want to hear solutions? Yes." He handed her a sheet of paper. "I've hired this company, Eagle Productions, to look after everything, so there'll be nothing for you to worry about."

"But Max, the link-up to transmission?" The look on his face stopped her. "I know, I know, solutions." She got up to leave. "Is Desmond Tang a big Jimmy Chancellor fan, by any chance?" she asked with a smile.

He looked vaguely amused. "Go change your schedule and quit worrying," he told her.

She read through the documentation, which was fairly scant, and copied Derek on the details. She changed Saturday's schedule and pulled all the existing promos and, not having any materials to work with, asked her team to get creative with the relevant announcements. She tried to find out a bit more about Jimmy Chancellor on the Internet, to give them some background, but all she could see was that he'd had a few hits in the 70s.

By the time she got home she was tired and irritated. It was typical of Max to change the schedule at the last minute like that, without a thought for what the viewers may have been expecting or even wanted to see. She could see no point to the concert and no merit whatever in showing it.

She had made some pasta and was treating herself to the late night rerun of *The Pride and The Passion* when the phone rang.

She could hear background noise, which sounded like a bar, and then a voice a bit like Declan's came on the line. It sounded like him, but it wasn't really the Declan she knew. It was a drunken Declan, a giggly, singsong Declan, a Declan she'd never come across before.

"Now what are you doing, my lovely?" He half spoke, half sang down the phone.

"Just watching TV and getting ready for bed." She sounded like a schoolmistress and knew it.

"No, don't do that, come and meet me. I'm in, where am I? I don't know, some bar in Lan Kwai Fong. On the corner. Come and meet me."

"Declan, it's late. I'm not going out now to find you in some bar on some corner of Lan Kwai Fong."

"Come on, Catty, I want to see you."

He'd never called her that before—it sounded ridiculous, and she broke into a laugh.

"Declan, I'm not going out, and that's it."

"Then let me come to you, that's what I'll do. I'll come and find you."

"Don't," she told him half-heartedly. "Go home, take an aspirin. Don't come here."

"Nope, I'm on my way, if you won't come to me, then I'll come to you. I'm leaving now. I'm walking out." She heard some more noise. "Oh fuck it's not my phone, it's Charlie's." There was the sound of scuffling as Declan, Cat presumed, was looking for Charlie, one of the Chinese transmission controllers. "OK." He came back. "I'm giving the phone back to Charlie, and I'm coming over to see you. Be there in five."

He was gone. Cat laughed, quietly delighted that he'd rung and wanted to see her. Didn't they say you always get the truth out of children and drunks? And the truth was, he wanted her. She rushed to the bathroom, brushed her teeth and combed her hair, checking that she looked all right. She felt stiff in her business suit and quickly swapped it for jeans and a sloppy sweater. Then she paced up and down the living room, waiting for the sound of her intercom. What if he'd passed out, and someone had put him in a cab home? Or what if he'd changed his mind? She heard rain beginning to pelt down outside, and wondered if he might take a taxi straight home instead? She would give him fifteen minutes, she decided, and then she'd go to bed.

When the buzzer rang, she let him up, and then realizing that she'd been doing nothing but waiting for him, grabbed a magazine and opened it, trying to make it look like she'd been reading all the time. She arranged it by her chair, hoping it looked like she'd just tossed it down there when the intercom had buzzed.

She needn't have bothered. Declan was in no state to see or even care what she'd been doing before his arrival. He fell in through the door, his hair dripping, and threw his arms around her neck.

"There you are," he told her. "I so wanted to see you."

"Come in." She sounded like a benevolent auntie now. "Shall I make you some coffee?"

"No, no." He looked at her in disgust. "Do you have anything to drink perhaps?"

"No I don't," she told him quickly. "You know I don't drink during the weekdays."

"Too bad." He slumped on the sofa. "It was Charlie's birthday. I think we went into every bar in Lan Kwai Fong. You're not cross, are you?"

She laughed. "Why would I be cross? You're a grown-up, aren't you?"

"Can I just stay with you?" he said sleepily. "I won't do anything bad."

"I don't think you could if you tried. You want to sleep on the sofa?"

He shook his head. "Haven't you got a nice big bed in there?" He nodded toward her bedroom.

She shook her head and went to the bathroom, not knowing what to suggest. She didn't want to invite him into her bed herself, but would have been happy to have found him there on her return. Once she'd taken off her makeup and changed into her nightie, she came back out into the living room to find him gone. Inside her bedroom he was pulling off his jeans, not having managed to get his shoes off first.

"Declan, let me help you." Cat the nanny, now. She bent down and undid his laces, then pulled his jeans off. He struggled with his shirt and then slumped onto the bed in his boxer shorts.

"I just want to feel you beside me," he mumbled. "I just want to feel your skin."

She climbed in next to him and he turned, putting a heavy arm around her.

"It's so lovely being with you," he said gently. "You're so soft and warm."

"You should drink water," she remembered, but his breathing had become even now, and she knew it was too late. She shifted into a more comfortable position, rearranging his arm so that he didn't crush her, and slept peacefully, thrilled that he was there beside her, and thrilled that in spite of everything, he had still chosen to be with her.

Thirty-One

"**P**ussy, about that memo you copied me on." Derek's frame blocked out the light in her doorway.

"Come in." Cat smiled. Declan was still in her bed when she'd left her place that morning, and had promised to see her during the week. She felt capable of anything, and wasn't about to let something as trivial as a live show upset her.

Derek sat in the chair opposite her. "Until this point I'd heard nothing about this." He waved the memo she'd sent him.

"Me neither. Max just sprang it on me yesterday afternoon."

"Jimmy Chancellor, eh? I thought he was dead."

"Bloody wish he was. It would save me a lot of heartache."

"What do you know about this company, Eagle Productions?"

"Nothing, but Max says they can handle it. I'm more worried about linking up to transmission here, commercial breaks, all that stuff."

Derek paused. "How much do you know about Max's illustrious past?"

"Not at lot. Just that he was some lackey for Desmond Tang who hit the jackpot."

"Many years ago he fancied himself as a producer, did a bit in news, I gather. Didn't make the grade so he set off on his own, set up a production company but it never really went anywhere. Somehow though, through his contacts, he started working for

Tang, but never gave up hope that one day he might still be a big TV exec."

"Which is why he pushed through the idea of Frontier, and persuaded Tang that TV was the logical next move?" Cat asked. "I don't suppose I can guess what that company of his was called, though, can I?"

Derek smiled, heaving his ever-widening frame out of the chair. "Think I'd better have a word with our Max, check that Eagle know what they're doing."

He screwed the memo up and aimed it at the bin, a look of delight on his face when it landed straight in.

"D'you think we'd better meet with them to be on the safe side?" Cat suggested.

"I don't think that would be a bad thing. Flex a bit of muscle."

"I love it when you talk dirty."

"You know me, Pussy: muscles of iron, nerves of steel, knob of butter."

They met with Tammy Wu and Eric Lau from Eagle Productions in Derek's office later that day. It smelled of stale beer and old socks and was cluttered with stolen Vibe merchandise and technology catalogs. On his desk chintzy Hong Kong souvenirs fought for space with empty mugs and scattered files. At the far end sat a bright red in-tray. The top shelf was marked "In," the middle one "Out," and the bottom "Shake it all about." Cat wondered if his guests got the joke.

She sat uneasily throughout the meeting. Tammy Wu was a fierce-looking woman in a Chanel-style suit with close-cropped permed hair. She spoke in clipped, short, humorless sentences. Eric Lau was tall and thin and wore a grey suit and steel-rimmed glasses. He rarely spoke and had the edit-suite pallor of a man who hardly ever saw daylight. He had to be the creative side of the partnership, Cat thought, but was he strong enough to direct a live show like this? There was little she could contribute as Derek went over crewing, direction, an outside broadcast unit and satellite link-up, but it was good just knowing that he and his team would be on top of it. When the time came she approached the question of materials they would have to provide.

"Of course we'll need some kind of opening title sequence," she started.

"Opening title sequence?" Eric repeated as if this were a whole new concept for him.

"Yes, you know, a fifteen-second piece to introduce the show. Some graphics set to music?" she tried, at the sight of his blank, non-comprehending face. Derek, beginning to look bored, began rummaging in a drawer.

"And a freeze-frame to go in and out of the breaks, in the same graphic style," Cat continued.

Eric wrote notes on his pad furiously. Derek, frowning, leaned forward and tapped into his computer. Cat wondered whether he was accessing the transmission log to check break patterns or something. As Tammy Wu went through the running order, identifying parts of the show they could interrupt, Cat leaned back to see what had come up on his monitor. She could see a grainy image of a couple having sex, with a box in the top right-hand corner showing a close up of the proceedings. Derek stared at the screen as if deep in thought about the merit of a three-break format over a two.

Tammy and Eric continued their discussions oblivious to Derek's screen, which was well out of their sight. Cat could no longer hear what they were saying as she fought to keep a straight face.

"My only reservation," she tried as the meeting came to a close, "is that the rights holders may want to have a say about how their concert is interrupted for commercial breaks. "I've been trying to get hold of Max to ask his advice but he's been unavailable."

"But we're the rights holders," Tammy told her, with a look of surprise. "I assumed you knew that."

Cat stopped. "You hold them?" She paused to consider the significance of this fact. "So Frontier licensed the show from you?"

"That's right, yes."

"I see." She swapped glances with Derek. The couple on the screen had changed positions now; the woman was on her knees sucking him.

"I hadn't realized that," Cat said, subdued. "I wasn't involved in the acquisition."

"So there is no problem. I think we're agreed on all points." Tammy started to get up. The man on the screen suddenly pulled back and came over the woman's face and breasts.

"Thank you so much for taking the time to come in and clarify things." Cat smiled as she shook their hands. The woman was rubbing his cum over her skin, groaning with pleasure.

As they showed their visitors out, Cat turned to Derek. "Cigarette?" she asked him.

On the night of the production she felt more comfortable staying there to watch, just in case there were any problems. Ten minutes before the show was due to start she walked over to the operations area.

"Hello, Pussy. Declan's not on shift tonight, is he?"

He took her through to the transmission suite and they watched as the previous show finished, the commercials played out and the operator counted down to the outside broadcast unit. Cat's stomach lurched. She always felt nervous in a live situation, as if some form of technological Tourette's Syndrome would take her over, forcing her to press random buttons and create on-air chaos.

Eagle had prepared a fifteen-second opening title sequence which they played out from the suite. It was glitzy and overblown and wouldn't have looked out of place fronting a game show. The operator mixed out of this and into the studio, where a grand piano took center stage. "Ladies and Gentlemen," a voice announced. "Please give a big hand for Mr. Jimmy Chancellor." The great man appeared to the sound of applause. He wore a white *Saturday Night Fever*-style suit and a toupee. He took to the piano and started with a flourish. After the first few cuts: a close-up, wide-shot and audience, Cat began to calm down.

In fact the show went surprisingly well. It was terrible, of course, and brought no value to her channel, but the production was fine, if unambitious. When it was over she heaved a sigh of relief and went back to her office.

The place was almost empty by now, it was just after 10:30. She wondered how to get home, but decided on a taxi all the way. In the far corner she could see a Vibe producer pausing and playing a pop video, presumably looking for shots, and a production assistant typing something up. She noticed movement in Jerry Greenberg's office and wondered briefly if she should pop in, tell him how the show went. But it wasn't Jerry inside, it was Melanie Chan.

Cat paused, trying to see more clearly. Melanie was looking inside a file on his desk, then she bent down and leafed through more files in the drawer cabinet underneath. Cat stopped for a moment, wondering what to do. She could confront her, let her know she'd been seen. But wouldn't that just get straight back to Max? It was easier to ignore her, just as it was easier to ignore how Max had bought a pointless show from a company which he himself owned. What was the point in making a fuss?

"I have *so* sold my soul," she muttered, mimicking Lorna. "I have *so* sold out."

Thirty-Two

"I'm sorry about the other night," Declan told her.

"Don't be, it was funny." They were sitting in a bar in SoHo, as the area south of Hollywood Road had become known.

"I do love being with you, you know that?"

"So do I, you."

"It's just selfish, I suppose, wanting you."

"Declan." She stopped him. "All I can say is that my life is fine without you, it's liveable. But when I'm with you, when I know I can see you, or that we have a date lined up, it's just so much better. I wish there was no one else, believe me, I wish that badly. But there is, and I just have to get used to it. If I have to share you I will. It's better than nothing at all."

He stroked her hand. "You're sure it's not asking too much?"

"I don't know. I can't promise that there won't be dark days. I can't promise that I won't get jealous, and that my tongue won't run away with me." She drained her glass and he refilled it. "I just hate all this yoyo stuff. I see you, I don't see you, I'm with you, you go on holiday."

"I know, I know," he said quickly. "I'm sorry."

She took a deep breath. "When's the next trip?"

"Later this year, October, November."

So she had two or three months left. "Where are you going then?"

"Indonesia, I think. Island hopping."

"How nice." Cat took a large swig of wine. "But now at least I know." She tried to sound upbeat. "I know when you're off, so it won't come as a nasty surprise."

"You really think we can do this?"

"Declan, we are doing it, aren't we? Something keeps drawing us together. Just when I'm beginning to get you out of my mind, something else happens. Maybe it's time to give it a chance?"

He took her hand and kissed it. "You deserve better."

"I know I do. But until he arrives you'll have to do."

He frowned. "I hate the thought of you with someone else."

She laughed in outrage. "How the hell do you think I feel? Put yourself in my position."

"I'm sorry. You do deserve someone else. Someone more, I don't know, savvy. Someone who'll whisk you off for weekends and buy you expensive gifts."

"Is that what you think I want?" Cat teased, thinking guiltily how nice that sounded. "I'll settle for motor-biking around the New Territories and roast chicken on the terrace."

"And some pathetic drunk who turns up on your doorstep just in time for bed."

"He's welcome to do that any time." She smiled, relieved that finally they seemed to have reached an understanding.

There was a sudden knocking on the glass beside them, and Jo was outside, waving. She darted inside, dragging a man behind her.

"I've been dying to introduce you to Malcolm," she gushed. They shook hands. Malcolm was stockily built with dark, wavy hair and a big broad grin. He was wearing a pair of well-cut suit trousers and a white shirt, and was carrying his jacket over one arm.

"We're going to Burma at the weekened, to see the temples in Bagan. I am so excited I can't tell you," she trilled happily. "OK, just wanted to pop in and say hello, we're having dinner down the road."

When they'd gone Declan raised an eyebrow. "Burma?

Dinner somewhere nice? You see, that's the type of man you should go for."

"Please." Cat sipped her wine. It was a coincidence, though, after everything he'd just been saying. Maybe it was a sign? "I could no sooner date a Malcolm than you could date a, a—"

A Harriet, she wanted to say.

Thirty-Three

Max announced Desmond Tang's intention to float forty per cent of Frontier shares on the Hong Kong stock exchange later that year, to raise funds for the network's second phase, which resulted in a deluge of work for the department heads over the following few weeks. Each had to calculate the cost of subtitling and dubbing into numerous different languages, and to come up with proposals for various digital off-shoot channels—in Cat's case a repeat channel, a soap opera channel and a reality TV channel.

Brandon Miller worked around the clock trying to tie in joint venture deals with the film studios, all of which seemed to fall apart at the last moment, and with retailers for a shopping channel. Greg Sharp had to turn his mind to sports interactivity, including gambling, a choice of camera angles and an Internet site with up-to-the-minute results and news stories.

And then just as everything was beginning to look real, the flotation collapsed, the investment bankers disappeared and life returned to whatever normality there had been in the first place.

"What is going on in this place?" Cat asked Lorna and Jo over lunch one day.

"I don't know," Lorna began. "All I can imagine is they found serious flaws in the business plan. Max isn't good on details, as we all know. And so how are you?"

Cat couldn't hide her happiness. "Everything's fabulous. Last weekend I stayed with him at Sai Kung, and we went to the beach."

"When does thingamabob put in her next appearance?" Jo asked doubtfully.

"Later this year. Indonesia."

"And what about him leaving, any more on that?" Jo seemed determined to bring Cat down.

"He hasn't mentioned that for a while. I think he'll stay a bit longer."

"Well, I'm glad you're happy," Jo sighed. "Malcolm's being very odd lately. He's started cancelling things at the last minute, and being a bit vague."

"I'm sorry." Cat and Lorna exchanged glances.

"Probably just the pressure of work," Lorna said quickly. "Happens all the time. So, you have no idea what Max is making me do now? He wants to set up a dress code and ban jeans, spandex and sneakers."

"He'll have a riot on his hands, that's all people ever wear around here," Cat said.

"He says he was embarrassed by us all when the bankers were here. I think he thinks they only pulled out because we were all so badly dressed, the idiot. Nothing to do with a lousy business plan, of course."

They paid for their meal and made their way back to the offices. On entering the reception they were met by two security guards escorting Jerry Greenberg out of the building. They only came up to his shoulders, and were doing their best to look tough, and if it weren't so pitiful Cat would have laughed. Jerry avoided their eyes. He looked devastated.

Inside the office the atmosphere was subdued.

"We said it would happen," Lorna whispered.

"Yeah but you don't bring the heavies in to escort someone out whose only crime was to wear dodgy tank tops."

They congregated in Cat's office, their voices reduced to a whisper.

"What did Max have on him?" Lorna asked herself.

"Oh God," Cat remembered. "The night of the Jimmy Chancellor thing, I saw Melanie Chan going through his office. I knew she was looking for something."

"So she stitched him up at last? Took a little longer than I expected."

"She wouldn't have found anything." Cat felt suddenly defensive of Jerry. "I mean he was hardly doing dodgy deals." Unlike Max, she almost added.

"Like you say, the tank tops didn't fit in. We have to be stylish and dynamic from now on."

"What a bastard," Jo said angrily. "They're all sodding bastards." She stalked off.

Cat couldn't concentrate all afternoon. She kept picturing the look on Jerry's face. It had been a mixture of humiliation, confusion and sheer exhaustion. At six o'clock she got ready to leave the building. Max didn't deserve all the hours she put in for him. As she walked through reception two giggling Chinese models were signing in. Out of curiosity she watched them. They headed straight for Max's office.

Thirty-Four

Declan said no more about leaving, and they settled into their hopeless routine, based around his shift pattern. On his free weekends, around one in four, she would stay in Sai Kung, sunning herself on his terrace and eating in the nearby fish restaurants. As Cat had imagined, she had good days and bad. There were the days when she'd persuade herself that she could cope with the situation, with knowing that he was still with Harriet, and that they were arranging yet another holiday together. And then there were the dark days, the days when she could barely stop herself from yelling at him:

"How? How can you love her? How can you choose her over me? It's like test driving a Maserati and then going back to your clunky old Hyundai."

He would sigh patiently, or go and make a cup of tea, or fetch a beer and sit quietly on the terrace, waiting for her to calm down. Then, shamefaced and contrite she'd go after him, hold him in her arms and nuzzle the back of his neck, and tell him how sorry she was.

Harriet's presence never left her—it was always there, somewhere, waiting to have the last laugh. One day he popped out on his motorbike for some milk, and Cat waited breathlessly until she heard the engine roar into the distance, then stole into his bedroom and began searching. Where were the photos of Thailand? What had he done with them?

Feeling like a spy, she opened his bedside drawers and searched, being careful not to move anything. A bike magazine, some tissues, a few coins and a pen. The drawer beneath was full of socks; she rummaged slightly but found nothing else. There was a large chest against the wall, and carefully she pulled open the creaking doors, holding her breath as she listened for the sound of his return. She found socks, T-shirts, some books and ties, all tossed hastily inside, and thought how she would have loved to tidy them up for him.

In his wardrobe she recognized some of his clothes and stroked them lovingly. On the floor was a mess of boots, shoes and—there they were, photo envelopes. Her heart pounding, she extricated one from under a sneaker, and crouching on the floor began to flip through. There was a beach, a beach hut and a view of a sunset. Then one of Harriet sitting in a café by the beach. She was wearing a pale grey top and khaki shorts, and her legs looked pink and plump. She was drinking a glass of beer and squinting in the sun.

Listening out for the door, Cat worked her way through the photos. Some tropical scenery, an elephant, another beach scene. They weren't in order, she thought, irritated. Harriet again, this time done up for the evening, if you could call it that. She was wearing a dark pink sleeveless top over some baggy black trousers, and a couple of mosquito bites were visible on one arm. Her hair looked newly washed and was flying away in the breeze. She wore no jewelry, Cat scrutinized, and very definitely no rings.

She could hear Declan's bike returning and panicked slightly, desperate to finish her viewing and check the others for any sign of jewelry. Quickly she raced through them, allowing him a second to park his bike and remove his helmet before unlocking the door to the apartment. As she heard the door open she was stuffing the envelope back under the sneaker and closing the wardrobe door. She took one quick look around the bedroom, satisfied that nothing was out of place, and as she heard his footsteps coming upstairs, raced back into the living room, and from there on to the terrace.

Sometimes when they made love she wanted to cry. What was he doing to her? Could he really love someone else more than he did her? When he entered her, when he pushed himself harder and harder inside her, did that mean nothing? And when he held her face in his hands and kissed her eyelids, her nose, her cheeks and her lips, what was that all about? Didn't that mean she was special, or was this just some generic lovemaking stuff he'd trot out for Harriet as well? And when he groaned his soft, ecstatic breath in her ear, didn't it mean anything special to him?

One Sunday they rode his motorbike to the south side of Hong Kong Island, to a perfect little cove they'd found just past Repulse Bay. It was probably the last time, Cat reflected, before he went off on his trip and winter set in. She unpacked their belongings, carefully laying their beach towels on the sand and stripping off her clothes to reveal the white one-piece she'd bought in the Philippines. Declan went off to buy a couple of beers, and they lay together, enjoying the milder sunshine.

She was reading as he leaned across and stroked her hair. She rubbed oil into his back, massaging his taut shoulders and playfully picking at any blemishes she found. Then she rubbed oil into the back of his legs, concentrating on his thigh and the area covered by his boxer shorts. He groaned, knowing he wouldn't be able to get up for at least half an hour.

Then he was quiet, sipping his beer thoughtfully, and she knew something was wrong.

"You know I'm off in a couple of weeks," he started.

Silently she drank her beer before saying, "I knew it was coming up. What are your plans?"

"We're hoping to take in several islands." *We.* That tiny word so capable of crushing her. "Sumatra, Java, Bali, Lombok, tour around a bit."

"That'll take some time."

"A month."

"As long as that?" Cat fell silent, sinking into mild depression. A month felt like an eternity, four weeks of emptiness. "And when you get back, what then?"

He turned to her, a look of fear on his face. "I don't know, Catherine. It's so hard."

She looked out to the sea, not wanting to draw him any further, not wanting even to talk to him any more. She should go away, she told herself, she had plenty of vacation time. She should go somewhere intrepid, somewhere exciting, somewhere even slightly dangerous, so that he'd be worried about her safety. Burma perhaps, or Cambodia?

She had to laugh at her own stupidity. China. She thought about China. She would have loved to see Shanghai and Beijing, visit the terracotta warriors and sail down the Li River from Guilin to Yangshuo. It would be fun to travel like that again, alone, as she'd done on her way to Hong Kong. It couldn't be much harder, could it? Maybe she should even start learning some Mandarin in preparation?

"What are you thinking about?" he asked cautiously.

"Nothing," came the instant reply. "Actually I was thinking that I could do with a break. I haven't been away since April, and that was work. I was thinking I might go to China."

"Really?" He smiled condescendingly, as if understanding immediately what she was up to. Irritated at herself, she said nothing, just gazed thoughtfully at the sand. If she'd only have kept her mouth shut, he might still be wondering. To be really cool she shouldn't have said anything until she had the trip planned and booked. Maybe even not tell him at all, let him hear from someone else?

She looked around helplessly at the other sunbathers. Laughing, happy couples sharing intimacy and sun-lotion. And there they were, she thought miserably, looking like every other happy couple on the beach. Perhaps behind all of them there was unhappiness, secrets which tore them apart and lies which kept them together? Maybe every couple had problems they disguised; maybe every relationship was a façade?

In the distance, heading into the waves, she could just make out someone who looked like Malcolm, Jo's boyfriend. Hoping Jo might be with him she got up and began to walk out toward him. Anything would be better than lying there in silence with Declan. It *was* Malcolm, Cat was sure of it. He turned back to beckon someone in the water, and Cat followed his gaze to see not Jo, but a slender-framed Chinese girl with shoulder-length black hair.

She ran into his arms, squealing at the cold of the water, and he lifted her up and threw her into the waves.

"I don't believe it." Cat crept back on to her bathtowel, appalled, as Declan wondered what she'd just seen. "What the hell am I going to say to Jo?"

Thirty-Five

Cat felt guilty about taking a Saturday off but as Max was in Taipei with Desmond Tang she didn't bother to declare it. The way Frontier worked, a half-day Saturday off counted as a whole day, and she felt she had put in more than enough long hours to justify her absence.

Tiffany Cheung's course started at 9:30 and would last the day, with a break for lunch. Cat was a little early, and had enough time to pop into her favorite bookshop by the ferry terminal to read the front pages of the two-day-old British papers. This done, she was just reaching for the latest *National Enquirer* when she recognized Melanie Chan across the aisle, deep in concentration, her nose pressed in a magazine. She was about to hide, hoping that Melanie wouldn't suggest they take the ferry into work together when she spotted the magazine title. It was *Your Baby*.

If she was pregnant this was a story of epic proportions. Even if she wasn't, it was still gossip worthy of the *National Enquirer*. She watched as Melanie then picked up a *Healthy Pregnancy* magazine as well and made her way to the checkout. It was almost worth going into work, Cat thought, just to share the story with Lorna and Jo.

But she didn't, she made her way to the New Age Centre and joined the other course participants. She had no idea what, or who to expect. She was shown into an upstairs room in which there were a few scatter cushions and an overpowering smell of incense. There were seven of them in all, two Asians, Wendy and Fanny; three Americans, Nancy, Susan and Michelle; Mia, who was Swedish, and Cat.

Tiffany got everyone to introduce themselves and say why they had chosen this course. Cat became resentful, irritated even as she waited her turn. It made her feel needy and weak. "I'm Cat Wellesley and I have a problem. I'm a sad old spinster and my boyfriend's in love with another woman." She wanted to rebel, to cause a stir, to shake up the holier-than-thou atmosphere of chimes, incense and hushed reverence.

When her turn came she said pretty much the same as everyone else. "My name's Catherine and I work at Frontier television. Like the rest of you I work too hard and have little time to relax. I've snuck off today and am still feeling guilty about it." She laughed nervously. This was hardly the stuff of riots. "I'm in a re-lationship which isn't going anywhere and life can sometimes feel—well, meaningless."

"How do you mean, meaningless?" Tiffany asked her quietly.

"I don't know. I don't see the point sometimes. It all seems su-perficial. I work and I spend money. There's not much else."

"And what are you hoping to achieve today?"

"I don't know." To her immense irritation Cat's voice began to break. There was something in Tiffany's tone that made her want to cry, that wrought the emotion out of her.

"I've started reading a lot of books and am a believer in rein-carnation. I want to know if there is a path I'm to follow or whether I'm just supposed to run around blindly in the dark. I'd like to believe the first thing, though."

Some of the other participants nodded their heads in agree-ment, and thankfully Cat sat down. She felt a bit silly. She had wanted to rise above all the reverence; knock some sense into the session, make people laugh, but if anything she had been the most fervent.

Tiffany led them into a meditation which Cat found hard at first. She couldn't sit still and kept secretly opening her eyes to watch the others. Nancy had assumed the Lotus position and Michelle looked like she was falling asleep but in general every-one else looked comfortable. Cat fidgeted as Tiffany told them to visualize hot golden sand pouring into their bodies, a concept she found deeply disturbing.

When it was over Tiffany talked in broad terms about meditation and reaching out to one's soul, and the law of karma, or cause and effect. She outlined how incidents in past lives can affect the present, and gave examples of past-life regression, where a person is taken back, through meditation, to a significant past life, and how what they uncover there can help either physical or mental afflictions in the present. Nancy and Mia recounted personal stories, which everyone listened to intently.

After lunch, for which they were left to the mercy of the local sandwich bars, Cat was relieved to return, and instead of feeling alien on her scatter cushion, as she had before, she felt at home. Compared to the noise and heat outside, the room felt cool and peaceful, and she decided she rather liked the sound of chimes.

Tiffany showed them how to cleanse their auras and went through each of the chakras, and what they represented. She talked about creative visualization, and how the soul, or Universe, can create anything you request.

"So be careful of what you ask for," she told them. "Because you might just get it."

"What if you ask for something negative?" Cat asked, shuddering at the number of death fantasies she'd had over the years. "I mean, when you're down and not thinking clearly," she added, hoping it didn't sound too strange.

"You just cancel that thought," Tiffany replied simply. "You just say, 'Cancel that thought.' It's as easy as that."

She split them into pairs, working herself with Nancy, who seemed to be the most in tune with what was going on. Cat worked with Mia, guiding her with the written sheet Tiffany had given them. Then it was her turn. She knew without even thinking what it was she was going to ask for. Cat visualized being with him, laughing with him, making love with him. "I want to be with Declan." She told herself, her soul, the Universe, she wasn't quite sure which. "I want him to love me the way I love him."

After a short break for some jasmine tea, they ended the course on dream analysis, and Cat wandered home, trying to make sense of what she'd learned. Now at least she could add aura cleansing to her morning routine and waste even more time. She toyed with the idea of spending the next day in meditation, but suddenly remembering Melanie that morning, called Jo instead.

Happiness was a sea view and a chilled bottle. They arranged to go to Stanley Market the next day and have lunch.

"I so need to talk to you," Jo said gratefully. "I've done something completely mad."

Thirty-Six

Jo kept Cat waiting half an hour before appearing in a taxi in the appointed spot near Cat's apartment.

"Sorry, Cat." She kissed her on both cheeks. "The washing machine started leaking and I had to mop it all up and then I had to wait ages for a taxi."

Cat smiled indulgently. Jo's sense of time-keeping was legendary. If her friend weren't such good value she would have given up on her by now.

"Oh God, I've been so depressed about Malcolm," she went on, as if that absolved her. "I've been calling and calling him, but I only ever get his voice mail."

"Oh Jo, you haven't, have you?" Cat was appalled. "You should never call them."

"Why not?" Jo scrunched up her face like a child.

"You just shouldn't. You know I've never once called Declan? Sure, I'll return his calls, but I'll never instigate one myself."

"But why on earth not?"

"I don't know, I seem to be jinxed, but the rare times I have called a man, I've always learned something I didn't want to know."

Jo flinched as if in physical pain, and Cat went on. "There was this wild South African guy, Pat—funny, flirty and very, very naughty. We only ever saw each other once or twice a week, but I fell for him so badly. One Saturday morning I was wondering whether I might see him that night, so decided to call. Thought it was perfectly reasonable to be able to plan my weekend, rather than just wait for him."

"And what happened?"

"I got his roommate. Who told me he'd been out all night and hadn't got back yet."

"Ouch."

"Then there was this other guy, Steve. I met him at some TV shindig, promoting some exciting new piece of equipment or something. We drank quite a lot and he made me laugh, he had this wonderful quick wit, said all the things you or I would only think about half an hour later. And he was sensitive, you know? Creative, a director. Loved art, theatre, really, the perfect man. He gave me his business card and wrote his home phone number on the back, saying we should keep in touch, have dinner some time. So I called him."

"And?"

"His gay lover answered."

"Oh fuck, you hadn't realized?"

"No, he was so subtle. I felt such a fool."

"Oh well, you're not making me feel any better." Jo slumped in the back of the taxi, looking out at the view over the Tai Tam Reservoir.

"So he hasn't been taking your calls?"

"Nope. I've left umpteen messages." Jo paused. "And then I did something even worse. I followed him."

"What?" Despite herself, Cat burst out laughing.

"I know his routine. Every Saturday afternoon he goes to a gym just opposite the Hong Kong Shanghai Bank. He's there from one till two, and then he likes a bit of lunch somewhere around Lan Kwai Fong or SoHo. It used to be with me," she added glumly.

"So I hovered behind one of the pillars at the bank and waited for him to come out. And when he did I kept a bit of a distance but followed him as far as the corner of D'Aguilar Street."

"And then what?"

"There was this pretty Chinese girl waiting for him. But I mean, above average looks, the sort of girl Max would get in to do a screen test, if not better." Jo took a deep breath. "He put his arms around her and kissed her, right there in front of me."

Cat could see tears in her eyes and she patted Jo's knee comfortingly. She had decided against telling her about seeing Malcolm on the beach, and there seemed no point in mentioning it now.

"We were happy," Jo blurted out. "We had such fun together. I just don't understand it."

"I know," Cat soothed. "Who knows what goes on in their minds? I'm sorry."

"I just can't believe he'd drop me like that. Without even telling me why."

"Men are cowards," Cat said simply. "If they can avoid something nasty, they will."

"How do you cope?" Jo asked her suddenly. "With Declan, I mean?"

Cat looked out of the window as Repulse Bay spread out in front of them, and the very beach where she'd last seen Declan, and caught Malcolm with his new girlfriend.

"I don't know if I do, to tell you the truth. I've sort of decided that sharing him's better than nothing, and there's still a bit of me that hopes one day he'll drop her for me." She sighed. "But then there's always another trip, more plans, and it all seems futile."

"Is he in Indonesia now?"

"As good as. He's on night shift so I can't see him, and then he leaves. Four whole weeks away, and then I reckon another two to get over his guilt. With any luck I might see him by Christmas."

"I just hate being alone," Jo said glumly.

"Don't we all? But what can you do?"

"Comfort shop," Jo suggested. "And comfort eat and drink."

They could see Stanley Market ahead of them, and told the taxi driver where to stop.

"Couldn't have put it better myself," Cat said. "Oh, but I have some great gossip," she remembered. "That'll cheer you up."

They paid and meandered through the first group of stalls before reaching the market lanes proper. By the time they had reached Cat's favorite shop that sold good quality bedding and tableware, she had finished the story.

"Melanie's preggers?" Jo repeated incredulously.

"Keep your voice down, there could be anyone here."

"That has cheered me up. What on earth are they going to do?" She selected some matching sheets and pillowcases. "Malcolm would have looked great in these." She sighed wistfully.

"Save them for someone else."

Trawling through the rest of the market, they bought fake Prada bags and cashmere sweaters for the winter.

"Why don't we go to China?" Cat suggested. "And forget about these stupid men?"

"Malcolm talked about taking me to Beijing once," Jo said sadly, rummaging for a pair of jeans in her size.

"Well, screw him, why don't we go?" Cat brightened at the prospect of travelling with someone else. "Let's do it."

Jo turned to her. "Yes, you're right, we should. We don't need these men, do we? What was it I read the other day—women can fake orgasms, but men can fake whole relationships. Isn't that ever the bloody truth?"

Thirty-Seven

In November Cat and Jo went to China, taking in Beijing, where they marvelled at the Forbidden City and the Great Wall, and Yangshuo, near Guilin, which was surrounded by mysteriously shaped limestone mountains. There, they hired bikes and rode through farmlands and villages, pausing only to sip water and admire the incredible views all around them.

As the Hong Kong air grew cooler and cleaner, she learned to enjoy being alone again. It occurred to her that she only thought of Declan these days to congratulate herself on how little she was actually thinking about him. She had embarked on yet another self-improvement regime to keep her mind off him. She had to set her alarm for six each morning because what with her dream analysis, meditation, runes, aura cleansing, yoga and stomach exercises, she was rarely in the shower before seven-fifteen. There, she would exfoliate, pummel her buttocks against cellulite, wash and deep condition her hair and scrub the dead skin off her feet. No one could accuse her of letting herself go without Declan. She would always maintain high standards, even if it did take all morning to do so.

Next she would brush her teeth, floss and rinse, before starting on her skin. She deep cleansed, exfoliated and applied a vitamin-enriched moisturiser. Then came the sun protector, which was rich in AHAs and protected against free radicals, whatever they were. Then eye cream, throat cream and an under-foundation base. Then concealer, foundation, eye base, eye makeup, mascara, a little blush, then some powder. Finally she would top it all off with a spritz of rejuvenating vitamin-enriched orange water, for that dewy, natural, unmade-up look.

He was due back any day, she knew; he might even be back already. How long would it take, she wondered, before he called? Would he have missed her, or would he now try to avoid her for a few weeks?

"Why don't you call him?" Jo suggested one Saturday.

"You know my rule," Cat insisted.

"Yes, but come on, maybe he needs a bit of encouragement? It must be tough for a man to have to do all the running, let's face it. One tiny call, that's all it takes. It would probably mean so much to him. And it could make the difference of seeing him this week-end or not for a few more weeks."

Jo had a point, Cat reluctantly told herself. Maybe he did need a bit of encouragement. She let the idea float around for an hour or so, teased herself with it, tried to picture him in his apartment, to imagine what he might be doing. A load of laundry, she thought, and bracing himself for the start of his next night shift. He'd be feeling down, and a bit anti-climatic. Maybe she should call?

By midday she had made up her mind. She'd be leaving in an hour or so and a positive conversation with him would make her feel so much happier over the weekend. She was taking control of her life. She was a new, positive, confident woman, she told herself. A woman who wasn't afraid of a stupid phone call.

She dialled his number, her stomach tingling. The phone rang three times, and she was just bracing herself to leave a message when it was picked up, and a woman's voice said hello.

Quickly she threw it back down, her stomach now doing somersaults.

"I don't fucking believe it," she swore. "Every fucking time?" She picked up the phone again and dialled Jo's extension. "I am never, ever, ever going to call a man again," she told her.

"I'll be right there."

A moment later, Jo was looking apologetic. "Ouch. I'm sorry. So she's with him in Hong Kong?"

"I don't understand it. I thought she'd have gone back by now."

"What are you going to do?"

"What can I do? Piddle around, go shopping, keep myself busy. Facials, pedicures, get my hair cut. Same as ever."

"Changing the subject, you haven't seen Melanie lately, have you?" Jo asked. "She mentioned some revisions on the sales tape ages ago and now I've got time to do them I can't find her."

"No, I haven't seen her all week, come to think of it. Maybe she's in birthing classes. But this place is like a morgue today. Max is in Bangkok again, Lorna's not around and no one knows where Brandon is. It all feels unnaturally quiet. What are your plans for the afternoon?"

"I'm going on a junk trip with Nigel's firm. I think Malcolm might be on it."

"Oh Jo, is that a good idea?"

"I just have to know, you know? I just have to see him."

"Well, call me if you need me. Apart from a bit of shopping I'm not going anywhere."

She took a cab to Nathan Road to see a tailor Lorna had recommended. The shop was Indian-run and its walls covered in letters and photos of their satisfied international customers. It was crammed with materials of all descriptions, and Cat idled away a few minutes admiring them and fantasizing that she might look a little like Audrey Hepburn in a simple black shift.

She ended up ordering two dresses, one in taupe and the other black. They measured her carefully whilst Cat scrutinized her waistline in the mirror. Her tummy had flattened, she thought, because she was drinking less, but there was still a discernible bump. She imagined she was pregnant with Declan's child, but pushed the thought right out of her mind. It was an easy blackmail, and not something she would ever contemplate.

As she reached the Star ferry terminal, she recognized Jerry Greenberg standing alone, looking out across the harbor. He looked smaller somehow, shrunken. She hesitated, not wanting him to see her. A conversation might be awkward, and he might rather not hear her stories. He turned toward her and quickly she looked at her watch, pulling a frown as if she were running late for something.

As the ferryman opened the gates she felt bad. If Jerry had seen her he might assume that she was avoiding him, which of course she was, but not for the reasons he might think. She followed him on board, and taking a deep breath, approached where he sat.

"Jerry, d'you mind if I join you?"

"Catherine, what a pleasure, please do, I thought I saw you over there."

"I can't tell you how appalled I was, how appalled everyone was, at the way you were treated." She decided to get it over with straight away.

"Thank you, Cat, that means a lot to me."

"I don't think you're missing anything though; it's going from bad to worse if you ask me."

"Is that so?" His eyes drifted, as though he was remembering Frontier and not altogether missing it.

"It's gone very quiet since the flotation thing collapsed," she told him. "Weirdly so. But we have a great success with *The Pride and The Passion*," she enthused. "Fan mail from India and some pretty good sponsorship deals."

"I'm glad to hear it," he said quietly.

She paused, wondering if this was painful for him. "I have some great gossip on Melanie." She just wanted to make him laugh, to see that it was still possible. She didn't mention seeing her go through his office, though, it would be too cruel.

"My God." Jerry shook his head. "I knew she was ambitious but I didn't realize how much. You know I never entirely trusted her." He let the words drift before continuing brightly, "You know it's perfect for Max."

"How so?"

"He has big ambitions. China is a huge market and he has his sights firmly set there. And you know what they say?"

Cat shook her head dumbly.

"If you want to do business with the Chinese, you've got to become an egg—white on the outside, yellow in the middle. And one of the best ways to prove you're an egg is to marry a Chinese."

"Good grief. So you think he'd marry Melanie as a business move?"

"Could be very lucrative. She speaks Mandarin, she could open a lot of doors for him. You know what the opposite of an egg is?"

Cat shook her head.

"A banana." Jerry was in his stride now, enjoying his show of experience and knowledge. "That's what they say about Eurasians—yellow on the outside, white in the middle."

The ferry banged against the side scattering numerous Chinese with it. Why they never waited until it had come to a complete standstill was beyond Cat. As the gangplank lowered they joined the queue to get off.

"Mad place," Cat said, exasperated.

"But you know you can never leave? That's what they say. It gets into the blood. You thrive on the energy. So many people leave, and then find they have to come back."

"There are days when I don't think I'd have any trouble leaving," Cat assured him.

"We'll see." He smiled, turning to shake her hand. "It was a pleasure to see you again, Catherine."

"You too, Jerry. Do you have anything in the pipeline?"

"I've been doing some consultancy projects, and my résumé's with various agencies. It'll take a while."

"You wouldn't consider leaving, then?"

"I don't want to. My wife's happy, the kids are at school, it's not really an option."

"Well, I really hope something comes through for you." Cat hoped she didn't sound patronizing.

Jerry made his way toward the bus stop. She watched him as he queued to get on board, his face brave to the world, and kept watching until long after the bus had driven down Chater Road, past the Bank of America, and disappeared from sight.

Thirty-Eight

"**M**alcolm wasn't on the junk trip," Jo told her the following week. "But I did something really stupid all the same."

Cat tried not to laugh. "You followed him again? Hired a private detective? Threw a brick through his window?"

"Much worse. I slept with Nigel."

Cat burst out laughing. "Oh Jo, Nigel?" she cried, remembering the stodgy bore who had charged them for their New Year's dinner. "How could you?"

"Oh, don't you ever do things you're not proud of?" Jo snapped. "It was just a fuck-you fuck, but it's made me feel worse." She turned as the opening titles of *The Pride and The Passion* started. "Oops, can't miss an episode." She headed toward her desk. "It's a crap series, but I love it."

"Apparently it gets better in a year or so," Cat called out, remembering an event she certainly wasn't proud of.

She turned to the monitor as Jo disappeared. Lake's covert lover had failed to contact her, and she was working herself up into a frenzy of self-doubt and analysis. While she believed he had betrayed her, the viewer knew that he was being kept prisoner by a Cuban terrorist organization he had vaguely been involved with in his youth.

Cat smiled. He wanted to be with Lake but was blocked. Was there some sort of Universal message in this? Perhaps this was the key to Declan's absence? While she doubted he was being held prisoner by anyone, perhaps there were other blocks holding him back? Or maybe he felt imprisoned by his relationship, maybe that was what it was getting at? It didn't necessarily mean he didn't *want* to see her again, just that he couldn't right now.

Then again, the implication was that Lake's boyfriend was highly unsuitable. Cat frowned. Maybe there was another message in that? She was just thinking how perhaps she should stop thinking when her phone rang.

Within seconds her life had changed. Declan was back, and he wanted to see her. Cat felt as if a burden had been lifted, as if Max had been fired and she, too, had been given a set of full and quivering lips like Lake's.

They arranged to meet at the Mandarin Oriental. She ordered a Singapore Sling and tried to work out exactly what it was that she saw in him. What the power was that he had over her? She tried persuading herself that she had been managing perfectly well without him, but that his friendship was welcome. She wouldn't sleep with him tonight, she decided. She wouldn't make it that easy for him.

She chatted as if he were just an old friend, telling him the latest about Malcolm, Jerry's firing and Melanie's suspected pregnancy.

"Fuck, it never ends, does it?" He laughed into his pint. "You go away for a few weeks and the place gets even worse."

"So you had a good trip?" she asked eventually, toying with her glass.

"Yes, it was fine. Hard work." She could tell he didn't want to go into it.

"I fucked up," she admitted. "I tried to call you at the weekend and Harriet answered."

"Oh it was you? She did mention it. Presumed it was a wrong number."

"So she stayed on a bit?"

"Yeah, the show she's working on got delayed for a few days, so she changed her flights."

"That's nice." Cat nodded.

He leaned forward and stroked her hand. "It's good to see you." He smiled and she felt all her resolve trickle away.

That night, as they lay together, Cat congratulated herself on not interrogating him about Harriet. Declan had spoken at length about their trip, and she had managed to avoid making any sarcastic comments, or quizzing him too much. That was the way it should be, she reminded herself. The more she got at Harriet, the more she just drove him toward her. And there was nothing worse than hearing his defense of the girl.

But the next evening she wasn't quite as successful. He came to her apartment and she cooked, picking up ingredients on her way home. She made Thai chicken soup with coconut and basil, followed by a green chicken curry with steamed rice and noodles with prawns. She just had time to wash quickly and retouch her makeup before he arrived, holding a bottle of champagne. He took a deep breath at the cooking smells, impressed, and smiled at the delicate place settings on the table. She had put some white roses in a blue and white vase in the center, and was using the new Chinese crockery set she had treated herself to one Saturday when she finally tired of buying clothes.

"Does Harriet cook much for you?" she asked as they started. The question had been with her since she started chopping the vegetables, and wouldn't go away. The only way to get it out of her mind was to blurt it out, and suffer the consequences.

He sighed. "Catherine."

"I'm just curious. Does she?"

"No. She doesn't. If anything I do all the cooking."

That took her by surprise. No wonder it hadn't seemed strange to him to be making her lunch that first day. "You do? And what do you cook?"

"I don't know, the usual stuff. Roasts, curries, shepherd's pie, I don't know."

"And so Harriet doesn't cook at all?"

"No. She hates cooking."

"So what, does she do the dishes then?" She liked the thought of those plump fingers, squeezed into yellow rubber gloves, scraping dried food off frying pans in the sink. He just smiled and shook his head.

"I can't imagine not enjoying cooking," she continued, trying to make Harriet sound abnormal. Maybe her tactic should be to excel at everything Harriet was bad at?

"This is great, by the way." He tried to change the subject. "I'm impressed."

She smiled, tactic working already. "Does she do the housework?"

He didn't look at her, just paused before scooping a pile of rice into his mouth.

"OK, OK, I won't ask any more. I just can't imagine anyone not enjoying cooking," she repeated, wondering where she was going with this, wanting to discover more and play with it, yet still wanting to rescue their relationship before bedtime.

"Shall I put some coffee on?" she asked when they had finished. "Please."

Glad to get away for a second, she went to the kitchen to put the kettle on. She fussed around, tidying the kitchen and putting the utensils into the sink. She would always keep a tidy apartment, she decided. Harriet sounded very undomestic. Cat would cook and clean and be tidy and he would suddenly realize what he'd been missing out on. Suddenly he was standing next to her, putting his bowl and plate in the sink.

"You don't have to do that," she said quickly, the 1950s American housewife.

"It's only fair," he said before pulling her toward him and kissing the side of her neck. "You smell good."

"Cristalle, de Chanel," she said quickly, wondering what kind of perfume Harriet wore.

"Let's skip coffee," he whispered, running his hand up her thigh. She wondered if he might make love to her there, in the kitchen, up against the sink.

And so their relationship settled back into its routine. They saw each other whenever Declan was off shift, and spent their weekends at his place in Sai Kung. And Cat had good days and bad days, strong days and weak days. There were times when she felt that there was no future, and that she might as well give him up, and there were times when she felt he added so much to her life that it would be impossible to do so.

One morning it occurred to her that they had been together for almost a year, and yet nothing had changed. He had everything—a woman he loved and a woman he had sex with, and all on his own terms. And she had, well what did she have? Nothing, she admitted miserably. A life on hold when he went away, and a life of frustration when he came back.

She arrived in good time for the ferry, so stopped off at the booksellers to read the horoscopes in the English magazines, in the hope of finding some kind of encouragement. *A burden is about to be lifted, a huge problem about to disappear*, would have been nice. Or, *If you're yet to find your soul mate, he is just around the corner.*

They said no such thing. She dropped her dollar into the slot and made her way to the ferry's waiting area. Several colleagues were already there, including Derek, who was watching an American naval ship pulling slowly into the harbor, the officers in their white uniforms standing proudly on deck. Cat joined him. For everything that could irritate her about Hong Kong, the harbor still provided some stunning sights.

"U.S. Navy's in," Derek sniffed. "Busy night for you then, Pussy." Despite herself she threw her head back and laughed.

Thirty-Nine

Frontier's Christmas party had been left to Lorna to organize and, despite a tight budget, she called in a few favors and secured the poolside beauty of the Regent Hotel, overlooking the harbor. Cat found it breathtaking. The trees sparkled with fairy lights and enormous floating displays of lilies adorned the pool. Uniformed maids passed around delicately crispy wantons and spring rolls to an appreciative crowd. The air was pleasantly cool and filled with anticipation. Beyond the pool on the skyline neon Christmas lights were appearing on buildings and Cat once again found herself falling in love with Hong Kong.

Declan approached her as she arrived, and they chatted, standing beside the bar, their legs touching discreetly. She hadn't changed after work, but was wearing her soft beige pantsuit with a Mandarin collar jacket. She kept a vague eye on Max, who was chatting just a few feet away from her with Brandon Miller.

At eight o'clock he approached a microphone, and began a brief speech. Cat and Declan moved closer in to hear properly, and he caught her fingers in his hand, giving them a squeeze before letting go again.

"I would like to take this opportunity to thank each and every one of you for your dedication and hard work since Frontier's inception. I know you have put in excessive hours, often under enormous pressure, and I appreciate it. Our viewing figures are up, and advertising revenues increasing at a steady pace, which reflects the confidence the business world has in our service and its ability to reach its target markets. Two years ago there were those quick to dismiss us. Together, we have proved them wrong. Two years ago many said we were a fly-by-night operation, but let me assure you, Frontier is here to stay. I personally have every intention of taking the company into the digital era, with new channels, interactivity and many exciting Internet opportunities. Together, we will continue to take our leading brand name further into the Asian marketplace. And it's all due to your efforts, and for those, I toast you now." He raised his glass.

"To the continuing success of Frontier, and to the continuing health and prosperity of all those who've worked so hard to make it that success. I congratulate you all, and wish you a very Merry Christmas."

"Merry Christmas," murmured the crowd self-consciously, as Max paused to watch Derek MacDonald, uncomfortable in a grey tailored suit, quietly sneak in. The buttons of his shirt were straining, and his trousers seemed to pull at the thighs.

"Mr. MacDonald how nice of you to arrive," Max said into the microphone, looking pointedly at his watch. "And now everyone, let the music begin, and have yourselves a terrific party."

"MacDonald!" A cry came from the back as a group of tape operators leaped on to the engineer, lifted him off the ground and threw him straight into the pool. Cat watched in horror as he choked and spluttered and made his way back above the water, his suit drenched, a leaking cell phone in one hand and a size twelve shoe in the other.

There was a second of appalled silence before Max suddenly swooped around and grabbed the first person he saw, which was Cat, and dragged her to the edge of the pool. He jumped in, pulling her in behind him. She just managed to take a sharp, short breath before hitting the water, and was aware of the strange sensation of wet clothes against her skin. Her jacket lifted up around her back and her mules came off. As she surfaced amongst the waterlilies, still in shock, she heard a ribald whoop and Phil Tucker was thrown in.

Cat was trying to swim to the steps as a group of post-room boys threw first Trent Davies, then Greg Sharp, into the pool. She wondered if senior management, forever paranoid, now saw it as a necessary sacrifice. To fight would be to go against Max's wishes. And in some ways it would be worse not to be thrown in, because it implied that no one even knew you *were* senior. At the far end of the pool Brandon Miller was now standing with Lorna, looking nervously at his elegant suit and Italian shoes, and Cat wondered if he was secretly hoping to be the next victim.

Then anyone was game. It didn't matter who they were or what they did. Those who tried to run from the scene—mostly women reluctant to ruin their clothes—were hunted down, captured and unceremoniously dumped. It felt like a revolution, as if the back-room boys were finally getting revenge. Had someone ever complained about an incorrectly labelled tape? Into the pool with them. A package gone astray? Into the pool. Clipping at the end of a commercial? Into the pool. Cat saw that in this simple, immature act, months of frustration, low morale and resentment were finally being avenged.

Max hauled himself out and held out his hand for Cat. His hair had flopped over and she could see a large bald patch in the center of his head.

"I can't believe you did that," she gasped as he heaved her to the side.

"Lighten up, Cat, it's a party."

Cat saw Lorna struggling to get out, and recognized a couple of ad sales girls hiding behind the changing rooms. Minutes later they were dragged to their watery fate. She saw Max running to the pool, a Chinese girl under each arm, and laughed at Declan, who had climbed on to a producer's shoulders, and was play-fighting two others. The hotel staff looked on in stunned disbelief before wisely removing trays of canapés and glasses from the scene.

As a group of Chinese secretaries giggled, wringing out their party clothes, Cat wanted to cry for her ruined suit and lost shoes. She helped Lorna distribute some specially produced Frontier T-shirts, but the minute anyone looked remotely dry, they were only thrown back in again. She checked her makeup, which was of course now running down her cheeks, and took off her wet jacket and top, content to wear the T-shirt and her sodden trousers. The minute she was out of the changing rooms, though, she was just thrown straight back in.

"Can't I at least get a drink first?" she laughed as Declan dive-bombed into her in the water. How wonderful it would be, she thought briefly, if he were to kiss her there and then, in front of everyone. He didn't of course, but did manage to touch her breast as he pushed her under.

She climbed out, determined to get a drink, and he joined her. "I feel like I entered a wet T-shirt competition," she joked. "And lost."

"You look all right to me." He smiled.

They hadn't talked about staying together that night, and she was suddenly desperate that they should. "You'll come home with me later?" she asked.

"Looking like this? I don't think so."

"Oh come on, Declan, it'll all be dry by morning."

"No Cat, I can't, not tonight."

She shrugged, as if not to care, and watched the scene at the pool instead. How could he not want to be with her? she fumed. Didn't he, like her, want to make love right there, that very minute? Didn't he want to be with her every time he saw her? How could he not want to go home with her, to lie in bed beside her, to wake up next to her?

She tried to think of something to say, something that would show that it didn't matter, but just choked on her frustration, and drained her glass. Declan saw some friends getting ready for a pool fight, and saying nothing, went to join them. Cat turned toward the bar, where she reached for another glass and drank it quickly.

"Drowning your sorrows?"

Cat met Max's eyes. "I'm just trying to warm up."

"Let me give you a ride home."

"Oh there's no need." She couldn't bear the thought.

"Come on. I was the one who got you wet, it's only right that I should get you home safely."

"That's very kind, Max, but—"

"I insist. You're not going anyplace else, looking like that."

"True." It would be a relief to get a ride home. There was no point in hanging on there, after all. It was better that Declan suddenly realize she'd gone, or even saw as Max walked her to his Mercedes.

Gingerly she climbed into the passenger seat. "I hate to ruin this upholstery."

"It's not important." He noticed her shivering. "Are you cold?"

"A little. It would serve you right if the entire company came down with the flu now."

He pulled out of the hotel forecourt, saying nothing.

"This is very kind, Max." She softened. "I could have got a taxi."

"Not looking like that you couldn't." He crunched the stick shift and she wondered how much he'd had to drink.

"Whatever's happened to Melanie?" she asked, hating the awkward silence. At least she could try and get some more gossip for Lorna and Jo. "I haven't seen her for ages."

"She had to go back to the States," he said slowly, as if unprepared. "Health issues. Or family." He trailed off, and she knew he was lying.

"Oh, I hope it's nothing serious." Cat hoped she sounded sincere. "Will she be back next year?"

"No, she won't. I haven't made it public yet so keep it to yourself."

"Oh, I'm sorry. That's quite a loss to the company."

"Not really," he said. "She was weak in many areas. I thought it best to let her go."

"Weak?" she repeated, shocked. "That was never the impression I got." She could see how Max's mind worked, how he would continue to criticize Melanie until eventually he believed it himself.

"There's a lot going on you don't know about." He sniffed. "Is this where you live?" He pulled up outside her apartment block and to her dismay switched off the ignition. "You still look great, you know that?"

"Maybe compared to a drowned rat I do." A pool of water was gathering around her bare feet. She reached for the door handle.

"Come on." His left hand was around her neck and suddenly he was pulling her toward him, and Cat had no idea how it had happened. "You're beautiful and you know it." His face was close to hers and he was puckering his mouth for a kiss. She noticed how his hair was flopping on to his forehead, depositing a drop of water on his brow. His lips looked plump and repugnant as they made their way toward her own.

"Max, I—"

"Don't talk," he said quietly as his lips were on hers, his tongue suddenly unwelcome inside her mouth. She tried to pull away but he kept the pressure on the back of her neck, and there was nowhere she could go. She pushed at his chest, aware of the curls through his damp T-shirt. She was reminded of her neighbor's black Labrador, which would break into her parents' garden when she was a girl and force its affections on her. Max's breath was only marginally better.

"What's the matter, Catherine? You don't want to?"

"No, I don't, Max, you're my boss."

He laughed. "You crack me up. A lot of women would sleep with me for exactly that reason. Come on, Catherine, we'd be great together." His right hand was around her waist, pulling her toward him now, all the time working its way up to her damp breast. He tried to kiss her again, but she was able to turn her head, and his mouth landed on her jaw. His hand, however, had made it, and was searching for her nipple.

"Please, Max, no!" She squirmed.

"You have beautiful breasts, you know that? It was the first thing I noticed about you. And great legs." He dived in for a kiss again, as she fought to push his hand away.

"Please." With superhuman strength, she managed to push him back, and he sat still a moment, a shocked look on his face. "Max, this is completely inappropriate. You're my boss!"

He started to laugh. "Catherine. Such high moral values you have."

"And I'm seeing someone." There. It was out.

"Who? That Irish guy?" He jerked his head back, as if to avoid a bad smell.

"Yes, Max. I'm seeing Declan."

He laughed, shocked. "You're seeing an, an engineer?" He stared at her in disbelief. "An engineer? Catherine, what are you thinking of? You set your sights low, you end up in the gutter. An engineer?" He rubbed his forehead, as if finding it hard to believe. "Don't you know what you've meant to me all this time?"

For a second she saw herself in him: thwarted, rejected and

frustrated. And not being able to keep it to herself, either. She froze, hardly believing it was happening.

"You have no idea, do you, how I feel about you? In Cannes, when you turned me down, it killed me. I've wanted you since that first evening at the Regent, you know that?"

She listened in disbelief, willing it to be a dream, willing it to be a nightmare, praying to wake up and find she'd banged her head on the pool floor and had been taken to the hospital.

"Oh God," he groaned suddenly. "I've said too much. I've opened myself up to you, and I never should have done that. I should have kept my mouth shut." He clutched his head in his hands.

"Max, please. I'm sorry if I ever gave you the impression—" She started waffling, trying both to save her job and his pride. "Let's just forget about this, shall we?"

"Forget about it?" He looked at her incredulously. "Forget about it? Is that all I mean to you?" He shook his head.

There was nothing she could say. She was doomed—whatever she said now, whatever she did, she knew she would be punished.

"Max, I think I'd better leave before either of us says or does anything we might regret." She tried to sound level-headed. "Don't you?"

She opened the car door and he roused himself. She had barely got out before he switched on the ignition and crunched the car into gear. She threw the door shut and, fumbling for her keys, retreated to the safety of her apartment.

Forty

She didn't tell anyone, not even Declan. She knew that keeping her job depended on it. If she and Max were ever to get over what happened, it would be because she had made sure it never got out. But it festered inside her—the image of his mouth on hers would leap, uninvited, into her mind when she was least expecting it. She knew that Max would be going through the same thing, if not even worse. And she was realistic enough to know that he wouldn't be man enough to get over it, and to know that dealing with him would never be the same again.

As she had wanted to punish Declan for his rejection, so would she be punished. Suddenly she knew the meaning of the term "instant karma."

At the following department heads meeting his mood was vile. "Next victim," he snarled after Trent Davies had finished his report.

"That'll be me then," Cat started awkwardly.

"No, I don't want to hear from you." He told Greg Sharp to talk instead. "Next victim." He repeated, having yelled at him for failing to acquire a racing event. "No, Catherine." He turned as she started. "I'm going to save the best for last. Lorna, what's new?"

When everyone but Cat had said their piece, he leaned back, savoring her discomfort. "There's no need for you guys to stay for the blood bath, go get on with your work."

There was an awkward pause as the others gathered their belongings and pulled out their chairs. Lorna threw a worried look in her direction. Cat kept her head down, staring at her report.

"You know something?" he said brightly, as if he'd just come up with a great idea. "I need to go to the john. Cat, you can wait here till I get back."

Cat's stomach felt like a cement mixer. She felt humiliated, disgraced. When he returned, he sat down slowly, a satisfied grin on his face, and turned toward her. "And now for your report?"

She gave him her update, stumbling on words and getting a little lost in her notes. He sat back, his arms folded, relishing her unease. Halfway through he interrupted her.

"Catherine, you've been under a lot of pressure lately. So I tell you what I'm going to do. I'm hiring someone to help you out. A new promo manager, he's coming from London."

"We've never spoken about this before."

"I know, but he sent in his resumé, and he looks pretty good. You know I've never been especially impressed with the standard of your producers' work, it's piss poor compared to the other channels. You need someone strong, someone bright and creative. Someone on the cutting edge of technology who can whip those assholes into shape."

"I didn't realize you were so unhappy with them."

"Well, in any event, you should have done something about them earlier. No matter. Get his number from Lacy and call him tonight. I haven't made him a firm offer yet, so see what you think."

"Do you have his show-reel?"

"She can give you that as well. And Cat?" he started as she'd got up. "I promise I won't hit on you again."

Her throat tightened as if she were being strangled.

Determined to hate Jeremy Glover's show-reel, to her immense irritation Cat was impressed instead. He had a long history of promo-making for both terrestrial and satellite channels in the UK, but no international experience. She called him and they chatted. He had never been to Asia but relished the challenge it would bring. He claimed to be good with people on all levels, to be fair and straight with difficult producers and to have excellent organizational skills.

"On paper he looks great," she admitted to Max. "And his work's good."

"And you who doubted me so. I'll have human resources make him an offer."

"Don't you think we should see him first?"

"You mean go to London together?" he teased and she felt her face redden. "It's my call. I'll handle it."

"I have such a bad feeling about this," she told Lorna over lunch. "I just know I'm being set up."

"That's because it's been taken out of your control, that's all. Let's face it, why would Max set you up? He rates you, Catherine, and you know it. You'll be in charge of this guy. You're still the boss." She paused. "Or is there something you're not telling me?"

Cat ached to tell Lorna what had happened. She longed to bring it to life, to watch the expression on her face, to know that she'd trumped her on a good story. But an image of Lorna, a beer in one hand and cigarette in the other, recounting it to a mesmerized audience in Sam's held her back.

"No," she said. "It just doesn't feel right."

Cat got back to her desk to find an e-mail from Max. He was copying her on a note he had written earlier to human resources.

Offer him the terms we agreed. One month's hotel accommodation. Tell him to ask for Catherine Wellesley, who I'm sure will do her best to make him feel welcome.

She scrolled down, realizing that this was his reply to an earlier note asking whether he had reached a decision. Scrolling further, she saw that this was in fact the end of a long chain of e-mails between Max and human resources, and included details of the salary and terms Jeremy was being offered. Max was proposing that the producer earn around twenty per cent more than she did and he was being offered a week's extra vacation together with an annual return flight to London. Shocked, she read and reread the words.

"Lorna, take a look at this." She caught her friend as she walked past. Lorna walked behind her desk and leaned over Cat's shoulder to read.

"Jeez, that's generous."

"That's a fuck sight more than I'm making," Cat said bitterly. "And a return flight?"

"It's a hell of a deal. What are you going to do?"

"What can I do? I'm not supposed to have seen this bit."

"It's not your fault Max is stupid enough to have sent it to you. You just printed it out. Hell, tell him your secretary just printed it out."

Cat took a deep breath, trying to calm herself. "I have to say something, don't I?" She pictured Max's mouth descending on hers and flinched.

"Up to you, honey. I would."

Cat requested another meeting with Max. There were the usual false starts as he cancelled, rearranged and then kept her waiting twenty minutes, but eventually she made it into his office.

"Max, I received your e-mail about Jeremy Glover. I want you to know that I printed it out for my file and realized it was the end of a chain."

"A chain?" He screwed up his face. "What are you talking about, Cat?"

"Look." She showed him the printout. "So I couldn't help but see the package he's being offered."

Max looked flustered. "How dare human resources send this to you?"

"They didn't, Max, you did." She pointed to his ID at the top of the sheet, feeling suddenly bold. "And how dare anyone offer him more money than I make?"

"He's a talented guy." Max started to compose himself. "He makes a lot of money freelance, and I had to match."

"He wouldn't make that much. And don't forget he's taxed more heavily in the UK."

"Enough already, Catherine, it's done. This is what the guy's worth."

"And what does that make me worth?" she snarled, and feeling surprisingly in control, walked out.

Forty-One

Cat went home early that night, drank enormous glasses of vodka and paced around her apartment, frowning.

This feeling will pass, she kept reminding herself. *It's only natural you should be upset.* The man she loved was in love with someone else. Her boss was punishing her for not sleeping with him. As problems went they weren't much fun, but worse things happened to people all the time. She stared aimlessly at her CD collection, wondering if one might relieve her mood, but couldn't even be bothered to select one off the shelf. She flipped through a magazine but found the bright, enthusiastic articles simply pointless and depressing.

By ten-thirty she'd hauled herself into bed and had fallen into a deep alcohol-induced sleep. By midnight she was awake again, and lay miserably listening to the traffic outside. By two she was beginning to see the funny side, and by three o'clock had worked out a way of rescuing the situation. She kept rehearsing the lines she would tell Max; imagining what his response might be and coming up with even more compelling arguments for her case. She had just fallen into a deep sleep when the alarm went off.

Hong Kong was looking bright and clear as she walked to her tram stop. The January air was cool and felt almost clean. A crowd had gathered to buy some gelatinous white noodles out of a huge vat for breakfast, and she stopped for a second, watching the vendor shake different spices on to each pile before handing them, in greaseproof paper, to each customer.

She felt like such an outsider. She didn't belong in Hong Kong and yet couldn't see herself living anywhere else either. She clearly didn't belong with Declan because after almost a year together she still hadn't won him over. And now even in her job she was being made to feel an outsider, someone worthless, used up.

How long would it be before Max started telling people how weak she was, she wondered. Before she was dismissed and sent home in humiliation like Jerry Greenberg? She had to turn this around, she told herself, she *could* turn it around. She rehearsed her lines again. She would present him with a practical solution, and let him decide.

Before she could lose momentum she went to his office.

"Max, do you have a moment?" He looked up awkwardly, and beckoned her in.

"I've been thinking a lot about Jeremy Glover," she started. "I understand why you want to hire him and on reflection I think it's a great idea. My producers could do with more guidance, and I think the channel branding could do with an overhaul. He seems like a talented, energetic guy and I'm sure he'll bring immense value to the channel." She took a deep breath.

"His arrival," she continued, "will free me up to concentrate more on the bigger picture, and less on the day-to-day running of the production area."

She took another deep breath, trying to read anything into his reaction. If anything, he looked faintly amused, which irritated her.

"Every other channel has an overall manager, a program director and a creative director. To date Variety has just had me, and my title has remained program director. Now we are to have our creative head, I think the ideal solution to the financial differentiation would be if I were to be made channel manager and given the appropriate remuneration."

She took a final deep breath. "At least to put me in line with our new creative director."

"Catherine. You're saying you want to be channel manager?" She could see he was stalling. "You know I always wanted to fill that position with a heavyweight. Someone who could truly lead the channel and develop its programming strategy."

"But Max, I've been doing just that." She was aware of raising her voice. "I have been leading the channel, I have the respect of my team, we work well together. And I have been developing the programming strategy. I've incorporated new strands, I did that huge deal with Midland, I created a British drama strand which has been heavily sponsored—you can't tell me I haven't been doing the job already because I clearly have."

"Well, Cat, look, this is all very sudden. I did have someone else in mind, but—"

"Who? Who did you have in mind?" She knew he was bluffing.

"Catherine, it's not for me to say right now, OK?" He began to gather his belongings. "Look, I have a meeting, there's a lot going on. Thank you for putting your proposal forward, I appreciate and respect your candor and enthusiasm. I just don't want to make any hasty decisions now."

"Well, I just wanted to give you a choice."

"A choice?" He raised an eyebrow. "You make it sound like an ultimatum."

"Max, I don't want to leave. I just want to be treated fairly."

"I understand." He looked her up and down. His tone softened. "How's that suit of yours?"

"Ruined." She laughed in relief and felt a glimmer of hope. Maybe they could still return to their pre-pass days? Maybe it was still possible? "How's yours?"

"Seen better days." He smiled, and ushered her out of the office.

Forty-Two

Max never did come back to her. Whenever she asked, he would only say that he was considering her position, and that the decision was tied up with various other plans for the company's future. Not that Cat, or anyone else, could see much of a future. After the failure to get Frontier listed, all anyone could see were morale-damaging cutbacks. Instead of paying for late-night taxis home, Max had half a dozen foldaway beds brought in for staff to sleep on overnight. Free coffee was withdrawn and a coin-operated coffee dispenser installed. Phone calls were scrutinized, and personal ones charged to the caller. Every day a new rumor surfaced that Frontier was about to fold, or that Desmond Tang was going to sell, or that Max was to be fired. Cat found herself wishing that something dramatic would happen, if only to save them from this endless state of limbo.

She and Declan fell back into their hopeless routine, and as the spring rains lashed down, Cat wondered if she would ever be released. Her life felt as stagnant as the pools of rain which built up in the gutters. She dreamed that Declan might still one day tell her he'd given up on Harriet, and wanted them to live a normal life together. But every time she saw him, that dream felt even further away.

Her only source of amusement came, oddly enough, from *The Pride and The Passion*. Lake was going to pieces because her lover, Tyrone, had betrayed her by marrying the wealthy actress Zara Fine—a puffy-faced alcoholic with the body of a camel.

The show developed a huge following in India, and she received fan mail by the sackful. Her favorite letters she read out to her staff in channel meetings, as a kind of morale booster. They included one from a lady in Uttar Pradesh who was going on vacation for two weeks and wanted them to "kindly halt the telecast of the show" in her absence. Another wrote in complaining that Lake's tangled love life was giving her a stomachache, and asked that the scriptwriters change the plot for her benefit.

Jeremy Glover arrived as the March rains began to subside. He was tall, slender and classically handsome in a mail order catalog sort of way. He had floppy blonde hair and wore horn-rimmed glasses, and seemed laid back and talented. Cat decided that despite her reservations, she might grow to like him.

"He's cute." Lorna studied his behind as he passed Cat's office. "You know you and he would make a great couple."

"Don't even think about it. I wouldn't give Max the satisfaction."

Lorna shut the door and sat down in the chair opposite her, leaning forward excitedly. "Top secret, right?" She lowered her voice, checking behind herself before continuing. "Melanie Chan. He made her get rid of it and then he fired her."

"How do you know?"

Lorna shook her head. "I can't tell you."

"Come on, Lorna," Cat said irritably. "This is me, remember?" It was worse than someone turning the *Pride* off before the end of an episode.

"I shouldn't even have told you that much. So talk about the Icarus factor?"

"He told me she was weak and had to be let go," Cat said dully, the excitement of the gossip diffused by Lorna's refusal to name her source. "Jerry thought Max might marry her, impress the Chinese. But he made her get rid of it? Nice. Tell me how you know."

"Catherine, it's complicated."

The door opened and Brandon Miller dropped some documents on Cat's desk.

"No new deals for the immediate future," he announced, making quick eye contact with Lorna.

"That's the first I heard of it," Cat told him.

"Schedule more repeats, that's the word from the top. And no one's going to MIP this year. Cost-cutting." With a brief nod to Lorna he left, closing the door behind him.

"God, this place is depressing." She shook her head before suddenly realizing. "Brandon?" she hissed. "Are you screwing Brandon?"

"Keep it to yourself." Lorna smiled guiltily.

"Brandon Miller?" Cat couldn't decide if this was the funniest or the most appalling news she had ever heard.

"Come on, it adds a little interest to my fun-packed days."

"I don't believe this. So how long's it been going on?"

"A few weeks, not long."

"I can't believe you haven't told me. I mean, where? And when do you find the time?"

"Afternoons mostly. Saturdays. Love motels in Mong Kok. You can rent a room by the hour, you know."

"Yes I know about love motels," Cat snapped. "I stayed in one if you remember." She felt winded, and couldn't decided whether it was the shock of Lorna's revelation or just the hurt that she hadn't confided it earlier. "Are you, serious about him?"

"No. It's just a fling. I want to stay with Andrew. I do love him."

Funny way of showing it, Cat thought. If she had a full-time love she could never imagine betraying it. They sat in silence for a second, before Lorna looked at her watch.

"Oh jeez, is that the time?"

As she got up, Max appeared in the door, and she squeezed past him. He paused to admire her pert bottom in a clingy red skirt, before turning to Cat.

"How's everything working out with Glover?"

"Fine. He's settling in great." She felt sick just looking at him. What little respect she'd ever had was long gone. "I gather I'm not to do any more programming deals?"

"That's right, until further notice. Burn up repeats." He turned to leave, and then stopped. "Jeremy and I are having a drink tonight. Why don't you join us?"

It was the last thing she felt like, but refusing Max was not an option. "OK," she said warily. "I look forward to it."

Forty-Three

"So I was in Vietnam with a camera crew." Max shovelled some more peanuts into his mouth as he started yet another story. "The Viet Cong were firing at us from all angles. We'd been told it was dangerous but we pushed ourselves to the limit, and man, if you ever saw that footage we got."

"And no one in the crew was injured?" Cat knew better than to believe him. The closest Max had ever got to action in Vietnam was a weekend sizing up the bars in Saigon.

"I got a little shrapnel wound in my shoulder," Max boasted, rubbing it as if it had suddenly become inflamed. "Nothing serious."

"Amazing." Glover was impressed. "Sounds like something out of *Apocalypse Now*."

"One of my favorite movies. You know I used to know Francis Ford Coppola?" Max puffed his chest out. "We're both from Detroit. He used to live a few blocks away from me."

"That's incredible. Did you ever see *The Rain People*?" Glover asked earnestly. "You know I saw it recently at an arts festival and found it well ahead of its time."

"See it? I worked on it."

Cat tried not to yawn, wondering if Jeremy had noticed how Max would claim some level of involvement in every topic he raised. It was all lies, every word. She, too, could remember feeling impressed with him when they'd first met, but now all she felt was revulsion.

"Of course my favorite movie of all time has to be *The Godfather*," Jeremy offered. "Though I'd say two is a better movie than one."

"*The Godfather*." Were those tears in Max's eyes? "You wanna know why I love *The Godfather* so much?" He left an exaggerated pause. "Because that was the first movie my father took me to see."

Jeremy nearly choked on his vodka. "But it was made in '72," he said.

Max started to look flustered. "That was the first movie my father took me to," he insisted. "He died shortly thereafter."

Cat thought she should move the conversation on. "My favorite all-time movie has to be *Dr. Zhivago*," she tried. "Julie Christie was just so beautiful in it."

Max looked at her with scorn. "It's your favorite movie because the actress was pretty?"

"Seems like a strange criterion to me," Jeremy sneered.

Cat could have kicked him, and then herself. She should have left Jeremy to hang himself and have done with it. She listened as they continued analyzing and describing favorite scenes, and felt foolish, regretting having entered a conversation where she was clearly not wanted.

"*Citizen Kane*." Max was leaning back now, puffing on a cigar. "Now there's a fine movie." His eyes moistened again. "Ah, Rosehip," he whispered, a far-off look on his face. "Rosehip."

Stifling a laugh, she excused herself and went to the loo as Jeremy tried to correct him. "You mean, Rosebud, don't you?"

Even from a distance she could see a flash of anger in Max's eyes.

It was farcical. The only reason she'd been invited was to pit her against the new producer. If she stayed Max would continue doing just that. It was better by far to leave now than play into his hands.

The cloakroom attendant fussed around her, turning on the tap, squirting soap into her hands and then holding out a cloth for her to dry them on. How Hong Kong could pander to your ego, she thought. How it could turn losers into heroes. Someone like Max was so well suited to the place, she realized, he'd flounder in the real world. And what was she doing there? Would she, too, flounder elsewhere?

She returned to where they sat, made her excuses and left. There was a certain power in walking away, she noted again. She had taken control, and in doing so, somehow wrongfooted Max. She wasn't going to play his game, and by walking away, had just made that perfectly clear.

Forty-Four

A few days later Max called Cat into his office. "Jeremy and I have been talking and he has some valuable comments to make about the schedule. I'd like to go through them with you if I may."

She glanced at the producer, who simply crossed his chino'd legs and ran his fingers through his hair.

"You see, this really doesn't make much sense and I'm indebted to Jeremy for pointing it out. Why do you have first run sitcoms at eleven o'clock at night when no one can see them? It makes no sense, Catherine."

"Well, I'm at a disadvantage here because I don't happen to have my schedule in front of me," Cat said slowly, stalling for time. "But I assume you're talking about Hong Kong time." She looked for an acknowledgement, and got it. She also got what she thought was the sign of a light coming on in Max's brain.

"I've been working to the directive that you issued last year that the majority of our audience is in India, which is some two and a half hours behind us, and in the Middle East, an hour and a half after that. A sitcom playing out in Hong Kong at eleven p.m. reaches India at eight-thirty, which is prime time, and the Middle East at six or seven, depending on exactly where you are. So to me it makes pretty good sense."

There was a brief pause as Max gathered himself. "But Hong Kong, Catherine, what about Hong Kong?"

"It's never been raised before," she said. "But if we suddenly have an audience here I can look into adapting things if you like."

She could see Max backing down. She turned to go, but couldn't stop herself from adding: "But perhaps I could suggest that rather than Jeremy wasting your valuable time on these matters," she turned to face the cringing producer, "why don't you come straight to me in future? I'm a little surprised this has even arisen as all our promos are versioned for Indian and Middle Eastern time, and not Hong Kong. Hadn't you noticed?"

"That's all right, Cat, you can leave us now," Max said quickly. "Thank you for your input."

Furious, she walked out without acknowledging either. She knew this was a war she could never win. Max was determined to force her out. She had humiliated him, and now he was getting his own back. She slumped in her chair. There was only one person she wanted to talk to. She picked up and replaced the receiver twice before bullying herself into dialling.

"I'm breaking my own rule," she said.

"I'm glad to hear it," Declan told her. "How's your day going?"

It was odd how in the days she didn't see him Declan would become an ogre, someone who was out to hurt her and who took pleasure in inflicting that pain. But once she got talking to him he was just Declan again, a normal guy who sounded pleasantly surprised to hear from her.

"Piece of shit," she told him. "I'd do anything for a drink and a chat, any chance you're free?" Again, the ogre reappeared in her mind, mocking her for daring to ask, and she felt small and insignificant.

"Of course I'm free," he told her. "It's nice of you to do the asking for a change."

She laughed aloud in relief. "You mean this is all it takes? I could have had you any time?"

"Catherine, you know you can have me any time."

He was already at a table when she arrived. She paused for a second, wondering how she might feel if this were the first time she'd seen him, trying to picture him as a stranger. His hair looked a little damp, as if he'd just come out of the shower, and the top two buttons of his shirt were undone. He was wearing faded jeans and a battered old pair of Docksiders.

His face lit up as she approached. There was so much love between them, she thought, so much unspoken love. How could he possibly not want to be with her for the rest of his life? She bent down to kiss him as he jumped up and they laughed awkwardly before kissing each other quickly on the lips.

"I was just having a quick beer, but do you want a bottle of wine?"

"More like two," she told him as he ordered it. "Jeremy Glover's becoming a real jerk. Seems to think he reports directly to Carnage." She told him what had happened. "But maybe he'll calm down after a couple of months. Right now he feels he has everything to prove. He can't see yet that Max is a madman. Maybe he'll learn."

"Why has Max suddenly got it in for you, though?" Declan asked, puzzled.

She had drained her glass and he refilled it. She was burning to tell him the truth. Discretion had got her nowhere, after all. So she told him.

"Jesus," he whistled when she'd finished. "So Carnage did make a move, then? That'll teach you to get in a car with a strange man."

"Well, I wasn't going anywhere with you then, was I?" Suddenly it had all become Declan's fault—if he had only agreed to go home with her none of this would have happened, she thought irritably.

"You know, I could see you two together," he teased. "You're a classy lady, Cat, you need a rich man. He'd give you the lifestyle you want—expensive clothes, flashy restaurants, smart foreign resorts . . ."

"Talking of which, when are you next off on vacation?" she snapped.

He paused, as if caught for breath, and she knew there was bad news coming. "June," he said finally. "To Vietnam."

"I thought it was time," she said quietly. "It'll never change, will it? I'm just wasting my time. I keep thinking that maybe, one day—" Her voice trailed off and she sighed. "But it never happens."

"I'm sorry." He squeezed her hand. "I never made any promises."

She felt vaguely patronized, and pulled it away. "I know you didn't."

They sat in silence. Which made her feel worse, she asked herself, the thought that he'd be away again in a few weeks' time, or the thought that they could end now, that very moment?

She forced herself to brighten. "You know, I could do with a break," she said. "Maybe I'll go to Vietnam? You know, Saigon, Hanoi, China Beach—wouldn't it be funny if I turned up? We could pretend we'd never met."

"She's met you already."

"Oh, that's true," Cat remembered. There went that fantasy. "So if I turned up by coincidence, would you sneak off to meet me?"

"No, Cat, I would not."

"You wouldn't even try?" She felt a stab of hurt. A strange joke was turning into a row, and she knew she should kill it now but couldn't stop herself. "You mean, you wouldn't even be tempted?"

He laughed, knowing he couldn't win. "Of course I'd be tempted, but I wouldn't do it."

"But, say she wanted a nap one afternoon, say she had chronic diarrhea, then you would?" she persisted.

"Oh God, Cat, yes, all right? I'm sure I bloody would." She was pushing him too far. "As long as you hadn't been going on like this the whole time."

"That's all I needed to hear." She felt a vague triumph of sorts.

"Why do you do this, woman?"

"Well, how the fuck do you think I feel?" she snapped, and immediately regretted it. "I'm sorry. Everything's getting to me at the moment."

He took her hand. "You know we could stop any time."

They were the words she least wanted to hear. "We could? Would it be that easy for you?"

"Of course it bloody wouldn't, who do you think I am?"

"I don't know."

The tears bubbled in her eyes and she despised herself for making a scene. She could feel him slipping away now, slipping away to Harriet and Vietnam. She could feel a cold world without him. He could walk away this moment, she thought, panicking. He could get up, pay for the wine and say goodbye. And she would have driven him to it.

"So." She took a deep breath, trying again to lighten the tension between them. "If I had shagged Max that night, would you be jealous?"

"Oh for fuck's sake, Cat." He laughed. "Yes. All right? Yes, I would be deeply fucking jealous."

"Thank God for that." She drained her glass.

"Can we change the subject now and go and get something to eat?"

"Yes," she said gratefully. "I think we should."

Forty-Five

The next few weeks saw memos being issued about wage freezes, hiring freezes, budget cuts and travel restrictions. Rumors were constantly being spread that Frontier was about to close, and as Asia staggered toward a general recession, Cat thought they seemed increasingly likely. All around her, companies were folding. Stories circulated about private jets being sold with free Rolls Royces thrown in, and the closure of a cake shop near Frontier's offices spurred the most bizarre thing she'd seen, a cake-run.

Lorna talked of a move to Tokyo with Andrew, Jo wondered whether it was time to return to London and Declan hoped there would be a severance package worth waiting for. Cat scheduled repeats and dreamed of island-hopping in the Philippines, or heading down toward Australia. She toyed with the idea of seeing Tiffany Cheung again for some inspiration, but somehow knew already that something was about to happen; she could feel that her life was about to change.

And then, very suddenly, it did, during a department heads meeting.

Max seemed uncomfortable throughout, and she assumed he was under immense stress. Desmond Tang must have been piling the pressure on, and for a brief moment she actually felt sorry for him. He said little during Trent Davies' report, incapable even of coming up with lewd comments about presenters and whether they should wear less clothing or not. During Greg Sharp's summary about an Indian cricket tournament he looked like he was hardly paying attention at all.

Cat had sat next to Jo, and found herself watching Lorna and Brandon's interaction throughout. Her friend had become more distant, and despite her insistence that she would never leave Andrew, Cat wondered what she really felt about the lawyer.

Max turned to Jo. "When will the next sales tape be ready?"

"I should have something to show you by the middle of next week."

"The middle of next week? Why is this taking so long, Jo?" Suddenly he was animated again, the old Max. "After all this time it'd better look so good I'm gonna wanna come all over the screen."

Jo paused. "Right oh," she said, deflating him. Cat was full of admiration and even Trent Davies stifled a laugh.

"Now, Catherine." He gathered himself, as if he'd been waiting for this moment a long time. "You'll be pleased to know I've finally appointed a channel manager for Variety."

The air shifted in the room and Cat felt every vein, muscle and organ in her body freeze.

"You have?" she managed. With all the cutbacks that were going on that made no sense.

"Cat, you were always a caretaker, you know that. You did a great job, and I appreciate your efforts, but it was time to bring someone in who could lead the team forward."

Her mouth felt paralyzed. "When do they start?" she managed.

"Effective today. You carry on with acquisitions and scheduling, but Jeremy Glover now has overall control and the final say on all decision-making."

Max might have rammed his fist in her stomach for the effect it had on her. She felt his boot against her head, kicking her again and again until she was lying crumpled in a dingy alleyway.

"Jeremy Glover?" The tip of her nose started tingling and tears welled in her eyes.

"That's right. He will attend these meetings from now on, and will report directly to me. That should be a relief to you, I'd have thought."

Through the blur in her eyes, she could make out that everyone in the room was studying a different artifact: a pencil, a pen, a notebook, the grain of the wooden table.

"I didn't think," Cat started slowly and carefully, trying to regain herself, "that he had any management experience. He's a promo-maker. Creative."

"I've been pretty impressed with him since he arrived. He's the kind of guy who can turn his hand to most things. I appreciate his intiative with scheduling and marketing issues."

What initiative, she wanted to ask. But she couldn't start now. She had to retain some sense of dignity. She felt like she was sliding down a rock-face, that she had finally lost her grip.

"It's a done deal, Catherine," Max continued. "If you have a problem with it, I suggest you speak to your manager."

"D'you want to get a coffee?" Jo whispered as they left the meeting room.

"Nope. I wanna get the fuck out of here." In cold fury she walked back to her office, picked up her bag and left the building.

It was only when she was outside in the hot midday sun that she lost her composure, and collapsed against the wall.

"Catherine, there you are." Lorna had rushed out after her. "What are you doing?"

"I needed some air. I'm not going back today. If ever." She was heaving, huge, heavy sobs pounding out of her lungs.

"I'm so sorry, Catherine. I don't know what he was thinking about." Lorna went to hug her.

"So he didn't share it with Brandon, then?" she snapped, stepping away.

"Look," Lorna tried. "I know we haven't been that close lately, and I know you don't approve of my relationship with Brandon, but, can we get over that?" she pleaded. "I admit, Max told Brandon two days ago, and then Brandon told me. What was I gonna do, give you advance warning? I'm sorry, Catherine."

"It's because I wouldn't fucking sleep with him," she spat. "Did he tell Brandon that? He's punishing me. He wants me out."

"Well, don't give him that satisfaction. Stay. Glover will fuck up and you'll be reinstated. He doesn't have the first clue, you can run rings around him. But don't quit. Don't be the loser here."

"If I stay I'm the bigger fucking loser. It'll look like I need this job. It'll look like I need Max and his fucked-up company." She paused to rub the tears off her face. "I don't know, I need time to think." She started walking away.

"Cat, you can't just walk out—"

"I just did."

"So what do I tell anyone?"

"Who cares? Just tell them I left for the day. What's Max gonna do, fire me?" She bit back her tears. "He already has."

She caught the next ferry, got herself home and quickly changed into her bathing suit and some shorts. Back in the street, she hailed a cab and made her way to Repulse Bay. She needed a drink, and sat in the Veranda café with a glass of wine, staring hopelessly out at the view.

Then she wandered barefoot down to the little beach she and Declan had found months ago and sat on the hot sand, digging her toes in, and watched the sea. The horrors of the meeting stayed with her, and she kept hearing Max's bitter words over and again: *If you have a problem, I suggest you speak to your manager.*

She knew Lorna was right, but Cat couldn't stay after this. There was no point in even thinking about it, her path was obvious. *Her path.* As the Universe had wanted her in Hong Kong, so now it wanted her out. Maybe it was meant to be, maybe this was exactly how it was supposed to happen? She didn't understand why, but it was easier to believe that it was a higher force kicking her out when she'd overstayed her welcome, and not her boss. Life should be an adventure, full of change, opportunities and lessons. Life was not about endless hours, high stress levels and humiliation at work.

Cat knew her mind. She remembered the power she'd felt by walking away that evening with Max and Jeremy. What had clinging on ever done for her? She'd clung on to Declan for what, over a year now, and where had that got her?

She was tired of it all. She knew what she had to do.

Forty-Six

She stayed on until the end of the week. Declan left for Vietnam without calling her. The way news travelled at Frontier there was no way he wouldn't have heard. So that was how much he cared, Cat thought. It was another sign, if she really needed one.

She did little work during the week. She packed her belongings, photocopied documents and organized the business cards she wanted to hang on to. A stream of visitors entered her office to sympathize, from Trent Davies and Greg Sharp to members of the operations team she hardly even knew. One afternoon Derek popped in.

"I'm sorry, Pussy," he said awkwardly. "It's very unfair." He squeezed into the chair opposite her. "How are you doing?"

"I'm OK." She smiled bravely. "Just sorting a few things out."

"You're not leaving, are you?" He could see the business cards in piles on her desk. "Catherine, don't do it."

"It's obvious Max wants me out," she sighed, resigned.

"Then don't make it easy for him. If you quit you're doing just that. If he wants to fire you then he's got to pay you off, but don't let him off lightly."

She sighed. "I've had enough. This place isn't going anywhere. I'm tired, I just want out."

He heaved himself out of the chair. "I'll be sorry to see you go." He held out his hand, and she shook it. It was only after he'd gone that she realized he'd called her by her real name for the first time.

Jeremy Glover himself was breezy, as if his promotion seemed perfectly natural and he saw no reason for Cat to be upset. He asked her for documents, studied the schedule, criticized her inventory and made a few misguided programming suggestions.

"We need a really strong drama series for this slot," he'd say.

"Jeremy, d'you think I *want* to fill the schedule with old crap or something? My budget's been slashed in half, and the most cost-effective thing to do right now is schedule repeats. I don't like it either, but I have no choice."

He'd nod his head vaguely and go off again, only to return later with more implausible ideas.

Max avoided all eye contact. Cat ignored him, wanting to make it clear that she found him beneath contempt. At the end of the week she typed the letter she had been mentally writing for days and strode into his office, depositing it on his desk.

"Catherine, can we talk about this?" he called out to her after reading it through.

"Like we did about your plans for the channel? I don't think so, Max. I'm on three months' notice. I intend to work them."

The following day, as she'd expected, she got a call from human resources telling her there was a check for three months' salary in the mail, but that she wasn't to come near the building again.

She gave notice on her apartment, booked a flight to Thailand and studied maps and routes. From there she would visit Vietnam and Burma, see Angkor Wat in Cambodia, go to Bali and Lombok and maybe head down to Australia. She had no desire to return to London, and if she were honest with herself, no desire to leave Asia either. But all around her companies were folding and people moving on, and she felt she was leaving the party at the right time.

Lorna and Jo took her out for dinner at an Italian restaurant, where Cat told them about her travel plans.

"So does Declan know anything about all this?" Lorna asked.

"You know that's what I find the hardest to take. I can't believe he didn't call."

"Cat, maybe he hasn't heard?" Jo tried. "He was off shift after all."

"Come on, Jo, you know how gossip flies in this place. What about poor Phil Tucker, that wasn't even true but it went around in five minutes. I get shafted like this and you don't think he's heard? No, I think it's better this way. I wasted well over a year on the false hope that he would choose me over her, but it was never going to happen." She paused to sip her wine. "Cat Moran, imagine! I'd sound like a frigging boat."

"Top secret." Jo lowered her voice. "But I've been approached by DigiSat in London. My old boss got a job there and wants me to work for him. I've had a phone interview and should be hearing any day now."

"God, London?" Cat wondered what it would be like to go back.

"There's a lot going on there now," Jo enthused. "Loads of start-ups. You should think about it."

They drank more bottles than was good for them and told endless Mad Max stories. In the loo, Cat had to steady herself, as if caught by surprise that the two bottles she personally must have drunk were having any effect. She walked deliberately and carefully to the basin, feeling dizzy, but not just from the alcohol. In the last ten days she'd lost her job, her income, her boyfriend, the country she lived in and her lifestyle. She felt as if an unseen force had scooped her up and was about to drop her into another adventure. She forced herself to be positive.

It was hard to believe that she would never wake up with Declan by her side again. That the struggle was over, she had given him back to Harriet. She had no intention of maintaining contact; it was better this way. She liked the idea of leaving suddenly, the idea that he would return to Hong Kong and find her gone. It would be as close to the death she had fantasized about as she could get without actually dying. He would never have said goodbye, and would have no way of contacting her. She liked the poignancy of that. Maybe then, just maybe, he'd begin to appreciate what he had had? What he could have had.

As her plane took off she looked long and hard out of the window at the mad, wild, extraordinary place that was Hong Kong. Jerry Greenberg's words were starting to make sense—it got in the blood, it sucked you in, its energy was addictive. Tears began to prick her eyes and she blinked them back. She'd shed more tears in the last few months than she cared to remember. There could be no looking back. This was the start of a new adventure, of new opportunities, a new life.

One day it might even make sense.

PART THREE

London
Later That Week

Forty-Seven

"So what made you come back, then?" Dominic asked her.

Dominic! Cat could hardly believe it—there she was, sitting opposite him in a wine-bar and telling him her story.

"A number of things, really." It was incredible how calm she could sound when she concentrated. "The Asian recession was hitting hard, but London was buzzing, especially in the media." She liked the way that sounded—it made her seem sensible and aware; someone who'd read *The Economist* rather than *The Enquirer.* "But there was one day that really clinched it," she continued. "I was staying in Ubud in Bali, you know it?"

He shook his head blankly and she was surprised. Someone like Dominic, she'd thought, would almost certainly have been there.

"I used to go to this Internet café, catch up on my mail. And one day I got two e-mails which settled it." There had been three, actually, but there was no need to go into the third right now.

"The first was from my dad, who'd had a minor heart attack. He was fine, but it was like a wake-up call for all of us. It made me think how little I'd seen of my parents, and how I should spend more time with them. And the other was from my friend Jo, telling me how great things were in London, and how many new companies were starting up, and with them, new jobs."

She drained her glass. "So it felt like it was time. I decided against heading down to Australia, and bought a flight home instead. The lease on my place was coming up, so the timing felt right."

"And your dad was OK?"

"He was fine. Shaken, and he's gone on a strict health regimen, but he's fine. Drinks less booze and plays more golf."

"And what happened to all those jobs?"

"Well, good question." She laughed awkwardly. "For some reason, nothing ever quite worked out. There were three things I was up for at one point, but they just never came through. There was always someone else, someone better connected, someone on the inside they felt more comfortable with. I think it's hard to break into the UK market once you've left it," she added, wanting to sound reasoned and intelligent rather than emotional and self-pitying.

"But you had an interview this week, didn't you?"

"Yes I did, with Trafalgar Broadcasting. They're launching some international channels. I'll hear soon if I've got a second interview."

"Good. I hope it works out. I'll get another bottle, shall I?" He headed for the bar. It was strange to watch him, out of context, in a wine-bar; strange to think that they were finally alone together, and that after all her fantasies and daydreams, there he was, on a Friday night, buying her a drink.

She'd run into him that evening as they left the building. She was saying goodbye to the security guard as she spotted him ahead of her, finishing a conversation. She'd walked past, smiling shyly, and suddenly he'd called out.

"Catherine!" He'd looked around awkwardly, as if worried that he'd drawn attention to himself. "I just wanted to check that you're coming back next week."

"Yes I am." She'd smiled. "I'm still doing all this data inputting for Jackie."

"Good, good. I'd hate to see you go just yet." He'd looked almost panicky. "Um, I don't suppose you fancy a drink or anything, do you?"

There had been no bells, no doves, no angels bursting into song, but the rest of the world seemed to fade quietly into the background, and there were just the two of them.

And now, watching him at the bar, she could feel that this was it—the new start she'd been waiting for. She would get that job at Trafalgar and have a wonderful life with Dominic. She almost wished that she was working tomorrow, so that she could whip off an e-mail to Lorna.

Lorna. She could picture her friend as if she'd just seen her last week. She was pleased they'd become close again. They'd kept in touch throughout Cat's travels, and the resentment she'd once felt had slowly dissipated. She could hardly blame Lorna for wanting to keep an affair private: it had just been Cat's ego that was hurt. As everything seemed to be crashing down around her, Lorna seemed to be challenging her own security—abusing both her relationship and her job, practically willing herself to get caught.

But she'd got away with it. Andrew, oblivious of her affair, had turned down the offer in Tokyo and signed another contract in Hong Kong, so Lorna had stayed on at Frontier. Her fling with Brandon fizzled out, and Cat sometimes got the impression that Lorna was embarrassed it had happened at all.

As Cat had wandered from beach or temple to internet café writing of her travels, she'd noticed an element of sadness in Lorna's replies; the feeling that all around her people were moving on.

Derek had started dating a Filippina girl and stopped spending so much time at Sam's; Phil Tucker was offered a job in Singapore, Trent Davies returned to New York and even Lacy Fok left to get married.

And then, the day in Ubud that Cat learned of her father's heart attack, there was the third e-mail, the one she didn't mention to Dominic; the one that told her that Declan, too, was going home.

It wasn't that she thought they might get together again—she was past that hope by now. She was never going to share anyone again, she had made that a new rule. But just the thought that they might find themselves in the same city comforted her; that they could bump into each other at any time, that he would be close by. Declan's decision to return to London gave her more assurance, a feeling of safety in numbers. If he'd returned, if he thought it was time to go back, then surely she could, too?

Dominic returned with another bottle and topped up their glasses. "We could get something to eat later, if you like?"

"Why not?" She sank back, dreamily, enjoying the warmth of the wine, as out of the blur of the last few months, a clear new life was emerging.

Forty-Eight

He had a hairy chest. Cat lay quietly beside him as he slept, admiring the shape the dark curls made as they crept in and then flowed down to his stomach. She thought it was perfect, not too coarse to be overwhelming, but dark and strong enough to have definition. She studied his form, the moles on his skin, a small scar, and immersed herself in the sound of his breath. If her head wasn't throbbing so much and her mouth dry like sandpaper she could have lain there all day watching him. His hair was ruffled up and the corner of his eyes full of sleep, but she thought he had never looked more gorgeous than he did there, his head on her white linen pillow.

Carefully she climbed out of the bed and tiptoed across the floor, taking her silk dressing-gown off the hook and wrapping it around herself. In the kitchen she downed a large glass of water and two aspirins, staring out at the dead plants on her terrace. When she got her job, she reminded herself, she would replenish them all, filling the tubs with geraniums and pansies, and she and Dominic would sit out there in the evenings, drinking wine and enjoying the harmonious surroundings she had created.

Dominic. What exactly had happened between them? There had been two bottles at the wine-bar, that much she could remember. Then they'd made their way to a Chinese restaurant nearby. He'd ordered lavishly, and she remembered thinking this was going to be the best meal she'd had since returning to

London. But all she could remember eating was the odd prawn. They must have had another bottle—perhaps even two?—and he'd sat sideways from her, their legs touching.

But from then on it was a bit of a blur. What had they talked about in the restaurant? She could remember him looking animated and lively, but hadn't a clue what he'd been saying.

And then what? Jumping into a cab home, kissing in the cab, she couldn't remember how they decided that he was to come home with her, but evidently they had. She couldn't remember exactly what had happened once they were inside, but could see her clothes were strewn over the sofa and her chin was sore, so she assumed there had been a lot of kissing.

She made a cup of tea and slunk back into bed beside him. He had rolled over by now, and she found herself looking at his back. His shoulders were strong and broad, his torso long and well toned and his bottom was neat and covered with a fine growth of dark hairs.

What had they done? She could not believe that she had finally had sex with the man she had been lusting after for weeks and then totally forgotten the experience. If he would just wake up and do it again. She'd always loved morning sex: sleepy, sober, lazy sex that could last for hours and end with two thunderous orgasms and a scrambled egg breakfast.

Despite her adoration, even Cat grew tired of studying his back and listening to the sound of his breath. It occurred to her that it would be better to be up and about, clean and made-up and busily getting on with her day when he woke up. What did she want, for him to wake and find an unwashed woman with streaky eye make-up beside him, desperate for sex?

Gently she climbed out of bed, tiptoeing to the bathroom. In the wastebasket she could see a scrunched-up piece of toilet paper, and just make out a fragment of flesh-colored rubber.

"Good one, Cat," she muttered irritably. Never again would she drink so much that she forgot everything, she told herself. Never, ever again.

She showered and washed her hair, brushed and flossed her teeth and put on some makeup, expecting to find him up when she came back out into the living room. But no, he still lay there, fast asleep. Now Cat began to feel impatient. There was nothing worse than a man who needed a lot of sleep. She wanted to buy a paper, fix some breakfast, start vacuuming the flat. She was making coffee as the phone rang.

"Cat. I didn't wake you, did I?" It was Jo.

"No, no, I've been up for a while. I'm so glad you've called." Glad and relieved.

"Well, I'm still pissed off with you but I've got to talk to you about something."

"Look, I still don't really understand why you're so upset, it was nothing. But anyway." Cat sank into the sofa, excited to be able to share her story. She lowered her voice. "Dominic's asleep in my bed right now."

"Oh my God, you didn't waste your time, did you? So what happened?" Cat told her what she could, irritated about the lack of detail.

"You must have been completely bombed," Jo reassured her.

"Yes thanks, I'd pretty much come to that conclusion myself. I just hope I didn't make a fool of myself."

"Well, he shagged you, didn't he, so you couldn't have been all that bad."

Cat laughed. "Look, Jo, I'm sorry if you were pissed off with me before—"

"Well, yes I was. You put me in a really awkward position."

"I think it would have been worse if I had've told you. I didn't know Max was going to take that stupid message seriously."

"Cat, I told you something in confidence, and you took advantage."

"In confidence? A monthly network meeting is confidential? Oh come on, Jo. Had I told you I was doing it you'd have spent the entire meeting worrying and waiting for him to arrive. As it was, it was much better that you were as surprised as everyone else." She couldn't understand why Jo failed to see the funny side. "So on a scale of one to ten, just how embarrassing would you say it was for him?"

"Twelve. Thirteen. He looked mortified. He was all puffed up with his own importance, only to realize that no one even knew who he was, let alone was expecting him."

"Tell me exactly what happened again?"

"The receptionist had walked him down to the meeting room

and introduced him. She said he said he had an appointment at that time, and Suzi just looked puzzled. He insisted that he'd had a call inviting him to a breakfast meeting. She told him there had to be a mistake and apologized for him going all that way so early in the morning. She asked him which company he was from, like she'd never heard of Frontier, and you could see that he totally resented having to introduce himself. He kind of went red and made noises about shabby behavior and unprofessionalism."

"Because he would never behave shabbily of course."

"Of course not. And that was it. He was led out and looked completely pissed off."

"And he didn't see you?"

"No, thank God, I must have merged in with a crowd of faces."

Cat sank back, laughing. "I'd have loved to have been a fly on the wall."

"It was pretty extraordinary. Listen." Her tone changed. "The reason I'm calling you is that I've been thinking about what Max could be doing here. You don't think he's involved in this Trafalgar thing, do you?"

"What?" Cat's chest tightened.

"Well, think about it. Trafalgar announces these big international plans and how they're trying to find a head and Max shows up in London. It could be."

"No, I can't believe it." In one brief suggestion Cat's future took a sudden nose-dive. "I mean, why would the CEO of an Asian network take up a management position at a British company? Why would he do that?"

"Maybe because he knows something we don't? Maybe Desmond Tang's finally about to pull the plug and this is Max's face-saving way out? Head up an international division of a major, reputable company that has money and the respect of the industry. It makes sense to me."

It *was* beginning to make sense, Cat thought in horror. It was actually starting to make sense. "Well, if that's the case I'm fucked."

"I know. I'm sorry."

"Talk about what goes around comes around." There was a sudden cry of pain from her bedroom. "Oh look, I have to go."

"Why, is he up now?"

"If he isn't he will be in a moment," she whispered and hung up. In the bedroom, Dominic was rubbing his head and frowning at a pink rock.

"What the hell is this I just banged my head on?" he asked her. It was the rose quartz crystal Cat had taken to putting under her pillow to attract love.

"Oh there it is," she tutted, putting it in her bedside drawer as if it were nothing out of the ordinary. "D'you fancy a coffee?"

"I tell you what I fancy." He pulled her toward him. His hair was roughed-up and his eyes bleary. His chin was dark and he smelled of sweat, sex and cigarettes. He kissed her, and she thought she had never loved anyone more. He peeled off her jeans, kissing her and admiring her smooth, clean body. Perversely she liked the fact that he smelled bad; it made it more illicit, like Lady Chatterley and her gardener. They made love again, slowly, with affection.

When they finished, he showered and pulled his suit on. "I'd better get going. Can I see you again, tonight?"

"Tonight would be wonderful."

"Give me your number, I'll call you later." As she wrote it down the little cat Precious appeared on the terrace, keen to get inside.

"That's a sweet one." He smiled with a look of sadness in his eyes. "I love cats."

"So do I," she cried happily. It was another sign.

Forty-Nine

"**S**hall I get the papers?" Dominic kissed her forehead. They'd finished making love for the second time that morning, and the corner store was about to close.

"Please. And I'll fix brunch." Cat smiled happily. It had been hard to keep their relationship a secret in the office when all she'd wanted to do was shout about it from the photocopier. They'd spent two weeks almost exclusively in each other's company. He'd moved two spare shirts, some underwear and a suit into her flat and she'd feel warm inside every time she opened the wardrobe and saw them hanging there. They had become a symbol of their relationship. Dominic was hers. Dominic Pryce—enigmatic, controversial and fiercely intelligent Dominic—was all hers.

And he was bringing her luck. She'd got a call from Trafalgar asking her to attend a second interview with the yet-to-be-announced division head. And there was her only misgiving. She kept imagining meeting Max in their offices and the idea filled her with horror. She'd tried getting a clue out of David Boyd, the director who'd first interviewed her, as to the identity of her potential new boss, but he would only divulge that the person was "a highly regarded industry professional with a wealth of international experience."

"Well, that counts Max out," Jo had joked.

She broke four eggs in a glass bowl and started whisking them with a little salt and pepper. She would scramble some eggs, make toast and they'd spend the day lazing over the papers. Perhaps a walk down Kings Road to the cinema, she wondered, a late lunch over a bottle of wine somewhere warm and cozy?

Again, the image of Max Carnegie jumped into her head.

"Fuck off, Max," she snapped. "Leave me alone! You are not the new head of Trafalgar International, you are not, not, not."

"Who are you talking to?" Dominic had come up the stairs, clutching the newspapers, a puzzled smile on his face.

"Just fretting over my ex-boss," she told him sheepishly. "Jo's planted the idea in my head that he might be involved in the Trafalgar thing." She poured the eggs in the pan and started heating them. "You know, it is a coincidence that he's in town just as they're announcing their plans. It does sort of add up."

"I don't think it's likely," Dominic told her. "He sounds like he's got too big an ego for that. He's used to running his own show."

"I hope you're right," she said, unconvinced. "But you know when something nags at you? When you just know that something's wrong?"

He looked at her blankly. "It's called nerves, it's a good sign."

"No, it's more than that." She searched for the right words. "It's something deeper than that. Nerves I can deal with, but this is, I don't know, a feeling on a soul level."

"What are you on about?" He frowned, checking the toast.

"That there's some upset in store. A nasty surprise." As she said it her stomach lurched yet again, as if to confirm her suspicions.

"Cat. It's nerves. It's just a coincidence that he's in town. Stop beating yourself up about it."

They had their breakfast and Cat was pleased for the distraction of the *Sunday Times* and the *News of the World*. She tried to show more interest in the former, reading the review section and the magazine before flipping through the tabloid, tutting occasionally as if in disapproval. The minute Dominic went to the loo, though, she reached for the magazine and turned to the horoscopes, where her sign read:

Love sizzles and is here to stay; someone from the past points the way to your future.

She read the words in disbelief. Max again! She was reluctant to dismiss the forecast as the love bit was too positive. But a contact from her past? That could only mean one person. It could have been the eggs but Cat suddenly felt sick. Wordlessly Dominic came back and resumed reading.

"If it were Max he'd have nixed me by now, wouldn't he?" she tried after a few minutes.

He looked up, irritated to be drawn away from the financial pages. "I'd have thought so, yes," he said wearily.

"Unless, unless he wants to see me humiliated." It was becoming disturbingly real. "He wants to watch me squirm at that meeting, he wants to enjoy my suffering. Then I bet he offers me the job because he knows I'll have to turn it down. Now that's his style."

Dominic shook the paper violently. "Cat, just go to the interview and do your best. There's nothing more you can do. It won't be him, it's just a coincidence."

There are no coincidences, she wanted to tell him, but now was not the right time for an esoteric discussion. She sat quietly, willing him to wrap her up in his arms and tell her that everything would be OK, but it was clear that all he wanted to do was read about foreign exchange markets.

"I hope you're right," she told him. "And this time on Thursday I'll know for sure. But hey, what's the worst that can happen? Max starts working over here, so I go back to Hong Kong? That wouldn't be so bad."

She looked for a flicker of reaction, a sign that that was an outcome he didn't want, but all she saw was the makings of a smirk, and with a heavy sigh she went back to her reading.

Fifty

"**I** have a fantastic job at Trafalgar," Cat recited to herself in the shower. "My boss is a dynamic, highly regarded industry professional from whom I am learning a lot. He is not Max Carnegie." Her stomach lurched again.

She dressed in a slim-fitting navy blue suit. The skirt shimmied down to her knees and the jacket covered a multitude of sins. She hung a simple sapphire cross around her neck and applied a discreet amount of makeup, skipping the perfume.

"Life is a series of transitions," she told herself. "I have just gone through a negative one, and am about to enter a positive one. My boss will not be Max Carnegie."

Cat had just finished reading a book that Lorna had sent her, the optimistically titled *Life Has No Happy Endings* by Leonora Schwarz, a New Yorker with a PhD in psychotherapy and a butch haircut. In it she claimed that from childhood women are conditioned to believe in the myth of the happy ending. Fairy tales where the beautiful girl gets her man and lives happily ever after merely help to create false hopes and an unfulfilled sense of reality, when more often than not, women end up disillusioned because their princes turn into motor mechanics with bad breath and an alcohol problem. Schwarz's theory was that life has no happy endings, merely positive and negative transitions, neither of which necessarily last a long time. Instead of expecting happiness as a birthright, she concluded, one should simply appreciate the positive times and learn from the negative.

Her theory had resonated with Cat. She was coming out of a long, negative transition and would enter the positive one with a profound sense of appreciation. And not a boss called Max Carnegie.

"Who are you talking to?" Dominic was knotting his tie.

"Myself. Confidence-boosting affirmations." She smiled, hoping he'd think her delightfully kooky.

He rolled his eyes instead. "They're going to get you the job, are they?"

"I believe in the power of positive thought," she told him. "And I am going to get this bloody job."

"I hope so," he told her. "I could do with a secretary who doesn't give me a hard-on every time she walks into my office."

They walked to Fulham Broadway together and he fumbled for coins at the ticket machine. It disappointed Cat that he hadn't yet started buying weekly travel cards, even though he left from her station most days. He kept his suits in her wardrobe all right, yet was in denial over a train pass.

"I'll see you tonight, won't I?" she asked on the platform.

He frowned and looked away, guiltily. "I suppose so," he said.

"What? Is there something else you need to do?" She so wanted to see him after her interview, to relax over a bottle of wine and talk him through it, step by step, asking for his opinions and misgivings.

"Oh, I should see the kids." His eyes stayed fixed on the rails. Sometimes she got the feeling he might throw himself on them.

"But you're seeing them at the weekend."

"I know. I just feel guilty. I should be there, helping them with their homework, that sort of thing."

Cat sighed. She could hardly argue with that. "Would your wife let you?" she tried.

"I doubt it."

Their train came in. Cat fell silent, wishing he could be more supportive on her big day. Wishing he didn't have a family to think of, and that he was making suggestions about dinner and some new restaurant to try out rather than looking hopelessly up at a no smoking sign.

She had to change at Embankment and he kissed her lightly on the lips. "I'll see you in the office then. Good luck. I'm sure you'll knock 'em dead."

Despondently she changed trains and resurfaced at Tottenham Court Road.

"Spare some change please, love?" a beggar asked her outside the station. She shook her head guiltily, telling herself that once she had a job she would buy *The Big Issue* every week and carry a packet of treats in her bag for the dogs. *Please God*, she urged. *I am a good person. If I get this job I'll give to charity. I'll give to the homeless. I'll do anything*.

She arrived at Trafalgar's offices a few minutes early, and sat in the reception area watching people come and go. One day she would belong here, she told herself. One day she'd be greeting the receptionist like an old friend and striding purposefully toward the elevators. What did all these people have that she didn't? She was just as good as any of them.

She was called up to David Boyd's office where he greeted her warmly. "I must apologize for all this cloak and dagger stuff," he began with his slight lisp, sitting back in his red leather chair. "But until our new director was released from his position and we'd got the announcement in *Broadcast*, I really was in no position to name names. Have you managed to see a copy this morning?"

"No, I'm afraid I haven't yet." Cat's stomach flipped over.

"It's front-page news, quite a coup for us to poach such a high-level individual." Cat smiled weakly as there was a knock at the door. "Ah, that'll be him now." He started to rise. Cat wasn't sure that she could. "I believe you two already know each other?"

Cat turned to face the smiling figure that was walking through the door. He wore a Paul Smith suit, a crooked tie and a smug smile. It was Mark Gilmore. "Yes, of course." Cat forced a warm smile and an unwavering handshake. "Mark, how are you?" In twenty seconds of blind panic Cat's stomach had done a triple somersault, her cheeks had flushed pink and her knees had almost betrayed her. Her smile was one of relief and horror.

"Catherine, how nice to see you again." Mark leaned toward her and kissed her on both cheeks, still holding her hand. She decided in that instant to act as if nothing had ever happened between them. Not just now, not just for this interview, but for ever. They had been extremely drunk after all—there was always the hope that he'd even forgotten about it himself. Cat knew instinctively that for their working relationship to succeed she had to persuade even herself that nothing had ever happened; reinvent the past as Max Carnegie was so fond of doing.

Mark turned to David Boyd. "Cat and I signed a major deal in Cannes a couple of years ago," he told him. "It was a memorable evening."

"We had an excellent dinner, didn't we?" Cat jumped in.

"Excellent, excellent." David Boyd looked pleased. "Well, I suggest you two have a chat and I will see you shortly."

Mark led her out of the office and into the corridor. "Fancy a coffee?" he suggested. Cat nodded weakly as he ushered her into an elevator. As they rode down she thought blindly of things to say.

"Congratulations on getting this job," she started. "A bit of a departure isn't it?"

"D'you think so? I've been in the business of selling programs world-wide for years, selling channels is just the next step."

"Yes, I suppose so." Cat let her voice trail off.

"So you?" He asked as the lift doors opened. "What happened to you then?"

"I left Frontier last year," she began as he walked her down the corridor. "It was time for me to leave Asia."

"Really? Why was that?"

"Oh you know, the recession, the feeling that Frontier wasn't going anywhere. I did some travelling and got back a few months ago."

"And what have you been doing since?" They had just walked into the bar. Cat ordered a cappuccino and had a moment to think as it was being made.

"Gardening leave," she told him. "Or rather, home-improvement leave. I did some major work on my place and have just about finished it all now." She hoped it didn't sound lame.

"So you're ready to start work again, are you?"

"Oh yes, I can get on with things without distractions now."

They sat down. Mark leaned back in his chair and seemed rather to enjoy her discomfort. He outlined his plans for Trafalgar and the key areas for development.

"So I need an assistant. Not in the secretarial sense, I've already got that, but someone who can support me in the regions we launch. You know, I go in and do the deal, but someone else has to come up with the programming, the schedule, all the operational stuff. The research beforehand. Does that appeal to you?"

"Definitely it does. I'm a launch person. I love start-ups, sorting things out, setting systems up, that sort of thing. It sounds right up my alley."

"You don't see yourself as the deal-maker then?"

She flinched. "No, not really. I mean, I've done it, but I like to get my hands dirty, you know?" The words 'as opposed to my mouth' jumped into her head and she cringed. "Get things straightened on the operational side."

"D'ya know anything about the Eastern bloc countries, or Africa?"

"Not really, no, but it wouldn't be hard to get to know them. I have a wealth of research material and some pretty good contacts." Neither was true, but it sounded good.

Mark slurped his coffee thoughtfully. "And when could you start?"

"Whenever. I have no obligations."

"What are you doing at the moment?"

"Some consultancy work for my boyfriend's firm," Cat tried awkwardly. "An investment bank. Nothing to do with TV, but it's quite fun."

Mark was interested, and so Cat expanded a little on Rubens, claiming to be project managing a relatively straightforward system upgrade. To her relief, he looked impressed. Had he any idea she meant inputting names and addresses on a huge database? As Cat had suspected, if she said something with enough confidence, he wouldn't question it.

When she finally arrived at Rubens, Jackie was waiting for her. "Dominic was just looking for you," she said with a knowing smile. "How did the interview go?"

"Fine, I think. I actually knew the guy from a while ago. I think that helps, hard to say, really."

"Of course it helps. I bet you've got it," Jackie added confidently before having to answer her phone.

Cat logged on and found an e-mail from Dominic. *Hope it all went well*, it read. *Sorry about this morning. Dinner tonight?*

She beamed. It was typically short and to the point, and she loved him for it. She reached for her organizer, looking around to check no one could see the message, and opened the page to the day's entry, writing *Dinner—Dominic* down. She was hardly likely to forget, but loved the way it looked, and imagined her diary in the months to come, full of entries of his name. *Dinner—Dominic; Cinema—Dominic; Theatre—Dominic.* She imagined their life in these pages: the restaurants, the movies and the times they would share. A week in Greece, a weekend in the Lake District, Christmas in New York.

Catherine Pryce. It had a certain ring to it.

Would love to have dinner, she typed back. *Think it went well, turns out my potential boss is not Max but someone I did a big deal with a couple of years ago. Fingers crossed!*

She read it through a couple of times before sending it. She couldn't bring herself to tell him the truth about Mark Gilmore—what was the point? It was a stupid mistake, and something she was far from proud of. Why stir up trouble and jealousy over a drunken night that didn't mean anything? But as she hit the send button she couldn't help but feel guilty that in some way she was deceiving him. It was sad to start their relationship off on a secret, but what else was she to do?

She hadn't even been offered the job yet, anyway. She would wait and see if she was, and then she'd consider telling him.

Fifty-One

Mark Gilmore offered Cat the job the following week. She was to be Head of Programming and Program Planning, Trafalgar Channels. Despite herself, she felt rather sad to be leaving Rubens. It had been a learning experience in her life, and one that she felt she'd become stronger for. Dominic took her out to celebrate, but the minute he turned up she could tell he was in no mood.

"I shouldn't be doing this," he started. "The system screwed up this afternoon and I should be with them fixing it."

"Dominic, you're a senior manager," she said. "And senior managers delegate. Your staff won't learn anything if you take over all the time."

"I don't know, I should be there." He checked his cell.

"They'll call you if there's a problem," she tried. "But I'm sure they're capable of fixing it."

He rubbed his eyes. "I've been taking too much time off lately. Now you've got your job I'm going to have to start putting the hours in again."

"Well, I won't stop you," she said, disappointed all the same. She'd hoped he might consider her more important than work, but clearly this was not the case. "You know I'd never get in the way of your work or your family."

He shrugged as if this was another source of discomfort. "I have to see them this weekend," he told her.

"But you saw them last weekend?"

"Doesn't matter. My wife wants me to have them on Sunday. I think she's got a date."

"Well, good for her." Was he jealous? She looked at him closely. "She deserves her own life."

"Yeah." He studied the menu, and ordered a steak. They sat awkwardly for a few minutes. She didn't know what to say. She'd always thought he had a dark side, but had hoped he might keep it to himself a while longer.

"Does it bother you? That she's seeing someone?"

"That someone else will bring up my children? Live in my house, you mean?"

"Dominic, it's a date, not a wedding."

He paused, taking a slug of wine. "No, it doesn't bother me. Like you say, she deserves something. I've ruined her life, after all."

"You have not ruined her life," Cat tutted. "Marriages break up all the time. It's sad, but true. It's not as if you left her for someone else, is it?" She thought quickly of Sandy, and wondered if that wasn't strictly the case. "It's not, is it?"

"No." He sighed. "There wasn't anyone else, not really."

Not really? She felt a stab of jealousy. Had Sandy broken his marriage up? She wished he'd just tell her and get it over with.

"So right now your wife's doing fine. She's got the family house, she's got the kids, and you pay for everything. Does she work?"

"She's a teacher."

Cat tried to picture his wife, a teacher. She must be what, in her late thirties? She thought she might dress sensibly, in beige, or perhaps floral prints. She imagined how tough it must have been to walk into school the day after he'd left her; to go through the motions of lessons and books and discipline, all the time feeling empty inside. It was strange how she felt no jealousy toward the woman who'd shared Dominic's life for ten or fifteen years, yet was enormously insecure over someone she only suspected he'd been involved with at all.

"Dominic, I know you feel guilty, but she'll find someone else. It was better to make a clean break rather than leave her hanging on indefinitely, wondering where her marriage was going."

"That's what I keep telling myself." He sighed and lit another cigarette, drawing hard and staring glumly at his phone.

Cat drained her glass, trying to think of how to rescue the evening. Perhaps now wasn't the best time to admit to having once given her new boss a blowjob, she smirked, wishing suddenly she was with either Jo or Lorna, and that they were laughing and having fun.

"So here's to a new start," she tried, raising her refilled glass.

He tried a smile. "I'm sorry. Congratulations. You deserve it. I'm sure you'll do well." He drained his glass and checked his cell again.

"So I won't see you this weekend?" She was almost glad that she wouldn't. Perhaps they'd seen too much of each other lately? Perhaps they needed a bit of a break, and he needed to miss her?

"It's only Sunday I need to get back," he told her. "But I don't want to do much otherwise, maybe get a pizza on Saturday?"

She smiled weakly. Her point exactly. They were just coming up to their first month's anniversary, and already he was suggesting take-out pizzas on a Saturday night?

She tried to rally. There would be good and bad days, she'd told herself, and this was just one of the latter. She must give him space, and never complain. She'd arrange to see Jo on Sunday, and go to a film or something. She would keep up a separate life for herself, and never get demanding or clingy.

"You'll find someone else at your new company, won't you?" he said suddenly, refilling his glass.

"Where did that come from?" Cat asked in surprise. "Of course I won't." Despite his mood, she still couldn't imagine being with anyone else. "I'm not interested in other men."

"You will." Their food arrived, and he tore into his steak.

She sighed. "Dominic, I have no intention of finding anyone else. I'm happy with you. I've wanted you for a long time, and now I've got you I'm not letting go without a fight." She paused. "I'm realistic about our relationship. I know you have a family to think about and a pressurized job. But I will always be there for you, OK?"

"OK." He nodded. "Thanks, Cat." He stretched his hand out to hers across the table. "That means a lot to me."

"Can we lighten up a bit now?" she pleaded, a smile on her face. And just as she thought they might, his phone rang, and he was gone again.

Fifty-Two

On her last evening at Rubens, a few of them decided to go to the local wine-bar for a farewell drink. Dominic was to join them later. At last, Cat thought, they could be open about their relationship in front of his colleagues. But as she and Jackie were approaching the down escalator they saw Dominic and Sandy sitting together in the atrium, smoking furtively.

"They're working on some project together," Jackie reassured her.

"You know, Sandy's about the only person who hasn't said goodbye, or thanked me?" Cat mused. She caught Dominic's eye, and he waved, signalling that he would see her later. Had he told Sandy about them? she wondered. Or was he doing so right now?

She had often wondered how it would feel to walk out of Rubens for the last time, knowing that she was to start a new life on Monday. In her fantasies the walk out had taken on a huge significance, like the end shot of a movie, and she'd thought she'd feel like a different person altogether. Instead the act had been marred by Sandy's presence.

She bought the first round and watched nervously for Dominic to appear. Every moment he was away meant more time spent with Sandy. She started to picture him even bringing her along with him, but scolded herself for being so negative. When he finally did arrive he looked drawn and exhausted. He bought a round and chatted to Graham Clark, barely acknowledging Cat in front of the others, and she felt let down.

When everyone else had gone he suggested they eat at the wine-bar. Cat was a little disappointed—the food was nothing special, but she settled for a Caesar salad with grilled chicken. He looked troubled. He was breathing heavily and lighting one ciga-rette after the other, stopping occasionally to chew at a fingernail.

"Did something happen today?" Cat asked impatiently. "Do you want to talk about it?"

He shook his head and she thought she could see tears welling in his eyes. She reached out for his hand. "Tell me," she tried more softly. "I'm here for you, you know I am."

"You'll hate me." He began and Cat felt a twisting, knotting dread form in her stomach.

"Try me."

"It's Sandy."

The world stopped for a second. "Yes?" she said cautiously, feeling like a boxer waiting for a right hook to the stomach.

"She's getting married."

Cat paused for a moment. "And that's a bad thing?"

"I'm sorry, Cat. You don't deserve all this." He took a deep draw on his cigarette.

"Look, Dominic, I always guessed there'd been something be-tween you two. It's no big deal. We all have a past." She cringed, reminded of her own.

"No, it's not like that." He ran his fingers through his hair. He looked like a criminal giving evidence to the police in a TV drama. Guilty as hell.

"What is it then, Dominic? Oh God, I think I can guess. You had an affair and you left your wife for her. Is that what hap-pened?" She urged herself to be strong and brave, to get it out into the open. "But what, she dumped you for this other guy? Is that it?"

"No Cat, you don't understand." He looked up at her. "I never had an affair with her."

"You . . . didn't?" Cat slumped back in her chair, thrown.

"No. I know everyone thinks I did, but I didn't. I've never so much as laid a finger on her."

Beyond Cat's immediate sense of relief there was a feeling that he was about to tell her something far more disturbing.

"Then what's the problem?" she asked cautiously. He poured himself another glass of wine and then almost drank half of it before drawing deeply on his cigarette.

"You . . . cared . . . about . . . her?" Cat spelled the words out slowly, trying to take them in herself.

"Yes." He drained his glass.

"And you still do?" Her voice felt like it was being pulled down inside her stomach.

"I'm sorry."

"Can you tell me about it?" She felt like his shrink.

He sighed. He poured what was left of the wine into his glass and then signalled to the waiter for another bottle. Cat was glad he did. She needed some kind of anesthetic.

"I've known her for what, six years now. The first couple of years she was just another colleague, you know? Just another person who worked for me. I wasn't particularly attracted to her or anything. And then something happened." He paused dramatically. "She had taken on this big project. I'd warned her about the way she was handling it, I could see it all going wrong, but she was headstrong and convinced she was right. And then late one Friday afternoon we met to discuss it and she realized she'd fucked up. Weeks of work completely useless and she was about to miss her deadline. And as we went through it all she started to cry. She looked so vulnerable, she was crying out to me, asking for my help."

"So what did you do?"

"I rolled up my sleeves, ordered a pizza and got to work." He smiled fondly at the recollection. "We worked through the night, gave ourselves Saturday morning off and then worked through till Sunday night. Got it all fixed."

"And during that time?"

"Nothing happened." He shrugged. "We just worked."

"But something did happen. To you anyway."

"Yes." Dominic nodded hopelessly. "It did." The bottle arrived and he refilled their glasses.

"And that was when you started having feelings for her." Cat couldn't believe she was counselling her own boyfriend about his desire for another woman.

"Yes. It was that weekend. From then on I knew I loved her."

"Loved?" There was the right hook. "That's a bit strong, isn't it?"

He shook his head. "I loved her, Cat. I'm sorry. To tell you the truth, I still do," he choked.

"So let me get this straight." Cat gathered herself. She'd had enough of playing counsellor. "She fucks up her job and instead of just firing her like any normal person would, you sacrifice your own weekend to help her out and then fall in love with her?"

He laughed. "You could put it like that, yes."

"Dominic." She held his hand, feeling slightly guilty for her outburst. "What kind of a man are you?"

"A fool, I know. But I never felt like this about anyone else."

"Dominic, you married young. You had kids quickly and were stuck with a huge mortgage and school fees to pay. You outgrew your wife. Suddenly this attractive girl from this office reaches out to you and wham! It's love! It wasn't love, Dominic, it was infatuation. Flattery. You enjoyed the fact that you could rescue her; that you could sort out the mess she'd made. She learned from you and she looked up to you. You were flattered."

"Maybe. But that was four years ago, and my feelings haven't changed."

Four years! Another right hook sharp in the stomach. "And have you ever tried to do anything about them?"

"Oh yes, I've tried. Over the years. But she was never interested. She knows exactly how I feel. I've taken her out, I've given her presents, I've been totally straight with her, but she's not interested in me."

"She accepted invitations and gifts?"

"It was hard for her not to."

"Dominic, you're her boss, for God's sake! What she should have said is 'Dominic, I really appreciate the thought but I find it wholly inappropriate for me to accept this because you're my boss, and as such, we should be working on a professional basis only.'" Cat cringed at the thought of her own upcoming work situation. "Instead she took advantage of you—accepting your gifts, no doubt, what, promotions as well, pay raises, all the best projects?"

To her horror he nodded, laughing at himself. She had hoped he might at least deny her last suggestions.

"It's hard for you to understand, I know. I've tried, Cat. I've tried to distance myself, get her out of my system, but I can't. I'm sorry."

"Oh Dominic." She was at a loss. "I don't know what to say."

They sat in silence for a moment before Dominic's face lit up. "Do you remember when you first started? I walked out one day?"

"Yes, I do."

"It was because she told me she could never feel for me the same way as she does her boyfriend. Fiancé, now. She told me there was no hope, that no matter how much I cared she would never feel the same way." He lit another cigarette.

"I remember that time," Cat said quietly, studying her untouched salad. "In fact," she laughed gently, "that was the day I fell in love with you. Only I imagined you'd stormed out of a meeting because you didn't like the way it was going, or something noble like that."

He reached across the table for her hand and they sat in silence. Through the pain something was strangely assuring her. It was too much of a coincidence that Dominic's storming out that day could have been so significant for both of them. Nothing happened by chance. It was another sign from the Universe that their relationship was worth working at.

"I'm sorry to do this to you," he tried. "But now I'm with you it feels easier. You're making me stronger. Please Cat—give me some time. I will get over her, I know I will. You're breaking the spell. Please—give me a chance."

Cat smiled sadly at her broken wreck of a boyfriend. She could walk away now, walk out of his life. But it was stronger to stay—to work with him, to help him through it. That, she thought, was what the Universe wanted.

As she'd hoped it would, the wine anesthetized her and she felt capable of anything.

"Of course I will," she said tenderly. "Of course I will, Dominic."

Fifty-Three

"**W**hat kind of presents anyway?" It was like an itch that wouldn't go away.

"I don't know, jewelry, scarves, that sort of thing." Dominic shrugged. Cat felt a flash of anger. They had been dating for a month now and he hadn't bought her a single thing.

"So she's shagging someone else yet she accepts jewelry from her boss? Hmmm, says a lot about her integrity, doesn't it?" If she could just make him see sense.

"It wasn't like that," he said quietly.

Then how was it? she wanted to yell at him, but took a deep breath and reached for the Sunday supplement instead. She would have liked him to think that none of this bothered her; she would have liked it not to bother her, either, but it killed her that he was blind to what she saw as Sandy's manipulation.

"I'll make some more coffee." He disappeared to the kitchen and Cat flipped through to the horoscopes. *Someone you're close to needs your support. Give it to them unselfishly.* Cat tossed the magazine aside. Dominic could have written it himself. She sighed heavily. It was another challenge from the Universe—Cat had to learn to put aside her jealousy and to support Dominic. That was her karma in this life. Maybe in their last lives together she had let him down badly, and now had to right certain old wrongs? Looking at life from the Universe's point of view, everything made sense. The Universe set the challenges and then allowed clues like astrology and the tarot cards help those who were aware.

But it was just so hard. Tomorrow was the start of her exciting new future and all Cat could think about was Dominic's strange past. Had he actually had an affair with Sandy it would have been easier. But this strange, melodramatic unrequited love was much harder to deal with.

"Last week she was wearing some earrings I bought her," Dominic said casually, as if mentioning an unusually wet summer. He seemed oblivious of her feelings. "I've never seen her wearing any of my things before."

"And did you take it as a sign?" Cat hissed.

"I suppose I did at first, but then she made it clear she'd forgotten where they came from."

"No woman would forget where they came from. She probably suspected you were seeing me and wanted to keep your interest. Or is there a new project coming up she'd like?"

"There is, actually." He looked vaguely puzzled. "In a few weeks."

"Dominic, can't you see?" She felt like hitting him. "She's manipulating you. She has been all this time. And it works. You're like a puppy around her. One click of her fingers and you come running, offering her presents and all the best jobs." She took a deep breath. "So who were you thinking of giving the project to?"

"Cat, don't."

"You were, weren't you? Can't you see you're doing yourself down? Everyone knows you treat her differently, it's a bit of a joke around the office." It was a lie, but from the look on his face, an effective one. "You can't keep giving all the high-profile stuff to her."

He turned away and took what looked like a deep and painful breath.

"Let's face it, she's getting married soon," she continued. "That'll mean wedding preparations, a honeymoon, and then probably a baby. Her time will be divided from now on, you know. She won't be able to work all night with you in the future."

She hated herself for her spite, but the words streamed out before she could stop herself. They were instant gratification, but, like a bar of chocolate in the afternoon, something she immediately regretted.

"I suppose." He looked downcast. Cat held her head in her hands. She felt like she was suffocating, stuck in the middle of something she really didn't want to get involved with. She longed to walk in the open air, to feel cleansed by a fresh cold wind.

"Can we get out of this place?" she asked him. "Let's go for a walk, maybe around Parson's Green? You need to get going soon anyway, don't you?"

He nodded, and Cat thought he was probably feeling just as stifled as she was. Silently they headed toward Chelsea. The air hung cold and damp, a bit like Cat's own spirits, and she tried to concentrate on her first day at work tomorrow, and how it might go. It struck her as ironic that only last week she'd been worrying about whether to tell Dominic about her and Mark Gilmore or not, and now he'd sent her reeling with a far worse confession of his own.

Which would you rather, that your partner was having sex with you and thinking about someone else, or having sex with someone else and thinking about you? Lorna's words rang in her ears. Did Dominic think of Sandy while they were making love? Did he dream of her at nights? Was he even thinking about her now?

As if sensing her discomfort, he took her hand. "Thank you for being here," he told her. "Thank you for taking me on."

She squeezed his hand. "I want us to be happy. I want us to get over this, you know?"

"So do I." He sighed. He looked at his watch. "I should go."

"I know. You must sort this out, you know? Organize clear weekends. She can't expect you to drop everything whenever she wants."

"Yes, you're right. Maybe I'll mention it later."

She said nothing, just enjoyed the feel of the cold on her cheeks.

"I love you," he said suddenly, and she turned, surprised. They were the words she'd always wanted to hear, yet they just felt unrealistic and inappropriate. "I do, you know. I love you."

She turned her face to the wind, not sure what to say next. He was becoming a different man, and she no longer knew how she felt about him.

Fifty-Four

Her first week at work was surprisingly uneventful. Cat saw little of Mark Gilmore, who had secured an office for her some four flights of stairs beneath his own. It was a large, open space with scuffed grey walls and worn furniture that reminded her a bit of a classroom. He promised that she would only be there until the new department had significantly expanded, while office supplies warned that they might have to use it to store excess furniture. Cat ordered bright red office accessories to dispel the gloom. At least her view was fantastic, and at lunchtime she would gaze out over Soho Square, eat a sandwich and play cards against the computer.

Alone in her office, she had too much time to think about Dominic. Mark had given her a couple of projects—she was to research the markets in South Africa and Eastern Europe, and to liase with the sales team and the rights department as to what programming she could possibly deliver. Her research took her on the Internet, which inevitably led her to mystic and psychic websites. She added three new horoscopes to her current list, and printed out every forecast she could find on love and romance.

None of them filled her with much hope.

By the end of the week she was ready for a drink. She felt flat and deflated. For months, a year even, all she had wanted was a job like this. Now she had got it it wasn't living up to her expectations. In total she reckoned she'd spoken to some four people all week: Mark's secretary Sally, someone from human resources, the sandwich bar girl and a man who wanted to dump a broken lamp in her office.

"It'll pick up, Cat," Jo reassured her as she filled her glass. "First weeks are notoriously bad." They had chosen to meet in an unassuming Thai place on Old Compton Street.

"I hope you're right. It's just a bit soul-destroying, that's all."

"Of course it is, but it'll change. Didn't you say you've got some things lined up for next week?"

"Yes, a couple of meetings about program rights. Once I start to build up an inventory it'll get more fun. And I suppose it'll be interesting to see what goes down well in each territory, but I don't know. It's so quiet. I never thought I'd say it but I almost miss Rubens."

"Cat, I can't believe you just said that."

"At least there I chatted to people." She moved out of the way as the waiter brought a basket of shrimp crackers. "At least there was someone to say good morning to, someone to have a coffee with. Here I'm completely alone. I'm on nodding terms with a guy down the corridor and that's about it. I'm going out of my mind."

"And how's blowjob boy?" Jo bit at a chip.

Cat cringed. "I'm acting like nothing ever happened, but I hardly ever see him anyway. We met for ten minutes on my first day and had a quick cup of tea this afternoon but apart from that he's been in meetings all the time. So it's not been a problem. He is bloody good-looking though, I'd forgotten."

"He is?"

"Yes, in a don't-give-a-damn, ramshackle suit sort of a way. His tie's never straight and his hair always looks like he's just got out of bed. But don't worry, I'd never sleep with him."

"Just give him blowjobs?"

"Perfectly acceptable behavior," Cat countered, before slumping down into an embarrassed pile on the table. "I'm just hoping he's forgotten. But he makes me laugh, you know? When I met with him today he'd just got out of some heavy-duty meeting and was mimicking everyone. He's got David Boyd's lisp off to a tee. He doesn't take things seriously, I like that."

"Till he starts taking the mickey out of you." Jo was always the voice of reason. "And are you seeing Dominic this weekend?"

"He's with the kids."

"D'you think you'll ever meet them?"

"I don't know." Cat sighed. "It's all so complicated. More so than I'd realized."

She hadn't wanted to tell Jo about Dominic and Sandy; it was too strange, too hopeless. It would mean admitting her own poor sense of judgement. But she needed to talk. After her week of isolation in the office, she needed to tell someone, to share it with someone. She took a deep breath and came clean.

"Oh my God, Cat, that's just not normal." Jo frowned. "I mean, how do you cope with it?"

"I'm not convinced I do. He comes around, smokes, worries, has supper and then we go to bed. But we have great sex." She lowered her voice as the waitress arranged dishes of green chicken curry, fishcakes, noodles, mixed vegetables and rice on their table. "There's this," she searched for the right word, "heat between us."

"Yes all right, spare me the details." There were times when Cat found Jo prudish. Sex was just another thing she discussed with Lorna, like gossip or Andrew's many failings, and she didn't understand her friend's reticence.

Jo shook her head, beginning to pile food on her plate. "Well, I don't know. It all sounds like hard work to me. I don't think I could stand it."

They were distracted for a moment by noise from the next table, where a girl must have been celebrating her birthday. No less than six waiters dressed in orange Thai silk uniforms had gathered around her to sing Happy Birthday accompanied by an Oriental banjo. The centerpiece of this humiliation was an enormous ice cream piled high with whipped cream and several sparklers. The noise and color obliterated all other conversation and most other tables had to stop for a moment to watch the poor girl gamely laugh off her embarrassment.

Jo shivered. "I would rather die than have all that fuss. So where were we? Oh yes, your nutty boyfriend."

Cat picked at her food. "I have to give it a go. I do feel for him, it's almost as if we were meant to go through hell to be together." She paused. "He even told me he loved me the other day."

"And you believed him?"

"Of course I believe him," Cat snapped, but as she did she acknowledged the doubt which had been nagging at her. "Why would he say it otherwise?"

"Sounds like he's in love with the idea of being in love." Jo helped herself to more green chicken curry. "Where does he live again?"

"Don't remind me. Tooting."

"Cat, I cannot see you in Tooting. Have you seen his apartment?"

"Not yet, he always stays at mine."

"So." Jo laughed unhelpfully. "You're seeing someone who says he loves you but who won't let you see his flat or meet his kids and has been in love with another woman for four years without ever having touched her."

At this Cat had to laugh. "I'm doing well, aren't I?"

"Why do you bother?"

"Because something's pushing me on. Something stronger, something deeper than logic. I think we were meant to be together, I've always felt that. I think we have a connection. Maybe I cheated on him in a past life? Maybe my soul's chosen to go through all this in this one? It just feels like it's my karma now to rescue him."

"From what?"

In the background another Happy Birthday chorus started up. "Oh for fuck's sake," Cat snapped, irritated. "Can't anyone have a quiet fucking meal around here?" She drained her glass. "Where was I?" She tried to remember but things were getting hazy. "If it doesn't all tie up, then everything I've believed for the last few years is false. I'd feel betrayed by the Universe."

"You haven't been betrayed. You've allowed yourself to fall back on your funny theories because they made the reality easier. It wasn't just that Cat couldn't get a job and so ended up temping, it was that Cat was guided by the Universe to temp for a certain Dominic Pryce at Rubens because he was the soul mate it was her destiny to find." Jo shovelled a fishcake into her mouth triumphantly.

Cat said nothing. Maybe Jo had a point. Maybe she'd led herself along, got totally caught up in a false belief system just because it was easier. But then, without that, what did she have?

"I mean, is it worth all the effort?" Jo continued. "What will you get at the end of the day? A divorced workaholic with two kids who lives in Tooting? That's not for you. Before I knew you I really admired you, you know? I mean I'm not saying I don't now, of course," she added quickly. "But you were always elegant, always well dressed, you had loads of respect in the office and you were having a dirty little affair with someone we all fancied. I could always see you marrying some rich lawyer type and living in a fuck-off villa somewhere, having kids and nannies and appearing in society pages. You were not destined to live in Tooting."

Cat drained her glass, quietly flattered. As Jo had spoken she'd found herself transported back to Hong Kong—they could have been sitting in a Thai restaurant there, she thought, a tram-ride away from home rather than a double-decker bus.

"If I could have found a wealthy lawyer, believe me, that would have been my chosen lifestyle too. I don't know. Nothing seems to be turning out the way I'd imagined."

Jo softened. "Things will pick up."

"Funny," Cat remembered. "Tiffany Cheung told me I'd end up with some businessman type. Someone I'd meet abroad. I was convinced it was Dominic."

"But you met him in London."

"Yes but that's abroad when you're living in Hong Kong."

"I'm sorry, Cat, I just don't get a good feeling about Dominic. Still, I can talk, I have no boyfriend, I work in the middle of nowhere and I'm about to get saddled with an enormous mortgage. Shall we get another bottle?"

"Definitely." Cat was surprised she had even asked. "So it's all happening?"

"Well, I've applied; it hasn't actually come through yet. What are you looking at?" Distracted, Cat was frowning at the cloakroom.

"Sorry, Jo but, isn't that Carnage checking his coat in?"

Jo strained to look. "Fucking hell, you're right. What on earth would he be doing here?"

"Hang on, he's turning around—" Cat hid behind a potted palm tree.

"I don't think he can see you." Jo leaned down as if reaching for her bag as Max and a middle-aged woman in a knitted cream suit were led to a table toward the back of the restaurant.

Jo strained to watch them. "She's not his usual type. It's OK, he can't see anything, he's got his back to us."

"Thank God for that. Why on earth would he come here?" Cat returned to her meal.

"It's got a good reputation, but it's nothing special."

"God, that was creepy, seeing him again." Cat shivered.

"Imagine how I felt that other morning. Don't you dare ever do anything like that again."

Cat laughed guiltily. "He deserved it, Jo. Do you think he stays awake at nights thinking about what he did to me or Melanie Chan or Jerry or any of the people he fucked over? He gets away with it all—no one ever stands up to him. Come on, there must be something we can do to him."

"Like what?"

"I don't know, more bogus appointments? Just harmless things, nothing terrible."

"I don't feel the need," Jo told her blankly. "And anyway, where does all this bitterness and anger get you with all your karmic stuff? I mean, you talk about forgiving Dominic because it's your karma, well what about Carnage? Don't you think there's a chance he was just getting even for something you did to him in a past life?"

"I hadn't thought about that." Cat laughed. "But no, he's affected a lot of people, not just me. He'll get his comeuppance in the next life, he's creating all this hatred himself."

"It all sounds very far fetched," Jo said. "Oh, changing the subject, did I tell you about the Frontier reunion thing? Tony from Vibe has just got back and it's his thirtieth, so he's rented a room in some pub on Dean Street for a party. You should come along."

"I don't know," Cat said uneasily.

"Well I'm going, and I'll give you all the details when I get them."

Jo excused herself and disappeared to the loo as Cat pondered over what she had said. She, too, believed she deserved a better life, a wealthy husband, and a scenic view from an elaborate but tasteful villa. It all seemed a distant dream now. She turned to watch Max as he started his first course. Could she justify blaming him any more? Maybe it was time to let go, to concentrate on what she had now.

Or maybe, an idea popped into her head, maybe she could still have some fun?

When Jo got back they paid the bill and made to leave. At the doorway though, Cat suddenly stopped. "Jo, you go on ahead, I need to pee. Don't wait for me."

They air-kissed goodbye and Cat made a quick dash for the loo. Her heart started beating fast and she wondered if this was how it felt to be an assassin. She gathered her composure and tried not to seem too drunk. As she headed back to the counter she stopped.

"The gentleman at the back there." She pointed. "Mr. Carnegie. He's a friend of mine. It's his birthday and I was wondering if you could organize that special birthday dessert for him? I'd like it to be a surprise, and I don't want him to know it came from me."

The cashier took Cat's money and after a quick discussion the surprise was confirmed. Cat almost ran out of the restaurant, her heart was beating so fast. It would have been fun to have stayed and watched the show, but it was too dangerous.

Laughing as she walked toward the bus stop, Cat began to remember what life was all about. It was about having fun and doing something so ridiculous it made you laugh whenever you thought about it. It was about being unpredictable and adventurous. It was about being interesting enough to be gossiped about. It was about earning money to fritter away on restaurants, clothes and makeup and, of course, books about how to lead a more spiritual life.

That was what it was all about.

Fifty-Five

On the surface Cat was working well. She delivered Mark the required reports on Eastern Europe and South Africa; she met with the sales team and rights clearance people and began a detailed inventory of the programs that were available to her. Underneath, though, something was clearly wrong. Dominic wasn't changing. He'd come to her place late, smoke cigarette after cigarette and drink endless bottles of beer or wine. He'd tell her about his work problems, about worries he had for his children and about how difficult or easy his wife was currently being.

But there was no sense of him moving on. She urged him to settle a divorce agreement, but he held back, afraid of the disruption such finality might cause. Cat saw no sense. As things stood his wife sent him all the bills and asked constantly for money for clothes, school trips and household repairs.

"She needs her independence as much as you do," Cat tried. "Agree a fixed sum every year and pay her monthly, when you get paid. Let her account for herself. The way things stand she's still totally dependent on you, and even she can't enjoy that. She needs her freedom too. Maybe even," her face clouded at the thought, "for as long as you go on like this she'll think there's a chance you'll come back."

"I'd never do that." He looked appalled at the idea.

"I know that and you know that, but she doesn't. And it almost looks like you're clinging on too. And as long as she can call you every time a window needs fixing, she has a hold on you."

"She's the mother of my children, of course she has a hold on me."

She began to tire of these constant discussions. They weren't what a new relationship was supposed to be about. But then Dominic would show occasional flashes of normalcy that gave her hope. The day he announced he'd like to go to the theatre and would she book tickets to the play of her choice, for example. Or the evening he rang her from a meeting in the city, announcing that he had no intention of going back to the office, and would she meet him in a pub nearby. Or when he mentioned how he'd like to buy a new apartment, and settle somewhere permanently.

"Where would you choose?" she asked curiously.

"I don't know, around Docklands somewhere? A room with a view, you know, something over the river."

She'd caught her breath—so there was still a chance! Deep down he had the same dreams as she did, the same outlook. She would just have to be patient and see him through the rough patches. Life couldn't be all smooth—it was just those good and bad transitions again. One day Dominic would feel more relaxed about his family. One day he'd have finalized a divorce, settled financially, and would feel less guilty for having left them. One day he'd realize that he didn't love, had *never* loved, Sandy, and begin to appreciate the woman who'd been there for him through the bad times. And when that day came, it would be Cat who'd benefit, it would be Cat who'd won his love and respect, and no one else.

She could picture them, in their loft-style apartment overlooking the river, holding elegant dinner parties for friends they didn't actually have right now. City types, elegant, coffee-commercial types, who owned beautiful apartments and had second homes in France. And in this fantasy he'd lean across the dinner table, take her by the hand and tell them all how much she meant to him, and how he couldn't imagine life without her.

He'd be worth the wait, she'd tell herself. He'd be worth it.

But he didn't make it easy for her. Just as she was beginning to see some light, something else would happen. One evening he told her he had to attend a cocktail party in the city and that he would go back to his own place afterwards. Cat missed him, but also enjoyed the time it meant she had to herself. She did some yoga and tried the manifestation exercises she'd learnt from Tiffany. She sat on her bed surrounded by candles, thinking about what it really was she wanted. Love, commitment, financial security, and that spacious apartment with its beautiful view. And Dominic. But not the Dominic he was, the Dominic she wanted him to be, the Dominic she saw occasional glimpses of. A Dominic who was dynamic, funny, warm and extroverted, and not the morose, brooding Dominic she knew and tolerated.

She did some deep breathing exercises and began, visualizing her home, her view, her happiness. She spelled it out, one aspect after the other, until she had completed the picture. And in the beautiful home she had created, with the warm relationship she imagined, she felt at peace; she could have sat there for hours and probably would have, had the phone not started to ring. It was Dominic, and he sounded terrible.

"I know I wasn't going to, but can I come over?" he asked her.

Cat told him that of course he could and prepared herself for bed, elated. He wanted her! When he was a bit drunk Dominic's heart was pulled toward her. Maybe this was his first step to realizing how important she had become to him? When he arrived he fell into her arms, but not out of passion. Dominic had tears in his eyes and was fighting to control them.

"I'm sorry," he kept repeating. "Can I get a drink?"

"Let me make you some tea," she told him virtuously. "More alcohol isn't going to do you any good." He nodded forlornly like a boy with a grazed knee. "What happened anyway?" She put the kettle on.

"I'm sorry." He held his head in his hands. "It was wrong of me to come here."

"No it wasn't, Dominic. You can share things with me." She came back into the living room.

"I don't know. I don't think I should be putting you through all this."

"All what?" Cat's chest began to tighten.

"Sandy," he said quietly, before taking a huge gulp of air to calm himself.

"Ah." Cat steadied herself. "What about her?"

"She brought her fiancé along. I'm sorry, Cat."

His face crumpled and he rubbed his eyes. She went back into the kitchen. As she poured boiling water over a tea bag she watched him. She loved every bit of him, and that was what hurt her so much. She loved his hair, his dark eyes, his broad shoulders, his flat stomach and his lean legs. She loved the dark curls on his chest and arms and how they crept out from under the cuffs of his shirts. She even loved his suits.

But did she love the man himself? Cat no longer knew that for certain.

"So did you talk to him?" She tried to be matter of fact about it.

"I shook his hand." He took a deep breath. "I've met him before, he works for another bank."

"And what bothered you most, seeing them together?"

"She was showing off her ring to people. And smiling. She looked radiant." Cat couldn't quite imagine it. "The way she looked at him." He broke off, unable to finish.

"She looked like a woman in love with a man she's going to marry." Cat handed him the mug.

"Yes." He took a sip of tea. "She never loved me. She never had any feelings for me."

"No, she didn't, but she led you on by accepting your gifts. Still." She tried to be fair. "Maybe she felt awkward that it was her boss offering them, maybe she felt she had to accept them? Maybe you put her in an awkward position?"

She felt a certain power in saying the words—they made her look impartial—using them she rose above the situation. He said nothing, just drank his tea thoughtfully.

"You're very good for me, you know? I do love you."

He held her as they fell asleep, but she couldn't help wondering whether he was holding on to her out of love, or whether she had just become a security blanket. She didn't sleep well. As she dozed she drew a comparison with Declan. A different relationship with a different cast of characters and staging, but the same theme. She was falling into the same pattern—in love with a man who was in love with someone else. It felt like a challenge from the Universe. Was she to get trapped in the same cycle over and over until she herself broke out of it?

She had made a new rule, hadn't she? Never to get involved with a man who loved someone else. And yet there she was, doing just that.

The next morning, Dominic seemed to have got over his pain. As he was getting dressed, he picked up a book from her bedside table. It was called *Past Lives, Past Loves.* "What on earth's this?" he asked, frowning.

"It's about past life regression, and people discovering they'd had past lives together," Cat told him.

"What a load of rubbish," he muttered.

"I don't think it is, I think it's fascinating," she countered.

"So you believe in all this, do you?" He waved the book before dropping it back on the table.

"I believe it's a fascinating theory, and the more I think about it, the more it makes sense."

"It does, does it? So who were you before, then, Cleopatra?"

Cat thought for a second how she preferred him when he was depressed. "No, I was not Cleopatra, and anyone who ever thinks like that is deluding themselves. But yes, I think we've all had other lives, and that those lives have an influence on who we are, what we do, who we meet and what happens to us in this life."

He slurped some tea, an amused look on his face.

"It makes sense, Dominic." She tried to draw an example out of the air. "For instance, you and Sandy. You have these—extraordinary—feelings for her," she began, enjoying seeing his face fall. "Why do you think that is? I bet there's a past life connection there somewhere."

"What nonsense." Irritated now, he began knotting his tie.

"Why is it nonsense? Why? Because there's no scientific explanation? It's a basic tenet of two world religions, you know, you can't just dismiss it out of hand."

"So what do you say happens, then? You die and what, you come straight back?"

"No, I don't think so, not straight away. It's all about learning and experience. You have to go through the mistakes and lessons you learned in the last life. And from that, from that basis, you create your next life."

"With whom? With whom do you do all this?"

"Spirits, spirit guides, I don't know exactly. I think there's a whole team up there, probably of more experienced souls who are in between lives and there to help others."

"Oh come on," he scoffed.

"Why not? The Universe is far more complex than life here, you know."

"Oh, Catherine." He laughed, and she could see he was tiring of the conversation. She was disappointed, but not surprised, at how closed his mind was.

"Dominic, come and look here." She pulled him by his tie to the French window that led onto the terrace.

"See the little cat, Precious? What do you think the world means to her, eh? The world is what, this terrace, the garden, the neighbor's terrace, let's say this whole block. She might be aware that every now and then she's bundled into a car and taken to the vet, and so there might be a bit more to the world than this bit here. But if you tell that cat that this is in fact just one street of many in a huge city, and that this one city is just one of many in one small country, and that this country is just one of many in one continent, and that—"

"Yes, yes, I get the picture."

"It's too complex for the cat to understand. It's way above her levels of comprehension, just as there are undoubtedly things that are way above our level of comprehension. But it doesn't mean they don't exist," she ended triumphantly. "Absence of evidence does not mean evidence of absence."

He smiled and shook his head. There was nothing he could say, so instead he drew her toward him and kissed her forehead. "Very clever, Catherine. And now I think we're late."

They took the tube into work together and she changed trains at Embankment. She was pleased with the way she had fought her argument, but felt inherently disappointed at the same time. He was on such a different wavelength to hers, and she couldn't decide why the Universe had so wanted her to be with him. Maybe she was to teach him these things, to lift his mind out of the daily drudge and make him focus on bigger, wider issues? Or maybe, as she'd feared, the Universe had brought him to her as a test. The parallels with Declan were shouting at her, laughing at her, and she felt like she was falling into a trap.

If she let him go, would she be passing the test?

She couldn't bear the thought. What would life be without him? Life would be a lonely job in an oversized office full of broken furniture. Life would be total isolation, with the odd e-mail and card game to keep her company. It would be a meaningless void.

Once at her desk she turned to her favorite horoscopes. None offered much inspiration. She screened programs until midday, then played cards for half an hour until it was time to pick up a sandwich. She'd discovered that at one o'clock they showed *The Pride and the Passion* on satellite, and it became a fixed appointment in her diary. The story line had moved on a bit, with Fire engaged to be married to Esselle, one of the fitness instructors at the health farm. But his former girlfriend, the supermodel Brandy, had arrived suffering from a booze and drug problem. Fire was yet to find out that years ago Brandy had been told by her agency to dump him for her career's sake, but that it was something she'd regretted all her life. Cat liked Esselle and approved of the upcoming marriage, but it was obvious that Brandy was going to fight to get Fire back.

Another love triangle, Cat thought, biting into her shrimp salad sandwich, and therefore another sign.

"OK, Universe," she muttered heavily. "Tell me what I should do next."

Fifty-Six

To Cat's surprise, Dominic suggested she spend the following Saturday night at his place in Tooting Bec. She took it as an indication that he wanted to share more of his life with her, and was pleased. She allowed herself an hour to get there on public transport, and went through alien areas like Stockwell and Balham before getting off at his station. He lived in a quiet street behind the main road, full of semi-detached houses with large bay windows. His looked no different from any other, even down to the floral curtains which billowed out in the wind.

He greeted her at the main door. "It's not as nice as your place by any means," he told her sheepishly, and she quickly saw why.

A dirty beige carpet led her through to the living room. In it were two oversized floral armchairs, a sagging brown sofa and a small Formica coffee table, on which he used old CD ROMs as coasters. On one side of the wall he had a computer, sound system, TV and video set up. It was the only area that looked clean and orderly. In his bedroom there was a double bed covered in a dark blue comforter pushed against one wall, a wardrobe against another and a heavy dark chest of drawers opposite that. A beaten-up armchair, covered in old clothes, filled one corner. Through a tiny window she could see an unkempt garden and the back of another house.

"I'll get some wine." He feigned cheerfulness as Cat tried to disguise her disappointment. She had come to terms with the thought that his place wouldn't be the minimalist haven of urban chic full of African artefacts that she'd once imagined, but she hadn't expected it to be quite so depressing either. She followed him into the kitchen where he was reaching for a bottle of wine out of a fridge with a broken handle. He opened it and filled two tumblers. What was it about men and decent glasses?

He ordered a greasy Indian take-out which they ate watching TV. Cat watched, but paid no attention. What was she doing here? As much as she had feelings for Dominic, the package he came in was becoming less and less desirable. In his suit, in his stride, he looked every part the type of man she'd always envisaged for herself. But sitting there on the floral armchair, in a pair of oversized jeans, some beaten-up moccasins and a fading green sweatshirt he looked undistinguished, someone who'd disappear in a crowd of three. She settled back on a sofa she suspected was giving her fleas and imagined life without him. She would drink less, practice yoga more and eat healthier food. She would read books rather than listen to Dominic's woes and concentrate on work rather than Internet horoscope sites.

She sighed heavily. How dull. And how superficial of her to want to pull out on the basis of the man's apartment—a place he had rented because he needed to escape his marriage. It was a start, nothing more than that, and she shouldn't judge him by it.

But as she watched him smoke and drink his way through an obscure 70s B movie while she herself was longing for bed, she began to waver. He was taking her for granted. She had given him so much leeway he no longer had any impetus to get over Sandy. As far as he was concerned, Cat was warm and understanding, and there was no need to even try to move on. He needed a shock. And she needed to break a pattern. She needed to end their relationship, make him realize how untenable the situation was. She needed him to need her, to value her, to realize how much she meant to him and brought to his life. Right now she felt as worthless as his sitting room furniture.

Depressed, she started getting ready for bed. In the bathroom she was astonished to find that Dominic had exactly the same toothbrush as she. Exactly the same. Of all the brands, of all the styles, even down to the same shade of turquoise, they were a perfect match. Was it another sign? Brushing her teeth, Cat wondered why the Universe was so determined they be together. She stared at the child's toothbrush left on the basin. Was she meant to be a stepmother to his children, was that it?

Cat had never felt particularly maternal, had never felt the deep, intimate craving for motherhood. It was something for the future, she'd always told herself. She enjoyed her freedom too much, and would cringe at the sound of crying infants in stores. The thought of childbirth was abhorrent. Having spent most of her thirty-two years trying to flatten her stomach, the last thing she wanted was to watch it balloon up out of her control.

So was that it, the Universe wanted her to stepmother Dominic's children? Because she had never wanted children of her own, she was now being presented with two of them? Was that it? A challenge that she, herself, had chosen before this life began? The more she thought about it, the more it made a weird kind of sense. Didn't she read about people all the time who'd spent their lives overcoming their deepest fears—fears that must have been created by their own higher selves, their own souls, purely as a challenge to be overcome?

She took a deep breath. Was the Universe now challenging her to live in South London and look after two kids?

They couldn't live in South London, she decided as she removed her eye makeup. Maybe they'd buy a big house in Barnes, or Mortlake, somewhere green and civilized. It would still be a reasonable commute for both of them. Maybe she'd be quite a good mother; maybe she and Dominic would even have a child of their own one day?

The couple next door started fighting as she climbed into his cold and lumpy bed. If she were to spend her life raising his children, she thought, she had to have one hundred per cent of his love. She couldn't commit to a responsibility like that without it. And in order to achieve that, her mind raced, she had to pull away, let him see what he was missing. They could only move forward if she did this. She could only move forward if she did it. If not, might she be condemned to a life of relationships with men who wouldn't, or couldn't commit; men who clung on to old loves and old feelings, oblivious to the love she had to give?

She had to break the pattern; she could see that clearly now. It was the strong, mature thing to do. It would focus his mind. It would hurt, and it might take a few weeks for the effects to filter through, but he would get there eventually. How many weeks, though? Cat felt a cold stab in her stomach. How long would it take him? A month, perhaps? God, a month seemed like an eternity. Four whole weeks without him; but then, she urged herself, then they'd be so much the stronger for it.

Cat lay there restlessly, unable to get comfortable, unable to sleep. The couple next door kept shouting. She would wait until the weekend was over. She would tell him over dinner next week. Or maybe on the phone? Wouldn't that be easier, wouldn't she just weaken face-to-face? *Give me a sign, Universe*, she pleaded sleepily. But hadn't it just done that? Weren't the matching toothbrushes exactly the sign she'd been looking for? Jo would laugh at that one. *What can I do?* she asked. *Tell me in my dream, give me a clue.*

She woke to the sound of the phone ringing, and Dominic's irritated groan. It was just 7:30. He got up and took the call as Cat strained to listen. He came back looking sorry.

"That was my wife." He sat on the bed heavily. "Something's come up. She wants me to have the children today."

"Dominic," Cat scolded. "You can't let her dominate your weekend like this. You are responsible for them on alternative weekends, she can't suddenly change the rules on a whim."

"You try telling her that."

She took a deep sigh. "So is she bringing them around here?"

"Yes. Around nine o'clock. I'm sorry, Cat."

"It's not your fault. You're a good dad." She climbed out of bed, almost grateful to be leaving. What had they been going to do with their Sunday anyway? They'd made no plans. This, perhaps, was the sign she'd been looking for, the sign to make a clean break. She took a quick shower, gathered her belongings and left.

She felt a mixture of things as she walked toward the station. Irritation, disappointment, but overwhelmingly, relief. She bought a paper, flipping through the headlines first before turning to the horoscope page.

It could have been written especially for her: *Like a needle stuck on a record, your life seems to be spinning around repeating itself, falling short on expectation and long on disappointment. What is needed now is a leap of faith—a bold act in which to re-evaluate yourself and your life. Others may disagree and find your decision unacceptable. But give them time, and like a rotating top, they will soon come spinning back to see your point of view.*

She was going to do it! She was going to call him on Monday and tell him it was all over. Tell him that until he sorted himself out she couldn't continue their relationship. She felt at once panic-stricken and elated. This was the thing to do! The short sharp shock he needed to refocus his life. He would thank her for it—the horoscope as much as said it.

As she changed at Embankment for the District Line, her feeling of relief increased. She jumped off the tube at Sloane Square and walked the length of Kings Road home, stopping off for some shopping. She felt unashamedly relieved to be back in civilization, to be able to buy luxury foods and wine again, and suddenly couldn't wait to get home. She would go to the garden center and spend the afternoon planting pansies and geraniums and puttering about on the terrace, and then she'd have a glass of wine in the cool spring sunshine.

And what would Dominic be doing—taking his kids to McDonald's? She knew whose life she preferred.

It was a risk, but everything was going to work out fine.

Fifty-Seven

"That Brandy's hot stuff, isn't she?" Mark turned to her suddenly as they rode down in the elevator.

"I can't believe you watch?" Cat said in delight.

"Well, I don't all the time, but I caught five minutes this afternoon."

"It's my lunch time fix," she admitted. *The Pride* and a sandwich."

The elevator stopped for more people to get in. "You all right?" he asked as they were pushed to one side. "I feel a bit bad that I haven't spent more time with you."

"I'm fine," she lied. "But it does get a bit lonely in that office."

"I'm trying to hire some more people to keep you company. A business analyst, for starters."

Cat nodded. Hardly the sort of person she could discuss her love life and horoscopes with. And would she still be able to watch *The Pride* over lunch?

They reached the ground and everyone spilled out.

"Did you get my e-mail about Hungary?"

"Yes I did, I'm putting some draft schedules together. It's a bit frustrating, though, it's all pretty old stuff."

"We'll see about that. Any plans for the evening?" Mark asked, nodding at someone in the distance.

"I'm meeting up with a friend." Cat followed his stare to see a stunning girl waiting for him in reception. She was elegantly thin, had a pale golden tan and Scandinavian blonde hair, and was wearing a cream cashmere turtleneck over some expensive-look-ing suede trousers.

Mark introduced her as Emma, who was Swedish, and a model. Cat was stunned that he could be with someone quite so beautiful. Somehow it elevated him in her mind, he became more interesting because of her. How long had they been together, Cat wondered, or did they even live together? She knew so little about her boss.

"What about you?" she asked.

"Some fashion benefit or other," he told her. "Benefiting out of work models or something." He winked.

Emma tutted. "It's an AIDS awareness benefit," she corrected him with a resigned smile, as he gently put his arm around her shoulders and escorted her out. Cat watched as he hailed a cab and then held the door open for her. What a dark old horse Mark was, she thought to herself.

Walking down toward Soho she wondered whether they'd ever get to the stage where she and Dominic and Mark and Emma would become friends, go to dinners and functions together?

She got to the wine-bar a few minutes late, to find that Jo still hadn't arrived. She ordered a bottle and wished she was waiting for Dominic, and had a brief fantasy that he'd suddenly appeared, coincidentally, with some American clients. He'd pulled away from them to see her, and begged her to take him back.

She was just deciding whether to be firm or to back down completely when Jo arrived.

"Sorry I'm late." She kissed Cat on both cheeks. "The tube was delayed for a quarter of an hour. Oh good, you've got a bot-tle." She sat down on the stool next to Cat's and poured herself a glass. "So tell me about Dominic?"

"I don't know what to say, really. He went very quiet."

"So what exactly did you say to him?"

"I just said how I've been doing a lot of thinking. How I don't think he's ready for a relationship yet, because he still has feelings for Sandy and is too entangled with his wife. I told him I thought we needed some time out. That I've been as supportive as I could over his children and his wife and even the Sandy business, but that I can't take any more."

"And you think this'll bring him back to you?" Jo asked.

"I think he needs a short sharp shock. I don't want to be taken for granted. And I told myself ages ago not to have anything to do with an attached man, not after all the Declan nonsense."

"Well, I hope it works," Jo said doubtfully.

"He just went so quiet. He kept saying 'I know.' It was a bit frustrating that he didn't protest. I mean, he could have insisted that I was exaggerating about Sandy. But he just agreed with everything I said."

"That doesn't sound good," Jo said.

Cat sighed. "I mean, he could have asked me to reconsider, to give him more time, see him again and talk things over."

"You caught him by surprise," Jo tried. "And let's face it, he was in the office. You've no idea what he was doing, whether he had to go into a meeting or was expecting a call or anything."

"True. I hate the fact that I no longer know about his days. I used to enjoy it when I was in control of them."

She tried to picture him sitting at his desk as she broke the news. Would he have fallen into despair, told Sophie to cancel his appointments and gone home, buying a bottle of whisky on the way back? As if.

"Well, give him time. That was the whole point of this, wasn't it? To give him time to sort his life out, and then come back to you even stronger?"

"Yes, that was the idea." His acceptance had been unsettling, and Cat had a nasty feeling that it wasn't going to work. She tried to rally. "But at least I've done something. I had to make some kind of stand after all this." She paused. "So what's your news? What's happening with the apartment?"

"Nothing, I still haven't heard. Why does everything have to take so long?"

They finished the bottle, Cat only half-listening to Jo's house-hunting stories. There could always be a message waiting for her when she got home. *He* might even be waiting for her when she got home.

Stop! She told herself. Give him at least a week, and then maybe he'd call.

"I'd better order another one," Jo said, and Cat nodded in relief.

Tomorrow, she told herself, she would remain alcohol-free and practice yoga, meditate for a while and start on her new book about near-death experiences. But tonight, at least, she was allowed this indulgence.

Fifty-Eight

"So I've got this proposed deal in Budapest," Mark started. "And the schedule Cat has given me, with no disrespect to her, is a piece of crap."

He was sitting in Cat's office with the head of program sales, the head of rights clearance and two sales managers.

"I cannot walk into a meeting and offer them a channel that's made up of nerdy detectives running to their crappy sedans, their flared trousers flapping around their ankles."

"Mark, you of all people must understand our position," the head of sales started. He looked like a government official denying his involvement in an arms-dealing scandal. "It's a growing market. We simply cannot give away product that we could be selling for a profit."

Mark rubbed his forehead. "What exactly have the Hungarians been buying up to date? Dramas? Soaps? Sitcoms? What deals have you actually done?"

"Several stations have expressed interest in our product. I can't jeopardize relationships like this."

"Expressed interest? Any old moron can express interest. How many actual deals have you signed?"

Cat loved his directness, but was sure he was ruffling too many refined Trafalgar feathers, and wondered how long he'd get away with it.

"That's not the point and well you know it. We've been in

talks for some time, and can confidently expect deals to start coming through any time now."

"Nuggets," Mark said abruptly. "Give me some nuggets then. Two or three lead shows amongst all the crap. Give me short license periods—three months' exclusivity and then you're free to sell them on, Cat. Tell us what nuggets you want."

Cat jumped up, reaching for the papers she'd drawn up. "Well, here's my first draft schedule," she said, offering everyone a copy. "I've shaded in three different priorities, drama being the highest."

"And very nicely shaded they are too," Mark quipped.

"Say you give me two of these nine o'clock dramas." She tried to compose herself, citing two of the longest-running series she could think of.

The head of sales was about to answer when Cat's phone rang. Noting Mark's irritation, she picked the receiver up and shrank into it.

There was an agonized pause. "Hi Cat. It's Dominic."

She had waited over two weeks for his call, and it had to come now of all times. He sounded terrible. "Is this a bad time?"

"I'm afraid it is," she whispered. "I'm in a meeting."

"I was just wondering if I could see you."

"Of course you can." She tried to sound warm, but not desperate. More importantly right now, she had to get off the line.

"What are you doing tomorrow?"

"Oh, damn, I've got this Frontier thing to go to." She hoped that if Mark was listening, he might think it was work.

"Never mind," he said sadly. "Maybe another time. I'll talk to you soon."

He hung up. Damn him! Couldn't he have come up with another evening, tried just a bit harder? Cat turned back to the meeting to find everyone getting up to go.

"Thanks for your contribution," Mark smirked.

Cat felt like slapping him. "I'm sorry. That's the trouble with having meetings in an office."

She wanted to berate him for mocking her, and to find out what she'd just missed. And more than anything she wanted to turn the clock back and to have been sitting there alone when Dominic's call came through.

"Is it time for *The Pride* yet?" Mark looked at his watch.

"It will have just started." Cat picked up the remote control and found the channel, and he sat down next to her.

"Did Esselle find out that Fire was boffing Brandy yet?" he asked.

"He hasn't boffed her yet," she told him. "We've moved back to Lake and whether she's going to marry that boring accountant or not. I hadn't realized she's been married before and has kids?"

"Yes, that's right," Mark remembered. "She married a phony plastic surgeon who botched a face-lift and then mysteriously disappeared. They found his clothes on the shore but never his body."

The phone rang and it was Sally, trying to find Mark.

"I'd better go." He got up reluctantly. "So you'll action all that, will you?"

"Action what? I missed that last bit."

"Nuggets," he told her. "We're allowed four nuggets for the first six months until viewing figures take off. But choose them in the next couple of days, as I want to go down there pretty soon."

"To Budapest?" Cat asked.

"Where else?" He smiled, looking at her for just a bit too long before walking out.

Fifty-Nine

"I'm not convinced I can do this." In a crowded Soho wine-bar, Cat took a hit on her glass of rosé.

"Of course you can," Jo scolded her. "It'll be fun to catch up with everyone. Once we've finished this bottle you'll feel better."

"I don't know," Cat said glumly. "I won't know anyone." She knew as she said it that she sounded like a child.

"Will you stop? You've been so obsessed with Dominic lately you've forgotten that anyone else exists. You know loads of people, Cat, you've just never bothered to keep in touch."

That much was true and Cat knew it. She'd deliberately avoided old friends when she was temping, and now she had a job it felt too late, she'd fallen out of the habit.

"It's going to be a good turn-out," Jo continued. "I bet you have a much better time than you expect."

"I don't know. I keep thinking I should have said yes to Dominic." Cat drained her glass and refilled both of theirs.

"No," Jo wailed. "Why make yourself so available? You did absolutely the right thing. You want to make him want you more, and you're not going to do that by always being around. Treat 'em mean, keep 'em keen. You've got to make him realize that he might lose you if he's not careful."

"I suppose." Cat remained unconvinced. She had a bad feeling about turning Dominic down when he'd finally made an effort.

And now another day had passed without so much as a call, a message or an e-mail. It was hard to take.

"You know Simone's back?" Jo went on. "She should be there tonight."

"Oh really?" Cat tried to sound pleased. She didn't really give a damn if the Queen herself turned up. She didn't much feel like talking to anyone who wasn't Dominic.

"You never know, maybe even Declan will show." If Jo had wanted to shock Cat out of her inertia, she managed to do just that.

"Oh God, that'd be all I need." Declan! She hadn't thought about him for a long time. "I thought he was shacked up with Harriet in the country. He wouldn't come, would he?"

"I don't know. There'd be loads of people there he'd know, but he seems to have gone underground these days. No one's heard anything about him."

"Still, it would be funny wouldn't it?" Cat felt herself rallying, and topped up their glasses again. "And would he bring the lovely Harriet, I wonder? And would she have washed her hair for the occasion?"

"That's the spirit. Should we have another bottle before we get going?"

"Why not, I'm going to need all the alcohol I can get tonight." As she said it Cat knew the second bottle was a mistake. But what did she care? What was one more mistake after a long succession of them?

They left the bar an hour later and headed for the pub, and the private room upstairs which Tony had rented. Cat hated pubs at the best of times but this one seemed particularly grimy. It was also packed full of people whose names she couldn't remember. She headed for the bar and ordered a drink. The wine was vile but it gave her something to do as Jo disappeared to circulate.

Cat chatted aimlessly to a couple of tape operators she remembered who were back working for a Soho facilities house. Simone the makeup artist was pretty far gone and greeted her like a long-lost best friend, and Cat enjoyed their drunken gossip. The wine was tasting better and she had another glass. At the bar Tony approached her. He'd added another tattoo to his collection and had shaved a stripe through his right eyebrow.

"Cat, great to see you. Where are you now?"

"At Trafalgar, doing international channel development," Cat told him self-consciously, trying not to sound too corporate. "You?"

"Freelancing. Let me give you my card, in case you ever need a producer."

"Thank you, I might one day." They chatted about different people, events in Hong Kong and their adjustment to London life. Cat was surprised how well they got on, but as her third glass of wine slipped down, she reckoned she could make friends with the antichrist if she wanted.

Suddenly Tony was telling her, "You're great, you know that? So easy to talk to. I always thought you were a bit of an ice-queen."

"An ice-queen, me?"

"You know, unapproachable. Wearing your sexy designer suits with those long legs of yours. I always had such a crush on you."

"You did?" Cat was astounded. She had always felt rather self-conscious around him, straight-laced and conservative.

"Why are you so surprised? You're gorgeous." She began to realize how drunk he was. "I still fancy you, you know. So what d'you think? Do I stand a chance, then?"

Cat froze, sobering up quickly. "Well um, I'm really flattered, Tony, but, I'm afraid I'm seeing someone else."

His face fell. "Yeah, I should have known. No one's going to leave you alone for long." A friend of his approached and awkwardly Tony turned away.

Little do you know, Cat thought to herself, still not sure whether his declaration had been a joke or not. She moved to the window to get some air, and looked out over Dean Street. Opposite was a bar she'd once met Dominic in before going to the cinema. She remembered waiting for him excitedly. She'd just got her job and her man and life had seemed so optimistic. And just as she'd thought it was all going so well, so it had turned to shit. *Be strong,* she told herself. *You've done the right thing. He'll come back, and things will be stronger and better than ever before. If someone like Tony can think you're so fucking great,* she shuddered at the thought, *then you must be doing something right.*

In the corner of her eye she could see Simone clinging on to a graphic designer, and she smiled. Life seemed so uncomplicated for some people. Or maybe Simone was just as capable of getting depressed as she was, but was just better at disguising it?

"Cat, is that you?" It was a warm, familiar voice that spoke right to her heart. She turned around. His hair was cut shorter, and looked a little darker, as was his skin paler. Maybe he'd grown slightly older even, but his eyes still twinkled, and his smile still looked like it had been reserved especially for her.

"For fuck's sake, Declan Moran." She smiled, and he kissed her warmly on both cheeks, though neither of them moved their heads much, and their lips touched both times. He held her hand, and she thought how funny it was that after all those months of avoiding public contact, they could now be open. "I wasn't expecting to see you here."

"Me neither. What are you doing?" He bought her another drink and she told him about her job, her apartment and her life, carefully missing out any reference to Dominic.

"So what about you?" she asked. "You're living out in the country now, I hear?"

"Berkshire, yes. In semi-retirement." He laughed. "I do a lot of work for one company but I make sure I get plenty of free time."

"To do what?"

"Fishing." He laughed again. "I've taken up fishing."

She pictured him fondly in a sou'wester eating cheese and pickle sandwiches on a riverbank.

"And how's Harriet?" She had to ask, had to destroy the moment. She couldn't let the evening go without finding out. His face darkened slightly.

"That's all over," he sighed. "A few months now."

"I don't believe it." Despite her shock, Cat laughed. "All those months of hell you put me through and *now* you finish?"

Declan smiled, as if remembering the months of hell Cat had put him through. "I know. I moved in with her when I got back, but it didn't work out."

"Why on earth not? You've known each other for years."

"She was having an affair," Declan told her sadly. "She'd started seeing someone at work."

"A colleague?" Cat was fascinated. She no longer felt that raw,

bitter pain which ripped through her stomach, just a lurid fascination for the woman who looked like the 'before' in a plastic
surgery ad. "Which one?" She dug out the only name she knew at
World Daytime Network, memorized from a card she'd picked
up at MIP.

"No, no." Declan shook his head. "It wasn't him. It was a
woman, to tell you the truth."

Cat leaned forward in shock as he continued.

"I think it's just a fling, I don't think she's become a full-time
lesbian or anything. I think she's just going through an experi-
mental phase."

"Declan, I, I don't know what to say." Cat clasped her mouth
in case she began to laugh.

"Declan, my darling, give us a big kiss." Simone had just spotted him, lurched across and clung on to his waist as if she'd fall
over without it. Cat smiled affectionately, though she felt Declan
looked sad and slightly lost.

Could they possibly get back together, she wondered? Oh how
strangely the Universe worked. She'd lost Dominic because of
this reunion, but might she just have gained Declan back? She
watched him talking to Simone and wondered if it wasn't too late
for them. She tried to picture herself in a cottage in Berkshire
with a fridge full of maggots. It was a far cry from the loft she was
supposed to be sharing with Dominic. *Stupid cow!* She scolded
herself for her overactive imagination. *You stupid cow.*

Simone finally moved on and Declan turned back to her. "So
what about you then, any man on the scene?"

Was he fishing now, she wondered? "Yes, sort of. I've been
seeing a banker." She laughed at the look of disapproval on his
face. She wasn't sure what more to say. She wanted to give Declan
the idea that he could see her again if he wanted to, yet couldn't
quite bring herself to write off Dominic just yet.

"I wanted to call you." Declan's face changed. "When I heard
what happened, I wanted to call. But there was never the time,
and when I got back from my trip, you'd already gone. I hoped
you'd write, or call, or something, but you just vanished."

"I thought it was better that way. To make a clean break. We
weren't going anywhere, let's face it."

"Look at you, Catherine," he said admiringly. "You're out of my league. You'd never be satisfied with someone like me. A banker, now that's more like it."

Cat blinked back the tears. "It's not that great a relationship, to be honest." She tried to laugh, tried to make it look like it didn't hurt.

Then a woman appeared. Unfamiliar to Cat, she had a slim body encased in tight black jeans and a leather jacket. Her hair was dark blonde and fell into her pale green eyes. She had a small, upturned nose and teeth that were slightly too big for her mouth.

"Found you at last," she said affectionately to Declan, linking her arm through his. Declan kissed her quickly then turned guiltily to Cat.

"Cat, this is Amanda." He introduced her. "Amanda, Catherine."

They shook hands, sizing each other up before Amanda turned back to Declan. "We've got to get going, the restaurant's booked for ten minutes' time."

"Oh OK. Sorry, Cat." Declan looked at her apologetically. "It was great seeing you again." He kissed her on the cheek.

"Great to see you too, Declan." So that was it, then. He had found someone else already, and had no intention of seeing her again. She covered her feelings up, smiling warmly at both of them. "And to relive some happy memories," she added for the hell of it.

The smile fell from Declan's face as Amanda led him out. How long would it be before she started plaguing him with questions? Cat wondered. At the top of the stairs? Downstairs as they left? On the walk to the restaurant? Or would she fall silent over dinner and sulk until he drew the jealousy out of her, like the venom from a wasp sting?

"Cat, you OK?" It was Jo.

"Fine, thanks. Fuck her," she heard herself slur, and felt suddenly very drunk and deflated.

"Who was she?"

"Declan's new girlfriend, Amanda. Harriet's become a dyke."

"Oh my God, are you serious?" Jo was stunned. "Do you want another drink?"

"No, you know, I've had enough. I should be getting home."

"Are you sure you're OK?"

"Yes, just bombed and tired. Fucking hell, I just saw Declan Moran." Using his surname alone seemed to distance him from her. Cat shook her head in disbelief. "I'll call you tomorrow."

The walk out took longer than she expected, with lots of kissing of people she didn't expect to see again. As she got closer to the door she caught her breath at the sight of Jeremy Glover walking in.

"Cat, what a surprise. How are you?" He smiled.

"Fine, thanks. What are you doing here?"

"I'm over here doing some recruitment, and I heard that something was going on. What are you up to these days?"

"Trafalgar Broadcasting." Cat tried to sober up. "Doing international channel development. You know, assessing new markets, potential joint venture partners, strategic partnership analysis, assessing programming needs and developments, that sort of thing." She tried to make it sound important and fulfilling.

"That sounds great." To her relief he actually looked impressed. "You know, Variety isn't the same without you," he added with a condescending smile.

"So what kind of recruitment are you doing here?" She held on to the wall to steady herself.

"Promo makers. I fired those two clowns you hired."

"Eddie and Darrell? You know, I never hired them, I inherited them from Max."

"Whatever. I've redesigned the whole look of the channel and our viewing figures are really going up. Though I must say it's been a bit weird lately, with Max out of the country for so long." He ran his fingers through his floppy blonde hair.

"Yeah, what's going on there?" she asked. "How's the company running without him?"

"Probably more successfully." Glover laughed. "Though I shouldn't be disloyal, Max and I get on really well, he gives me a lot of freedom. But it is odd that he's been away so long."

Suddenly Cat felt acutely irritated. Jeremy was leading *her* life, the life that she had created for herself and yet somehow thrown away. She would never know how she came up with what she said next. The idea just popped into her mind and was out of her mouth before she even had time to think about it. It felt like it wasn't even her speaking it; it was as though it was coming from a disembodied voice that had simply used her as a vehicle.

"Well, the story I've heard is that some triad gang has got a contract out on him. He daren't go back as he'd only end up floating face down in the harbor."

"What?" Jeremy looked incredulous. "Are you serious?"

"That's what I heard." She shrugged. "From a couple of very reliable sources." She wanted to give the impression that she still had connections; she wanted him to believe that she was still tied to Hong Kong and to Frontier itself. She enjoyed seeing the look of shock tinged with admiration on his face.

"That's extraordinary."

"Not really. He was always shagging vulnerable Chinese girls on the promise of a big TV career that would never materialize." *Where was it all coming from?* "He just shagged the wrong woman this time. A triad daughter, or sister or something." She wobbled against the wall and hoped she hadn't just given herself away.

"Jesus Christ," Glover whistled. "But you know, come to think of it, it all makes sense." He looked thoughtful for a second, as if piecing a mystery together.

Cat nodded wisely. "Keep it to yourself of course," she said, knowing that he wouldn't. "And for God's sake you didn't hear it from me."

"Of course." Jeremy looked shocked. "Of course I didn't."

Feeling more pleased with herself, Cat went to the loo and then left, walking down Old Compton Street toward Piccadilly. She began laughing as she remembered snatches of the evening: Tony's surprise infatuation, Harriet's lesbianism, Amanda's imminent jealousy and the look of shock on Jeremy Glover's face. She kept giggling, burying her face in her scarf so as not to look like a madwoman, until crossing Piccadilly to the bus stop she noticed she'd been trailing two sheets of toilet paper from the heel of her left shoe. She disentangled herself and laughed again, for the sake of anyone who might have been watching.

She dozed on the bus, waking just in time for her stop. Walking up the stairs to her door, she was reminded again of Dominic and her stomach heaved. Gingerly she looked at her answering machine, but the light wasn't flashing.

"Bastard," she hissed, and steadying herself, picked up the receiver and dialled 1471. The last number was Jo's from the day before. Feeling a sudden need to talk, she pressed three. After a couple of rings Jo picked up.

"Oh good, you're home. Dominic still hasn't called, the creep."

"Yeah, I've just this second walked in. Look, he knew you were going out tonight." Jo sounded as tired and as drunk as Cat was.

"But even so, he might have tried. I mean it's late." She tried to look at her watch. "Isn't he worried that I might have stayed out?"

"He probably is, but doesn't want to show it."

"Maybe," she paused, before rallying. "Bloody hell though, what a night. I'm so glad you made me go." Cat's brain was working but her mouth couldn't quite keep up. "So Tony from Music's in love with me, Harriet's a dyke and Declan's got Mandy." She spat out the girl's name. "But Harriet's a dyke!! How humiliating can that be for a man? I knew it couldn't last, it just didn't feel right, you know? What was he thinking, seeing her in the first place? I mean what?"

"Cat, can we talk tomorrow?" Jo stopped her. "I've just had to pee in an old mug because I couldn't make it to the loo. I think I'd better go to bed."

"Oh sorry, so should I."

Cat hung up, lost her balance and stumbled on to the phone table. At least she knew that Jo had probably just done the same thing, only she had a mug full of pee to deal with as well. Slowly Cat stumbled into bed, congratulating herself on an excellent evening.

Sixty

Dominic didn't call. Cat jumped whenever the phone rang in the office and checked her answering machine every evening when she got home. She'd dial 1471 and if she got the number-not-known message, convince herself it had been him, blocking his call by dialling 141. She checked her e-mails throughout the day, devastated not to be hearing from him. How was he living, she wondered constantly. How was he surviving without her?

The weekends when she knew he didn't have the children were the hardest. Could he really be happy on his own? How was he filling the long, empty evenings without her? Didn't he miss her company, her observations and her humor? How was he surviving without her sex? Didn't he go to sleep thinking about her, dreaming about her, longing for her? Didn't he even miss her cooking, for God's sake?

And then it struck her one day in the bath. She had just finished exfoliating her face and applying a thick pink moisturising mask and was sinking back into a tub full of neroli-scented bubbles when it came to her. He wasn't happy, and that was the whole point. Dominic couldn't *be* happy. He had destroyed his marriage, after all, abandoned two children. He couldn't allow himself happiness. Happiness was anathema to him. Should it appear in his life, he must do his best to destroy it. Cat began to understand. He was in pain, of course he was. He was as cut up as she was, probably even more so. But somehow it felt right to him, this un-happiness. It was what he deserved. And while he continued to revel in his self-inflicted misery, there would be no chance for either of them.

"What do I do?" she asked the tarot later. *Wait on the guidance of your soul*, came the frustrating reply.

Weeks passed. Cat lurched from one horoscope to another. Her morning routine consisted of checking her e-mails to see if he'd written, and then continuing her analytical discussions with Lorna when he hadn't. Then she would go onto the Internet to see if there was any joy to be had from any of her four favorite websites, which there rarely was. This took until around 11a.m., when she did a little work until 12:30. Then she'd nip to the cafeteria, buy a sandwich and return to watch *The Pride and the Passion*. After that she'd check the teletext horoscope and then call a numerology phone line. When none of these forecasts told her anything she wanted to hear she'd hit a slump, at around 3 o'-clock, and withdraw to the chocolate machine by the cafeteria.

Mark gave her occasional projects but none were terribly ful-filling. She would sit alone in her dilapidated office and stare glumly out across Soho Square. Every now and then he would surprise her with a visit. Sometimes he'd come during *The Pride*, and would stay and watch for a few minutes before handing her a channel proposition to go over, or a *Dear John* letter to write. Occasionally he'd do something to make her laugh out loud. She had been watching an episode where Lake's children, who had mysteriously gone from being toddlers to teenagers overnight, were upset at her decision to remarry, when an e-mail popped up. *Did she put those kids in a grow-bag or something?* it read. She had spent the next twenty minutes trying to come up with a sponta-neously funny response, but failed.

But it was twenty minutes spent not obsessing over Dominic, so that was something. If she were part of a team, she thought, she might get over him. If her office were full of people; if there was chatting and gossip and laughter, then maybe she wouldn't think of him all the time. But there was nothing: no team, no fun, just a handful of lifeless projects and a corner of broken furniture.

She would fantasize about how he might come back—about a

storm, an urgent ring on the doorbell and Dominic standing there, *her* Dominic: drenched, his teeth chattering, a hopeful look on his face. She would be wearing a thick cream towelling dressing-gown she didn't actually possess and be smelling warm and clean from her bath. He would wrap her in his wet arms and kiss her: her hair, her face, her neck and then he'd scoop her up, because of course she was about fifteen pounds lighter, carry her up the stairs and throw her on to the bed. They'd make love and then, then . . .

Curiously, she was unable to fantasize about much after that point. What happened next didn't matter, it was just the getting him back that did.

She didn't eat much. She hadn't noticed that she was losing weight until she tried on a pantsuit she'd bought in Hong Kong and found it way too big. She wondered why she had bought such a large size, not having noticed how much more prominent her ribcage had become and how much flatter her stomach.

Dominic. She had to have faith, had to believe in the power of their love, and she had to believe in the power of the Universe. Twice a day she'd draw a card to see if it brought any cheer. But inevitably she'd end up with the Hermit (wait and reflect), or the Hanged Man (let everything go). Then one morning as she was about to leave she drew The Tower, the twenty-sixth card. *The destruction of your life as you know it*, she read to her dismay. *You have outgrown your situation and it is time to move on. The ways of the past are restrictions, and no longer apply. The more you resist, the more painful this change will become—liberate yourself now.*

She sat on the top of the stairs and wept, pitifully, unable to stand, unable to move, unable to catch a tube and get on with a proper day's work. Was she having a nervous breakdown? she asked herself. She felt incapable of doing anything at all. She just sat and cried until there were no more tears and she began to feel faintly melodramatic. Then she rubbed foundation on her cheeks, reapplied her mascara and got on with her day.

One morning she found that Lorna, who was obviously tiring of her misery, had e-mailed her: *Why don't you call him, Cat? Why don't you suggest a meeting? You dumped him, remember, and he's hurting bad. Why don't you invite him for a drink? Anything would be better than this waiting game. That's what I'd do if I were you. I know you have this thing about calling, and I know you want him to do the running, but get over it. He needs some encouragement. CALL HIM. Oh, but here's something that'll cheer you up. There's a rumor going around that Max is staying out of Hong Kong because he's in trouble with some triad gang. I heard it the other day when I was in graphics and I dismissed it, but yesterday I got a call from a journalist asking if I knew anything. Strange but true.*

Cat's stomach churned, she'd almost forgotten about her conversation with Jeremy. What if it were traced back to her? As a story it was plausible enough to be taken seriously, though, and if she hadn't made it up, she told herself, someone else could.

Maybe she had even created it, she wondered, her mind racing, maybe he really was in trouble? Maybe she had unwittingly manifested it using the power of her own mind? She rather liked the idea, it made her feel omnipotent and mysterious. But then again, if she were capable of manifesting Max's decline, why hadn't she been able to reach Dominic's inner consciousness yet? Why was he still resisting her?

That evening she paced around her flat, wondering whether to call him or not. Lorna had made it sound so simple and logical. Cat couldn't help thinking she would be giving in, though. It was she who had set the challenge after all, she could hardly cave in on it now. But it would be fantastic to hear his voice again, and to think that he could be back in her life within hours. Within hours! That was all it would take. Her stomach churned as she rehearsed what to say.

She decided to wait until late, around ten o'clock. He'd be at home, he'd have finished his pizza, or his burger, or whatever he was eating these days and he'd be drinking beer and smoking. Restlessly she wandered around her flat, tidying a few things up, pulling the occasional rune and sipping nervously on a glass of wine. She drank enough to steady herself, but not enough to blur her words. The last impression she wanted to create was that this was just drink'n'dial therapy.

She couldn't call exactly at ten, it would look premediated. At three minutes past she dialled his number, her fingers relieved to be finding the familiar buttons on the keypad. It rang three times and she took a deep, calming breath. Then his answering machine clicked on and she listened to his voice in disbelief. She hung up quickly, dialled 141 and redialled. As the phone rang again she hung up.

Where could he be? He never went out. Of course, she reassured herself, taking another deep calming breath, he was buried in work. He'd be back doing those endless nights, making up for all that time he'd supposedly lost when he was seeing her. She could call his cell, but decided against it. She'd never called him on it before, after all. She hated not knowing where he might be, or what he might be doing when it rang. He could be at a business dinner, she told herself, he could always be entertaining his American counterparts.

But Dominic was now living a life Cat knew nothing about. It chilled her. Her Dominic was becoming more and more distant and Cat swore at herself for allowing it to happen. He was too fragile to be treated like a normal person, she should have realized that from the start.

Everything she did was wrong. Every decision she took, every choice she made, every gut feeling she followed, everything was wrong. She'd blown it with Declan, she'd blown her job in Hong Kong, she'd blown Mark Gilmore (at least she could still see the funny side) and now she'd clearly blown it with Dominic.

The following evening she hired the film *Sliding Doors* to cheer herself up. Cat loved it. She watched entranced as Helen's life split into two and moved on in completely different directions. The movie seemed to echo exactly her feeling of having turned left when she should have turned right. It was yet another sign. But the conclusion the film seemed to draw was that the girl who had been pro-active, who had pushed her way through the sliding doors and into a different life, simply found her true love slightly earlier than the one who had waited a few minutes for the next tube. That much, it seemed, of their lives had been predestined. The movie echoed the messages of the runes—that by waiting on the will of the Universe, and not by trying to make things happen, she would reach her destiny in due course.

Cat felt it was a sign not to ring him, but it was a process she had already started by trying the previous night. She was awake to it, alert to it, and it nagged at her. So when the movie ended and she'd rewound the tape, methodically putting it back in its box and placing it somewhere she wouldn't forget, she tried again.

I am not afraid to make this call, she told herself as the dial tone started. *Nothing bad is going to happen.* This time he picked up after the second ring. Her heart leaped. "Dominic, it's Cat."

"Cat, hi." It was hard to read his tone. He sounded surprised, certainly, but not emotional.

"Look, I'd love to see you. It feels like such a long time and I'm really hating this distance between us."

"Oh, OK." He could have sounded more enthusiastic.

"You know, I thought we were going to meet up a few weeks ago, when you called me at work."

"Oh yes. I'm sorry about that, I got you at a bad time. Well, when do you want to meet up, then?" He sounded like he was making an appointment with a sales rep.

"I don't know, what's good for you?" She had been hoping he'd suggest the next day.

"Oh God, let me see," he sighed. "Wednesday?" It was almost a week away.

"OK." She wrote in her diary, relieved to see his name on an entry again after weeks of blankness. "Where shall we meet?"

"The usual?"

"OK, why not?" She laughed. So the wine-bar had sentimental value for him too! It was the place of their first date and the start of many subsequent evenings. It had to be a good sign.

They said goodbye and Cat hung up, elated to have accomplished so much. He could have sounded keener, she thought, but then she had caught him off-guard. He was still in shock about her having ended things and was now keen to protect himself. Of course, it was obvious when she thought about it. He was as sensitive as a woman; he wouldn't want to sound desperate. They were both being cautious—it was only natural.

He would be hers again, she told herself. That night she visualized the two of them, entwined by a golden thread, drawing their bodies closer and closer together. Her Dominic. Her Dominic would be coming back.

She would count the days.

Sixty-One

Cat was an hour late for work that Wednesday. She stood for the duration of two cups of tea in front of her wardrobe, cursing it. How did she really want to look? What was the image she was trying to convey? Her soft pink was too quiet and might give the impression she was hurt, or vulnerable. But too much black and she might look ruthless and uncaring. Beige tones reeked of indifference, and that was the last thing she felt. The new ice-blue suit she'd bought at the weekend specially hung enticingly on its rail. It was sexy and slim-fitting and she knew he'd adore it, but as she peered out of the bedroom window to study a threatening sky she knew she couldn't risk arriving at the wine-bar with rain-splattered legs and an inappropriately summery outfit.

She finally decided on a navy blue suit with a pale pin stripe running through it, matched with gold accessories. She pulled her hair up into a French pleat, which had been Dominic's favorite style. It would look as if she'd just come from some high-level meeting, and he'd respect her for that. She couldn't reveal that she played cards and read horoscopes all day.

Too tense to think, Cat played cards and read horoscopes all day. She had discovered that some of the tabloids had websites, and had started to read their forecasts as well. Now she was up to seven a day, none of which seemed to tie in with the others. One talked of financial worries, another of interesting career opportunities and a third of a family matter which needed sorting out. But Mystic Myshwana, whose forecast now popped up on e-mail from New York at three o'clock every afternoon, brought tears of relief to Cat's eyes.

She read: *We all make mistakes from time to time, but we don't all get an opportunity to correct them. The stars now are giving you that opportunity. Someone thinks more highly of you than you realize. He may be disguising it, but have faith, and things will resolve themselves in a wonderful, dramatic manner.*

Cat's whoops of joy echoed around the office. She felt vindicated. She had kept the faith: faith that Dominic would return and faith in all her various fortune-tellers. She had always believed they would show her the way. And now the hours she had spent chasing for that one, elusive, message, had paid off. She forwarded it to Lorna and Jo for their approval. Dominic thought more highly of her than she realized! Things were going to resolve themselves wonderfully! She had always had faith in Mystic Myshwana, Cat persuaded herself. She had always been more accurate than the others.

By six she was more than ready to leave. On Friday she had to deliver a detailed analysis of the various South African television stations and their programming—today at least she'd printed out some schedules and created a file for her document. She'd begun selecting her typeface and wondering whether she wanted her headings emboldened or italicized or both—but really, what did any of it matter? Her future, her life as she had planned it, depended on the outcome of this evening—what did she care about what the average South African watched on a Tuesday evening, or about which typeface Mark Gilmore found pleasing?

Tonight was to be the most important night of her life. Tonight was the night that Dominic would tell her he loved her, and mean it. Tonight he would tell her that he'd had a breakthrough over Sandy, that he'd finally started seeing her as everyone else did. And he'd tell her how it was all because of her, and how much he appreciated her warmth, her love, her support and her honesty. Tonight he would tell her he'd decided to divorce his wife and make a clean break. And tonight he'd suggest that in time they move in together, and make a long-term commitment.

Cat took a deep breath. It was going to happen! She could see it, she could feel it, her entire being craved it. And at last she would tell him how much she loved him, how she had always loved him, but that she'd held it back because of his feelings for Sandy. And tonight they'd hold each other, cry into each other's hair, kiss each other and plunge into bed, where they'd make intense love and sleep with their arms and legs entwined.

She arrived at the wine-bar ten minutes early and checked her appearance in the loo before ordering a glass. Should she have made herself late, come rushing in full of apologies and excuses? No, that would be insincere. And tonight was not a night for insincerity, theirs was an honest, open relationship. Instead he would come in and find her sitting there in navy blue and gold, looking like a woman for whom this evening was important, a woman who'd take their discussions seriously. He might even think she'd excused herself from her high-level meeting early, wanting to see him on time, respecting his time. That was the sort of image she wanted to convey.

The bar was full of laughing people. *Like Dominic and I used to laugh*, she began to think before remembering how rarely they had ever laughed together. She'd spent most of their relationship trying to understand his problems. But there would be laughter. After a tense beginning, there would be plenty of love and laughter.

He was late. He was always late of course, but this of all evenings? She studied her nails (clear polish) and flipped through a discarded *Evening Standard*. She didn't want him to see her reading the paper, though, didn't want to appear casual.

Then he was there. She was tucking the paper into her bag as he walked through the door. He was wearing what he always wore, a navy suit, Oxford blue shirt and a tie she recognized. It would have been more thoughtful to wear one she'd bought him, of course, but she knew his limitations. In the five minutes it took him to dress every morning, such a gracious act would never have occurred to him.

"Hello Cat," he said. She tried to read the look on his face. If anything he looked tense, and she remembered how it always took him a couple of drinks to shake off the day's events.

They kissed awkwardly on the lips.

"How are you?" She smiled. Had he put on weight? All those take-out pizzas, she assumed. His body seemed so familiar, and yet so strange.

"Fine, fine, you?"

"I'm fine, thanks." She worried that they were acting like strangers. After two months apart, they were awkward in each other's presence. Someone watching them now might think they'd been set up. *She'll be in a navy suit. So'll he.*

"Shall we get a bottle?" he asked anxiously, looking like he might down it in one.

"Silly not to." She tried to sound light, but already was beginning to feel something was badly wrong. He ordered a bottle of house white, which she thought was disappointing and strange. Was she no longer good enough for expensive Pouilly Fuissés and bottles of Chablis?

"So how's work going?" he tried.

She told him about Mark and the various projects she'd been given, trying to make them sound interesting and challenging.

"I'm glad you're enjoying it," he told her. She hadn't said she was.

"How's Rubens?" she asked.

"You know, same old same old." He shrugged.

And Sandy? She would have liked to have asked, but stopped herself. She couldn't drag her up tonight, at least not yet.

"Have you seen any films lately?" he asked.

"One or two, yes," Cat answered, sinking. It was worse than talking to a forgotten cousin at a family funeral. They had become two people who used to be close and who now felt as unconnected as if each spoke a different language.

"Did you see *Sliding Doors?*" he asked her. "I saw it the other night. What a great film, I almost cried at the end."

"Yes, I saw it," she told him dully. Who had he seen *Sliding Doors* with? It wasn't the kind of film he'd take his children to see, or the kind any man would watch unless his girlfriend had suggested it.

"And wasn't she wonderful, Gwynneth Paltrow?" he continued as she sunk lower and lower. "Her English accent was so believable." *Who had he seen it with?*

They moved on to a Chinese place in Pimlico, and Cat let Dominic order. Once they were alone with a bottle of Chablis and some nibbles, she began.

"The reason I needed to see you is that, well, I've hated this distance between us. I thought you needed time to sort yourself out, and that was why I called it a day, but I thought you'd want to see me again. And you did, once, didn't you? I never understood why you didn't call me back that time."

"That time?" He looked puzzled, as if trying to remember.

"When I couldn't talk to you properly, remember? I was in a meeting." Cat tried not to sound too irritated. Throughout their relationship she had busily memorized dates, days and even times, while Dominic wasn't even capable of remembering their last conversation.

"Oh then," he sighed, looking pained. "Yes, I wanted to see you then. I did." His face darkened and he looked like he was bracing himself for something. "But then more time passed and—I don't know, I have to be honest with you, Cat." He sighed again, and in that sigh Cat knew her world was about to fall apart. "The truth is, I fell in love a few weeks ago."

She almost snapped the stem of her glass in two. She held it tightly, as if the glass alone could prevent her from falling. A sword through her heart would have been less painful. A bullet through the brain, preferable. "Fell in love?" she repeated.

"I'm sorry, Cat."

"You fell in love?" Why did he have to be so dramatic about it? *I started seeing someone* would have been bad enough, but *I fell in love?* Did he have to be so Mills and Boon about everything?

Dominic picked at a cracker, knowing he was going to suffer.

"Who with?" she asked. The sword had plunged into her chest, its cold steel burning inside her.

"No one you know. A consultant we use sometimes. I wasn't expecting it, Cat, it came right out of the blue."

A few weeks, Cat calculated. The last time they'd spoken he'd sounded like he could barely get up in the morning. And then just a week or so later he'd fallen in love? How could that have happened?

"How did you meet her?" she asked.

"She came to discuss a new project her company's been handling for us. We ended up having a drink. I wasn't expecting it, but you know what it's like. The brush of a leg, the touch of a hand." His face softened as he remembered.

"Yes, spare me the details," Cat snapped. So while she'd spent sleepless nights crying he'd been relishing a new love, and with it new stories to discover, a new body to explore. A different mouth, a different voice, a different person. "She was who you saw *Sliding Doors* with."

He smiled, realizing how he'd given himself away. "Yes."

All Cat could think of was how the one film which had spoken to her recently, the one film which had made such an impression, was now ruined.

"So you met her, what, a week after we spoke?"

He frowned. "A week, two, I'm not sure."

At least he had the decency to be vague about it. Cat was sure the girl would have written the date in her diary and have been counting the weeks ever since. "And what's her name?"

"Lindy." He smiled, unable to disguise his affection. A waiter brought their food, laying out hotplates, serving dishes, bowls and hot towels.

Lindy? Cat leaned back, taking a large slug of wine. What kind of a girl was Lindy? And what kind of a name was Lindy, anyway? Her eyes froze on her glass as she tried to picture her. A girl called Lindy has short dark hair, slightly greasy skin and wears overly sweet perfume. A girl called Lindy is sporty; she was captain of the basketball team at school and still plays hockey twice a week. She has a childlike enthusiasm for life and an infectious laugh. A girl called Lindy has never known depression. She prefers pubs to wine-bars and downs pints with the boys. A girl called Lindy buys her makeup from The Body Shop and her panties from a chain store. She has lower-middle-class parents. A girl called Lindy excels at a mediocre job and laughs at her boss's worn jokes. She holidays in the Greek islands and wears an unflattering one-piece. A girl called Lindy lives in a Clapham back street and boasts a large collection of ceramic frogs. She keeps soft toys in her bedroom and likes it from behind.

"Lindy," Cat repeated when the waiter finally left the table.

"It's short for Melinda." Dominic helped her to rice, some steamed seafood and a clump of noodles.

"So you got over me like that?" She clicked her thumb and middle finger. She felt dangerous. She felt like she could do anything. This could be the only time in her life when she could reasonably throw a glass of wine in his face, or knock the table and its contents to the floor, or speed around to his flat and throw a brick through his window without being in the wrong. Because she herself had been wronged.

He paused, sensing her anger, and chose his words carefully. "Cat, it wasn't like that. My relationship with Lindy is different."

Relationship with Lindy? Her Dominic? The sword burned again inside her chest, it struck her lungs and she had to catch her breath. It sliced into her stomach and she laid down her chopsticks, defeated. "Different? How different?"

"I don't know, Cat, please don't ask me to explain. I'm sorry."

"What does she have?" she asked, her eyes stinging. "What does she have that I don't?" As the cliché tumbled out she felt vaguely embarrassed.

"You'll hate me, Cat." He smiled sadly, and she prepared herself to. "She pays for things."

"What?"

"Dinners. She insists on paying. I never felt you paid your way."

"What?" Cat repeated. She almost laughed. She no longer knew what to feel. A searing hurt that he'd found someone else, repulsion that he could be so shallow and even pity for the hapless Lindy, who was apparently buying her way into his affections.

"Dominic, I don't believe you." Stronger now. "She pays for things? I didn't pay my way? You make quarter of a million a year and I was a fucking temp. How can you say that?"

"I'm sorry." He drank his wine. If he wanted to make her hate him, he was doing a good job. Suddenly he looked cheap; a man who only ever bought suits in the sales and counted out the price of every meal. Cat wished she'd ordered the lobster.

"There must be more to her than that."

"She makes me laugh," he told her. "She has incredible warmth and affection." He couldn't disguise his pride. "She adores me. What else can I say? She swallows." He probably added it as a joke, Cat told herself, but neither of them laughed.

She stared dejectedly at the scallops on her plate, and then excused herself and went to the loo. The tears flowed but she no longer knew why. Was she crying for Dominic: the sensitive, tortured, misunderstood Dominic, her lost love, or just for the Dominic she always thought he was? Was she crying because he was out of her life for ever, or because Lindy was now in his?

Dominic. Her Dominic, meeting Lindy in wine-bars or maybe pubs, taking her to dinners (or was she taking him?), holding her hand, making love to her. Making love. The pain was too much. This was meant to be their big reunion—Cat had even bought new underwear specially. But here she was, crying inside a claustrophobic loo full of plastic flowers. Her Dominic had betrayed her, and all her dreams were shattered. As if in commiseration her hair began to fall out of its French pleat, and she pushed it back roughly. She patched up her face and returned to the table.

"I thought you'd got stuck there for a minute." He tried to sound cheerful, but she could see he was hating this. Everything he said was crass and inappropriate, and Cat knew he knew it.

She said nothing, just drained her glass. A big chunk of hair fell down again and she felt ill and exhausted. She leaned forward heavily.

"You're not going to eat anything, are you?" His voice a little softer now. She shook her head. "You've lost weight," he tried, looking at her admiringly.

"You've gained it," she snapped. "Must be all those meals Lindy keeps buying you."

He asked the waiter to clear the untouched dishes. Cat drank heavily. Her pain had given way to anger—anger at Lindy for indulging him and anger at herself for having once done the same thing. And anger at Dominic for his deceit. The tortured soul had become the torturer.

Looking at him now, she could see that his sensitivity, the sensitivity she'd once found so appealing, had never been anything more than self-pity. He was incapable of applying it to anyone else.

"Does she know you're seeing me tonight?"

"Yes, I explained it to her. She understands."

She wondered how he'd have put it to her. Would Lindy now be worrying that he might return to Cat, or had he convinced her that their relationship was long past its sell-by date? How would he have spoken about her, described her, she wondered? Ex-girlfriend, she thought with horror. It sounded so final, so loathed.

"And does she know about Sandy?"

Dominic sighed. "No. I haven't told her about that."

"So she has that to look forward to, then."

"Cat, it's been difficult, but I've been trying really hard to get over her. Lindy doesn't need to know about that."

"Lucky old Lindy, to be spared that. What kind of age is she?"

"Twenty-four."

Cat nodded. "I thought she'd be young. Where does she live?"

"Cat, do we have to?"

She thought of him commuting with her. Did they hold hands on the train? Did they giggle together over her copy of the *Sun*? Would he fondly kiss her goodbye in the mornings?

"Totteridge and Whetstone." He sighed, and she tried to place it.

"And has she met the children?"

"No, no," he said quickly, and she felt oddly relieved.

"I need to go now." She stood up. He paid the bill quickly, tossing a few notes on the table, and walked her outside. She felt numb, in a state of shock. This was supposed to be an evening of laughter, of relief and of love. They were supposed to leave the restaurant holding hands, to stumble into a taxi together, to make love and hold each other in her bed all night. Lindy wasn't supposed to have happened.

He flagged down a taxi and she paused, prolonging the moment before she left him for ever.

"Cat, I'm sorry." He looked at her sympathetically as if she were a plump teenager who'd come last in a beauty pageant. She slapped him, hard and fast on the cheek.

"Don't tell me you're fucking sorry," she snarled as he recoiled, holding the side of his face. Satisfied, she jumped into the cab and turned away as it drove off. She couldn't bear to look back at him, to watch him grow smaller and more distant, to see him hail another taxi and get on with his life. She sank back, allowing the greyness of the South London streets to consume her. All she could think about was how life would be nothing but a bleak, impenetrable greyness from now on, and she fantasized about finding a loaded gun somewhere, pressing it to her temple and pulling the trigger.

Sixty-Two

What was the point of getting up? Cat stared bleakly at her alarm clock, the time it told meaningless in her world. She hadn't slept much, just dozed a little between bouts of wakeful depression.

She could get up. She could make a cup of tea and watch the news—it might lift her out of herself. Or she could lie there, hugging her knees to her chest, and wait for the world to change. Yesterday she'd had hope. Yesterday she'd woken with a clear head and a dream to fulfil. Last night she was in pain, her insides ripped up, and her stomach in shreds. But today? Today she just felt numb, cold inside—dead. A moving body sheltering a dead heart and a dead soul. If she lay still long enough perhaps her body could die as well; the numbness could swallow it up, her eyes could close and the blackness last for ever.

But she had things to do, responsibilities, a report to finish. Cat hauled herself out of bed, turned on the TV, filled the kettle and poured some orange juice. She washed down her vitamins, including a couple of extra St John's Wort for good measure. Then she channel-hopped her way through bickering politicians, brightly colored breakfast TV sets and a couple with an irritating three-year-old complaining about the state of their local amenities.

Everything was futile, meaningless, and she wondered how people had the energy to put this worthless stuff together every morning. Did any of it matter? Today's big story was tomorrow's old news, the drab-looking couple might or might not get their improved amenities, politicians would continue to bicker. In the big scheme of things all of this was trivial, none of it mattered. She turned the TV off again and tried the radio instead, allowing the 60s-sounding jingles and the patter of an over-enthusiastic DJ to wash over her.

She went through her routine slowly and methodically, as if wading through tar. She brushed and flossed her teeth, ran a shallow bath and did some stomach exercises. She sank into the tub knowing she was late but not caring. Mark would not give a damn anyway, he hardly ever saw her. What did any of it matter?

She washed her hair, telling herself she would feel better once she was clean and dressed. She listened to music, marvelling that so many pained love songs were written and sung by men. Had any man ever felt so strongly about her? Had they; fuck. No matter how loving or giving she could be, no matter how well she took care of herself, no matter how great their sex life was, they could always walk away.

She stared at her wardrobe, sighing deeply. What did she care what she wore? What did anyone care? She couldn't cope with skirts, couldn't struggle with hose today. She chose a dark grey pantsuit, austere and business-like. The waistband felt loose and she studied her ever-flattening stomach.

On a sudden impulse she reached for her tarot cards and shuffled them, whispering *Give me some inspiration, Universe, give me some hope.* That was all she'd ever wanted. Up until yesterday she'd had plenty of it; today she had nothing.

She drew a card, the eight of swords. A woman with long black hair wearing a red dress was tied up and blindfolded. On either side of her four swords were plunged into the ground, making eight in total. Swords, she knew, represented mental and rational functions, communication and thoughts. They were indicative of struggle or conflict and pointed to separation from past attachments. The number eight represented balance and a renewal of energies. Then she remembered how last night she'd kept imagining a sword piercing her chest and slicing up her insides.

To the ceiling, she suddenly snapped, "Oh thanks, Universe, very fucking funny. Thanks a lot." She fought back the tears.

"That's all I am to you, isn't it? A fucking joke." She was angry now, and needed to release that anger. She'd put so much faith in her beliefs, in following her intuition and signs, and what had she got for it?

"A plaything, that's all I am to you, isn't it?" she cried, sinking to her knees. "Someone to have fun with. Lead her down the wrong way, give her false hope and then shove her down a blind fucking alley." The tears started pouring down and she slumped in front of the bookcase. "I listened to you! I had faith in you! And what for?"

She gave way to her tears now, oblivious of time, the radio, her neighbors, of anything. She slumped on the floor and cried like a child. How had she managed to get everything so wrong? she kept asking herself. How had she fallen so badly off her life-path and into a place where everything she touched fell apart? She felt abandoned, betrayed, and worse still, she had no idea how to get back on, how to reach the good times again.

"I give up," she whispered. "I give up. There is no happiness, there will be no love. I will live my life. I will go to work and I will pay my bills. There is nothing else."

The tears started to subside, replaced with heavy, deep breaths. A life without expectations would be a simple life. Cat would learn to enjoy it. She would take pleasure in books, TV shows and good food and wine. She would no longer strive for anything, stop trying to figure anything out. It would be OK.

As she hauled herself up, a book on the shelf drew her attention. It was another of her self-help manuals, and she reached for it, letting the pages fall open. In bold italicized print the heading read: *If someone breaks your spirit, someone else will restore your hope.*

Cat smiled with a sense of resignation. Maybe the Universe was coming through for her after all? That was the sort of inspiration she'd been looking for. At least it was enough to get her out of the apartment.

She dried her hair, put on some makeup and a rose quartz ring that was supposed to draw love and harmony into her life, and finished the look off with a lilac-colored pashmina around her shoulders. She shook her head. She looked like a successful career girl, someone who might draw attentive looks on the street. The sort of person who'd got life sorted, who had everything she wanted.

Cat saw her bus coming and wanted to throw herself under it. London itself depressed her. The architecture, the grimy shops, even the smarter shops just looked pointless and wasteful. At Fulham Broadway she fantasized about throwing herself under the train, but remembering how often she'd cursed rush hour suicides that had disrupted her plans, thought the better of it.

Letting herself into her office, Cat found two battered old desks and an ugly lamp had been added to her collection. She didn't have the energy to complain. She logged on, wrote long e-mails to Lorna and Jo and got on the Internet. She read her seven different horoscopes, none of which seemed particularly relevant, and then surfed through a number of travel sites. Would she feel any happier, she mused, if she were digging her toes into the sand on a Thai beach right now?

She stared glumly at her screen, willing something good to happen. She looked out across Soho Square, as if she might catch a glimpse of Dominic in the distance. The sun began to break through the clouds and Cat studied the early summer scenes— hanging baskets were once again getting filled and pansies popping up beneath the trees. So Dominic and Lindy were enjoying a happy spring romance. Lucky Lindy would be revelling in the warmth of the sun, the warmth of his affection and the warmth of his body.

Cat wished that thick dark clouds would block out the sky and that a heavy winter would descend upon the city, shrouding everyone else's hopes and dreams. She wanted everyone to share her bleakness, everyone else's life to be in ruins.

And more than anything she wanted not to have to live out her winter, her unhappiness, alone.

Sixty-Three

"Thanks for that South African thing, by the way." It was typical of Mark to dismiss a detailed report that had taken Cat two weeks to prepare as a "thing." They were standing in the queue for the carvery in Trafalgar's canteen. Cat watched in fascination as the knife sliced through his pink roast beef, imagining what kind of cut it might make on her wrist.

"Glad you found it helpful," she replied, trying to hide her irritation.

"Very. But I'm afraid I'm going to have to put all that on hold right now. Something else has come up," he said with a mysterious smile. "That's why I asked you to have lunch."

They were jostled through the queue to pay. Cat looked down at her coagulating pasta. What did it matter if it had gone cold, she thought, she wasn't going to eat any of it anyway. It was only twelve, and too early for her, but Mark was in a hurry.

"You know there's a TV market coming up in Johannesburg in a month's time," she tried as they sat down. "I thought that would be an ideal time to strike."

"I know. And we might still be able to. But Sir John's got other things in mind at the moment."

"Such as?" She watched him tear into his beef hungrily.

"Asia. I need a general status report. But think big. I don't just want to know about television companies. We've got to get thinking about the Internet, Internet applications and the interactive business. Do you think you can get much about that?"

"I guess a lot of that kind of information would be available on the Internet itself," Cat thought aloud, prodding at her spaghetti carbonara. "And of course you need it by yesterday afternoon, don't you?"

"You read my mind." He heaped a forkful of beef, mashed potatoes and peas into his mouth. "You all right? You seem a bit down."

"Yeah, I am a bit," she sighed. "My boyfriend and I are going through a bit of a weird patch." She still couldn't admit the truth. "And I have too much time to think about it. I mean, I'm just so isolated in that office."

"I know, it's not ideal. The Budapest thing is looking close, and then we'll have a real channel to launch. We'll bring some people in, get you some company."

She cringed. He made her feel like an only child during summer vacation, and that he was her protective father trying to find her some friends.

Back at her desk, Cat turned on *The Pride and the Passion* and started her research. As Brandy set about seducing Fire in the sauna, Cat went on the Internet and trawled through a host of Asian websites. While Fire tried bravely to resist, Cat discovered relevant articles in the *Asian Wall St. Journal* and the *Asian Times*, and printed them. While Brandy uttered such incongruities as "Come on, Fire baby, you know you make me hot," Cat found company reports and numerous relevant corporate websites. As Fire finally gave in and Brandy climbed under his bath towel, they cruelly cut to a shot of Esselle making wedding preparations, oblivious to what was going on just two floors below.

Cat spent the next two hours pulling together as much information as she could, but before putting it into any kind of formal structure, made herself a coffee, willing the small envelope signifying a new e-mail to pop up in the lower right-hand corner of her screen. When she turned, there was still nothing new.

He could have contacted her. They had been close once, after all. He could have called to see if she was all right, or dropped her a line to make sure. She couldn't believe he had stopped thinking about her like that. She had to believe he was missing her, had to believe that his relationship with Lindy was a sham. She'd written to Lorna that morning, and quickly reread her words:

I cannot believe he is really happy with Lindy-who-swallows. I think she's a rebound thing. I saw how he looked at me; he still has feelings, I'm sure. I just mishandled things. I need to see him again. I can't help thinking if we could just do it again, you know? We used to have such incredible sex, and I just cannot believe it's so good with Lindy-who-swallows. And I miss it so much.

She couldn't bear the thought of him with another woman while she lay alone, aching for him at night. Summer was coming—the season for evening riverside drinks, dinners al fresco and chilled glasses of rosé, or champagne. It was the season for romance, for love, for hot, sweaty sex under a sultry night-time sky. And it would be Lindy who'd enjoy her summer with Dominic, Lindy! It was so hard to take in, it felt like a death of sorts—she could not believe, *refused* to believe, that he'd gone.

Maybe she should try seducing him, like Brandy? Cat laughed. As if.

An e-mail popped up. It was Mystic Myshwana's daily forecast, live from New York. Eagerly Cat read it:

Every now and then you realize the power you hold. Every now and then the planets align themselves to remind you of just that. You have been battered along by the ocean and dumped, bedraggled and confused along the shore. This weekend the stars are urging you to gain control. You have the power to achieve anything you want, to defeat the enemy, to win the coveted prize. Just follow your instincts and the skies will support you.

Cat read and reread the horoscope in disbelief. Never had one been so compelling, made so much sense to her before. She had the power! What felt like an outlandish, ridiculous idea a few minutes ago was beginning to seem plausible. Even her horoscope was urging her on to take a risk, and to gain control. *Every now and then you realize the power you hold*, she read again, *you have the power to achieve anything you want.*

"What are you doing, ordering a kebab?"

She hadn't even noticed Mark entering the office and walking up behind her.

"Oh, no, it's this stupid e-mail thing that just pops up." Cat closed the e-mail, embarrassed. "A friend of mine set it up for me, and now I don't know how to get rid of it," she added lamely.

"Mystic Myshwana?"

She felt like a twelve-year-old caught checking out bras in a shopping catalog. "It's just some stupid American thing." She blushed.

"I've brought you something, to keep you company." From behind his back he presented her with a potted plant wrapped up in paper.

"Mark!" She laughed. "That's so sweet of you." She felt genuinely touched. "Instead of talking to the wall, I'll talk to my plant." It was a miniature palm, green and elegant, and for a second it reminded her of Asia.

"Glad you like it. Don't forget to water it, now." He turned to leave, and then remembered. "So, hot stuff today, then? That Brandy in the sauna."

Cat sighed. "I feel so sorry for poor Esselle."

"Nah, she's boring. Brandy's hot. He should go with her."

Cat was intrigued. "So if you had a nice but dull girlfriend, and some hot stuff tried to seduce you, would you go for it?"

"It'd be hard to resist."

"Even if it meant betraying someone like Esselle?"

He sighed. "What can I say, when a woman comes on to you, it's a powerful thing. You'd have to be a saint to turn her down."

Cat looked away, suddenly appalled at the way the conversation was going. They were coming dangerously close to admitting what had happened in Cannes. Had Emma been his girlfriend then? she suddenly wondered. Had she, Cat, seduced the boyfriend of a woman like that?

"Anyway." He changed the subject, as if understanding her discomfort. "How are things going with the Asian stuff?"

"I have a pile of things waiting for me on the printer." She nodded. "I'm just about to start putting it together now."

"Great, thanks." He made for the door. "Esselle doesn't stand a chance, you know," he added as he disappeared.

She sank back, breathing heavily. If what Mark had just said was right, then she had the power to do anything. And if even she had managed to tempt him away from his stunning girlfriend, albeit only for the duration of a blowjob, then what more was she capable of? She could sit back, accept defeat, and let Dominic carry on with Lindy. Or she could be bold and make something happen. What had following her intuition and waiting passively on the will of the Universe ever done for her anyway? Maybe now was the time for drastic action?

"I think you're totally out of your mind," Jo told her blankly that evening. "You've been watching too many soap operas."

"But I have to do something," Cat pleaded, wanting her friend's support.

"No, you don't. Just accept that it's over, Cat. You dumped him, remember? That was the one strong thing you've done, you can't go back on it now."

"I took a risk and failed. So now I have to take another."

"Why do you have to? Cat, I know it's hard, and I know it hurts, but there are other men. You never thought you'd get over Declan, but you did. Right now you don't think you'll get over Dominic, but you will. It's time to let him go."

"That's good, coming from you, who bloody followed Malcolm and even went on that junk trip to find him. And then screwed Nigel."

"Yes, I know, I'm not proud of myself. I went a bit crazy; they drive you nuts, men. And I think this is driving you nuts. You're not yourself, and now you're about to do something totally stupid."

"I can't just sit back and let him go like that. This weekend I know he's got the kids. She lives a million miles away, there's no way she's going to see him on Sunday night after they've left. So there's my chance."

The next morning, though, she felt less enthusiastic. For the hell of it she drew a tarot card before she left for work. It was *The World*. Cat laughed in astonishment. The World represented maximizing one's potential and making the most out of life. The world was at her feet, that was her interpretation.

She would do it—she would see her plan through! She would get her Dominic back. He'd admire her guts and her spirit. And then he'd come back for good.

Sixty-Four

Cat hadn't felt this nervous since a Frontier department heads meeting. Her stomach fluttered as though a colony of butterflies had just emerged from their larvae inside it. She was going to get her man. She was going to prove to him that life was more exciting with her than with any girl-next-door type like Lindy. She was going to knock him out, win him back and make him adore her. There was no alternative. Without him she couldn't sleep, couldn't eat and couldn't be bothered to work either. The Universe had put them together, and Cat wasn't about to let a nobody like Lindy tear them apart.

It was Sunday evening, and the traffic toward Tooting Bec was light. Cat went over the words she was going to say, the routine she'd perfected over the weekend, the possible outcomes or problems. Taking her lead from Brandy, she had rehearsed an answer for more or less anything he might say.

She knew he would be at home. The children would have gone back to his wife and he'd be left to tidy up his apartment. Lindy would be tucked up in Totteridge and Whetstone, surrounded by fluffy toys and ceramic frogs and probably seeing to her bikini line in preparation for the Monday date Cat was about to ensure didn't happen.

The streets of Tooting Bec looked strangely familiar, welcoming almost, in a bleak, impersonal way. She paid the cab and approached his front door. One of the bay windows was open and a floral curtain fluttered behind it. She pulled her tummy in and straightened her dress. It was black and cut on the bias and looked as though it had been made for her body. Slightly see-through and deeply sexy, Cat could remember entertaining the thought that she might wear it for a heady evening out which had never actually happened. In the same fantasy Dominic had proclaimed his undying love for her and presented her with a diamond ring Ivana Trump would have been proud of. It was a scene far removed from the Tooting Bec doorstep on which she now stood.

She rang his doorbell and waited a few seconds until she heard him. "Pizza delivery," she called into the intercom.

"No, there must be some mistake," his voice crackled back.

"It's a special delivery," she cooed. She heard him laugh in recognition, a kind of an "oh no" laugh. He clicked off the intercom and she heard a door open, then the sound of his feet on the stairs. Yet again she checked her stomach, and the dress. She wore only black stockings and garters underneath. As Dominic opened the door she smiled at the features she loved so much yet which had already started growing faint in her mind.

"Hello Cat." He kissed her on the mouth, ushering her inside. He was unshaven and his hair needed a cut. He was in a faded orange Rubens sweatshirt, a pair of jeans and his moccasins.

She had deliberately not drunk anything. She wanted to be in charge and to stay sharp. She needed to listen to every word he said and to be able to counter his arguments clearly. She took a deep breath. What was wanted of her now was nothing less than an Oscar-winning performance. She was no longer Cat Wellesley, the vulnerable and wounded ex-girlfriend; she was Cat Wellesley, *femme fatale.*

"Do you know why I'm here?" she asked seductively.

"Let me get some wine." He shook his head, the makings of a smirk on his face.

She swept into his sitting room and then stopped abruptly, appalled at the state of it. He obviously hadn't started to clear up after the children, and the floor was strewn with magazines, papers and food packages. She turned toward the kitchen in disgust. "I don't want any wine," she told him slowly. "There's only one thing I want tonight."

"I'll get some anyway." He looked like someone who'd just remembered a dental appointment.

She said nothing. If in doubt, she'd decided it was better to stay silent. She was not to lessen the impact. *Seductive, cool and in control.* She took deep breaths. *He wants you and is on the rebound. Tonight you will get him back. You will not take no for an answer.*

He appeared with two tumblers and a bottle of red.

"I told you I don't want any wine."

"Well I do." He poured two glasses and took a deep swig of his.

"There's only one thing I want," Cat said again. "And I'm not leaving until I get it."

"Cat, you've got to understand—"

"Yes I know, I know, you've fallen in love with Lindy." She almost spat out the girl's name. "But we both know that's not true, don't we? You don't love her, and you're not in love with her. So let's stop this silly charade and be honest with each other for a change."

"Cat, I am being honest." He slumped on the sofa beside her. "I do love her."

"You do not," she scoffed. "If you loved her you wouldn't have spoken about her the way you did. She swallows? Is that any way to talk about someone you supposedly love? I don't think so, Dominic."

He shook his head guiltily and drank. "That was a mistake, it was stupid of me. I just wanted to lighten things up a bit."

To lighten things up a bit? the vulnerable Cat thought in amazement. The *femme fatale* said nothing. She swung her legs around and placed her stilettoed feet in his lap. They looked sharp enough to cut through the denim of his jeans.

"Please, I don't want to hurt you." He pushed them away.

"You're not going to hurt me." Cat sat back on the sofa, allowing her legs to fall over his. The dress started riding up her thighs. The garters were turning her on, and she longed for him to stroke her thighs, to touch her again.

"Cat, please stop this." He tried to push her away.

"You know you want me." This was one of her back-up lines in case she became stuck. "Dominic, you know you want me." As if on cue her nipples hardened under the fabric of her dress. She knew he could see them.

"Cat, please." He shook his head, raising his right hand to his eyes. She could see he was weakening. "I don't want to hurt you, but I love Lindy. I love her, do you understand that? She's good for me."

"And I wasn't?" Cat snapped, regretting it instantly. *Femme fatales* didn't snap, they just purred. She had to think Lauren Bacall in *To Have and Have Not* rather than Glenn Close in *Fatal Attraction*.

"That's not what I said," he said carefully, as if reasoning with a child. "Lindy is a sweet, young girl. She adores me. I don't want to hurt her."

"Well, I won't tell her if you don't." A stroke of genius. The *femme fatale* was back on track.

"Cat, please don't do this." He sank his head into his hands. "Please."

Her legs were still crossed over his, and she encouraged her dress to ride up toward her thighs. The tops of her stockings were now exposed.

"Dominic, I'm not going until I get what I want."

Carefully avoiding her thighs, he drained his glass and refilled it. "I'm not going to do this, Cat, I think it's best if you go."

"Shut up, Dominic, I'm the one in charge here." Another of her stop-gap lines. If she could just keep the pressure up, she told herself, he would crack.

Abruptly he stood up, pushing her legs away. "Let me call you a taxi."

The Cat beneath the *femme fatale* started to panic. Total humiliation was looming. "I'm not going anywhere," she told him coolly.

"Cat, why are you doing this?" He made it sound like she'd tied him to a bed and was wielding a pair of scissors at his penis.

"Because you're making a mistake. Because we've both made mistakes."

"Cat, please. I don't want to betray her. I can't hurt her."

He paced around the room, drinking, a tortured expression on his face. She watched him hopelessly. He was probably the only man ever to refuse a woman's advances. Cat began to feel defeated. She dropped her guard.

"Does she know about Sandy yet?"

He slumped to the floor at her feet and shook his head. "There's no point in telling her about that. She couldn't take it. She adores me."

Another glimmer of hope. "And you're not honest enough to share it with her? Come on, Dominic, this isn't a relationship, it's a stop-gap and you know it." She started to massage his shoulders. "You know you want me." She purred in his ear. "You know our sex was the best ever. Can you honestly tell me it's as good with her?"

"It's different," he said carefully. She thought he was about to cry.

"You know you want me," she whispered again. She felt him relax into her massage, weaken.

"I can't hurt her."

"I'm not going to tell her."

"I can't believe you're doing this to me."

"I can't believe you're resisting."

He turned around now and, rising to his knees, grabbed her, kissing her hard.

"What are you doing to me?" he whispered, rubbing her breasts so hard she knew she'd have nipple rash by morning.

She released the bulge that was growing harder in his trousers, and he groaned as she took him in her mouth. She teased him with her tongue, her lips and her hands, but only for a few minutes. She didn't want to give him a hasty blowjob and then leave. She stood up, pulling him up with her. He looked slightly ridiculous, she thought, his erect penis sticking out from beneath his sweatshirt. Urgently he led her to the bedroom, where he thrust her against the wall so hard she almost banged her head. With a smile she unhooked the top of her dress, and he pulled it off her in one go. She stood there, naked but for her stockings and garters, feeling excited and triumphant.

Quickly he shed his clothes and threw her onto the bed. Cat braced herself for the smell of cheap perfume but there was none. They had sex, quickly and brutally, and then he rolled off her with a sigh.

"I should never have done that."

Cat lay quietly, trying to work out how she felt. Not triumphant, as she'd expected. Strangely empty, if anything. She might have got her own way, but she hadn't made him love her.

"Does she stay here much?" she asked.

"All the time. There's even a pair of her panties in that drawer." He nodded toward the chest of drawers with a pride that reminded Cat of her own when he'd kept his shirts at her place.

And later, as she heard him drift off to sleep, she wondered what exactly she'd achieved. At most she'd fucked with them, that was all. Dominic would always know he'd been unfaithful to Lindy; and even if she never found out it would be a stain, a blemish on their relationship.

In the morning he woke with a cry of frustration and slammed his fist into his pillow. "I should never have done that last night," he spat. "Never!"

Sulkily he made her a cup of tea and disappeared into the bathroom. Cat leaped out of the bed and searched the chest of drawers. What kind of panties did Lindy wear? They would tell her a lot about the girl. Hoping to find a pair of greying size six-teens, she found a tiny black g-string instead. It had no label, and she wondered if it'd been bought at a market. For the hell of it she hid it down the back of Dominic's overstuffed chair. Just to fuck with them, she told herself. Silly not to.

In the bathroom she found a bottle of bubble bath adorning the side of the tub, boasting Lindy's existence in his life. Worse still, there was a sponge bag under the basin full of contact lens solution and an emergency makeup kit. Cat went through it carefully, getting an idea of Lindy's coloring and style. On impulse she dropped a nearly used-up lipstick of her own inside. It was the sort of thing Dominic would never notice, but Lindy certainly would. It was by Chanel: a mauvey shade of pink called *Malice*. It seemed appropriate enough.

"I've called you a cab," Dominic told her. "It'll be here in a minute."

He gave her a quick hug goodbye. "Next time I get a pizza delivery I'll be a bit more careful," he joked. As she walked to the taxi she saw him close the door and then open it again, to watch her leave.

She sank back into the lumpy upholstery, grateful for the cab driver's silence. What had she actually got out of all that? She hadn't won him back; from that angle the whole thing had been a failure, but now Dominic had a new source of guilt and Lindy a lost g-string and a lipstick called *Malice* to puzzle over.

So it hadn't been a complete waste of time, then.

Sixty-Five

Cat was watering her plant when Mark walked into her office, looking tired but jubilant.

"Budapest," he declared. "Signed the deal last night. A twenty-four hour cable channel starting transmission in September."

"September? That only gives us two months."

"I know, it's a bit of a rush, but they want a soft-launch then and the real thing at the end of the year. So what can we give them?"

Cat searched through her Eastern European file. "Well, not all these things were cleared, but I could probably start off with say, a four-hour block."

"Make it six, running to eight by full launch."

"You're asking a hell of a lot." She frowned. "Can I have some help? A temp or something? There's going to be tons of information to pull together—you know, scripts, marketing blurb, publicity photos, all that stuff."

"Take Sally," he offered. "I've got no need for a secretary anyway, I'm sure she's underused. It would be good for her to get involved in a proper project rather than just taking my calls. Have her three afternoons a week if you like." He paused, as if only just realizing what he had said. "Or at least arrange something with her; she knows how much spare time she's got."

For the next few weeks Cat felt alive again. She befriended two librarians, Terry and Rod, who rushed through the dubbing of all the obvious shows. The schedule was approved and Sally spent hours in a dusty storeroom retrieving and photocopying scripts. When the first batch of materials was finally sent off they felt like they had won a war.

She met with Mark every week to discuss their progress, and to raise more things he hadn't thought about. She quickly realized he hated details—he was the deal-maker, not the doer.

"Who's going to make promos?" she asked him one day. "We have to have responsibility for the look and feel of the channel—we can't leave that in their hands. I mean, we haven't even got a channel ident yet."

"You got anyone in mind?"

"Yes I do, a very creative type who's just back from Hong Kong. Worked at Frontier for the music channel. He's freelancing now."

"Great. When can he start?"

"I asked him to come in tomorrow."

Mark smiled, as if he'd already anticipated that answer, and she wondered if he was deliberately letting things slip for her to catch, if he was testing her.

Tony arrived, and despite Cat's misgivings about working with someone who'd once drunkenly proclaimed his lust for her, she enjoyed having a small team in her office, enjoyed hearing Sally and Tony's banter and listening to his moans about the shows he had to sit through. Mark would appear bearing gifts of pizza, or Chinese take-out, and in the evenings would smuggle cans of beer to them past a frowning human resources office.

When Sally dropped a pile of scripts on the floor, throwing them out of order, he rolled up his sleeves and helped to sort them out with everyone else. He praised Tony's design for the channel ident and made intelligent suggestions on how it might be improved. Cat began to look forward to his visits. He seemed to fill the room, to bring everyone to life, and if a day went by without him popping in, she'd feel disappointed, cheated even.

For the channel launch Cat accompanied Mark to Budapest, where they spent several days at the broadcasting center going over operational procedures and marketing details with the Hungarian team.

It was odd having breakfast with him every morning. It felt intimate, yet all they ever discussed was work. At night, they'd be taken out to different restaurants with the staff, who were clearly enjoying a welcome treat on expenses. Most of the time they would go straight from the office, but on the night of the launch they returned to their hotel to freshen up.

She had wanted to wear her black cocktail dress with her hair up in a loose chignon, but that, she remembered with a cringe, was how she'd looked when she'd first met him. She settled instead on a golden silk pair of Capri pants and a matching top that she'd had made up in Bangkok. She teamed it with gold strappy sandals and a small silk bag. She piled her hair up loosely and wrapped a shawl around her shoulders.

As she approached Mark in the foyer he looked as if he were seeing her for the first time. His face lit up and he made no effort to disguise his delight. She smiled. He had seen her too late too often by now—her makeup rubbed off, hair a mess and exhaustion on her face.

"You scrubbed up well," he told her appreciatively, taking her arm and leading her to a taxi.

She felt tense throughout the preliminary speeches until the network was finally announced, and the six show monitors whirred into action. She watched Tony's launch promo carefully as if it might all go terribly wrong. Only when the opening titles of the first show came up did she begin to relax and accept a glass of wine. Mark broke away from a journalist to see her.

"It's all down to you, you know that?" He hugged her. "I couldn't have done it without you. You've been fantastic, I can't thank you enough."

She felt tears of relief bubble up. Finally she had achieved something tangible at Trafalgar.

"Don't go all emotional on me now," he mocked, wiping a tear from her eye. "You've got work to do. Talk to journalists—spread the word. I want to see your name in every Hungarian newspaper tomorrow morning."

Cat did some interviews, accepted glasses of wine and ate canapés all evening with a sense of being watched. At times she would turn around just to see Mark's back as he laughed with a member of the press. Sometimes she caught his eye, and they'd smile self-consciously.

She only hoped he wasn't making sure she didn't get drunk and go down on every man in the room. They were a good team, she told herself. Because of him, because of this project, she'd almost stopped thinking about Dominic. What was that line she'd read? *If someone breaks your spirit, someone else will restore your hope.*

Mark had done just that, she thought as she watched him chatting to the president of the network. His timing had been perfect.

So something, or someone, had to be on her side, after all.

Sixty-Six

Back in London, Cat's euphoria quickly evaporated as her daily routine kicked in. A producer was hired in Budapest and Tony moved on. Mark began to resent Sally's time being taken away from him, and Sally herself began to complain about the tedium of finding, photocopying and despatching scripts. She hadn't gone to secretarial college for that.

This left Cat to deal with it. She was to run the channel by remote control from now on, simply forwarding schedules and materials. It was tempting to put in repeats just to avoid having to search out new scripts and blurbs in the storeroom, but she resisted. It was a dirty job, having to trawl through rows of filing cabinets to find the right series and episodes, and to climb a stepladder to reach many of them. It was there, up the ladder one afternoon, that the reality began to sink in.

The channel would continue and she'd fall into a weekly pattern. But then Mark would sign another deal, most likely with an even tighter deadline. There were enough projects in the balance after all—South Africa, other Eastern European countries, Asia. What was he doing all day if not working on them? And so there would be more crazy launches, which was fine by her, but then more scripts to retrieve, more materials to send, more of the routine drudge.

Most people's careers go upward, she sighed. Hers just got more mundane. What was she doing, gathering scripts in a basement storeroom? She could die here, she thought dramatically.

She could make a noose, throw a rope over one of the rafters, climb up on the ladder and then kick it away. She could hang there and no one would notice her missing for days.

Not that it would make any difference, though. She felt dead already. She felt like a ghost, a spirit trapped on the earthly plane, haunting the corridors of the Trafalgar building and communicating with only the tiny handful who could see her.

Cat watched the photocopier spew out pages of an 80s sitcom. Then she took the scripts back to her office, where she found a sofa she recognized from the breakfast show deposited along one wall. It was a bright orange check that only a TV company would ever use. She sat on it, pausing to think about what it would be like to work on a show like that. There would be a team of reporters, researchers and producers. People to talk to, to bounce ideas off, on-going jokes and banter.

And shagging. Cat jumped up, inspecting the orange check. How many illicit affairs had been started on that sofa? she wondered. She knew it happened—when the lights went down and the cameras were turned off, that sofa would have been a prize target. The crew would watch it in the morning, a pair of squeaky clean presenters sitting comfortably on its plump cushions, and sniggering to themselves, knowing how many sound men had nailed newsreaders there, engineers, production assistants.

How long was it since she last had sex? She couldn't bear to think about it. She'd gone the whole summer without. Oh to have a dirty little affair, she thought dreamily. An office romance, a naughty secret.

An image of Mark popped into her mind. His shirt, white and crumpled, was hanging out of his trousers. His hair was dishevelled and he looked like he'd just cracked a dirty joke. He was coming toward her, sitting beside her, kissing her. His hands were running over her breasts, his lips on her neck, and her skirt was getting ruffled up. The picture cut, like on a promo or in a movie, and suddenly they were naked, laughing and kissing, and exploring each other's bodies.

The phone rang. "Cat." It was Jo's voice. "I so need someone to talk to."

"Oh my God, I don't believe it," Cat said breathlessly. "I was just having a fantasy about doing my boss."

"Oh how mundane," Jo tutted. "Last night I married George Clooney and he was running for president."

They burst out laughing.

"So what do you want to do, have a drink?" Cat asked.

"I'm so pissed off I could drink rubbing alcohol. My fucking apartment's just fallen through. I was screwed. My bastard lawyer was taking so long, the sellers got impatient and accepted a higher offer. Can you believe it?" Cat was still reeling from the shock of her fantasy. "I mean, is *their* lawyer going to kick up a fuss about those things? Or was mine just being an asshole?"

She shook herself out of it. "Can you stay on much longer at your place?"

"I don't know, I've given my notice, I'm going to have to talk to my landlord. I'm so depressed."

They arranged to meet and Cat gathered her things, relieved at least to be able to escape at a decent hour. In the foyer she ran into Mark, and blushed.

"Night on the town?" he asked, holding the door open for her.

"Consoling a friend whose apartment's fallen through. You?"

"Just going home." They crossed Tottenham Court Road together. "Nothing planned."

He seemed quiet, and she wondered if he was a bit down.

"How's Emma?" she asked.

"That was over a long time ago," he said. "Sad really, but there was no heat, between us, you know?" Funny, Cat could remember using those very words herself, once. "She was more of an Esselle than a Brandy."

She turned to him crossly. "Fire just dumped Brandy, didn't you see? I'd stick with your Esselle if I were you. Brandys are nothing but trouble. Men don't marry Brandys, they marry Esselles."

They'd reached the entrance of the station, and she needed to cut through to Soho. He hovered, as if wanting to chat. "Sounds like you're talking from experience?"

She laughed, trying to look mysterious. "Of course I'm not. Have a nice evening." She waved goodbye.

If only you knew, she thought.

Sixty-Seven

Cat had read rave reviews about the telephone psychic Jack Dunne in a magazine. She had often considered calling one of those psychic hotlines in the past, but had had her doubts. But Jack, she had read, had got several extraordinary details right and a couple of things he'd told the reviewer had come true within weeks.

The night of Cat's appointment she felt exhilarated, as if she were doing something positive, in some way moving on. After a brief introduction—a bit about his psychic gift, the tape recording he was making and how he would send her a cassette in the mail—Jack began. He sounded paternal, his voice was mellow, comforting, and he had a slight northern accent.

"I'm picking up something about your work," he started. "You work in communications, do you, something to do with writing, scripts?"

Cat smiled. She'd photocopied enough of them lately. "Yes," she told him. "I work in television."

"But you're not enjoying it are you, love? I'm getting that quite strongly. Stay with it, it'll get better."

Cat doubted it somehow. She felt a pang of disappointment, as if she'd been hoping he'd tell her to take direct action and quit.

"Are you planning a trip, or have you just been on one?"

"I went to Budapest recently."

"No, not that, I'm getting something farther away. A long-haul flight."

"Well, I have been living abroad," Cat told him, wondering whether she was giving too much away. "I only got back last year."

"Ah is that it?" He paused. "Why did you come back, love?" he asked abruptly. "You're not happy here at all, are you?"

"No I'm not," Cat replied, slightly stunned.

"Where were you, Asia? I see Chinese faces around you, you were in Hong Kong, were you? Or Singapore?"

"Hong Kong, yes."

"But you felt you had to leave, was that it?"

"Yes."

"And it hasn't worked out for you back here, has it?"

"No."

"There's a man. I'm getting a businessman type, was he the reason you came back?"

She wondered if this was Dominic.

"I'm getting this man quite strongly, he wears suits. Someone you were close to. Is he an ex-boyfriend?"

"He might be, but he's not the reason I came back."

"There's some unfinished business there, I think, love. Do you still have feelings for him?"

"Yes, I suppose I do."

"I see you two together. I think it'll all work out. Is there a feeling around you both, a kind of awkwardness?"

Cat sighed. "You could say that. But I don't know, I was beginning to get over him."

"Were you, love? Sometimes these things just need time, you know. Rome wasn't built in a day. Did he hurt you?"

"Yes."

"I think he'll come back, you know. I think he'll want to make amends. He cares for you, far more than you realize." The words rang a distant bell, but Cat couldn't remember where from. "But I'm having a problem with you in England. I don't think it suits you. I think you need to go out East again, that's where your opportunities lie."

"You really think so?" Could she go back? The thought gripped her. Could she start again?

"I do see you taking a trip out there soon, and I do see you with this man. Would he go out there with you?"

She sighed. "I don't know." She thought about Dominic's family and saw little chance.

"It would be so right if he did," he added, as if he could see happiness and laughter and love and all the things Cat wanted so badly.

The reading continued; Jack talked about Cat's health, her past and the well-being of her family. He picked up on her father's heart attack, and assured her he would be fine from now on. Once she had hung up and reread her notes, Cat poured herself a celebratory glass of wine. It felt like her eyes had just been opened.

London wasn't right for her; she could see that now. She'd given it plenty of time and things weren't getting any better. Could she go back to Asia, she asked herself, could she start again? She began to plan. She could take some leave and fly out to Hong Kong, catch up with Lorna, sniff around for work, meet some new people and network. From there she could fly on to Singapore, try her luck there. Lorna would have contacts.

She would get to work on her résumé. Her job might have been tedious, but she knew she could make it look good on paper.

Then she would have a holiday, maybe take a week on the beach in Phuket. How she longed to feel the heat of the sun again, the sand under her feet, and the hot dark evening air, thick, like a blanket. What had she been doing freezing her butt off in London when Asia was so accessible?

And Dominic? What of him? Did they really stand a chance after everything that had happened? she wondered. She poured another glass, thinking it all through. Once she had gone out there and secured herself a job, she would come back to sort things out. And then it would be perfectly acceptable to contact him to say she was leaving, get on a friendly basis again. They could exchange e-mails for a few months, then, who knows? Rubens had an office in Hong Kong, it wouldn't exactly be hard for him to transfer. They could move to an apartment or villa on the south side and commute into Central together in the mornings. During the holidays his children could come and stay with them. It would be good for them to experience something of the Far East, and not just the South East.

It was all falling into place. She would see Mark tomorrow and ask for some vacation. Ideally she would need three weeks, which she was more than entitled to, but he'd need someone to cover for her. The thought of sitting alone in that ugly grey office sent a shiver through her. Why on earth had she stuck it for so long?

It had taken one simple phone call and a check for thirty pounds for Cat to see the light. She moved out on to the terrace to study her fading geraniums. The little cat joined her there.

"Presh, I'm moving back to Hong Kong," she whispered, burying her nose in its soft fur. "I'll miss you of course, but Hong Kong!"

She drained her glass, running through her day tomorrow. She would approach Mark about holiday leave and e-mail Lorna with her plans. She had a couple of schedule updates to do and then would be free to concentrate on her résumé. And trawl the Internet for cheap flights.

Suddenly life seemed positive again. Hong Kong! She was going back!

Sixty-Eight

When Cat arrived in the office the next morning she put a call through to Sally, who suggested she pop up to see Mark at noon. She spent the morning sorting out her schedule changes and then e-mailed Lorna with the news of her reading and new plans. She wrote a similar note to Jo before getting to work on her résumé.

Jo wrote back: *Christ, things move fast around you! My landlord called last night and told me I have to leave the apartment in two weeks, as he's got another tenant. I can't believe this has happened. So not only do I have to start house hunting again, I now have to find somewhere else to live in the short term! So pissed off I can't tell you.*

Come to Asia with me. Cat wrote back. *It's the answer to all our problems.*

Suddenly she was convinced that it was, and felt impatient to get out there. She wanted to have flights booked, a place to stay, some contacts to approach. It was a whole new project for her, and she was keen to make it happen.

A little before twelve, she climbed the four flights to Mark's office. He was sitting behind his desk surrounded by documents and spreadsheets and scribbled-out phone messages.

"Cat, you must have read my mind." He looked up from the mess. "Sit down. How's it going?"

"Fine," she said. "Everything's under control. Budapest now has all materials for the first three months and I've just released the first draft eight-hour schedule for December. We had a slight glitch with the quality of some of the tapes but I think it's all sorted now." She paused, preparing herself to ask about vacation.

He was looking bored already. "So I've got a new project for you," he interrupted. "D'you remember all the Asian stuff you did for me? Well the powers-that-be are getting interested. I need to know more about Frontier from an insider's perspective."

"What on earth for?"

"Nothing concrete yet, but as you used to work there, I'd like to know more about the day-to-day operations."

"Such as?" she asked guardedly.

"You know, the company's strengths and weaknesses. Its leadership and management team, especially that joker Carnegie. What's his story? I want to know about the company's strategy, the competition in the region, all the ins and outs. D'you think you could put something together for me?"

"Well, I could. But don't forget I haven't worked there for over a year."

"Got contacts, haven't you?"

"Well, yes." She thought of Lorna. "I mean, from what I've heard it's struggling on, despite everyone's predictions. We all thought it was about to collapse a year ago." She wished he'd tell her more, give her a reason why, instead of letting her guess what he was really after.

"So what's your problem?" He started to look irritated.

"Well Mark, I don't know why you want it, or who's going to see it." She felt like a nagging wife. "And, you know, I think it's a bit indiscreet. Disloyal of me."

"Bullshit, Cat," he snapped. "You work for me now. I know the company's got problems. That deal you and I did, it took six months and a lawyer's letter to get the last payment out of them. All I want is an overview of who does what, where they're going and what the problems really are. And I'll keep it to myself, so you can be as indiscreet as you like. And if you can get anything on the Carnegie rumors so much the better."

"The Carnegie rumors?" Her stomach dropped.

"Don't tell me you haven't heard, I'd be disappointed in you."

"I hear a lot of things." She tried to sound enigmatic. "Which one in particular are you talking about?"

"The one I heard the other night. About death threats and triad gangs. You know it?"

"Yes, I've heard that one." Cat paused. "It's been doing the rounds. Who told you?"

"A friend," he smirked, and Cat wondered if it had been Terry Johnson, who would probably have got it from Jeremy Glover.

"I don't know if there's any truth in it." She wondered if she could diffuse the rumor as easily as she had started it.

"Then why else has he been out of the country for so long?"

She had to laugh. "I don't know, a few months ago I was wondering if he was up for your job."

"Would you have preferred that?" he teased.

"No, Mark, I would not." There were times when he looked at her in a certain way, when everything he said seemed to remind her of Cannes; when he taunted her, enjoyed her discomfort.

"But in Max's defense," she continued, trying to ignore him, "he gave me a hell of a break and I always respected him for that. But the more I got to know him the more I realized there was always a hidden agenda. And now I wouldn't trust him farther than I could throw him."

"And it's exactly that sort of statement which gives credence to the triad rumor."

"I suppose it does, rather." She'd tried to diffuse it. But now it had a momentum of its own, and like Frankenstein's monster, had grown stronger than its creator.

"I can probably get you something in a couple of days." She began to get up.

"Be discreet with your contacts, won't you? I don't want anyone in Hong Kong getting suspicious."

It was only when she got back to her office that Cat remembered why she'd gone to see him in the first place. It was funny how he'd made her forget.

She'd get him the report the following evening, she decided, and then bring up her vacation plans. How weird that Mark was suddenly interested in Asia, now what was that supposed to mean? Absolutely nothing, she told herself crossly. It meant nothing. She was to stop looking for clues and signs in everything from now on, stop deceiving herself.

She started her report and the words flowed; it was as if she was purging herself as she wrote. She skipped lunch and missed *The Pride.* She managed to stay objective but felt that her prose read like a soap opera, which was how Frontier had always felt. And what a bizarre cast of characters it was. They jumped out like the opening titles of Dallas, with JR becoming meaner and uglier as the story unfolded. She wrote about the dismissal of Jerry Greenberg and the disappearance of Melanie Chan, knowing that Mark would smile at her intimations and pick up on the words she'd left unwritten.

By the following evening she had written it, read it through, made revisions, rewritten parts and presented it as the damn good story it was. She took it to Mark, who was slumped in his chair watching the news. He skimmed through it, pausing to read bits as she waited.

"I dare say I'll come up with more as the week goes on," she told him, before bringing up her vacation plans.

"Asia, eh? You never know, I might end up asking you to do some work for me over there, would you be open to that? If we put something toward your flights, say?"

"Business class, I assume?" She smiled. "Of course I'd be open to that. What kind of work?"

He gave her a scornful look. "I could tell you, but I'd only have to kill you later." She rolled her eyes. "Don't rush to book anything just yet, though, will you?"

Cat left his office and walked down the empty staircase to her own. She wondered what was really going on, and wished he'd be straighter with her. It probably wasn't going anywhere, like so many of the other reports she'd done for him. Whatever happened to South Africa? The rest of Eastern Europe? All the other Asian markets? None of them seemed to have come to anything.

The building was quiet now, most people had left and the offices were locked up and in darkness. All Cat had to do was to log off her computer and jump on a train. She was fantasizing about a huge plate of pasta and a glass of chilled wine as she reached her desk, when she stopped, letting out a faint cry. She had received a new e-mail.

It was from Dominic.

Sixty-Nine

Cat got into the office to find a message from Mark asking her to see him at 11:30. That gave her two and a half hours to reply to the in-depth analyses Lorna and Jo would hopefully have sent her, read all her horoscopes, ring her favorite numerology hotline, give herself a quick tarot reading and reread the report she had given Mark the previous night.

She logged on and made herself a coffee, beaming inwardly at the thought of the awesome, incredible, meaningful and life-changing e-mail Dominic had sent her. It read: *How have things been going? Don't suppose you fancy a drink some time?*

Jo and Lorna were strangely less enthusiastic about it than she was, but both agreed that he must have broken up with Lindy and was missing her. She had written back last night, hoping he'd notice the time, which was 7:45, and see her for the hard worker she was. Her reply said: *Have been rushed off my feet launching a Hungarian service which has meant 14-hour days and a very successful business trip to Budapest. Busy planning a trip to Hong Kong, part business, part pleasure, but in the meantime, yes, why not, let's have a drink.*

She read both e-mails again, approving of her response, which she had also forwarded to Lorna and Jo. She liked the tone: she sounded busy, hard-working and career orientated. She in no way sounded lonely or unhappy. Breezy. She sounded breezy, like he was just an old friend to hook up with between business trips.

He hadn't responded yet, it was a bit too early for him. Cat reckoned she'd get something back after her meeting with Mark. But she would get something back. He'd finally seen the light, and life was falling into place. All she'd had to do was make the decision to return to Asia—it had been as simple as that—and the Universe was now rewarding her.

The coincidences were flowing faster than Niagara Falls. She'd mentioned it to Mark and suddenly there was a business opportunity, with the chance of getting her fare paid as well. And Jack Dunne had said that Dominic would go with her, and suddenly there he was, wanting them to get back together. It was extraordinary.

"Fascinating stuff," Mark enthused, waving her report. "Great reading. You should have been a journalist."

Cat beamed. It meant a lot when he complimented her.

"Tell me more about Carnegie." He stretched. She was beginning to see that when Mark was really interested in something he tried to play it down. She smiled. Suddenly everything was getting clearer; she felt as if she had tapped into some Universal knowledge and was becoming more intuitive and in touch than ever before.

"What do you want to know?"

"How did he get the job in the first place?"

"He was a crony of Desmond Tang's. He was his corporate communications person, or something like that, but in truth I think he was a glorified gofer." She changed her tone, trying to sound fair. "Maybe he's a launch person, he's certainly driven, but I don't think he's the sort to take the company to the next stage."

"That's exactly the impression I get. But he did all the channel deals, did he?"

"Yes, he did. How great they actually are I don't know, but he got them done, and he launched five channels in record time."

"Programming deals?"

"A few. A bit dodgy, though."

Mark sat up straight. "Dodgy?"

Cat faltered. "There were a lot of things he was cagey about, he never let me see any paperwork or finances." She could see Mark taking this in.

"And why did you fall out with him?"

Cat's face reddened. "What d'you mean, fall out?"

"Well, why else did you leave? You were making decent money, you had a great job, why leave?"

She took a deep breath. "He set me up. He made a drunken, stupid pass after a party one night, and was humiliated when I turned him down. From then on I became a target. Nothing I could do was right. He hired a promo manager on a salary far higher than mine, and shortly afterwards promoted him above me. I couldn't stay after that."

"Nice," Mark exhaled. "So we've got dodgy dealing, sexual impropriety and triad connections. Hot stuff."

"Where is all this leading?"

"I have a meeting this afternoon with the powers-that-be. Sir John's been in direct talks with Desmond Tang."

"My God. So this is quite serious then?"

"You could say that," he smirked. "But I couldn't possibly comment."

Cat smiled, disguising her irritation. "There are a lot of good people at Frontier," she tried. "They've just been horribly mismanaged."

"Thanks again." He nodded. "I'll let you know what happens."

Cat raced downstairs to see if Dominic had written back yet. He had. She took a deep breath before opening his mail. It read: *Are you free Friday night? To get you in the Asian mood we could always go to Jim Thompson's over the road from you. Shall we meet at the bar at 7:30?*

Perfect, Cat beamed. How thoughtful of him to choose somewhere Asian. He really was making an effort. And interesting that he should pick somewhere so convenient for her.

Two days. In just two day's time she and Dominic would be reunited. She forwarded both e-mails to Lorna and Jo and celebrated with a sandwich over *The Pride and the Passion*. Fire had confessed his affair with Brandy to Esselle, who was devastated. Most of the episode was taken up with her tears and hysterics, and Cat wondered idly if there had been tears and hysterics with Lindy? What could have happened? She must have discovered Cat's hidden clues and demanded an explanation from Dominic, who would have been forced into confessing the truth.

There would have been tears, hysterics, things thrown and

Dominic's face slapped. They would have broken up immediately, and Dominic would probably have gone through a period of anger toward Cat. But by now he was over it. And in just two days' time it would all come right. Now all she had to do was persuade him to quit his job, leave his family and move with her to Hong Kong.

And then everything would work out.

Seventy

The next two days Cat stayed restlessly at her desk. She received words of encouragement from Lorna, words of warning from Jo and no words at all from Mark. Everything seemed to be happening at once and yet still she had to wait. She felt like she was living under a volcano—she could hear it rumbling but was yet to receive official warning to move on. She knew that by the weekend she and Dominic could be together again. She also knew that she still wanted to move to Hong Kong. Somehow it would all fall into place—the only things that had really bothered her about Dominic were his squalid flat and his mundane lifestyle. Once she'd removed those, they could be happy together. Hong Kong was the solution. She would find them a beautiful apartment which she would then decorate. And he would finally be happy.

But what was happening in Hong Kong? Cat longed to get her trip sorted, book her flights. She had trawled numerous websites and found an idyllic-looking beachfront hotel in Phuket. Would Mark come up with a reason for her to go, or would she have to pay her own way? It irritated her that he still hadn't contacted her since their last meeting, but maybe it was a sign that she should concentrate on her upcoming evening instead?

She was going to leave at five, go home, fill her vases with fresh flowers, tidy up a bit, have a shower and fix her hair, and then get dressed for tonight's date. What to wear? The ice-blue suit? Too business-like. Jeans and a T-shirt? Too casual. She got it—she'd wear the golden silk outfit that had proved such a success in Budapest. She'd had a nice time that trip with Mark, she remembered fondly. He'd been great company.

By ten to five she thought her stomach was about to explode. Still no word from Mark, she thought irritably. What was he doing? She thought about popping up to his office but decided against it. If he were busy she'd feel a fool hanging around, getting in the way. It was three minutes to five. She logged off, tidied her desk and made for the door. One minute to . . . Oh fuck it, what was the point in waiting any longer?

As she got to the elevator the doors slid open and there was Mark. They both jumped and then laughed nervously. "I was just coming to see you," he started. "Fancy a drink?"

"Oh damn it, Mark, I'd love one, but I can't. I have plans."

"Too bad." He called the elevator back. "I'm going to the bar anyway, we can ride down together. I need to escape."

"That bad?"

"Tell me about it. I'm sorry I haven't been keeping you up-to-date but so much has been going on. But your report's been incredibly useful, don't worry."

They got into the next elevator, but as it was almost full she didn't like to ask what was happening. They stood awkwardly until they were deposited on to the ground floor.

"Are you sure you won't have a drink?"

She looked at her watch. Could she manage one? She was dying to hear Mark's news. "Oh all right then, just a quick one."

He led her to the bar, which was heaving with Trafalgar staff, and bought her a glass of wine. She liked the way he looked. He stood out from the crowd, who seemed to wear a uniform of faded jeans with their shirts hanging down. She liked it that Mark wore a suit, albeit a fairly shabby one, and that his shirt was tucked in properly and he wore a tie.

"So what are your plans for tonight?" he asked.

Cat could barely control the beam that spread across her face. "I'm seeing my ex-boyfriend." How she hated that term. "We're having a reunion dinner."

"I didn't know you'd broken up." He didn't seem very pleased for her. "So it's all back on again, is it?"

"I can't say for sure, but I think so, hope so."

"Congratulations," he said after a pause. "I hope it works out for you."

He looked rather sad, she thought, as he downed his vodka and tonic. Was he missing Emma, or was the pressure of work just getting to him?

"So do you have plans for the weekend?" she asked. She wanted to know more about Hong Kong but the bar was too crowded for her to risk asking.

"Please," he laughed. "The way things are going I'll be here most of the time."

"Do tell me, won't you? What's going on?"

"I will when I can. Though right now I just need a break from it all."

They shifted to a quieter spot where Cat felt freer to talk. "So what about you? You're not seeing anyone then, since Emma?"

"Oh yeah, there've been a couple of people. Nothing special, though."

"That's so strange, Mark. You're such a catch and there are so many single women out there."

He laughed. "Maybe there is someone," he said carefully. "But you know, there are always complications."

"Oh." Cat felt the wine relaxing her. "Complications are bad. To be avoided at all cost. My last two boyfriends, including this one tonight." *TONIGHT! She was seeing Dominic tonight!* "Both had complications. Never again."

"But you are seeing him again."

"Yes, but only because I'm hoping the complications will be over."

"Well I hope they are too," he told her, frowning, and Cat felt suddenly bad for him. So he was in love with someone who was in love with someone else too, then? She wouldn't wish that feeling on anyone. Who were these women who couldn't see a decent man if he stood right in front of them, anyway? People like Sandy or Mark's woman? She couldn't imagine being so blind.

"I should go," she told him apologetically. "I've got to get ready."

He leaned forward and kissed her on the cheek. "Good luck, Cat," he whispered. "Knock him out."

At seven-thirty she headed across the street to Jim Thompson's to see Dominic arriving. He'd made an effort, she thought proudly. He'd really pushed himself to get there on time.

"You look great," he said with a bashful smile. "Let's get a drink."

He ordered champagne and Cat eased her way to the bar beside him. He looked the same as ever. His suit was navy, shirt Oxford blue, tie a conservative blue and green. He kept staring at her appreciatively, as if he was proud to be the one buying her drinks. As the bar filled they were pushed closer and closer together, until she could smell the champagne on his breath and make out all the different colors which made up his hazel-green eyes.

He told her about work, about new developments, about members of staff. She didn't ask about Sandy, or Lindy, and he didn't volunteer information. They didn't need to, Cat thought. They were together now, and that was all that was important.

They were shown to their table in the vast area filled with tropical plants and Asian artefacts. For Cat it was the perfect setting to tell him about her plans. Maybe he would even go with her, she thought excitedly. When was the last time he'd ever had a vacation? Maybe she could tempt him with descriptions of golden sands, fabulous food and the energy of Hong Kong?

He listened attentively, pausing every now and again to stroke her hand, or to gently push a stray hair out of her eye. They ate Thai food and drank a bottle of Pouilly Fuissé. As the meal ended he suggested they have coffee at her place. She laughed, and they held hands across the table. He put his arm protectively around her as they crossed the road, and then once in her doorway as Cat fumbled in her bag for the keys, he pushed her gently up against the door and kissed her. For a second she worried about getting dirt on her clothes, but then she relaxed into the kiss. What did it matter if her outfit was ruined? The only thing that mattered was that they were together, and that they had a future together.

They made love. And it was making love, Cat reflected, rather than the aggressive sex they'd last had. What a ridiculous time that was. What a ridiculous thing she had done. As Jo had said, she'd gone crazy with it all, quite crazy. But those days were long gone now, and she was thinking with new clarity. She wouldn't rush into anything. She'd carry on with her plans for Asia and gradually tempt him to join her there. It would be a romantic story to tell everyone: how they lost each other for a few months, and how by the time they'd got back together she was leaving the country, and then how finally he realized that he had to go, too.

They lay in each other's arms and Cat felt completely secure for the first time in months. In Dominic she had a strong and protective lover, and in Mark a dynamic and protective boss. Throw in a trip to Asia and what more could she ask for? She began to doze to the sound of Dominic's reassuring, even sleep beside her. She was going to miss Mark. She hadn't thought of it before, but she'd miss him. How would she tell him she was leaving, and however would he take it? She hoped he'd understand. Maybe they'd become friends and e-mail silly jokes to each other and go to each other's weddings. Wouldn't it be wonderful to marry in Thailand, or Bali? As she slowly fell asleep, Cat imagined the scenery, the heat, the dress she'd wear. The ceremony, the flowers and the honeymoon . . .

Seventy-One

"What about going to the cinema tonight?" She breezed into the living room carrying a tray of coffee, orange juice and croissants. She'd washed and dressed in a white T-shirt and knee-length skirt and her hair was pulled loosely off her face. He was on the sofa, fully dressed now and pulling on his shoes. It looked worryingly as if he were about to leave.

"Oh no, Cat, no." His face darkened and he rubbed his eyes. "I can't do anything like that."

"Why on earth not, do you have the kids?"

"No, it's not that." He took a deep breath. "I just can't see you again."

"What?" She slumped down on the armchair. It had to be a joke. Then she remembered that Dominic never joked.

"I'm sorry." He looked away, started tying his shoelaces, and instinctively Cat knew.

"You're still seeing Lindy, aren't you?"

"I'm sorry. I should never have contacted you."

"Why did you then?" She stayed calm, poured coffee and fantasized about throwing his in his lap.

"She's away," he said quietly.

"So you thought, 'Good old Cat. She's always up for a fuck.'" And as she said it she cringed, knowing that that was exactly the impression she must have given before. She sipped her coffee, trying to take it in. He was still with her? "Did you ever tell her about the night I stayed?" she asked eventually.

"She was suspicious. She found something, a lipstick?" Cat tried not to react. "I told her you'd come around, but not that you'd stayed. I said you were upset and that it was probably an attempt to break us up."

"And so where is Lindy now?"

"On vacation with her mother," he mumbled.

"She vacations with her mother, does she?" Cat made it sound like a failing. "So where have they gone?" More ammunition was needed.

"To Rhodes, if you must know."

Strangely, Cat felt relief that they were going somewhere European and safe. Trekking in Peru or seeing the Great Wall of China would have been far more threatening. Instead she could almost picture Lindy and her mum, pink-skinned and excitable, drinking retsina in a very average taverna.

"And so you thought you'd see them off at Gatwick and then enjoy a quick fuck in her absence?"

"It wasn't like that—"

"Then what was it like?" she snapped. "What?"

"Cat, I." He could say nothing. Regret was etched all over his face like the pre-op markings of a plastic surgeon.

"So last night you buy champagne and talk to me as if I was the most desirable woman on the planet. You make love to me like I'm something special and now this morning I'm nothing, nothing at all."

"I'm sorry. I got everything wrong." He started to get up. "I think I should just go."

Cat turned away and focused on the Balinese masks that hung on either side of the fireplace. She would go to Asia. She would meet someone else. She would forget about Dominic; this time she really would.

He gathered his belongings. Cat stayed dully looking at the masks, wanting him out of her life and yet desperate for him not to leave just yet. Once he'd done that she'd have nothing, just a long weekend and all the questions she knew would only come once the pressure of his presence was lifted.

"I'll say goodbye then."

"So you really can just turn it on whenever you want to, then?" she snapped. "Last night you were all over me. You pushed me up against the door and you kissed me, remember? And yet it meant nothing to you? You could have been doing it to anyone."

"I should just go." He paused. "I'm sorry." He started walking down the stairs and she panicked, wanting to make him feel worse before he left.

"You actually planned the whole thing—that's what's so despicable," she shouted. "It's not as if we ran in to each other somewhere and had a screw for old time's sake—you planned it. It was premeditated."

"I'm sorry. I didn't think—"

"Think what?"

"That it would bother you. I didn't think for a moment that you were still interested. I blew it, I'm sorry."

She willed herself to think of something cutting and funny, something that would stay with him for months, but she couldn't. Her mind had gone numb. She listened as his footsteps continued down the stairs, and then heard the door open and close. On impulse she jumped up to watch him from her bedroom window, but as much as she strained she couldn't see him; he'd all but disappeared among the Saturday morning crowds.

She switched on the news, hoping a tragic plane crash or the untimely death of a celebrity might rouse her from her impending depression. Neither had happened and she scolded herself. How shallow had she become, that she seriously wanted others to die in order to put her own problems into perspective? Who did she think she was? Was she so self-obsessed that other people's lives had become meaningless?

Had her years of spiritual development resulted in nothing? Had she just become a wreck who clung to horoscopes for security? What had it all been about, any of it? The stars, the tarot, the psychics—what had any of it been about? She felt empty and worthless. She didn't watch the news for its news content every day; she watched it to alleviate her boredom. She took no real interest in the Middle East peace process or in the spread of AIDS in Africa; they were simply a distraction from her own pitiful circumstances.

She stared forlornly at the breakfast tray. Just an hour ago the future had seemed so different. All those dreams and fantasies, and every one of them a waste of time. And now Dominic would return to his smug little relationship and Lindy would kid herself that he was treating her with respect. If only she knew.

Cat no longer cared that she had lost Dominic. Dominic wasn't worth having in the first place. All she cared now was that someone else had got him, and that that someone else believed he was worth having. If only Lindy could find out. Cat poured another coffee and called Lorna. She got her answering machine. Then she tried Jo with the same result.

She felt strangely calm as she cleared away the breakfast things, and then it came to her. She dialled Dominic's number. He wouldn't be home yet, but she would leave a message. His voice came on the line—it had always reminded Cat of a vicar, there was something pious about it—and at the beep she said, "Dominic, it's Cat. I'm still in shock at the way you've treated me this week and the more I think about it the angrier I become." The lies flowed fluently. "I know Lindy's number, I've known it for some time now, and once she's back from vacation I'm going to give her a ring and let her know exactly what you've been up to, including that Sunday night. She has a right to know. I'm sure she'll find it all fascinating."

Triumphantly she flung the phone down, her breath quickening.

Seventy-Two

The first call came shortly after eleven o'clock. Cat picked it up, heard Dominic's voice and dropped the receiver again. A minute later the phone rang again. She let it go to the machine.

"Cat," came his anguished cry. "I know you're there, please, pick up. Cat. Pick up. Please." She picked the receiver up and promptly dropped it again. A minute later it rang again and she let it go.

"Cat, please. I know you're angry. But please, don't do this. I beg you. Don't do it. Come on, Cat, let's talk about it. Pick up, please."

She walked out on to the terrace and dead-headed the geraniums. "Cat," his voice wailed in the background. "Please let's talk. Don't do this. Don't do it. I beg you." The answering machine switched him off. Cat erased his last messages and the phone started ringing again. She picked it up and dropped it.

Cat rearranged her flowers. "Please. Don't do this. Don't ruin my life. I love her. I know you don't want to hear it but I love her." The words stung but she carried on. "I love her. Please, don't do this." The machine cut him off again.

He called several more times, repeating the same strangulated sentiments. Cat made up a shopping list, changed her sheets and got ready to go out. She was beginning to feel imprisoned by his calls, and it irritated her that Jo and Lorna wouldn't be able to get through. In the end she pulled the phone out of the socket.

It occurred to her as she left that he might come around later, try to dissuade her in person. She had to remember to keep the light off in the bedroom and close the door, so he might think she was out. It worried her that he might do something stupid. She felt like she was in a movie and having to enter a witness protection program to evade a boyfriend who'd gone over the edge. She had a brief fantasy that she was Julia Roberts in *Sleeping with the Enemy*, and looked behind herself a few times, urgently tossing her hair over her shoulders.

She walked the length of Kings Road and turned left into Sloane Street, ending up inside Harvey Nichols. Nothing bad could ever happen to her there. She bought makeup, glossy hose and some sunglasses to cheer herself up. She didn't want to go home. Couldn't bear the thought of listening to more of his messages all night. What if he were waiting for her when she got back, what then? She imagined a struggle; she might hit her head, fall down unconscious in the street.

No, she told herself. She just had an overactive imagination. He wouldn't come around. He would stay in his squalid flat, drinking beer and whisky. He'd revel in his misery, come up with more and more ways to blame her and refuse to accept responsibility himself. She had nothing to fear.

Cat walked back up Kings Road, her legs beginning to tire now. It felt good just to be among people. If she ever were in real danger, she decided, she would head for Harrods. It wouldn't take much to lose someone there. She popped into the supermarket and then continued home, stopping off at Heal's and fantasizing about living in an apartment so stylish she'd get requests to appear in interior design magazines. Not unlike the loft she had once wanted with Dominic. How old and tired that fantasy seemed by now.

When she got home, Dominic was not prowling around on her doorstep, nor had her flat been trashed. Life was as usual. She kept the phone unplugged and enjoyed the calm of the television instead.

She felt numb, blank. Too lethargic to meditate, too bored even to care about her tarot cards. It really was all over. She had been a fool to think they could ever have got back together.

The next morning she lay heavily in her bed, willing the day to pass. Exhausted in defeat, drained of emotion and, she realized with a sense of relief, beginning to be bored with it all. She felt like a jaded story-line in a soap opera. If there were viewers of her life they would have switched off by now, tired of watching her throw herself from one humiliation to the next under the misguided belief that Dominic had been her destiny.

She got up, plugged her phone back in and went across the road for the papers. Coming back, she was relieved to hear silence. He'd given up. It was over. She made coffee and out of habit turned to the horoscope, which read:

You are at the top of the world right now, and deservedly so. Everything you've ever wanted is now dropping into your hands like overripe fruit from the trees. Catch it, grasp it firmly, and don't let go. The path might not be an easy one, but it's yours, and no one else's.

"What crap," Cat said aloud as she read it through for the second time. Wasn't this the same astrologer who'd told her that Max was about to become her new boss? "Total and utter crap." Her voice began to break now, and she could feel the tears, which had surprised her by their absence, beginning to well up. She took a deep breath. She would not cry. There was no point in crying over that man; no point at all.

She turned on the TV and watched the headlines, then started channel-hopping. She came to an American talk show where the hostess was reviewing a self-help book about the search for happiness. A group of tearful disciples described the impact it had had on their lives. Cat watched with the same kind of detached fascination she reserved for anthropological documentaries. These people could have come from a different world in a different time. That anyone could expose their vulnerabilities at all was beyond her. That they could do it on national TV, to be syndicated around the world, just left her feeling deeply unmoved and cynical.

The phone rang and she stopped, hoping it was Lorna or Jo. How wonderful it would be to sink on the sofa and describe in glorious, if not slightly exaggerated, detail, the events of the last two days. She let the machine pick it up, and then sighed as she heard Dominic's voice.

"Cat—are you there? I'm sure you are. I didn't sleep last night.

Listen, Lindy's back Wednesday night. I don't want you to speak to her. I've decided to meet her at the airport and tell her myself. I think that's the best way. I suppose I should be grateful to you for forcing me to be honest with the woman I love. Yes, Cat, the woman I love. I want to marry her, you know. These last few hours have made me realize how important she is to me. I just hope she can forgive me and that we can get over this. Like I said, maybe I should be grateful."

The phone clicked down and Cat caught her breath. *The woman he loved. The woman he wanted to marry.* Dominic would never be happy. He would continue to chase happiness and then let it go the minute he'd found it. Misery was his happiness and depression his ally. He would only make Lindy unhappy. Maybe Cat had even done her a favor.

"Happiness is our birthright," the show hostess was proclaiming. Cat laughed at the irony. What *right* did anyone have to feel happiness? She tried to remember the last time she'd ever really felt it. It was probably when she was still at Rubens, before her relationship with Dominic had taken off. Then she had had hope. At the lowest point of her life she'd had so much to look forward to. Her happiness had come from dreams and fantasies, none of which had matured. The reality that developed certainly hadn't brought her happiness.

The woman he loved. She no longer cared about Dominic; that pain was leaving her. It felt as if she was shedding a thick winter coat for the spring; every now and then there was a nip in the air and she wanted to pull it back around her shoulders; but now summer had come and it was stifling her, rubbing against her bare skin, and she knew she was better off without it. He was never the man she'd loved. She had had a fantasy of the man he might be, and when he'd turned into someone else she'd simply made excuses for him.

She went back to the kitchen and began emptying the dishwasher. It was good to be doing something menial as her mind raced. It felt like a wheel of a car, stuck in some mud and splattering unsettling thoughts around her.

So what *was* getting at her now? She tried to sort through her feelings. If she no longer cared about Dominic and Lindy, what was the problem? Why was depression hovering over her like a lost soul? *Get away from me*, she wanted to shout. *Leave me now! Go into the light!* Wasn't that what they always said? She should get an exorcist. She had enough demons after all; she just couldn't figure out what they wanted.

She was still in shock, that was her problem. Everything had happened so fast—on Wednesday she'd become pregnant with a new dream, on Friday she'd given birth to it and by Saturday it had died a sudden and violent death. Of course she was going to feel mixed up and depressed.

But there was more. She had to focus. *To admit the truth was to start the process by which you release it*; she was sure she'd read that somewhere. What got to her more than anything was the fact that someone else was loved. Dominic loved Lindy. Lindy had succeeded where Cat all her life had failed. Other people found love all the time—some made it look as easy as buying a bus ticket—yet all she had ever managed was a string of brief and irrelevant flirtations—unsatisfying snacks to stave off a life-long famine.

Then there was Declan. He hadn't loved her enough to leave Harriet. But whenever things had been going well—whenever they'd shared a wonderful weekend, or a romantic dinner—all she'd done was sabotage it by bringing up the girl's name. The few times she'd ever been offered happiness all she'd done was snap at it, tell it to fuck off. So he'd moved on and hadn't looked back. And now he had Amanda.

Cat cringed as she remembered. What had she done there? What was it with this destructive streak she had? Was that what was holding her back? If she could just have been happy for him, shown him some generosity, then maybe things would have turned out differently. Maybe the Universe would have rewarded her. But oh no, fired up by jealousy and spite she'd deliberately set him up. If Cat Wellesley couldn't be happy, then neither should anyone else. And now it had come full circle. Cause and effect. You only get back what you put out in this world, and Cat could see now she had put out a lot of shit.

She didn't deserve love, or happiness, or any of those things people crave. In this life she would be alone. It was what her soul had chosen for her. In this life there would be pain and hurt and disappointment. She had brought it upon herself.

"Happiness is our birthright," the hostess repeated with gravitas as an excited audience clapped.

"No, it's fucking not," Cat hissed. She felt imprisoned along a path that she had not chosen. She slid down the kitchen units, her legs suddenly useless, and as she reached the floor, knocked over the dish of milk she'd left out for the cat. "Oh very funny, Universe," she snapped at the ceiling. "Very fucking funny."

She buried her face in her hands and sobbed. There were no tears—they'd dried up long ago—just painful, heaving sighs that pulled on her ribcage and felt tougher than a hundred crunches on a full stomach.

"Happiness is not our fucking birthright," she hissed at the television. There was no claim on happiness. Life was about pain and suffering and misery. It was about illness and famine and repression. Loss and betrayal. If you found happiness, cling to it, because it wouldn't last long. You didn't learn from happiness. Happiness would only turn into despair again.

Life was about learning and experience, that was all, and you only learned through suffering. Cat pictured the millions who had suffered over the centuries. Victims of war, famine, crime. Since time began there had only been one recurrent theme—suffering. There was so little happiness in life, who was anyone to demand it as a birthright? Who was Cat to demand it? She had had her moments of happiness but that was it—moments within years.

And she hadn't suffered half as much as most.

She sat straighter now as her thoughts began to clear. "It's about strength," she realized. That was what it was all about. The strength to go on. The strength to wake up each morning and to live your life, be it in the face of tragedy or depression or hardship. It was such a simple message Cat had to stop to think it through. But it was so clear to her now she wondered why she'd never got it before.

Life was about strength. That was all there was to it. The soul's journey, the soul's path, was all about becoming stronger. And then the stronger you got, the more the world threw at you. Life wasn't about hiding under the covers or crying on the kitchen floor. Life was about picking yourself up, staring hardship in the face, and just carrying on.

She got up and wiped up the spilled milk on the floor. The more she thought, the more it made sense. She only had to think about all the disabled people she'd seen on TV running marathons or climbing mountains or painting portraits with their feet. They had become stronger and more resilient because they were evolved souls—souls who'd experienced much already and were prepared for the hardest reality of them all. They had an inner strength. Cat thought of the women who'd lost husbands in wars, or mothers who'd lost children. They could easily have slumped back into their armchairs, surrounded by their photos and immersed in their grief. But they'd got strong and fought on—fought for their rights, or for justice, or to create peace.

Cat's troubles were nothing in comparison. So she'd never found love, so what? Get over it. She was capable of living alone. She could earn a living and she could feed herself. What right did she have to feel sorry for herself? It would be an insult to all the others.

She sat out on the terrace, listening to the birds. The little cat joined her there, jumping timidly on to her knee.

"Survival of the fittest," Cat whispered as she stroked her cheek against its soft head. Everything was falling into place. The survival of the fittest! How fitting that nature itself had held the key to what philosophers and theologians had been struggling to determine for centuries. The meaning of life! She had just figured it all out, there on her kitchen floor on a Sunday morning.

Life was about strength. It was not about happiness or love, they were mere rewards. It was a test of strength. In the big scheme of things, Cat herself had not been tested that much so far. There would be other problems, other difficulties, other tests. And then there would be other lives, Cat was convinced of that now. For it all to make sense, she would have to experience everything: a life in a third-world country, a life of repression, a life as a member of each religion, a life with disability. Then and only then would she achieve the highest reward—perfect, unconditional happiness. Life wasn't about happiness; death was.

So what had she learned from the Dominic débâcle? She tried to make sense of it. What had she got out of it, not in a material, earthly sense but on a deeper, soul level?

She couldn't think of a damn thing. Had she grown from it? Grown more cynical, maybe. Had she learned anything? Not to trust men? Had the experience led her anywhere? Not that she could think of.

She made some herbal tea and sipped it thoughtfully, returning to the garden. Were they stuck on a treadmill now, her and Dominic? Would this war continue for another life? Maybe that was even it in the first place, maybe they had just been continuing a fight from a past life? She sipped her tea thoughtfully. So perhaps it was time to break the karma? Perhaps she should call him and admit that she had no way of contacting Lindy?

A bit dull and worthy, that. She could always call him on Wednesday, let him sweat it out a bit. It might teach him a lesson.

Declan too—maybe all that was about unfinished business being carried over? Maybe in this life she was supposed to let go, detach herself from all karmic ties. Release them all. She closed her eyes and tried a visualization. She imagined Declan and Dominic (two Ds—that alone might signify some karmic link) attached to her by two long pieces of thread, like dogs on a lead.

She tested it, pulling them closer for a second, and then letting the thread loosen, until finally she let it go altogether, and watched them slip away. "I release you to the Universe," she whispered, slightly self-consciously, hoping her neighbors weren't out gardening. "I release you both."

Precious dug her claws into Cat's thigh, and she smiled, easing them off. She felt surprisingly calm and mature. She felt she had raised herself to another level, a level where petty jealousies and thoughts of revenge no longer existed. She would call Dominic on Wednesday. She would put him out of his misery.

"Oh, I'm sorry, is she bothering you?" Her neighbor appeared in the garden, nodding toward the cat.

"No, no, not at all, I love her visits." Cat smiled warmly.

"Well, just kick her out if she gets too much, won't you?"

"She's fine, I enjoy the company." They smiled at each other and Cat wondered how they had managed not to meet after all this time. Precious jumped down to be with her mistress and Cat smiled peacefully, having enjoyed the human contact, however slight it may have been. That was what it was all about, moments like that. You get knocked down, you get back up again. Not because you think that love will be just around the corner, not because you're entitled to happiness at the next stage, not because something fantastic must be about to happen; just because. That was it. Just because.

Seventy-Three

She got into work the next morning to an urgent call from Mark. She picked up her pen and a notepad, running through everything she had done for him recently and wondering nervously if she had got any of it wrong. She was sure her report would have been scrutinized by senior management—what if she had made any mistakes? She took the stairs two at a time, running over anything vaguely controversial she might have written and trying to make up her defense.

Mark was at his desk, which was covered in files and documents as usual, wearing a crumpled white shirt and a tie that looked like it had been knotted in the dark.

"How was your weekend?" he started. "Oh, how did the date go?" He sat up, as if suddenly remembering something of huge interest.

"It was a disaster, thanks," Cat joked, a sense of relief flooding over her. He wasn't angry with her then, it wasn't that. "But I'm fine. I'm over it."

"Glad to hear it. Maybe it just wasn't meant to be, eh?"

Cat smiled. After the day of revelations she'd just had, his naivety made him all the more human. Deal-maker *extraordinaire* he might have been, but he still had a long way to go. She felt suddenly calmer, more mature. "How was your weekend?" She had no wish to reveal more about hers.

"Busy. That's why I wanted to see you straight away. I just bought Frontier."

"What?" How typical of Mark to throw away a line like that.

"Or at least a controlling share of it. I spent the weekend on the phone down at Sir John's delightful weekend cottage in the New Forest. Lady Maudsley does a lovely roast pork."

She could picture Sir John in tweeds and Lady Maudsley in a twin set. The scene was more *Country Living* than corporate raiders.

"So Desmond Tang finally wanted to sell?"

"Couldn't wait to get shot of it. Felt he'd been throwing good money after bad."

"And Trafalgar wouldn't be?"

He raised an eyebrow. "It's an opportunity," he told her. "We have the programming expertise and the management know-how. We can turn the company around."

"And so, all this happened at the weekend?" She had so many questions she didn't know which to ask first.

"It was finalized over the weekend, but Sir John's been in talks for a while now. All very hush hush."

"For goodness sake." It was hard to take it all in. "So what about Carnegie?"

"Given his marching orders last night."

"So who's going to run the company now?"

He sat back and clasped his hands behind his head. "I am."

"Oh my God, Mark, congratulations." It was hard to take in. "You're moving to Hong Kong?"

"That's right. I nearly called you last night, you know. Thought we could celebrate, and then I thought you probably were already."

"I wish you had called." She shook her head. "I was just sitting on my terrace with the neighbor's cat."

How nice it would have been to have spent the evening with Mark, she thought. To have heard the revelations over a bottle of champagne, to have had time to digest them, to have talked them over at length, comfortably, over food and wine. She felt a stab of disappointment. "So they're going to replace you here?"

"They've got a couple of people in mind, apparently."

"And, I hate to ask, but where does all this leave me?"

"Well, as your report said, strictly speaking there's no programming head. I need someone I can rely on and trust. Someone who knows the people, the systems, the problems. Someone who can help me turn the company around and drag it into profit." Irritatingly, he paused to top up his coffee and take a sip. "You want the job?"

"Mark, you're offering me head of programming?" Cat asked incredulously.

"Call it Vice President if you like. Bit more gravitas."

She smiled. Under the arms of his shirt she could see dark patches of sweat, and she knew he wasn't as calm as he made out.

"You do realize they make a hell of a lot more money out there than we do here?"

"I've been checking it all out, don't worry. How much d'you want?"

She paused. He needed her badly, she could see that now. She had the contacts, she had an understanding of the region and she knew the company well. Without her he would be vulnerable. Cat knew she had all the power right now. She thought of Glover's salary and doubled it. He didn't flinch. "And I'll need a decent housing allowance," she added quickly.

"Yeah, yeah, you'll get it. You want a car too?"

"Silly not to." She laughed. *A car!* With a car she could get a villa in Sai Kung overlooking the bay. She could live on the south side of the island. She could feel her eyes widen like a child's. "When do we leave?"

"I'm on a flight out Wednesday, I need to do an all-staff session straight away. You want to join me then?"

"Of course." Her mind raced to thoughts of her apartment and her terrace, and all her plants wilting.

"Good girl. I think the tickets are already booked." He winked. "We'll go for a few days, soothe and schmooze, and then you can come back and collect your stuff. That sound OK?"

"Sure." *Jo!* Jo could move in. "And who would do my existing job?"

"I was thinking about that, at least for the short term. Now the channel's up and running, you're not exactly taxed, are you? So I was thinking about Sally. She doesn't want to come to Hong Kong but is terrified of having to work for some jerk. Could she do it, what do you think?"

"It would be perfect for her! I can show her everything over the next couple of days. She'll pick it up really quickly, it's hardly brain surgery. And they already know her in Budapest. I think it would be a great opportunity for her."

"Excellent. I'll suggest it to her in a minute. So, get yourself sorted. You've got three days."

"Unreal." She stood up, and he moved with her. "I'm thrilled, I really am. Thank you." She reached up and kissed him, and he pulled her in toward him.

"Couldn't have done it without you."

"Please."

"Seriously. The inside info. That's what got Sir John going, and gave us the edge over Tang. It made a big difference."

She started to feel emotional and was beginning to leave when another thought struck her. "You know something? Can we kill off bloody well working on Saturdays?"

"Good idea. First thing we do. Make everyone realize we're good guys. We'll work on my speech on the plane."

At her desk Cat logged on to her computer to find five new e-mails, including one from Lorna. It read: *Cat, when you get in, call me. Word is around here that we've just been bought by your company. Do you know anything? What's the deal here?*

Her mind raced. There was so much to do. She typed back a quick response: *It's all true. Announcement Wednesday. Things crazy here—will type later.*

She called Jo, who simply repeated "I don't believe it" four or five times as the story unfolded. "Take my flat, Jo. Look after my geraniums."

"Oh my God, you have no idea how depressed I've been about finding somewhere. I looked at a few on Saturday and they were awful. I'm sorry I didn't call you back but I was so feeling so low. I would love your flat."

"It's yours from Wednesday." They agreed to have drinks on Tuesday.

"Thank you, Universe," Cat kept saying, not quite believing her luck. At the window a fly kept buzzing against the glass. She watched it for a minute as it repeatedly knocked itself in frustration. All it had to do was move to the left and it would have flown clear through the open side window.

And that was all Cat had had to do. She'd been banging her head against block after block, and finally she was turning left. "Thank you, Universe," she whispered again and again. "Thank you."

Seventy-Four

So much to do, so little time. Cat took Sally through her old job. It felt like she was unloading a great weight, a part of her life that she had never felt particularly comfortable with. She drank champagne as she showed Jo around the apartment, pointing out all its idiosyncrasies and promising to clear out more things on her return. Lorna kept in constant touch, telling Cat the rumors that were going around and how people were reacting to the news. On Wednesday morning she called again.

"You'll never believe this, but I just found out what the story was behind Carnage. Turns out his mother was dying of cancer."

"What?" Cat's stomach tightened.

"She lived in London, married a Brit after Max's father died."

"Hard to imagine him even having parents. So he was, what, looking after her?"

"You got it. All the time he was in London, trying to arrange better treatment, getting hold of specialists, all that kind of thing. Refused to leave."

"You remember I saw him at a restaurant once?" Cat's voice trailed off as she thought of the birthday surprise she'd fixed. "I remember thinking the woman he was with wasn't his usual type. So who was she, I wonder? A relative?"

"I guess. His sister flew over from the US."

Cat felt terribly, terribly guilty.

"And then this fucking rumor starts up about triad connections," Lorna continued. "It went out of control."

"Tang must have known the truth," Cat tried. It couldn't all have been her fault, surely?

"I guess so. Catherine, can you imagine the irony here? I mean, for the first time in his miserable fucking life Carnage does something utterly unselfish, and *that's* the time he gets shafted?"

Don't rub it in, Cat thought. "How do you know all this?"

"Brandon told me. Don't worry, there's nothing between us, we're just friends, that's all." She paused for breath. "So Carnage was just on the phone to him. Wanted him to clear out a couple of old documents, imagine! Destroying the evidence."

"Just as I was beginning to feel sorry for him."

"Oh, he's a broken man. His mother passed away last week. I mean, no matter how much we all hated the guy, when you hear something like that you can only feel bad."

You don't know the half of it. "Really. Like you say, the only unselfish act he ever did."

"Out of your control, though." Lorna brightened. "Imagine, honey, Hong Kong! I've missed you! We'll go celebrate."

"Absolutely we will." Cat could picture herself, Lorna and Mark in a bar somewhere. She could imagine showing Mark around, taking him to the best places, looking after him, getting closer to him.

"And this new guy's good, you say?"

"Oh yes," Cat said confidently. "You'll love him."

"Passport, tickets, suntan lotion." He was suddenly in her office, slapping her ticket down on the desk as she hung up. "I'm off soon, so I'll see you at the airport. Check-in desk, nineish?"

"Perfect." Cat paused. "Mark, did you know about Carnegie?"

"What about him?"

"About his mother dying?"

"Oh that, yes, I meant to tell you. Bit sad really."

"So Desmond Tang screwed him over? I mean, selling the company under his feet like that?"

"You could look at it like that. He wanted to get rid of him a long time ago, I think, but didn't want to lose face. It's all worked out rather well for him."

"But Max thought he was close to him. I mean, he must be devastated."

"Probably. Not my problem, though." He shrugged. "Nor yours. Check-in tonight." He nodded and walked out.

She cleared out her belongings and handed everything over to Sally. Her conscience was clear, at least as far as Trafalgar was concerned.

She walked towards the station, trying to make sense of it all. She couldn't hold herself responsible. The rumor only worked because so many people wanted it to. And what difference had it made anyway? Tang had wanted to sell. If anything the rumor had just given him a convenient smoke screen. Maybe Max would learn from all this, be humbled by it? Maybe he would learn that human relationships were more important than deals and long hours and treating other people badly? Maybe she would even have done him a favor?

Suddenly she was seeing everything differently. She hadn't fallen off any life-path at all—the path itself was to take her through good and bad experiences. The bad were to be learned from, the good to enjoy as a gift. You couldn't fall off your path, she realized. You had free will, and you had choices, but they were all part of the soul's plan. The individual chose the route, but the destination was the choice of the soul.

And her new destination was Hong Kong. She took one last look at central London before disappearing down to the train. London had been a place of struggle for her—but she'd learned from it. She would come back from time to time, and she would always appreciate it as a world city, but miss it? No, she had no regrets about leaving. There was a better life for her elsewhere. As there was for Mark, too.

Seventy-Five

Mark was waiting for her as arranged at the check-in desk.

"I took the window seat," he smirked.

"I hate window seats," she said.

"Bit of duty-free, a glass of champagne or two, get that speech over with and then we can relax," he was saying as they walked toward passport control.

"Sounds good to me," she replied, thinking how lucky she was to be travelling with such a laid-back boss. Someone like Max would have had her drawing up useless reports or making unnecessary schedule revisions for the hell of it. Gently Mark put his hand on her back, guiding her through the control area and helping her put her hand luggage on the conveyor belt. Beneath the roguish exterior he really was quite a gentleman at heart, she mused.

"So you got yourself sorted, then?" he asked her once they were through. "Sally, your place, you've tied up all your loose ends?"

"I think so," she replied. "Had a long chat with my mum this afternoon. They're planning to come out for Christmas."

Suddenly she remembered—there had been another call she'd meant to make. Dominic! He would be at an airport now, perhaps even this one, waiting to break the news to Lindy. With everything that had happened she had completely forgotten to call him.

"Anything wrong?" Mark asked with a look of concern.

"I just remembered something else I meant to do."

"Is it urgent? You want to make a phone call?" He offered her his cell.

"No, it's OK." She paused to gather herself. "It'll be fine." Saturday morning now seemed a long, long time ago. She'd never understood what people meant by time being an illusion before, but right at that moment she did.

Mark went off to look at magazines while Cat's mind raced. She could always call Dominic now. She could borrow Mark's phone, find a quiet corner and call him. But it might be too late already. The more she lingered, the less her inclination was to do anything. She had no desire to hear his voice even—the thought of it alone filled her with revulsion.

What would happen if she did nothing? she wondered. He had probably told Lindy already. It would be too late. And she had genuinely forgotten, that was the strange thing. Once Mark had told her about the takeover, she'd genuinely forgotten all about it.

What had it all been about? she asked herself. She slumped on a chair, waiting for Mark to choose his reading material. What on earth had it all been for? And then something came to her.

If the world were full of souls, each individually needing their own experiences, then some of them, some of the time, had to create those experiences for others, getting nothing in return. And maybe that was what she had just done. Maybe their entire relationship hadn't been about furthering *her* soul's journey, but his? Maybe in this life he had chosen to learn to appreciate women, to treat them with respect? And Cat had just given him the chance to experience the full effect of his wrongdoings. That was the only way he would grow.

Somehow it made sense. She hadn't wilfully neglected to call him after all—the Universe had created an extraordinary set of events that had simply led her to forget.

Or was she now creating more bad karma for herself, and would Dominic be back in the next life to taunt her? She smiled, watching Mark flirt with a shop clerk, a sense of strange pride that he was with her. That was something to worry about in the next life, not now.

They had been airborne for two hours by the time they wrapped up his all-staff speech.

"We'll have one last look at it before we land." Mark pulled his blanket up around him. "But now I need some sleep." He offered her a melatonin tablet and took a couple himself, washing them down with vintage brandy.

Cat took the tablets and went to the bathroom, where she brushed her teeth, cleansed her face and put on plenty of moisturiser. By the time she'd got back, he'd pushed his chair down and was almost horizontal next to her. She did the same, pulling her blanket up around herself. He was breathing evenly, and she turned to face him. It felt intimate being this close, but not embarrassing. They were lying together as if in a bed, and yet somehow it felt quite natural.

She tried to go to sleep, but there was too much going on in her mind. She was going back to Hong Kong! She could hardly believe it was happening. In less than ten hours her feet would touch Chinese tarmac again. How long would it be before she heard her first spit, and saw her first chicken foot? Mad, bad Hong Kong—city of extremes. No place like it on earth. Jerry Greenberg was right when he said you could never leave it, you would always have to come back. It had a magic, an energy of its own. Its spirit never left you.

Jerry, she remembered. Maybe she could even do something for Jerry now?

Had she somehow created this turn of events? she wondered. Had she manifested all this herself? *Be careful what you ask for*. Tiffany Cheung's words echoed in her mind. *You might just get it*.

But this time it would be different—she would be with Mark, and he was going to be the boss. Together they could right the wrongs, eliminate the insanity and reward the deserving. And she would have money, a car and a decent home. And she would have Mark. And Frontier would have Mark. Instead of fear and loathing, the corridors would be full of laughter and enthusiasm. Mark would treat them as equals, and turn the company into something to be proud of.

Funny, irreverent, sexy Mark.

"What are you thinking about?" He stirred.

"Oh I don't know." She looked away, embarrassed at being

caught watching him. "Everything and nothing." She paused. "I just can't get over my luck."

"Luck? Don't do yourself down. It was hard work and skill."

"You think?"

"I know. I watched you launch the Hungarian service, remember? That was hard work." He closed his eyes, trying to bed down for the night. "And you have skill. Your writing skills are excellent, and as you know, I've long been a fan of your oral skills."

She covered her face in shame and laughed out loud, disturbing two elderly ladies in front of them. How long had he been planning that one? He'd probably been itching for the opportunity to say it. She could see he was smirking, pleased with himself.

"So you?" She had to say something to knock him down. "What about you, then? What happened to that girl, the one with complications? You decided to leave her behind, did you?"

"Don't be silly." He yawned. "I'm not that stupid. She's right here, beside me." His hand crept out from under the blanket, and held hers briefly. "Now get some sleep."

She sat there, winded, and to her irritation he drifted off. How *could* he leave it at that, she thought, how could he? Suddenly her mind was racing, searching for clues. Was it just the in-flight champagne or was one last piece of the puzzle revealing itself, having been hidden under some celestial sofa for weeks?

Cat traced back all the signs, all the horoscopes, psychics and cards, and how she had steadfastly misinterpreted every one of them. It was always Mark! The person from her past who'd point the way to the future, that was Mark. The man she'd once been close to, who'd go with her to Asia—that had to be Mark! The man who thought more highly of her than she realized, the man in a business suit, the fact that they'd meet overseas—it was always Mark!

She asked the flight attendant for a glass of port and sipped it slowly. As the velvety flavor of berries fought against the toothpaste remains in her mouth, she marvelled at her own stupidity. Everything she'd heard, everything she'd read, every card she'd drawn, she'd twisted and turned to fit in with her desire of the moment. And all the time Mark had been there, waiting for her. All the time he'd cared for her just as she had someone else; but more cleverly, he'd taken his time.

Could she have an affair with her boss? Could they actually be lovers as well as colleagues? All in good time, she told herself. It was not for her to force through. Every time she had tried to force something through—she cringed at the thought—it had turned to disaster. She would do nothing, just let the Universe, and Hong Kong, work their magic.

As the plane headed farther east, Cat drifted in and out of sleep, lulled by the sound of the engines and air conditioning. At some point she saw a crack of daylight somewhere in the world peeking through the shutter of Mark's window. What had she read once? *The darkest hour comes before the dawn.* For Cat, there had been many dark hours. But now, right now?

She no longer believed in happy endings. She no longer expected her prince to turn up and lead her happily ever after toward his castle, or loft-style apartment on the river, or villa overlooking a South China Sea bay. She had learned enough to know that life wasn't like that. It was just a series of transitions, a series of good and bad experiences. The only constant in life was change.

This was just another transition, she told herself, the port finally dragging her toward sleep. But, she knew deep inside, it was going to be a good one.